Leapfrog

Peter Hawes was born in Westport and spent his youth in Bradford, England, where his father was a pro league player for Bradford Northern.

For many years Peter worked in television as a researcher, journalist, writer, presenter and director. He presented *Today in History*, *Hawes for the Asking*, *Against the Law*, *W-3*, and various documentaries and children's shows. He was associate director, interviewer, writer and translator (into Spanish) of *Neglected Miracle*, a full-length documentary on the politics of the seeds of the world. He wrote *A Week Of It* together with David McPhail and A. K. Grant and has written a number of plays, including *Alf's General Theory*, *Armageddon Revisited*, *Ptolemy's Dip*, *Aunt Daisy* and *Goldie: A Good Joke*. He has also been writer in residence at the Downstage Theatre, Wellington.

While teaching English in Spain, Peter wrote *La Hoguera* (*The Bonfire*), a farce about the Spanish Inquisition. He has also written a number of children's books, including *Animals for the Asking*. In 1995 *Tasman's Lay* was published, a novel exploring New Zealand's discovery.

Peter lives in Palmerston North, where he was writer in residence at Massey University.

OTHER BOOKS BY THE SAME AUTHOR

SHORT STORIES

Animals for the Asking

More Animals for the Asking

NOVELS

La Hoguera

Tasman's Lay

Peter
HAWES

Leapfrog with Unicorns

VINTAGE

This is a work of fantasy. No such companies as Agrisync and Acomazuni exist and the events are fictitious.

Special thanks to Massey University, whose writing fellowship gave me the time and facilities to write this book.

Vintage New Zealand
Random House New Zealand Ltd
(An imprint of the Random House Group)

18 Poland Road
Glenfield
Auckland 10
NEW ZEALAND

Sydney New York Toronto
London Auckland Johannesburg
and agencies throughout the world

First published 1996

Printed in Malaysia
ISBN 1 86941 284 2

To Lizzie,
my wife

'Never play leapfrog with a unicorn.'

[MURPHY]

Two kinds of unicorn there be
There's FINANCE
and there's STRICT PC.
We leapt, and now
we find our afts
impaled on both
their crooked shafts.

[HAWES]

BOOK ONE

PROLOGUE

Before the Potlatch: A Parable

The Hohokam Indians, it is said, could not differentiate between cheese and bumblebees because both were yellow. So important was the colour yellow to them that it transcended all shape. Yellow was the colour of the sun, of corn and of gold. The sun caused the corn to grow, and from corn came gold.

Of all the Indians of the Sonoran Desert — the Salado, Hopi, Mogollon, Anasazi and Sinagua — only the Hohokam knew the secret of growing corn, and without it the tribes would have died. For there was nothing else to harvest in that ragged wilderness but the pads of prickly pear, the greasy buds of cholla cactus . . . and the gold of the encircling mountains.

So the value of corn was immense.

In what has been called their post-Classic period — AD 1450 through 1530 — the Hohokam established a trading system of incredible complexity. Not only could corn be purchased for gold, but next year's crop could be bought, and sold at great profit, a season ahead of time.

So important did this buying and selling become, that corn began to affect the price of gold. And from this interdependent cycle grew another: the right to buy — with corn — the right to buy and sell gold. Fabulous fortunes were made by those who invested shrewdly in the corn market of the Hohokam.

To conduct the business of buying and selling, the Hohokam built a mighty bourse — later mistakenly identified by archaeologists as a stadium for elaborate ball games. From plates of red rock, caliche mud, and from ponderosa pine and white fir dragged across the desert from the Superstition Mountains, the Hohokam built their temple to transaction, their fabulous Corn Exchange. Here multitudes of bidders stood, shoulder to shoulder on high embankments overlooking the trading floor, shouting their offers, haggling prices up and down, arguing their commissions.

Across the mesas, gulches, bajadas and mountains of the Sonora, the sounds of crazed speculation joined with the burlap-breasted winds.

THE NAME HOHOKAM was probably bestowed posthumously; it means 'those who have vanished', although a closer approximation is 'all worn out' — as in old tyres.

For at the very height of the corn-market boom, the Hohokam died of starvation.

PART ONE

First Corn

Corn is an acquired taste. Morgan Moran acquired it at the age of ten, the year she became a Sinagua Indian.

Newly braided, she watched her mother wrench the sunflowers from the plot which they had inhabited since Morgan began, then sprinkle the battered soil with yellow seeds.

Within a month they sprouted — these seeds — and grew with great urgency into a phalanx of rustling praying mantises, much taller than she. Her two brothers ran squealing through the ranks of rasping stalks, but she did not, and was secretly pleased when access was banned upon pain of a whupping. In the solidarity of sibship she of course mourned the loss of this exhilarating playground and joined the resulting run-away project.

They were back by sundown and, to the best of her recollection, the supper they returned to was the first corn-on-the-cob of their lives.

Oh she'd experienced popcorn and — yetch — hominy grits, but the only other time she'd seen real corn was when Hank had grown some in the 'Threaten Field'; the one in which the 'scare-crow' always hovered on its pole, even when there were no crops. One year there was a new sort of plant under the scare-crow, which she later realised was corn. It had not seemed so skeletally tall and alive then, and it came vividly to her attention only after the flood.

The Flood

They'd watched from the porch, warm and rather deliciously insulated from the elements. The rain was so heavy it was difficult — at age eight and a half anyway — to work out whether the rain was coming down or the river was going up. The tractor was up to its rusty belly in water, but then it wasn't theirs and it hadn't gone since she could remember; and she could remember back to about age one. The cottonwoods down by the creek bank stuck up like organ pipes, a hundred yards out across the new lake. The water had reached the wire fence that kept the dogs in or the wolves out (they fought like cats and dogs if they met), and water was rushing — rather treacherously, she thought — from underneath the house to meet it.

Her mother had been glaring at the rising lake, ferocious, as if it owed her money. Then she stumped inside. There had been a squall of cold air and they thought she'd gone for a shawl, then they heard scrapings on the kitchen floor and seconds later she appeared on the inside of the glass at the top of the coloured window, climbing up into the trapdoor to the roof. They didn't rush inside and ask her what she was doing — she wasn't the sort you questioned — and almost immediately they heard banging and thumps, and shingles came plummeting down from the roof. They looked like holes in the rain as they fell, then they tobogganed down to the flood and floated round its rim. More crashes and falling dust. A block of ceiling fell to the floor, followed by rain.

The falling ceiling had knocked the chair off the table. 'Morgan!' bawled her mother. 'Put that chair back!' Morgan did so, and held it as her mother climbed down, baring her big white flourbag knickers when her hem got caught in a jagged bit of ceiling. She was puffing a bit when she reached the wreckage-strewn floor, but viciously triumphant. She stumped back onto the porch and leaned on the split-larch railing watching the advancing lake with its wooden hem of shingles.

You can evidently make an insurance claim on falling water, but not on rising water, so her mother had bashed the shingles off the roof to get some falling water going. But that's where the plan backfired; the rising water never reached the house. It stopped at the bottom step, then lay around long enough for all its mud to fall out and for catfish to suck the buckwheat out of the silo, then it crept back into the river. They had to put two more months on the bill at the general store in Carson City while the roof was paid for; but still, it was a very imaginative try.

IT WAS AT the clean-up a week later — the first time the water was low enough to make the two-mile journey up to the ranch house

— that she saw Hank's cornfield again. Its wire fence had been flattened, but perversely the corn had not escaped. Still plugged into the soil, it sprawled there like pick-up sticks, like spilt dry spaghetti (she'd spilt a packet of Martha's).

The scene became a permanent memory; her touchstone image of total devastation. Tangled limbs, like in the Belsen photos at school, wrapped in their little shrouds of husk. And presiding above the carnage, on its now slightly buckled pole, the monstrous, black bat-shaped scare-crow.

ALL THIS WAS happening on the Break-a-Heart Ranch, Silver Springs, eleven miles off the main road out of Carson City, Nevada; owned by Mr Hank Hodges, whose first name was really Henry but who was called Hank by everyone. Not by her and her brothers of course, because at their age it was impolite to call old people by nicknames. (Except 'Hoppy' Sideways, and that was only because they didn't know what else to call him and nor did he.)

Hank had a thousand acres of land, most of it flat, though pitted with gulches and dry arroyos. Most of the hills were so far away they just looked as if the horizon had turned up a bit at the edges, but there was one little range close by, yellow, knobbly — like the knuckles on a Chinese fist. 'The Jumbled-up Downs' Hank called it. Beef cattle grazed carefully between the bayonets of yucca on Break-a-Heart and it also had real horses, not just actors' ones (they'd made a film with Marilyn Monroe and some horses on Hank's ranch once, in the olden days); but really and mainly it was a vehicle-testing station; the Nevada Vehicular Research and Developmental Centre. NVRDC. All across Hank's property were roads, really rough, steep, torturous, dangerous tracks, and up and down them Hank's technicians hurled jeeps and trucks and cars and machines of all kinds, to test them for all sorts of things; to the death. From the porch where she'd watched the flood rising, she could often see stripped-down chassis bucking across the plain behind the cottonwoods, hauling vapour trails of bricky dust behind them; or screaming up the Jumbled-up Downs in lunging, rocking movements, as if constantly pouncing down to bite at the ground.

They said Hank also tested jet engines; bolted them down to the rock, way over behind the turned-up bits of horizon, and let them blast. That's what her brothers said anyway. Hoppy Sideways said the noise was just the Manitou.

SHE LOVED THIS place greatly. 'Within half a day of here, Morgan,' Hank had told her once, 'you've got every environment on earth.' Well, she hadn't been quite sure what environments were at the time, but they were all down there at the end of Fort Churchill Road, and her aim in life was to help Mr Hodges — Hank — put them into automobiles.

It would help in a way to make up for the undignified career of her father, who had left town when she was two.

HE'D BEEN A trick golfer; a brilliant one evidently. He could hit the ball off the end of Hoppy Sideway's tongue; he could curl the ball round a tree and make it come back nearly all the way; and he lined up his drives then hit them backwards down the fairway for two hundred yards! Hoppy Sideways was his caddy and partner in the tricks. Her father'd run out on Hoppy as well and they had sort of inherited him.

A bit like Hank had inherited them, because they'd all been on a tour of the WMR — the Western Mountain Region — when her father had run away, and Hank had kindly given them a place to live in on his ranch and they'd been there ever since. Even more kindly he'd given Hoppy Sideways a separate shack to live in, further down the creek so they didn't have to put up with his ways every time he had some.

Hoppy was still amazingly talented: he could spin a golf ball on the tip of his tongue like basketballers do on their finger; he could dodge a drive from about three paces; and he could catch an eight iron from so close he had to jump up to get it as it rose off the club. On the flip side, he was a collapsible drunk who reeked to high heaven of oldness (although he wasn't really) and peyote tobacco. These things — probably minus the smell — made him into what was called a 'character' and there were lots of stories about him.

Like the night that Mr Baum, who owned the Noosa Lodge bar, got so fed up with Hoppy falling off his stool all the time he took him home — which was sixteen miles away.

Mr Baum dropped Hoppy off at his shack but then had to carry on down Fort Churchill Road to turn round, and on the way passed Hank on his way into town. Hank then saw Hoppy standing right where Mr Baum had left him because he was too trashed to move, and said, 'You waiting for a ride somewhere, Hoppy?' and Hoppy said, 'Yep.' And got a ride back to the Noosa Lodge bar, where he was just falling off his stool when Mr Baum walked in . . .

THE SCARE-CROW

EVERY FEW MONTHS or so there was a new one. She'd thought at first that 'scare-crow' was a crow that scared people, which is why she spelt it with a hyphen. Anyway, it wasn't such a silly thought — it scared her more than it scared crows. Every model was put in the same place, on a metal pole in the middle of the flinty field which sometimes bore rye, sometimes nothing, and once, corn.

The first scare-crows — all of which were made out of wood — were sleek, like the heads of eagles. Then they got bumpier somehow; the eagle turned into a buzzard. They weren't really bumpy, more as if they'd been made by someone who cuts the shape into diamonds. And they were always black.

Half a mile away, just beside the porch of the ranch house, Hank had set up a radar. The idea was to build a scare-crow the radar couldn't see, which struck her as what she would later recognise as 'counter-productive'. To build something that wasn't there. Then Hank started making kites in the same shape as the scare-crows and they all crashed.

LAKE TAHOE

ONE DAY HANK said he was taking them all to Lake Tahoe. This was a high point of life up until then because she'd never been to this famous place. The only imperfection in the scheme was that her brothers were to come as well. And her mother of course. They sneaked a bit guiltily past Hoppy's place in case he wanted to come too. If cars can sneak, that is.

Lake Tahoe was over to the west about thirty miles — you could evidently pass it on your way to Reno if you weren't going the quickest way. There was going to be a convention there of national radar enthusiasts, and Hank was organising it. He was going up for the day to check that everything was ready.

From Break-a-Heart you had to go north towards Reno for a while, even though the lake was to the west, then left onto State Highway 431. Her first important memory of the day was at the top of Mt Rose, because as they turned right, round a bend cut into the hill, 'upwards' disappeared. Completely vanished! Suddenly she was looking down on the sky! The whole windscreen of Hank's big Wagoneer — beyond the two sun-visors and the compass that dangled down between them like an eye from Dr Seuss — was filled with sky but they were going downwards! And at the same time as she was staring into this upside-down geography, Hank was telling them how the lake was so cold that people who drown in it never rot, and that there was this man whose wife had fallen off the excursion launch and wouldn't float up because she couldn't putrefy and turn into gas, so he couldn't collect the insurance.

And they were heading down into it!

They turned right at the lake shore, although they could have gone to a place called Skunk Harbour if they'd gone left and she'd never seen a skunk in her life.

Hank went into the big hotel and said he would meet them later. The souvenir shop was a good place to start sightseeing, he told them.

The souvenir shop was made of fir logs, whole ones — a vertical raft. The souvenir man, whose name she forgot, told her brothers, 'They've cut down so much timber over the years on this side of the lake, there's more of it under the ground than above it.' It seemed to her that everything ended up under something in this place! In the window of the souvenir shop were small plastic stands with black cloth over them, and on the cloth were necklaces of turquoise beads. They were evidently from ancient local Indians who'd been buried in their finery eleven thousand years ago. Squirrels found the beads and took them back to their nests, and then ants raided the nests, stole the beads and built them into their anthills, and that's where they were found and sold to the man in the souvenir shop, who'd rethreaded them and put them in the window.

THEY LOOKED IN shops, they went to a lunch bar that didn't have hotdogs, they watched water skiers and Chris Craft mariners going up and down; they got bored. They hid, they fought, they went to the lake. Her brothers threw stones into the water. But she didn't, not while the lady from the excursion launch was down there.

At one stage, while she was fascinatedly watching heads of people floating in an outdoor hot tub, a man in a lumberjacket stopped beside her and said, 'You read your Bible, little lady?'

'Yessir, I do,' she replied politely.

'You'll know the end o' the world's coming then?'

'No, sir, I don't read that part,' she replied politely.

She re-found her mother, who was stumping along the road called Lake Shore Drive, glaring at the FOR SALE signs amidst the trees and muttering, 'Rush in, buy; cannot afford; sell to one more sucker' — or variants on this — at nearly every one.

It was getting dark and suddenly cold when Hank came out of the big hotel and said there were some last-minute hitches and would anyone mind if they stayed overnight. And nobody did. Hank stayed in the big hotel, and her mother and her and her brothers in a trailer behind the souvenir shop in the town. Hank paid for the trailer and also said he'd buy them all dinner in the big hotel.

Wow! It was a very plush restaurant! Mind you, it still didn't have hotdogs.

Morgan had ordered vegetables with her steak and was returning from the steam table. On her left were small palm trees in mahogany boxes, and goldfish bowls, brilliantly lit, filled with shoals of fishlets like fluttering tinsel. And on her right — and she stopped for a stunned moment to gaze — another goldfish bowl, far bigger, brilliantly lit, filled with . . . people! It was, said Hank, the casino.

Bed by nine thirty. Nearly midnight! — And once general rules have been broken, why can't they be broken by more . . .?

Fire regulations made it against the law to lock kids in trailers in those days, so that only left the power of the promise, and that of course was easily nullified by crossed fingers. So when her mother said she was 'going out for a while; no one will leave their bed,' they all nodded and promised and the trailer echoed to the sound of crossing fingers. As soon as she'd left, the boys were off down to the millionaire chalets by the lakeside to look in bedroom windows, and she was off to look into the aquarian casino in the big hotel.

The casino was easy to get into — after all, nobody in Nevada wanted to stop anyone gambling! Hank had told her that in Reno the room service in the hotels was deliberately so bad that no one would want to just stay in their rooms.

She stood on the dense green carpet, directly above the slight drop to the gambling floor; holding, for safety, a tassel of the silky red cord that was strung from golden posts across the front of the casino.

The scene was unbelievable! And also real, because there it was. The fantasy was caused mainly by the lights. They seemed to shine only on themselves, so there were violent blocks of glare — like slot machines and poker machines — and next to them, just darkness. Dazzling gold or blackness; nothing in between. On the far side, across this aquarium of unnatural colours and shapes, she could see her mother standing in front of a poker machine. On the hand that pulled the steel handle of the machine she wore a leather glove, like the ones riveters wear.

On top of the machine was a Daisy cup of coins. The light and the darkness behind it seemed to make her bulge, like a gibbous moon, half there — the front half; gloved hand raised, the other one clutching her black handbag like a throat — the other half not.

An incredibly tall black man in black and white and a black tie asked her if she was lost, and she said she was not, thank you. Then he politely asked her where her parents were, and she pointed vaguely into the human fish tank. As she later realised, she had pointed — with a statistical probability any gambler would be proud of — at the two fattest people in the room.

'Well, I'll tell you what, li'l ma'am,' whispered the very tall black man seriously, in a voice that was somehow bubbly and sharp, even under his breath, 'you's not allowed in there, on pain of death. An' some deaths can be mighty painful. But if you promise to be 'bout one foot taller than you are now, one day I might jus' be able to take you in. What you reckon 'bout that?'

'But I'm not,' replied Morgan, dazed, inexplicably near tears and resentful of her inadequacies.

'No, no, I don't mean now,' said the very tall man, 'I mean later; in about ten years' time. You promise me that, an' I'll let you go in to your folks. Okay?'

She nodded. He took her hand before she had time to let him

or not, and led her across the lightning-lit world, towards the huge outlines of the strangers who were now her parents.

'A li'l gift to you fine folks,' he said to them, and they instantly made cries and goos, during which time he said something to the man behind the gambling table. 'Now don' you let me down, ma'am,' he said. 'I want you to begin that growin' process from this very minute.' He wagged a finger from about three feet above her, then walked off into the stripes of light and darkness.

Her new parents were 'Penn' and 'Herb'.

Penn — she never did find out what it stood for — had three ivory chins; the only chins she'd ever seen with cellulite in them. She was a very nice person who bred Burmese, which are like Siamese in that they're also cross-eyed and mad, but brown, with a kink in the tail. While Herb went to the bar to get her a soda, Penn explained they were from Anaheim, near Los Angeles, and then propped her up on the thick brass rail to watch craps being played. Herb returned with a root beer, which she thanked him for with her fingers crossed. She hated root beer; it was like a mouthful of powder puffs.

From her vantage point on the rail she could see her mother, which meant her mother could see her if ever she looked up. But she never did. She was grimly at war with the glowing chrome device in front of her. Morgan later learned that slot machines here never take your last quarter, and she suspected her mother spent most of the night playing the same coin; just for the feel of it. It must have been the most money she'd handled in years.

Morgan quickly gained expertship in the language of craps — 'standoff, natural, pass, big six and eight, point' — and once, when the tall man returned, she threw a turn. And did she just dribble that come-out down the baize? Oh no! She belted those dice into the endplate with a venom that had them reeling backwards on their little round corners like tops! — Three! Twelve! Was she a millionaire? Craps! Total failure!

However, within minutes she was advising Penn and Herb on pass-line strategy.

The root beer had its effect and Penn escorted her to the Ladies, a nightmare of glowing black marble and gold trimming. The basins, the walls, the floor, the ceiling, all mirror black; all taps, handles, inners and accessories, gold. Black and gold, an echo, in colour, of the world outside. Would the . . . Yes! The bowl was black! The lid was golden! She pushed up the glowing lid, clamboured up to straddle the cold black rim and watched herself pour molten gold down the casino blackness.

Penn took some minutes to finish up, then they set off back, past palms, goldfish tanks and mirrors, to the casino floor. Suddenly she was getting tired. She was raw about the eyes, sounds came as if from under water. Then, as they were about to step down the green-carpeted stairs to the netherworld of dazzling tables, she saw a sight at which she would have screamed, had not horror drained all sound from her throat. There was their table, inside its teepee of golden light; there was Herb, billowing endlessly out from his spinal column, there were the other shakers she had come vaguely to know, and there was Michael the friendly dealer. All was well; all was as it had always been in her experience, at the craps table of a casino. Then Michael took a smooth step backward — and his head was sheared off! It disappeared! It vanished. It was completely severed from his shoulders!

Within a second she realised what had happened: he had stepped into the darkness outside the pyramid of light and been guillotined by the hypotenuse, but the damage was done. Nothing Penn could do would induce her to return to the table. They parted, Penn almost tearful, Morgan with eleven dollars eighty cents in the top pocket of her cotton dress.

Outside was bitter cold. There was a profound silence, the world was made of the Outer Space that glowed in the sky above her — and even on the lake. Lights smouldered through the Ponderosa pines by the waterside where millionaires were counting money or peeing inside each other (in a process known as sexual intercourse), with her vile brothers looking on through the window. She set off down the wide river-stone steps to the road that led to the souvenir shop. The hotel grounds, down to the roadside, were laid out in rock gardens and there were orange lights set into little cliff walls above flowerbeds that were labelled.

'Rubiaceous: gardenia, madder and bedstraw.' She was committing this interesting information to memory when there was a ruckus at the hotel door above her. The orange light of the rubiaceous garden somehow interfered with the light at the lobby doorway, and to her it seemed that a mad octopus had crashed through the doors. It sort of rolled down several layers of rock garden until it turned into the incredibly tall black man grappling with a monstrously small man.

Once she'd got the scene into perspective, it was apparent the tall man was a hopeless fighter and that the little guy was in no great danger of damage because of his quickness. In fact he gave the tall man a boot in the shin, which caused him to hop and make a strangled howl of pain — he was obviously trying to keep the battle as secret as possible from the patrons inside. The little man then turned to flee, and would have made a total getaway had not the tall one just tipped his heel with his toe and sent him ass over tea kettle down several more layers of rock garden. He did quite a lot of bouncing, and by the time he stopped she could see he'd hurt his leg. But he had hobbled off through the soda funnels of light from the street lamps before she could get to do her sixth grade first aid on him.

The whole battle had taken place in strange silence, but her attention was brought back to the tall man by the sound of clapping. He was slapping his hands past each other like cymbal players do in brass bands, and from his manner in the dimness he was mighty pleased with himself.

Suddenly she was outraged. She marched up the uneven grey stones of the steps, trembling with wrath, her untethered hair bobbling behind her. The tall black man was heading back inside and when he stopped at the sound of her voice he was in the light from the doorway. 'Why hello again, l'il ma'am! You bin doing any growin' yet?' he said.

She was trembling with protective indignation; she had no time for past friendships. 'Why don't you pick on someone your own size!' she cried, and put up her fists, ready to pummel this bully into a strip of pulp on behalf of tiny, oppressed people everywhere.

He took a concerned step forward, and paradoxically she could see him more clearly out here in the night. His hair was tightly curled, but in waves, and his lips pointed outwards like a beak, which was appropriate because his voice had a harshly melodic quacking quality. ''Cos they always win,' he said, 'that's why. You run away from your folks again?'

She was not to be distracted. 'That man you just beat up was little! He was a dwarf!'

'Nope.' And he shook his head, way way up in the

stratosphere above her own. 'He ain't no dwarf, ma'am; he's jus' someone who's got both legs shorter'n the other, that's all.'

'He could have hurt himself real bad!'

'Tell you what, you just used a couple o' words there that sum that genman up pretty well, ma'am, and they's "real bad". That li'l guy is a famous pickpocket; he's a back-pocket thief on account of he can't reach jacket pockets. So he specialises in back pockets, an' I'll tell you what, he's pretty damn good! He woulda got away with over three hunnerd dollars o' someone's highest quality gamblin' cash if I wusn't jus' that li'l bit better myself; 'cos you see, ma'am, I'm a gemmun who believes in saving money.' And from the small pocket on the left of his waistcoat he took out a wudge of bills. 'There, tha's what you call a withdrawal o' cash. Three hunnerd dollars, flipped back outa that li'l asshole's pocket, which I shall now return to a satisfied customer, who will in return, return it to me later, per medium o' my fine gaming tables, in compliance with the highest principles of modern finance in which money circulates at high speeds.'

Suddenly he extended a huge soft hand, purple on the back, pink in the front; 'Fergive my rudeness, l'il lady, but I di'nt introduce myself yet. My name is Harvey Latour, manager of this resort and casino.'

And at that very moment her mother emerged from the doors of the big hotel, about as pleased to see Morgan as Dracula is to see the dawn.

AND SO MORGAN and her mother met Harvey Latour. The amazing Harvey the Toot, who within two minutes had thawn her glacial mother, and within three had made her smile! And within five had invited them to breakfast next morning!

'Nobody pays for my family no matter how poor I may be,' stated her mother in a voice like a stamped foot, in reply to the invitation.

'You's poor?' quacked Harvey the Toot.

'Yes,' replied her mother.

'Well, I guess I jus' made a bad investment. I figured you for an heiress in disguise.'

Next morning, after a paid-for breakfast of eggs, sausage links and hash browns or cheese and mushroom omelettes (rumoured to contain six eggs), her mother and Harvey stayed talking in the restaurant of the big hotel while Hank took Morgan and her brothers to Skunk Harbour to find skunks.

Harvey had been somewhere around middle thirty at that time; tall, long-faced, and with great purple lips, which fell apart into cavernous smiles at frequent and often unexpected moments. Her mother was over fifty, with a face like the one that giant bagworm moths used on the backs of their wings to scare off enemies. So whether the 'nature of their relationship' was ever more than commercial she never knew, but it was certainly commercial. As she followed Hank and her brothers towards the door, the voice of Harvey the Toot drifted after her across the green-carpeted lobby: 'Thing is there's two kindsa capitalism in the US, Mizz Morgan; there's yo' state capitalism, an' there's yo' federal capitalism . . .'

Later that day, after zero skunks but several donuts, they all set off home up Mt Rose, turned the corner hewn into the mountain top and left behind the terrestrial sky, the unrotten corpses and thrice-stolen necklaces — but not, she felt, as she glanced at her secretly gleaming mother, the influence of the words of Harvey the Toot.

So when her mother told her, shortly after, to braid her hair and never unbraid it again because she was a Sinagua Indian, she somehow connected it with Lake Tahoe.

Although she also somehow connected it with Hoppy Sideways . . .

Hoppy

A VERY SHORT time later, a few weeks after her mother planted the corn, Hoppy Sideways died. Emphysema. It was not unexpected. His breath had rattled round in his chest for years, just below the hooking mechanism of his cough. It was one of the sounds, in fact, that Morgan later associated with 'environment'; the rolling, gagging thunder of Hoppy's cough, mingling with the notes of the moon bird and cactus wren. He had often sat with Morgan's mother on the porch of their home — the two of them silent; she with a granite uninterest in any topic of conversation, he with brain-fuddled incapacity for any sound beyond coughing. The two of them, bonded by silence.

Morgan had 'sat in' on Hoppy's sickbed on occasion — dutiful occasions it had to be said. There was nothing to do but sit in the pellucid gloaming of his shack and look down at his prematurely ribbed face; flat-cheeked, brown-skinned, and with an upper lip eroded into channels like the side of a butte. His eyelids, in sleep, came down over most of his eyes, but did not quite close at the bottom. His lids lay in two dark lines with gooey awareness between them. Was he watching from behind those lids, so thin you could see veins in them?

The place reeked of old fat, leather, wet-stove smoke, tobacco and baked sheet iron, and everywhere, from every dilapidated board and beam, resonated the sound of Hoppy's dreadful breathing. Only by staying centred in herself could these moments be made bearable; to be drawn out into the world of that wheezing, rattling, coma-like sleep would be to enter nightmare. Morgan invented sprightly derivations for the sounds; the best she'd come up with so far was a nest of young baby bagpipes cheeping for their supper as Mummy bagpipe arrived. They were hideous hours quite frankly, these hours of 'sitting in', but it seemed — well, so her mother blood-curdlingly attested — that Hoppy had a 'special fondness' for her. How on earth this was manifested Morgan had no idea.

Hoppy had no known relatives, and yet when he died a group of a dozen silent Washo braves arrived and silently bore him away — in the fairly expensive coffin Hank had provided. Technically it was theft, but no one said a word.

ONE DAY, AT about the time when the scare-crows were changing from sleek to faceted, the creek had been infested by a lime-green cloying weed called hydrilla. It was the biggest word she could handle at the time, but it soon came easily, so often did she hear it used. Hydrilla weed had all but brought the creek to a standstill and no County efforts to clear it had worked. Then a new phrase arrived — grass carp — and soon it was rolling from her tongue as easily as hydrilla. (At about age eleven she learned it was two words.) Grascarp could evidently clear an acre of hydrilla a month — each! The flip side was, they cleared out every other form of river-dweller as well.

At this stage the issue got complicated because Hank wanted the river slowed down — it was threatening to consume one of the few cultivable bits of his land, the Threaten Field (which she now realised was the 'threatened field'). So Hank was not really anti-hydrilla. Most other neighbours were, however, and the County listened to them. One day a County tank truck came thundering down Fort Churchill Road, halfway to the homestead, and dumped about a thousand foot-long black fish into the stream.

After that you could almost see the weed going down; you could see grooves appearing in it; you could see it being plucked down out of sight like when eels got a fix on a swimming duck. Before long the weed was at least half gone. But then the trout started disappearing as well. And every other sort of fish. You even saw the skeletons of fair-sized catfish glowing on the slimy brown stones of the riverbed. And at this point the situation came to the bleary notice of Hoppy Sideways. No one had known how Hoppy felt about fish; he ate prawns in the bar and there were tins of tuna in his shack, she knew, but no one had known Hoppy had this deep mystical relationship with fish. Well, he did.

One night there was this wailing from his old shack, which was about two hundred yards upstream from their cottage. You couldn't see anything (Morgan snuck out to look); you just heard this really sad cry. Then nothing. She waited, shivering on the porch, for events. There weren't any. Nor the next night, nor the next. But the next night, standing in the river, still as herons — and glowing just as whitely in the moon — were figures. And she recognised them, these years later, as the Washo shamans who turned up to take Hoppy away. He disappeared forever, and so had the grass carp.

SO WHEN IT came to her 'formative influences', a lot of them were built into Lake Tahoe and Hoppy Sideways, and she'd never, at any later stage, been able to quite untangle them. On the day her mother told her she was to braid her hair — which was a few days before the corn got planted, which was a month or two before Hoppy died, which was a few weeks after they got back from Lake Tahoe — she had an image of Hoppy lying waxily still, his hair in thick grey plaits with uncaught wisps coming off them like spray. He'd had them that way for the golf act — she'd seen posters — and had kept them ever after.

Then squirrels sneaked into the vision and stole the turquoise beads from the rotting string around Hoppy's neck, and suddenly he was an uninsurable corpse staring upwards from the lake bottom into the face of his wife, who was leaning over the bow and weeping: 'Honey, I cain't collect neither the state nor the federal insurance . . .' And then fronds of lustrous black hair, intertwined in graceful dolphin-back patterns, floated past Morgan's eyes and either up or down — whichever way it was — towards the sky. It was Hoppy, in the most handsome of the posters that lined the walls of his shack. And she knew they'd taken Hoppy to the lake.

FLAGSTAFF

THINGS LOOKED UP after that. It was as if Morgan's braids had brought them luck. More money came in from somewhere, there was more to eat, more trips into Carson City. Her mother even muttered about a vehicle, although who would have driven it remained a mystery.

And then one day she was granted a scholarship to Christina Leahman High School for Girls. How remained as powerful a mystery as the drivership of the projected car; she had never applied for such a scholarship; in fact had never heard of the school. But she went. Evidently it was at the centre of the spiritual home of the Sinagua Indian.

Hank drove her to Weed Heights, where you could intercept the bus down Alt 95 to the border, where she arrived thirty hours later, having pulled her blind down as sun rose over Scotty's Junction and not having put it up again for three hours, on account of the radiation from the atomic-testing site to her left. She changed at Boulder City and again at Kingman, and arrived in Flagstaff next morning.

It was a seven-hundred-girl, private institution, set in the Coconino Forest about four miles out of Flagstaff. It was made of shingles, rather like the ones her mother had once belted off the roof to collect insurance, but they continued down the sides like scales on a chicken's leg. And the complex was completely surrounded by firs. Even from the third-storey windows (she discovered in her second year) all you could see was further up the tree. The view was of long yellow grass for about a hundred yards in all directions, and then it was a hundred percent tree. Above you was a sky, blue in the morning and grey in the afternoons at thunderstorm time. It was like being trapped in a crater made of wood, and very cold. Which is preposterous when you think that the next city down the road, Phoenix, is the hottest non-Islamic city in the world. But then Phoenix isn't six thousand feet up, as Flagstaff is.

Her first teacher was Miss Waterhouse, who must have been emotionally disturbed because, although she was very pretty and no older than the hordes of rampant males at the Northern Arizona University down on South Malpais Lane, she rarely went out, often took other people's dorms when they wanted weekends off; and if she did go out, it was only down to that goddam Dexterville at the Peace Surplus. Presumably she ended up as a nun or a campaign worker for Jimmy Carter, but in the meantime, she taught Morgan all about herself. About Morgan that is.

They entered the classroom that first day, she and Miss Waterhouse (Philippa). On the walls, bad drawings of moonshots; at the desks, pimples and braces, arranged on dull faces in varying degrees of malevolence. 'Good morning, class,' said Miss Waterhouse. 'I want you to meet Morgan. Morgan is going to join our class, and I want you to make her feel very welcome.' She recognised Beverley Hall and Adrienne Code, whom she'd met that morning in the corridor and who had already asked her if she smoked or did it. And Sonya Heald, who had the adjoining locker and said she'd smoked once and done it three times, which, when you look back on it, was going to give her an interesting lifetime average. 'Morgan is a Sinagua Indian, whose tribe used to live in this very region many years ago. The word Sinagua comes from the Spanish "sin" — without — and "agua", which of course means water. Without water. The without-water Indians . . .'

'Did that mean they didn't have to go to the toilet, miss?'

And thus the ethnic albatross was put in place. It dangled from her body like the braids; presumably for the rest of her life.

To her astonishment Morgan found that Humphrey's Peak, which you could see to the north of Flagstaff (when you could get out of your damn volcano of trees) was deeply sacred to her. Miss Waterhouse told the class this in the second term. It was evidently riddled with Kachina spirits, but she'd never gone up there — although many of her classes did over the years — in case she didn't recognise them. It would be extremely rude to walk past a spirit of your ancestors without recognising it, and so she went to Mount Agassiz instead. She could glance across to the sacred slopes from there; and anyway the skiing was better. The next year they did an essay on Sunset Crater, just north of Flagstaff, which she discovered was even more sacred to her.

Over the next year and a half she went home once, and her mother passed through twice on her way to mumbled destinations in the South. Then her mother telephoned to announce the family was moving from Nevada to Arizona. To their Spiritual Home. They would be passing through Flagstaff in two weeks.

This was upsetting; Break-a-Heart was to be abandoned without farewell. Morgan knew what 'environment' was now. It was walking the two miles down to the end of Fort Churchill Road; past the high sheds and wired enclosures and the TOP SECRET signs, past the kennels and joyously baying watchdogs, down the porch, through the screen door and under the high gallery of brass pans of Martha's kitchen. Past Nellie the Puerto Rican drying plates and placing them like great minims on the bars of the Welsh dresser; past Martha herself, although she was generally resting; past the glassed sideboards of jade and porcelain; the zigzag Indian rugs; the silver thing off the Pullman dining car that dismantled into about six different ways of eating; the five thousand books — to the photograph of the stag.

He's standing in the shallow water of a lake and would have had his back turned if the flash hadn't attracted him. His long immobile face can't register his shock, but every nerve of his body is engorged with desperate energy; and every hair of his body and every pore of his antlers is emblazoned onto the camera's retina by the light that has discovered him. He stands appalled, outstaring forever a flash of gunpowder, ignited in 1890.

That was environment: that and a mental image of an angular black scare-crow hovering over a field of smashed corn.

Roots

SHE WAS AT the Greyhound station in Malpais Lane, to meet her migrating family on the two thirty from Kingman. Her two brothers swaggered off the bus, surprisingly taller, portentous;

more self-conscious about hugs from sisters. Then came her mother.

'Ollas, ollas! Gash as den shaaa ka ia nerekowa! Lakota, lakota!' she cried; 'Ho ya neh, ho ya neh!'

Her lank old fronds were woven into two stiff grey sticks that drooped juttingly — like Eeyore's ears. She clenched her arms into a crab's pincer of welcome and stumped forward. They embraced. Their braids touched and almost intertwined. Mother and daughter, Sinagua forever.

They stayed two nights — in a motel! On the second day, a Saturday, there was to be a pilgrimage. They ordered a rental. Farrell, her eldest brother, with an Adam's apple like their mother's nose and who now shaved, was to drive the 'hire-car' as her mother called it. They would head first to Sedona.

'Hey, Mom!' — a passionate chorus of siblings. 'We gotta go to the Grand Canyon, Mom! You can't come to Flagstaff and not go to the Grand Canyon.'

'No to all canyons grand and small!'

'But, Mom!'

'What is a canyon? Huh? A canyon is a goddam hole in the ground. We have not come to see things that are not there, boy, we are come to look at things that are there! Get in.'

She sat in the front seat, right hand on the Pontiac's automatic gear stick, ready to wrench it into neutral at the first indication of a northerly bias to their travels. They headed south, down Highway 17.

YOU HAVE TO face it, Arizona does have a higher class of desert. Nevada, in comparison, is just a gigantic riverbed, with stumpy vegetation in grey drab — flora made by the army. Arizona uses colour to stupendous effect: blue-black volcanic domes, rafts of bright red, blue granite, white limestone, scarlet ironstone — in stripes. And shapes: buttes — desert gothic in crimson; saguaro cactus — a vast army surrendering. They dash silently in their 'hire-car' through a tumult of petrified creation; conversation as rare as beryllium.

They are nearing Sedona. It blazes in the sun ahead; orange tiles on cream walls — Indian Gardens . . . sinagua! There is a place called Sinagua! A mental finger presses REVEAL CODES and for a second she looks into the heart of things.

Her mother is glaring at a map. 'Turn off next right,' says she.

They turn, at a Y junction that announces itself as 'The Y', down a highway lined with cafés. 'You will turn right into Coffee Pot Road,' says her mother. 'Here we will take lunch.'

They turn into the caféless Coffee Pot Road and travel silently down its length. Directly ahead of them looms a vermilion butte; beside it a sign: COFFEE POT ROCK. 'You will turn back,' growls her mother dangerously.

They lunch at the Desert Sage, which they can do, announces the menu 'in comfortable, simplistic fashion'. Morgan smiles as she reads this, then finds herself glancing at her brothers. 'Enjoying your meals?' asks the waitress. Tall, eighteen, nice hair. Saxon features; orinasal Midwestern accent.

They wait for their mother to reply on their behalves.

'Perhaps,' replies her mother. 'Probably it is better than the meal that I actually ordered.'

The malevolence has no effect. This was not the answer programmed to be received and is therefore unheard. 'Are you going to a Special Place?'

'No we are not. Nowhere special.'

'I mean — are you going to one of the Special Places?' There is a tense pause. 'A vortex, you know? There's five or six quite close by. None of them's drive in, but Cathedral Rock is a short hike and has clean restrooms.'

At last even the surface of the waitress' pleasantry begins to blister under the gaze.

'Perhaps you could get me some more syrup for my waffle?' replies her mother.

With these few words she announces that she and her family will not, thank you, become Special People. They will not buy crystals, incense, Birkenstock footwear or natural-fibre clothing; neither will they visit floatation tanks, talking circles nor vision quests. It is more than unlikely that they will dress as clowns on Earth Day, or subscribe to the magazine that tells them how to build their own Tibetan mangola. And they will take a rain check on the herbs that regulate the metabolism. Thank you.

'She was pretty,' said Gordon as they left.

'I think she was from Minnesota,' said Farrell.

'You can get pills for that,' muttered their mother.

To the Verde Valley they trundle in their rental; across Beaver

Creek to Montezuma's Castle. Seventy-five cents entry fee, plus a dollar for an information pamphlet. The Castle is a series of scalded bricks, looking like old Lego, hanging from a high cave in a cliff. 'Your ancestors lived there,' says her mother. She glares down at her information pamphlet. 'Until it burnt down,' she adds.

Burnt down? A cliff? They exchange a glance, mother and daughter. It is likely her mother sees the doubt in her eyes. A pause. Is she going to say, 'Fire was hotter in those days'? If so, Morgan will certainly agree. The moment passes.

'Come, I want a cup of coffee.'

They drink bad coffee, her mother reads page four of the guide book aloud, then they progress to Montezuma's Well, a pea-green pond surrounded by yellow cliffs pitted with emmenthal-like holes. Many of these holes hold walls of ancient brick. Obviously she lived here too, in a hole beside the pond.

'Bottomless,' declares her mother as she turns away. Ducks bob in the middle of the bottomless lake, sometimes upending to graze on lakebed weeds.

The spiritual quest ended here and they returned, along the same highway, to Flagstaff.

She saw her family off next day with mixed feelings.

Racial Recognition

There are certain things that are severely taboo to a Sinagua Indian. One of these is being leg-upped back into your second-storey window by two palefaces from the Northern Arizona University at four in the morning. In fact, so taboo is this behaviour that it leaves one in the limbo of 'suspended for three days pending investigation', the conclusions of which could well be expulsion. On being summoned to the principal's office (Mrs [Helen] Silverman) for interrogation, Morgan explained that she had been to a meeting, at the NAU, of the Indigenous People's Research Institute, at which she had learned for the first time that Andrew Jackson had issued her ancestors with army surplus blankets, deliberately infested with smallpox. Her seemingly inebriated condition had in fact been the result of trauma.

In her third year at Leahman High, the Race Relations Authority conducted the first of a series of studies into her racial prejudice. A man and a woman, both bright white and both in their earnest forties, arrived at the school with a huge portfolio of photos of black/white, male/female college students, taken from high school yearbooks. The class looked at these photos, then it was lunch break, and after that they were shown some slides of more students from old yearbooks. The class then had to indicate if they'd seen any of these people before; that is, in the pre-lunch photos. Evidently this had much to do with what the earnest sociological couple called 'cross-race recognition'.

Then the rest of the class was given time off while the researchers talked to Morgan. She was asked to call one of them Mrs Brigham and the other Mr Barkowitz.

'Now, Morgan,' said Mrs Brigham, who had fantastically clear glasses that blasted her eyes into white-out every time she looked towards the windows, 'it is important you remember what we told the class earlier; Mr Barkowitz and I are not racists. People who investigate racial differences, while at the same time appreciating the difference between races, are not racist.' She glanced at Mr Barkowitz, who nodded over his folded arms. 'Now, let me ask you . . .' and the motor went out of her voice, dropping it to a whisper, 'have you ever heard people say things like "they all look the same to me" in reference to you?'

'No, Mrs Brigham.'

Mrs Brigham was not entirely pleased. 'Never? In your whole life?'

'No, Mrs Brigham.'

Mr Barkowitz, who was leaning against the main desk, now cantilevered forward across his knee. 'Have you heard it said in reference to anyone in your family?'

'No, Mr Barkowitz.'

'No one, in your whole life, has said "they all look the same to me" about you?'

'No, sir.'

'What . . . tribe are you part of, exactly, Morgan?' says Mrs Brigham.

'Sinagua, Mrs.'

'And they were a local tribe, I believe?' says Mr Barkowitz.

'Yes, Mr Barkowitz.'

'Are there many Sinagua around here?' — Mrs Brigham.

'No, Mrs.'
'How many?' — Mr Barkowitz.
'None.'
'None at all?'
'No, Mrs Brigham.'
'What about where you used to live?'
'No.'
'Do you know any other Sinagua?'
'No, Mr Barkowitz.'
'Do you know of any other Sinagua?'
'No, Mrs Brigham.'
'So it's just your family?'
'No.'
'How do you mean?'
'My brothers aren't either. It's just me. And my mother. I think. I think we're the only two who aren't extinct yet.'

Sociologically she was a flop. She failed every known avenue of prejudice: she did not qualify as the recipient of 'they all look the same', as there was no one else to look the same as; she was not the victim of 'intergroup conflict', because she wasn't a group; and no one had 'acquired negative responses' about her race during their 'socialisation', because there wasn't one. As a minority she was a disaster. For several heady years it seemed likely she would be stricken from the roll of minorities for being too few. But then, alas, the advent of Jimmy Carter; the myopia of positive discrimination was enlarged by the power of ten and the parameters of prejudice imploded to encompass anything over about 0.45 percent of a human being.

AT SEVENTEEN SHE was ordered to a powwow at her mother's surprisingly well-appointed house near Papago Park, some five miles east of downtown Phoenix. It was one of the staff buildings of the botanical gardens, and was her mother's in exchange for a small state rental and right of access — for meteorologists — to the barometers and water gauges in various sections of the garden. Above the ranchslider doors that gave onto a cool porch of the oiled, wooden bungalow, her mother had affixed the title MOOS-O-MEN, which, she told Morgan, meant the 'crossing of the paths'.

Her mother was nearly seventy and looking more like Willie

Nelson by the day. Well, a beardless Willie Nelson with no voice, but with everything else that constituted the famous man — a nose profile like an arthritic forefinger, lips like a miser's purse, eyes that could cut diamond, and a bright bandanna with long, grey, intertwined strips of hair dangling from it.

Beside her on the porch, seated in a buckskin armchair far too low for her, was Ms Bird.

Ms Bird was, speaking geometrically, an isosceles triangle; getting bigger all the way down. At the top her body entered a youthish, washed-blue, muslim frock, trim-shouldered and diminutively breasted: it emerged at the nether end with calves sculpted by Michelangelo. She sat uncomfortably forward on the ridiculously low chair — all the furniture was built for Morgan's mother and no one else — with a white yoghurt shake in her left hand. Above her: MOOS-O-MEN, in angular white capitals. On the brittle lawn in front of her, competing weathermen trudged past each other, clutching beakers of rain. Beyond the lawn, the botanical desert and the Suspicion Mountains, opaque and low on the horizon, like the last shards of glass in a broken pane.

'You will meet Miss Bird,' said her mother, 'she is from the Ethnic Alternatives Commission. She is here to make you a deal.'

'Well,' said Ms Bird in a tiny voice, 'hardly a deal.'

'Oh?' Her mother was suddenly suspicious.

'An offer. A suggestion.'

'Yes. A suggestion. So you will listen and speak politely to Miss Bird.' She lay back in her seat. The porch threw a Zorro-mask of shadow across her face. Her eyes were half closed; all the better to see you with, my dear.

'The thing is, Morgan,' said Ms Bird, and held the yoghurt glass with both hands in her Zeppelinesque lap like a phallus, 'statistics show a mounting interest — nationwide — in the art and history of the Black Sand Indians. An urge to know them better, to make contact. Hands across — the desert, I suppose.'

Morgan could see Ms Bird looking into her eyes, and in her mind's eye could see her seeing her own image mirrored in her impassive pupils; her own smile — like the opening of a suburban letterbox. The smile stopped, maybe she had seen herself. 'We feel a need to respond to this demand, to make positive steps to create the links people are seeking. To empower that contact. Consequently —' and the consequence was a putting down of the glass, a rummaging through a handicraft-type hempen bag at her side, and the extraction of documents, 'we have instituted a new degree, the Art of the Sinagua Indian. There is to be a grant of $8000 and an accommodation allowance as well. We are obliged to advertise the grant publicly, but — there is provision for us to take superordinatory measures . . . If you were interested in the position, I could assure you your application would be treated with very favourable attention.'

Ms Bird had soft pink skin and a pretty little mouth. Her eyes were startling blue and of the type that are naturally held so wide you can see the white underneath. It was a vulnerable face somehow; it dared your Id to suddenly shout 'Boo!' knowing that Ms Bird would probably wet herself.

There had obviously been a waiting silence, for her mother now growled, 'You do wish to go to university, don't you, child?'

That was not a question, that's a loaded revolver! Just try saying 'no'. Go on, do it; say: 'No, Mom, I don't want to go to university. I want to work for Hank in the middle of all those environments.' Go on! Do it! Tell her what you really think! — 'I mean what's a university, Mom? University's a class full of biophysicists studying for a career in real estate . . .'

'Guess so, Mom.'

'I truly wish I had your opportunities.'

Morgan looked at her braided, enigmatically well-off mother, and inside her head she said, 'I think you have.' But outside of it she didn't say a word.

'The degree would include a study of the major epochs of world art as well,' pleaded Ms Bird. 'It would result in a very well-rounded grasp of the history of art in general.'

'I was thinking more of going into mechanical engineering,' said Morgan politely.

Ms Bird's demeanour spoke of worry and confusion. 'I'm afraid it's not on the syllabus,' she said.

'Since when have we been mechanics? Huh?' bawled her mother. 'We know corn, child, we know nothing of engines!' She glowered; Evil crouching. 'Tell me what Phoenix means!'

'It means the bird that rises from the ashes.'

'Do not forget it, and sound more respectful. This place rose from the ashes of the Hohokam. That is why we're here.'

It seemed there had been a tribe near here who'd learned how to make canals and therefore grow corn. They'd mysteriously died out. Then, hundreds of years later, along came refugees from the Civil War who cleared the sand out of the canals and got the town going again, so they called it Phoenix. Because it rose out of the canal? Aren't we talking King Neptune or something here?

She silently tried to sound a bit more respectful.

'I believe the U of A have made overtures?' said Ms Bird.

Her mother sat up; the shadow slid down her body like a Batman costume. 'You said nothing of this to me!'

'It didn't seem relevant, Mom. They offered me a course in Native American Dance and Role-playing.'

'Did they mention a grant?' Her mother's voice was conspiratorially sotto, as if she were trying to slide it past Ms Bird.

Morgan shook her head without looking at her mother.

'Huh. You stick to Miss Bird's pots.'

'I'm sorry, Mom, but pots are not me. I want to work with machinery.'

Ms Bird creased from the middle with studious concern. 'Look, Miss Morgan — Morgan; perhaps what you need is more contact with the culture. We — frankly, we see you as a very valuable part of our project; to have you — a real member of the tribe — well . . . Look, look at it the other way; what if you didn't accept? What sort of impression would that make, when a member of the very tribe turns her back on a study of her own culture? You see the impression that could give?'

'Yes,' said Morgan's mother, rapaciously alert. 'I see your point, Miss Bird; I see the unfortunate impression it would give if my daughter didn't play ball.' She sat up and swung her legs from the leaner. 'Morgan,' she said, 'go inside and . . . make us something.'

Attempted Rebellion

Morgan returned to Arizona and enrolled at the Greyhound Bus Maintenance School, Gallup, Arizona. Her application was accepted, then superordinated by Provision C, Section A of the Ethnic Alternatives Act of 1979, which decreed that 'employment initiatives forwarded by the Ethnic Alternatives Commission superordinate all other employment opportunities offered, and non-compliance with this provision will result in prosecution under Provision C, Section A of the Ethnic Alternatives Act of 1979'.

It was signed by various unknown dignitaries, along with Ms Bird and her mother.

Morgan was enrolled at the NAU in the Art of the Sinagua Indian, majoring in pottery. Her mother visited her in her new Thunderbird, driven by a Navajo named Errol.

THE SINAGUA INDIANS never made decorated pottery of any kind. To the detriment of art and splendour, the Sinagua were, to a peon, of the working class. Those who made the pots, used them, and thus the indigenous workers of the Sonoran Desert produced plain, round, brown, sturdily utilitarian ollas of no artistic merit whatsoever.

Consequently there was almost nothing to study and Morgan acted in plays, went to motor races and wrote articles on gambling strategies for the campus newssheet.

She graduated Phi Beta Kappa.

Her brothers were by then both directors of a new, Pheonix-based fashion house by the name of Acomazuni Fashions, specialising in beadwork jackets worked into geometric zigzag patterns interspersed with stylized crab-like shapes — rather like Space Invaders. Business was riotously successful. The company had soon expanded into ethnic articles of many kinds and changed its name to Acomazuni Enterprises. By the time of Morgan's graduation, it was being groomed for listing on the New York Stock Exchange.

CEO of Acomazuni Enterprises was Morgan's mother, who at the end of 1981 had changed her name from Mavis to Acomazuni.

AND THAT'S ABOUT the end of Morgan's formative influences.

Except for one . . .

HOTWA VO

'I WISH TO travel to the South,' said a voice. 'You will purchase a hire-car and come down to me.'

'I was thinking about going skiing this weekend, Mom.'

'That is correct; you were.'

She aims her Renta Dodge down Highway 17 — a maddening road, laid in regular concrete slabs that don't quite fit, like riding along the back of an armadillo.

Phoenix. MOOS-O-MEN. Colonies of meteorologists labour over their anthills of instruments. Round and about the house lie the appurtenances of modest luxury. Business is booming. Acomazuni Enterprises can now furnish a newly arrived couple to Sun City with a range of ethnic houseware — Athapascan rugs, Pueblo pots, Hopi kachinas, Anasazi black and white pottery — that would otherwise have taken generations to accumulate. A special low-budget range of ethnic treasures was currently being manufactured for the trailer-home market.

Instructions are given to a maid and a gardener. Why not a goddam chauffeur?

'Head for Casa Grande,' growls her mother.

They set off around Phoenix; the second-most boring trip in the state. The most boring trip is across Phoenix.

Through the suburban everglades of Mesa and Tempe, past the scruffy approach to the airport and the tattered, dusty pit that some say was once a ball court of the Hohokam and others say was their stock exchange.

They head south for Casa Grande, the four-storey mansion built by the Hohokam while Westminster Abbey was going up elsewhere.

They approach.

'Turn right,' says her mother at Eleven Mile Corner. They are not going to the ruins. Then where? The Hohokam-Pima Monument, sixty miles down the road?

No. There was no way of knowing where they were heading — her mother had hunched into noncommunication, arms crossed (she now wore rawhide jackets bearded with leather tassels), glaring at the road as if resenting its intrusion between her and their destination.

The desert accompanied them on either side; torn iron mountains, glimmering ceramic lakefuls of mirage, burnished red cores of bright rock that flashed like mirrors in the sun. Naked forked minerals; the bones beneath. Far too primal to be comfortable — who wants to know what it's all made of? But the nudity gave this world a terrible honesty, which asked awkward questions of you.

And across the sun-surgered rockscape, the regular starbursts of creosote, the Ghengis Khan of the desert weeds, which squirts poison from its roots into the soil around — vegetal scorched-earth tactics.

She thinks she sees a rattlesnake. She doesn't really, it's just time she did. 'Buzzworms' they call them out here; it shows a glorious disdain.

The desert giant, saguaro. In summer it lies like a U-boat, ballasts full of water, all systems shut down, waiting for the danger overhead to pass; the desiccating sun. Cholla — they say it jumps at you. Ocotillo — thorny, spider-like. Barrel cactus, staghorn, chain fruit, bursage, brittlebush . . . Long, wide, bonzai forests of mesquite, where once, say people from universities, grew broad savannahs of grass.

For some hours they travelled, with no indication from her mother of the nearness or otherwise of their destination. Is it an overnight journey? It will have to be soon.

Sand! How unusual. Strangely enough, sand in these deserts is rare. It was creeping into the landscape now, like an incoming tide; and like a tide it was swamping all else. Not only vegetation but also landforms. Mountains had been washed as flat as sandcastles, now buttes and mesas followed. Nothing projected; the land was levelling.

As if emerging from Coleridge's 'caverns measureless to Man' a green river rose out of the sand on their right. Its canyon had been wrenched from its sides by the elements, and like an exposed worm it writhed across the desert floor.

All around them was flatness; the horizon started on the outside of the car doors. There was nothing there.

'Turn right here,' said her mother.

'Here?!'

'Yes.'

'Holy . . .'

'Hold your noise, Morgan.'

The road quickly dried into a pair of ragged lines across the dust. No more was said. The horizon began to shimmer; a mirage hovered above the river — its departing soul? She drove slowly, to reduce as much as possible the clanging damage to the nethers of their vehicle. As they approached the dull river she saw that shallow grooves led to it, filled with unsettled blow-dust. What were they? Either ancient ditches or the desperate finger-straithes of some giant or god, grabbed from behind and grappling for purchase on the soil as it is hauled into the river by an unimaginable beast. Good grief, is that the sort of mood she was in?

Suddenly, on the crusty salinas around them, the stubs of civilisation; thin ridges of adobe that could have been walls; a wooden door frame, seemingly unaware the house around it had gone; timbers, mummifying in the sun. Amidst a grid of shallow corrugations, a ghost town was sinking into the sand. Even the ghosts had fled.

'Stop here.'

She did so. She looked to her mother and waited. Well pleased, her mother clambered from the automobile and looked around her. Ahead of them was the green river, which in the heat-buckled perspective seemed to be lying slightly above them. Behind them was nothing but the surreal vision of little white boxes traversing the horizon; Kenworths on the highway. Around them, grooved nothingness. There was nothing here! This was a void, bursting to the gunnels with Time, Space and Eternity. A place positively bloated with silent nullity.

It was hideous; somehow offensive; a vast, useless, stupid, vicious stretch of wasted planet. As if God hadn't finished; as if in his haste to get to Rest Day he'd forgotten to fill a bit in. Empty. A desert deserted by desert. Malpais; badland. This place was so bad it was evil! This was teetering on the negative, this was an unplace!

And her mother of course was smiling. Two old friends had just remet.

'Now, this,' she said, 'now this is desert.'

And that was it. That was all. They got in the car and drove home!

The sun, having evaporated another trillion gallons of water, set behind them. 'Where have we been, Mom?' she said.

'Hotwa Vo.'

'Where?'

'Hotwa Vo.'

'Why?'

'You were born there.'

And she huddled down into that anti-monde where meanness

and malevolence are negated by the meanness and malevolence of the landscape around them, and bad old ladies become good.

UPON A WHIM Morgan telephoned Hank. No, not a whim; a cure. Cure for a restlessness; the scratching of a mental itch.

'What sort of Indian was Hoppy?' she asked him.

Sinagua.

Where from?

He wasn't sure. But he thought it was from somewhere south of Phoenix. Somewhere called Hova Twa or something.

PART TWO

Early Work Experiences

After graduation Morgan was made Assistant Curator of the Arizona State Museum and joint Head Curator of the Black Sand section of the South-west Indian Artefact Department.

She was OICP, Officer in Charge of Presentation, and her exhibits were often described in official pamphlets as 'dynamic'. This dynamism was the result of what she would later recognise as 'hybrid vigour' — the combination of two elements to make a far more rigorous third. What she had done was simple; she had combined her knowledge of art with her love of fast automobiles. She had replicated, in Black Sand pottery, the courses of the more famous Grand Prix circuits.

Using paddle-and-anvil pots, she traced the complex curves and hoops of Watkins Glen and St Jovite, or the long straights and tight bends of Mosport, Ontario. Her favourites were the torturous ones — Monza, Monjuich, Brands Hatch — so dangerous they were now unused. For tunnels on the famous Monte Carlo street rally she used traditional southern Arizonian baskets of hilaria grass and yucca leaves; for the devilish chicanes of Le Mans she used horizontal representations of Kokopelli, the humpbacked flute player. It was in fact at the premier of her most ambitious project — a recreation of the infamous Nurburgring mountain circuit, using Sinaguan willowstrip fish traps as a mountain base — that she was head-hunted to Washington.

It happened like this:

The new exhibition was called 'Here Passed the Hohokam: a study of hematite pigmentation in the Golden Years'. Mid-morning on the second day, a very attractive man and his dazzling wife arrived. The very attractive man was moderately tall and elegantly bald, with sharply etched panels of brown hair at the sides, which curled fulsomely at the back. He had brooding eyes that snapped you to attention, and a jawline that would cut silk. Dark European suit, nacreous tie, brown shoes — with polished insteps, she later noticed. He and the dazzling wife parted ways almost immediately; she to the photographic print section, and he to look at the pots. She watched him. No, he wasn't looking at the pots at all. Not after a tactile inspection of the first one or two, anyway. He was looking at their positioning. He was examining the structure of the presentation.

Before long he came over to her: she knew he would.

'Did you do the layout?' he asked in a light, careless voice. No introductions, no preamble.

'Yes.'

He nodded. Taut cheeks, full lips; not a smidgen of humour anywhere.

'My name is Dole McCall.' In three snappy movements he had plucked a card from his inside jacket pocket and handed it to her. 'Why don't you contact me.'

He started to walk away.

'What about?'

'A job.'

The card explained that Dole McCall was Chief Executive Officer of McCALL, HOEHN & SYMMONS, Investment Bankers, Washington, DC.

Before long the dazzling wife came over: she knew she would.

'Did he offer you a job?' she asked in a sort of brisk sigh.

'Who?'

'My husband. The one who gave you the card.'

'No.'

This time she gave a little unvoiced cough. 'Do you know why, honey? Because you're beautiful, that's why. Because you're drop-dead beautiful. Take the job and you'll find out what I mean. My God you will.' And with that, she too walked away.

The wife, from up close, had been a revelation. Her super-allure was created by a combination of shockingly blonde hair and a radiant tan, but close scrutiny revealed the hair as piano-key green, the tan as a perplexing glow of artificial russet — make-up somehow subcutaneously applied. Morgan later learnt it was carotene, the pigment found — yes — in carrots, and which dyes you, inside and out, a pleasantly healthy reddy brown until it is absorbed into your liver as vitamin A.

The woman glanced once over her shoulder at the door, stopping for a second in what was almost a pose. She was looking to see if her husband was watching. He wasn't. She glared quickly at the now-beautiful Morgan Moran and departed.

It was true. Morgan had turned out beautiful. No, true was the wrong word; she was officially beautiful — there's a tremendous difference. She had the testimonials to prove it. She'd been asked to enter Miss Arizona by a tense deputation of Rotarians, and she had. At an informal rehearsal she met the other contestants and had blitzed them. It's a funny thing, competing in beauty; it's like some futuristic war in another galaxy where they use weapons you can't see. You just stand there, radiating beauty, and the enemy drops dead on all sides. Hey! Drop dead! That was it!

Then she resigned. Some local papers said she'd pulled out because she refused to unbraid her hair, which was partly true; her hair was fine, uncontrollable and incorrigibly wrinkled after a decade of confinement, and she wouldn't have had a snowball's chance with it in any other configuration.

Others said it had to do with the questionnaire for all prospective beauty queens, which said:

Tick:

☐ VIRGIN

☐ NON-VIRGIN

☐ PRACTISING NON-VIRGIN

But the real reason was her waist. Twenty-six. Her other two measurements were thirty-six. Two thirty-sixes joined up by this tree stump, this barrel called twenty-six! Directly underneath your waist, she'd been told, are your kidneys, and she'd offered to donate one to a needy human who was renally failing. One kidney out of the way would give her waist a chance to get more concavity into it. Her offer was politely declined. A diabetic somewhere died because of inavailability of kidneys and Morgan withdrew from Miss Arizona.

In Washington

On her first day, Dole McCall took her out to lunch. Well, he took her to lunch but not out. The restaurant was in the red-brick pile in Market Square, off Pennsylvania Ave, that was the home of McCall, Hoehn & Symmons.

There were in fact two restaurants at McCall, Hoehn Etc; a spacious, gracious, airy one on the fourth floor — in a splendid room built into the roof to save tax in colonial times — and a basement swillery squeezed between the seeping, mornay-painted, bulging brick cellar walls that held out Washington's Quaternary soil. The elevated restaurant was for company partners, vice-presidents and distinguished clients; the pit restaurant was for humanity. He'd shown her both, then, blessedly, taken her to the former.

'Apartment okay?' he asked.

'Wonderful.' She could hardly say anything else; it had been organised for her by the company. But in fact, unlike most solicited compliments, this one was true. It was a pretty little two-storey walk-up on a brick-paved street in the Rock Creek Park district of northwest Washington. The picture window of her lounge gave widely onto both the apartment buildings that blocked her view of the National Cathedral.

'Should be,' he said. Presumably he was referring to the rent bill. 'Henry Kissinger lives just two blocks over,' he added.

She watched Dole McCall eating his flat, grey stew. The sleeve of his charcoal suit stretched upwards a little. A golden Otis oyster watch came into view, over his shirtsleeve. And so did another. In fact she could have sworn there was a third. Three gold watches over his shirt. She glanced at the other arm.

'You like operas?' he asked.

Opera! He was going to invite her to an opera? 'I've never been, but I guess I would.' Hey! First day out and she's on a thousand-dollar date! She's in the fast lane to the fast lane!

'My mom used to take me when I was a kid,' continued Dole McCall, 'so I'd be cultured. Only time I screamed harder was at the dentist. You used to scream at the dentist?'

He seemed quite happy talking about dentists, then about screaming in general, and then how his brother had screamed when the neighbour's two elkhounds had eaten his guinea pigs.

'Wasn't the neighbour's fault, an' he was real cut up about it. Said he'd replace them. He asked where did you get them and how much were they? And when my mom told him ninety cents, he said that sounded kinda cheap, an' here was five bucks extra. After that my brother swore he saw him feeding his elkhounds on them. I never saw him feeding 'em guineapigs myself, but well, when you think about it, they were a helluva lot cheaper'n Chum.'

The subject of the opera was touched on again only briefly when he observed that he couldn't see how people could take watching people getting stabbed then singing instead of bleeding. Three weeks later she learnt that McCall, Hoehn had sponsored a Met season of *La Traviatta*. She wasn't invited and as far as she knew he didn't go anyway; not even with his carotene-tinctured, nearly cuckqueaned wife.

Cuckqueaned — glorious word: 'noun, a female cuckold'. How his wife was nearly cuckqueaned is another story. If the story were to be given a name, it would probably be 'The Night of the Glowing Carrot'.

The dessert arrived. A low square of off-white, coarsely textured pastry. A thin red horizontal line bisected it like a perfect clawmark. On its sugar-dusted top was a bird dropping of cream. The plastic-coated menu identified the dessert as 'strawberry shortcake'. Cunningly she poured milk over it, knowing that to attempt to divide the dry shortcake with her spoon would cause dangerous splinters to snap off the side and perhaps fly across the room. She reduced its breaking strain with milk, coaxing it down from the fragile volatility of a Princz Rupert's Drop to the soggy passivity of playdough.

He had a wedge of Black Forest cake, the shape, the colour and almost the size of the cutwater of an oiltanker.

'I read *Low-Risk Strategies for the Investor*,' she said as he picked up his cake fork. 'I read the whole thing on the train over from Phoenix.'

Dole McCall made no immediate comment. 'Good; great,' he said at last. 'Nothing you learn is ever wasted.' He seemed to have finished this thought, but he hadn't. 'Though it might seem as though it is sometimes,' he mumbled. She waited; he'd seemed to be leading to something. 'Oh?' she prompted.

He sighed and carved a shaving of prow. 'Lemme tell you 'bout the two restaurants here,' he said, then leaned into his forkful of cake and munched in front of her for about thirty seconds. She waited, keeping tight reign on her expression. He continued: 'See this one's okay; but the one in the basement's a cesspool. Thing is, food's exactly the same; here, there. Identical. Same food — well, no wonder, only room for one lot of cooking, see? Cost the earth to put in another kitchen, and it's against building regulations anyway — this building's got official heritage, see? We can't touch it 'cos it was built in the olden days. So what you get up here's what they get down there. Well actually, what they get down there's what we get up here's more like it; kitchen's down there. Problem is, no time for a lunchtime out. Traders can't afford to leave their desk, and if they send out, all they get is burgers or pizza or Chinese, and that stuff leaves a nex' day stink that blows the wax outta your ears. So we have to . . .'

She was leaning forward. She only realised this when she saw the blunt tip of her hair dangling at ninety degrees above the puggy remains of her dessert. 'May I ask why we're talking kitchens?' she blurted, already appalled with realisation.

'Well, thought you should have some background on the matter . . .'

'Do you mean to say you brought me two thousand miles from Arizona as a cook?'

His eyes flared like umbrellas. 'Christ, no, not as cook! You're in charge of the whole thing. You're listed as the Culinary Presentation Officer.'

'But this is an investment bank! This is where you buy and sell bonds and equity! I read a financial book, I know what LIBOR means, I know you call IBM "Big Blue", I . . . and all you want me to do is present food!'

'For forty thousand dollars a year. Yeah. Plus bonuses.'

'What bonuses?'

'I dunno right off. But everyone gets bonuses. The whole investment banking system works on bonuses.'

'I'll have to reconsider.'

'Reconsider what? Your salary? It's three times what you got in the museum. I checked.'

'I've got a first in Art History.'

'Yeah; maybe you have. What you really got is a good eye for presenting flimflam. I looked at them dumb pots in the museum, an' I said to myself; this presentation's got something, it's got — go, it's racy. Hell, if she can make an interesting presentation outa crap like this, she can do it outa anything. Even the food at McCall, Hoehn! — Look, forty-two five hundred with a review after six months.'

Somewhere in the distance, over the horizon of her brain, she heard the smashed crockery of standards of value. 'One condition,' she said.

'What's that?'

'I can redecorate this room. My talent, your chequebook.'

'Sure.' A shrug. 'Okay, sure. Why?'

'I reckon,' she said, sitting back, looking slowly about her, 'if you want to emphasise social difference, you've got to redecorate.'

'Yeah,' he said, sitting back also, looking round. 'I see what you mean.' He leaned forward, spoke hoodedly. 'Listen, now an' then I bring a trader up here for lunch; when he's made a big kill, when he's brought us a client from Wall Street or something like that. Thing is, that's fine, but I don't like them getting big ideas — you know, thinking it's gonna be on a regular basis. You redecorate, yeah; an' make it something that'll make them hamsters downstairs feel uncomfortable.'

Challenges of the Job

MORGAN FAIRLY QUICKLY decided on a Louis XIV motif. Not perhaps as imaginative as one would expect from an Hons in Art, but, well, what epoch more apt for the monarchs of trade? — Absolutism? Absolutely!

Polystyrene pillars were commissioned, and sprayed with polyvinyl marble; gilt-framed mirrors, large as lakes, were dangled from the walls beside pastel portraits of stags, young women with high breasts, and parties picnicking beside ornamental ponds. Sculpted seventeenth-century patricians in wigs and no eyeballs were set into thrush-egg-blue alcoves, next to free-standing black and gold amphoras and Japanese screens. An artificial fireplace of Caracas marble, and above it a portrait of — not Louis himself, but Molière, presiding genius of the Age of the Sun King. She'd read somewhere he'd died while performing in one of his own plays. *Le Malade Imaginaire*, it was called, which she found screamingly funny.

In all, she created a fourth-floor environment for aristocrats; for the nobles of Reaganomics.

A FEW MONTHS later she obtained permission to redecorate downstairs as well. She hadn't intended to, she hadn't even intended revisiting the accursed place; but she changed her mind on both counts. She wanted revenge.

She set savagely to work and daubed those dank, grimy walls

with late Palaeolithic ochre scrawls; the primitive rock art of the caves of Lascaux and Altamira. She gave the denizens of the Pit an environment that reflected their status: she gave them cave art.

TRADERS

SEXUAL HARASSMENT IS witty to traders.

Traders drill spy holes into the women's toilets. They have their compeers fired for fun. They call their customers 'victims'. They play bestial practical jokes. They lie, and treat others cruelly. They belch, and fart louder than Peter the Great. They scream and swear. The trading floor is like Hitler's Operations Room on a bad day in mid-'45.

The decor was no more than they deserved, cave art for cavemen; but it was obvious that her act of revenge was viewed with disappointment by management.

'See you painted the basement in mammoths?' murmured Dole McCall, distractedly forlorn and measuring the lengths of his nails against one another. Mind you, he always looked forlorn; his skin wore a perennial matte finish of prison-wall pallor. They were in his office. It could do with a motif. Pink Period clowns?

'It seemed apt.'

'Kinda hoping you'd do . . . something soothing. That European guy who does yellow birds upside down.'

'Klee?'

'No, Clee or somethin'. Saw some in a book the other day. Sorta stuff you get in kids' playrooms.'

'It was either Prehistoric or Goya's Black paintings, as far as I was concerned.'

'Idea was you'd, you know, calm them down a bit.'

'Only calm they're interested in from me is *post coitum triste*.'

'They're all right. High-spirited; it's just all the adrenalin.'

Adrenalin? Plus rocket fuel! But what Dole McCall's highly pigmented wife had told her that day in Arizona now made sense. 'Drop-dead beautiful'; it was the only means of control in the midst of this troupe of gorillas, cavemen, whooping, banana-munching neanderthals. Turn up on the trading floor as a mildly pretty young thing and you'll spend your time plucking fingers out of your pants. But turn up imperious, and these braying, doubt-wracked creeps will fold. Drop-dead, ferocious beauty;

beauty as mace; the only way. In the first five weeks of her tenure, four other women, all pretty, had come and gone — sobbing — from McCall, Hoehn & Symmons.

YET STRANGELY ENOUGH, it was to the Pit that Morgan was increasingly drawn. The executives who dined upstairs at the Sun King's golden tables were etiolated, troubled, smileless men, whose expressions were always strangely out of kilter with their surroundings; as if they were listening to messages from invisible headphones. Their faces, when in neutral, still held a faintly puzzled irritability, and they generated a sort of anti-charisma that made them so inconsequential she had nearly walked through one or other of them on several occasions. The Mighty Mirrorglass Men gave off barely a reflection.

THE NIGHT OF THE GLOWING CARROT: AN INTERLUDE

DOLE MCCALL SAT opposite Morgan, dark-suited, chartreuse-handkerchiefed; an effigy of immaculate desirability — gold cufflinks, dazzling wing-tip shoes, lustrous Studio 31 winter tan, good posture, dry hands, features with the gloriously chiselled severity of a Pharaoh. His fingernails, perfect as piano keys, curled around his double vodka, three olives. Morgan admired him over a double gin and twist. Pol Roget waited in a silver ice bucket.

Nice place; cubicles of plush red Pullman on the far side, little red-and-white-clothed pavement-society tables on this side. Behind Dole McCall, a hunting scene by E. J. Herberte; delirious dogs, riders in coats of runnerbean red, all posing for E. J. Herberte before dashing off to kill things. In for the kill.

The place was elegantly unfull. An artistic smattering of other couples dotted the sallow Impressionist canvas of the restaurant. Loud clashes of stainless steel from behind the far wall suggested there was either a joust or some cooking going on behind the kitchen door; browning garlic and olive oil deliciously stung the air. She quaffs an unladylike bumper of gin, rattles it round her head like Listerine and settles back, warm and accommodating, ready to be seduced.

Soft-shell crabs 'pour mademoiselle'; burger and fries 'for sir'

— (sir did not understand 'foreign languages'). The gorgeous Dole McCall: dumber than a barrel of hair. Who cares! Let copulation thrive! She dampens at the prospect of an interlude of imbecilic frottage.

He leans over, attentive. 'C'n I make a suggestion?'

Ah. Let battle commence. The first subtle thrust to be lightly parried.

'Anything.'

'Let's go to your place and fuck.'

THEY WERE SPRAWLED across her beige chaise longue. Sounds and actions had blurred into a delicious congress of divestment, skin was ecstatically exposed, touches exploded in veins, secret places widened like anemones. 'Rummage! Pillage! Make me disappear!'

Then, suddenly, there it was. She had slithered down his hard surfaces and was staring at it now; Dole McCall's triumphant maypole. She stared. Nothing in Morgan's experience had prepared her for such a moment; nothing within her cache of etiquette could be placed between her and her response. There it was. Did he use carotene too? Was it stained from confrication with his internally pigmented wife? Whatever. Whichever. There it was; glowing. Glowing in the dark like a carrot.

That had been the end; their relationship had never recovered from her whoops of manic hilarity.

The Pit

IT WAS IN the Pit that things happened, where life surged, where wheels were driven round, where fingers were put in pies, where worms turned, where pigeons came home to roost, where nuts were stored for winter, where the earth revolved. Life in the Pit was a primordial stew, lubricated by underarm sweat and flying spittle, from which these bloated, brachycephalic druggels — these Traders — emerged, semi-finished — like emotional axolotls — to do battle, powered by greed, with the forces of unmoney. They were crass, vile, repulsive — and invigorating! She would listen as they shouted through full mouths of beef stew (Boeuf Royale above), 'An' I dumped them, man, I dumped those mothers; "*meum dictum pactum*," I said to that plum-throated Oxford jerk, and he took it; three million nose-diving cruzados!

They'll be lower than whaleshit tomorrow! Jeezas, there's a customer born every minute!'

They came down only for dinners. At the end of their day, when the money had done its moonlight flit to the Bahamas and Grand Cayman, they relaxed with food and verbal violence in the Pit before going to bars to imbibe chemicals.

Lunches were consumed on the hoof. Trolleys of victuals were dispatched to the second-floor trading room, from whither emanated, diurnally, the odours of the trough. She had learned the rules of the trough from horrified experience.

Rules of the Trough

MEATBALLS, NO; MEAT loaf, yes — (it was aerodynamically unsuited as a projectile). Baked hash, yes; meat croquettes, no. Lasagne, yes; chili con carne, no — the resultant smell soon exceeded the Chicago holding pens. Pork chops, yes; spare ribs no, — boomerang time. And watch the veges: cabbage, yes; carrots no; beans, yes; peas, no; celery, yes; parsnips, no. Potatoes diced, yes; whole or mashed, no no no!

Antisocial Darwinism

JOHNNY PIETRAPETOSA WAS the Trader King. He was twenty-three — in age and stones — with a degree in industrial chemistry from Oberlin, and was probably about to speciate: become another life-form. He was at the end of the chain of *Homo sapiens* and ready to be transmogrified by Darwinism into *Homo tradens*. He had evolved the ultimate trader's body — both bullish and bearish — and had perfected Trader's Bray, which worked by simply opening the mouth and clenching and unclenching the buttocks. By this means he could anally propel his voice over six screaming salesmen. He had also been blessed with Trader's Ear, which meant that with the decibel content of a gamelan gong in each inner canal, he could still hear, in digits, to four decimal places.

From Johnny she learnt the history of finance: 'You know how these guys started out? Huh? McCall, Hoehn, Symmons? Caddies. They wuz caddies; ammo-humpers, junior wood-chucks, petunia donkeys. In those days all the finance was done on the golf course. They jus' listened up, that's all. Then '75, deregulation; the old white-shoe bankers went down like a row of shitcans. Spilled it to the runts who'd been listening. Caddies. McCall, Hoehn, Symmons. Annual millionaires. They'd been listening but they hadn't been playing, so didn't have no old-school-tie obligations and that crap; went into it properly; banking without honour, that's business.'

This discourse had got Johnny through his main. He wore wide ties to protect his shirt from the spillage of discourse: 'Gemme some of that dessert offa that trolley, Morg, willya? Huh? That's your job innit? Gettn off your scrumptious butt an' gettn me some two-crust?'

'No pie, Johnny; flan or gelatin pudding.'

'Stuff that schlock, Morg, I want two-crust!'

'It was a heavy main, Johnny; with heavy mains you have light dessert.'

'Fuck light dessert. I want heavy dessert; I want poundage in my dessert! I don't put four hundred million a year through this sonofabitch company so it can feed me bum fluff!'

ON OTHER OCCASIONS she would learn the philosophies of Wall Street: 'See, it's not education that makes you good; hell, I got so much education it'd make ya sick — I got education in how you make ammonia outa air, an' waddo I do with it? I trade money. See, I've got empathy, empathy with money. The guys up there on Floor Two, the ones that make the price of a nuclear fuckin' submarine every day, they make it because they are money, they are the nature of money. See, to create the sorta money we do up there, you gotta go back to the very roots of money; you gotta hook into its nature. See, now ol' Shakespeare of England, he believed crocodiles wuz born out of the mud of the Nile. Well, money is born outa the goo of wells, the sludge of mines, the treacles of untreated coca. Money is sleaze. An' that's what you gotta be up there: sleaze. You gotta fiddle with money like creeps fiddle with little boys. It's the way, Morg; the only motherfuckin' goddam way. Giz another coupla them woofie puddings then, Morg.'

SHE RELENTED. SHE redecorated. She expunged the mammoths and painted the Pit after the style of Paul Klee.

In fact, not a great deal of rearrangement was necessary; Klee, after all, spent his later years studying the art of prehistoric caves.

Anyway, she brought the fiscal cavemen almost into the present; she eased her mammoths, bison and stricken deer into Klee's deceptively simple, faintly ominous hieroglyphics.

'Jeezas! Them guys had another spaghetti fight in here, Morg?' said Johnny as he looked round at the spiderously cartooned walls on unveiling day in the Pit. But he was smiling semi-appreciatively as he sat beneath the 'Twittering Machine' and screamed for meat.

Plates

HER MOTHER HAD sent her a catalogue of plates from Acomazuni Potteries. Morgan ordered several dozen. The edges of the Hohokam-style plates were decorated with sculpted birds and animals, or incised with geometrical reliefs, often of snakes or toads. Strangely, these attractive designs had been used by the Hohokam only as offerings to the dead.

She used them downstairs. It seemed appropriate; the life of the average Pit plate was lamentably short.

Trading

GROWN MEN WERE howling, lights were flashing, telephones screamed. The reeking, sweltrous room glowed like kryptonite from the spill of an Argus of monitors.

Morgan pushed the stainless-steel trolley down the aisle, past rows of wide-eyed, frothing men chained to telephones like galley slaves. It was one thirty p.m. Filthy plates mixed contents with printout sheets and graph papers. Reefs of mashed potato clung to the fibroplaster walls, fleets of flattened peas had moon-landed on the ceiling, Canaveralled there by plastic rulers. She excavated plates from middens of used figures; bacterial fungi were growing from the congealed leftovers like usnea from skulls. Knives and forks, sealed to plates by three-week gravy — don't use force, you'll break the plate. 'Culinary Presentation Officer'? Huh! Slushy! That was her technical term! None of the other three women on her staff would dare to enter this den. She did it herself; marching amongst the mob of monetary Minotaurs, safe inside her force field of intimidating beauty.

'Up point seven seven!'

'Mine, mine, mine!'

'Fuck the put, it's a call, you stupid bastard; don't do this to me!'

'Revision!' screams Abe Wallenstein. 'The fucker's gone down!'

'God! No! Oh don't let it happen!'

'Yours, yours, yours!'

'Number's down by point four!'

'Jeezas, I'm up one sixty! I'm dead, I'm doing a dog!'

'I gotta high-roll fucker here who thinks Pornex is cheap!'

'It's long the mark!'

'Where's the reports? Where's the fucking reports, man! I can't do it without the reports!'

'Geneva's buying big, they're buying huge! I can't hold 'em; they're killing me!'

'Where's the proofs on the margins? I need margins!'

'Christ, I think I bought a wooden ticket!'

It was hysteria based on greed and fear: grear? freed? The most disturbing but poignant aspect of the frenzy was its self-revelatory nature; they wailed in public horror, they screamed their dread to the skies. They were stampeding through a vale of nightmare, disaster stalking their every step and driving them into ever-increasing, panic-stricken frenzy. And blow by blow they each shrieked their ordeal to the other benighted forexmen around them.

The stock trading pit was evidently much worse.

Morgan slams the last Hohokam plate onto the trolley, a gesture lost in the cacophony. She tosses her head, gives an unheard hiss of contempt and silently rattles towards the elevator. She reaches for the plastic button of the elevator, gingerly avoiding the statically electrified steel. A vocal sonic boom stops her; turns her round. The anally powered voice of Johnny Pietrapetosa envelopes the din of the room like a blanket over a parrot cage, smothering it into profound silence.

'Morgan! It's for you!'

He is standing, much as Mussolini does in posters, belly echoed in miniature by his prognathous jaw, holding out a white telephone in a half-mast Fascist salute. His face is a mask of contained outrage.

She walks down the corridor of silent traders towards him, awed, and mirroring the awed gaze of the many in her eyes. The clusters of telephones have fallen uncannily silent as well.

'It's for me?' she whispers; and it is audible. On the forex trading floor, during trading hours, a whisper is audible!

'It's your mother.'

'What?'

Morgan takes the receiver, stares at it dumbly as if lip-reading the caller.

'How many times have you told her not to call you at the office,' mutters Johnny Pietrapetosa, but there is no humour in his voice. A private call has polluted the trading room. Civilisation, as he knows it, is under invasion. He stands waiting. She can feel them all waiting. She puts the receiver to her ear.

'Mom?'

'Give me a rate.'

'Give you a what?'

'Is that not what you say? "Give me a rate"?'

'A rate on what, Mom?'

'Wampum.'

'Wampum?'

'Landsakes, Morgan child, did I not teach you how to hear properly? Must you echo everything I say?'

'I'm sorry, Mom, I don't understand. This is a currency trading room an' . . .'

'Exactly. So give me a rate on wampum! Do you prefer that I take my patronage to First Boston?'

'Hang on a moment, Mom.'

'Had I known of this delay I would have called collect!'

Morgan lowered the phone; turned a half-circle to encompass the traders, feeling for some reason a little like Alice in Wonderland.

'My mom wants a rate on wampum.'

The silence somehow intensified. Even the telephones awaited events.

'Wampum?' said Johnny. 'Ain't that some sorta clothing?'

'It usta be a currency,' said little Abe Wallenstein. 'Indians usta spend it.'

'Yeah, but if it's a dead currency, that'd be like buying Confederate dollars,' observes Nat Burns.

'Well, what exactly is it?' said Johnny.

'Mom, you still there?'

'Of course I am still here, child! That is not to say I will not have to go out on the streets shortly, to pay for this call!'

'What exactly is wampum, Mom?'

'Have you forsaken your entire heritage, child? Wampum is our traditional currency!'

'Yeah, but, Mom, I don't think we use it any more.'

'That is because there has not been any. Now there is; we are making it.'

'You're making Native Indian currency? You . . . entitled to do that, Mom?'

'I didn't do it, child. They did: the consumer. We were making wampum simply as traditional belts from beads and left-handed whelks, then one day a person offered it as currency for the other products they had purchased at the store. To us it seemed a good gimmick; we would accept wampum as currency in our store. And then the system spread. Now the whole of Phoenix deals in wampum — all the stores, the bars, the cinemas. Well, if wampum is to be a currency, it will be my currency.'

'I always sorta thought Congress did the money side of everything, Mom?'

'The Equal Rights Commission of Congress has given me the right to print wampum. But to do this I must have an official rate. Now landsakes, child, must I haggle with my own daughter over the price of my own money? Give me a rate!'

Her voice had carried across the silent room. Abe Wallenstein, five foot three (in built-ups) sidled forward. 'Morg,' he whispered, 'ask her, was it long or short the dollar last time they used it?'

'How do you mean, Abe?'

'Well, back in the Olden Days, what would the bank . . . jeezas, I s'pose they were trading posts then. Hell, what's something they used to buy in the Olden Days?'

'Elks?' murmured Taft Raye.

'Try beavers. They're smaller,' whispered Abe Wallenstein. 'Ask her how many beavers you got for a wampum?'

'No use asking what you got for it in the Olden Days,' observed Bradford Braddock Jnr. 'Ask her what you get for it now.'

'That's sorta what she's asking us, Bradford,' gritted Morgan.

'Are you still there, child? Give me a rate, godammit! Congress needs to know!'

Johnny Pietrapetosa took the phone from Morgan's bloodless hand. 'Mrs Moran? Johnny Pietrapetosa, trader, McCall, Hoehn & Symmons. Thanks for calling. How soon you reckon you could get us a wampum up here? Six o'clock courier tonight? Fine, I'll wait for it. I'll give you a price eight thirty tomorrow morning, Mrs Moran . . . Acomazuni? Fine, Acomazuni. You'll hear from me then.'

LATE THAT EVENING Johnny Pietrapetosa, Napoleon of the trading floor, general of the Greeding of America, drove his Opel into the petrol island next to Hamburger Haven on M St and ordered a gallon of unleaded. He told them about it next day.

'Poor schmuck didn't know what I was talking about. One gallon, Johnny?' Knows me see? "Yep," I says, "and I want change too." An' I hands him the wampum! Ahahahah!'

'So whaddid he give you?' asks Abe Wallenstein.

'Nuthin! But he took it. No change; didn' know how to. But he took it!'

'So . . .'

'So one wampum's a gallon of unleaded!'

And so the price was fixed, as these things are. At eight thirty that morning Johnny made an offer over the phone. 'I'll give ya ninety-three cents against the wampum, Mrs Moran.'

And a currency was born.

WAMPUM: THE BULL RUN

THE NEXT EIGHT months were all Up! Bonzo was back in Washington and times were propitious. Johnny Pietrapetosa explained why in a dinnertime lecture laced in equal measure with wisdom and gravy.

'See Reagan's devised this economic philosophy called the 'Dribble-up System'. It's brilliant. Money is sucked upwards outta the hands of the poor and tatty and into the coffers of big business so they can use it in an orderly fashion. Nearest thing we's ever had to 'pure economics'! For the first time just about the whole GNP is going into the places where it makes most profit, unadulterated by bits being taken out for hospitals an' schools an' wages an' all them unprofitable ventures. It's a terrific breakthrough. He could get the Nobel for economics! He's the first president to make a full-out attack on the invidious agencies that lie in the way of generating money!

'See, he was clever enough to realise that people and money aren't in the same category any more. Overall it doesn't really matter if people work, as long as money does. Cut out the middleman — the human being, see? — and you don' need cars, or steel, or textiles or machinery! Or any of them risky items, Morg. Jus' need money.'

'Brilliant,' she said a little coldly. 'So Reagan's put the country back on its feet by shafting the automobile industry?'

A loud pause. 'Yeah. In a way. Jeez, that's not bad, Morg! Very witty!'

'Thanks,' she said politely.

'You're welcome. Lotta irony in the situation of course. Here he is, Reagan, number one Commie hater in the whole world, and yet he's the one that's invented the rich few and the unquiet masses. He's the guy who's most making Karl Marx look good.'

WAMPUM HIT THE neo-Marxian dribble-up market with the force of a slam dunk. 'Hey, fierce! Lookit what I found!' squealed the Huppies, Chuppies, Guppies, Rumpies, Yumpies, Yippies, Yeepies, Dinks, Diks and Dewks. Wampum was 'it' — dinky, kinky, slinky; a new, nonfunky issue with quick-rise value, with none of the unchic connotations of greed or seriousness. A sure thing, 'the latest'; a must-have. Acomazuni wampum quickly rose to 143 against the Congress dollar. The forex floors were hot for wampum. 'The world, it is my oyster!' crowed Morgan's mother. 'I have a licence to print money!'

As Johnny Pietrapetosa said: 'Eighty-five'll be seen as the year of the Wampumisation of the Market!'

ACOMAZUNI ENTERPRISES FLOURISHED. A *Time* magazine cover story called Morgan's mother the 'Grandma Moses of the fiscal mart'.

And wampum had a desperately desired effect upon Morgan's career . . .

'Look, come into my office, willya, Morg?' said Jed Barrel one early afternoon in spring. 'Gotta non-comestible career-change proposition to put to ya.'

Her heart leapt like a four-chambered flea. Carefully, so as not to overturn the balance of Fate, Morgan abandoned her trolley and apron and entered the fourth-floor office of Jed Barrel.

The most famous thing about Jed's office was the increasing size of his fish tank. Old stagers like Johnny could remember when it was a melon-sized bowl with two fish, then it was promoted to basketball size with four, then it went square and gained dozens of tiny little somethings that looked like animated painted fingernails . . . and so on. The sad fact of the matter was that the fish tank had better advancement prospects than did Jed. He'd been waiting thirteen years to be made a partner, and every time he was passed over for the Board he promoted his fish tank. It was now a glass pillar that reached to just under the low grey ceiling; full of weeds, bubbling water, a plastic shipwreck and these red and black goggle-eyed fish that have fins like the goo that comes out of cracked boiling eggs. Jed stood beside his tornado of leaking fish.

'Could have some great news for you, Morg,' he said. 'Thing is, the Equal Opportunities Department's just had its first meeting . . .'

'I'd heard we might be getting an Equal Opportunities Department, Jed.' Flatter him, praise him, lick his bootstraps! Get that job! 'At your instigation, was it?'

'Yeah; well, partly. It had a fair amount to do with the District Equal Opportunities Board telling us of the fiscal disadvantages that could accrue if we didn't set up an Equal Opportunities Department before the end of the financial year, actually, but the rest of the impetus came from me — yeah.'

She smiled slickly. 'I can understand that, Jed.' She projected pheromones towards him, sucked in her waist, swelled herself pneumatically above and below it. 'And I bet you're the guy at the top too, Jed?'

'Yeah, I'm the guy at the top, I s'pose you could say.' If he wore braces he'd now be thrumming them and saying 'Aw shucks'. 'Equal Opportunity buck stops right here, I guess.'

Her heart thumped almost painfully in her throat and ears. 'Congratulations.'

'I appreciate that.'

'You're welcome. What's the suggestion, Jed?'

'Well, conversation at the first meeting got pretty quickly

round to wampum, an' we — the executive of the EOD — we thought, well, seeing as how wampum's sorta cultural for you — I mean, to us it's just bits of belt that happen to be hot on the forex market — but to you, when you were an Indian, like, hunnerds an' hunnerds of years ago, wampum were things you wore. Not just commodities; these were clothes, accessories; like bras an' suspenders . . .' His eyes alighted like tongues upon her breasts.

'And belts?' she added, deflectingly.

'Yeah, that sorta thing.'

'And so because they're part of my culture, you . . .'

'Yeah. Because you're more intimately associated with wampum than us, we thought you should be more associated with it here at the company . . .'

It had happened! Her own console, her own chair, behind her own Desk of Wampum! She hauled the slightly repulsive Jed from his magnified world behind the fish tank, hugged him into priapism and kissed his damp cheek. 'Oh wow! Hey! Gee thanks, Jed! I can tell you now, I've got to admit, I've wanted to get onto that floor for months! I really have. I can do it; I've been watching. I won't let you down, Jed, I promise. I'll be great. Really great. You won't regret this. When do I start?'

Her own desk! She was to join the brawling, baying, turpiloquent life of the second floor and the Pit! Fervently she propelled her gratitude across the prairies beneath the Rust Belt, the mobile-home parks and the five-diamond resorts, to the great Indian goddess — the Chac Mool — of Positive Discrimination. 'Thank you, thank you,' she whispered in her mind.

SOME WEEKS LATER, when she was established as HODWT — Head of Desk, Wampum Trading, just three down the row from Johnny Pietrapetosa and with her own bright screen and tentacle of phones, Johnny said to her, 'They din' mean a desk at all.'

She looked up from her screen, oblivious for a moment to its news. 'What? Who didn't?'

'Jed Barrel. Equal Opportunities wasn't going to offer you a desk.'

Her eyes narrowed; behind his broad, golden innocence was a smirk. 'What was it going to offer me?'

'A calendar.'

'What?'

'A McCall's calendar. You wearing wampum belts. If you see what I mean. If it worked out, there was gonna be a co-production with *Playboy*. You were gonna be the first-ever Sinagua centrefold. Equal Opportunities has bin onta *Playboy* too.'

SHE TOOK TO the business of trading like a dentist takes to pain. She had a God-given affinity; the prescience of the White Buffalo Cow Woman. Her anticipation was uncanny, and across the spittle-damp forex floors of the nation she gained renown as one who could 'read the wind'.

MARY

THE STORY WAS legitimised by appearing on television:

'Morgan, you're a North American Native Indian person,' said the interviewer, 'is it true you're bringing some deeply indigenous skills of prophesy into the modern world of business?'

'Well, I don't think so, Mary-Lee, but . . .'

'There's that story about reading the wind, isn't there? How does that go again?'

'Well, of course it's just a quaint folk tale, but they say there was a subtribe of the Sinagua Indians — the Q:onaguapai, who lived in the Grand Canyon. What they believed was that the wind contained everything it passed over. They could look up at the wind and read if there was a herd of buffalo on the plain above, or deer at the stream. So they'd know if it was worthwhile climbing up the canyonside.'

'And you just might be bringing those skills into the marketplace?'

'Oh I don't think so Mary-Lee. I'm just lucky I guess.' (Modest laughter.)

'Can luck be that consistent though, Morgan? There's plenty of traders who'll say it can't. They say your reading of the dollar is uncanny. There has to be something more than luck.'

THERE SURE DID. And it was called Mary Krueljack. Mary of the Irish skin, violently blue eyes (contacts) and rosebud mouth. Mary Krueljack, with whom she drank Black Russians in Strands, a few blocks down M Street from her apartment.

She'd been dreamily shopping round Georgetown one day,

wandering past the urban grunge shops with their windowfuls of whips and thongs for tying intimate friends to beds with, and the T-shirt outlets (TANNED RESTED AND READY . . . with a picture of Richard Nixon underneath); going nowhere really, simply floating on the tide. Well, at the corner of M and Seventh the terrain tilts sharply down towards New York Avenue, and as you cross the road you are tipped by geography into the doorway of Strands, whether you like it or not. Well dammit, now she was here . . .

Within another minute she had met Mary.

Mary was pregnant. Mary had been pregnant three times, to different men, and always because of contraceptive failure. Mary's fecundity had prevailed over rubber, creams and pills. It was possible that without contraception Mary would be childless.

'Look, look at this,' Mary had said, about four minutes into their relationship. She'd wobbled down from her high barstool, parted the bottom of her blouse and pulled her black slacks down to the beginnings of her tarantulous pubes. The handful of male patrons looked on. 'It popped out today.' She referred to her navel, which jutted like a tiny ear from her paunch. 'D'y reckon you can get cosmetic surgery for that sort of thing?'

They met often after that. Mary drank Napa Valley chardonnay, (the baby presumably took hers amniotically), and they discussed big issues such as whether Mary's inability to respond with fervour to 'God Bless America' should result in therapy for patriotism or atheism. Then, one night, over white wine and Black Russians, they began discussing careers. Mary worked in a supermarket . . .

Mary's Tale

She had been a checkout assistant, clocking her terminal ID — 10001125001 3 — into whichever register she had been assigned that day, running infinite purchases over its little beeping scanner, then expunging her identity at the end of the day and walking away from the machine, perhaps forever. Well, that's how it was supposed to happen. Mary developed a crush on terminal number eleven, which blossomed into an insuperable devotion. At first she would trade terminals, in order to be with Eleven, then, when her passion became apparent, unscrupulous checkout compeers would sell it to her. Ultimately she refused to leave Eleven's side at all, and became as resolute about staying nights as had Bartleby the Scrivener. She was taken to the company psychoanalyst, who cured her by transferring her across town to a job in the warehouse.

'The warehouse. One shed,' said Mary, 'one shed, big as a city block, and packed to the gunnels. An' you know what that mother is full of?'

'What's it full of?'

'Inflation. Raw, unprocessed inflation.'

'Of course! You've got all the prices there. Hey!' Morgan lurched forward, almost sharing Mary's lap with Randy or Candy or whoever was foetally developing in there. 'You can work it out, the whole thing! Jeezas, Mary, if I knew what inflation was going to be in my job, I'd know what the interest rate was going to be and . . .'

Mary's face was a scrollwork of contempt. 'That's not how you make inflation. Inflation, in the Commodities World, is made by consensus.'

'Yeah?'

'Yeah. You have all your commodity prices. They're all on a computer . . .'

'You got access to that computer?'

'Yeah.'

'Hey!'

'It's got a password.'

'Shit.'

'It's "Oliver Twist".'

'Hey!'

'Don't mean anything, those prices. You don't get inflation from them; you don't get inflation till you have the vote.'

'You vote inflation?'

'In the Commodities World you do, yeah. See, the big eight supermarkets have a teleconference every month. They all listen to the price hikes or dips, and then they have a vote on what inflation should be — based on certain equations; like, ten hikes of one-hundredth the value of a commodity will be one-tenth of a percent on the national index.'

'Hey, you know your stuff!'

'Yeah. Gotta know your stuff in the commodities world. Commodities world is responsible for thirty-six percent of national inflation.' Her face was bright with childish pride; the head around it wobbled.

'That right?'

'Yep. Only petrol's higher 'n that. Salaries is third; way back. Anyway, from all these equations and whatnots, the Pricing Co-ordinators work out what inflation should be, and vote on it.'

'Hey, that's price-fixing! Where's all this freedom of choice and competition the consumer's supposed to get?'

'That's there. Told you, you know nothin'! Jus' listen up.'

'Okay, okay.'

'Thing is, they have a vote on what they think the month's thirty-six percent of the inflation should be. But that's just a general inflation figure, see?'

'Sorta.'

'Look, say they all think it should be two point seven inflation that week, right?'

'Right.'

'Well, all that means is that each chain will put up prices two point seven — but on any products they like, not specific ones. See? That's where your competition comes in, they all put their inflation on different things.'

'That's sharp.'

'Yeah. Now that's jus' for putting inflation up . . .'

'Hey, come on — you going to tell me supermarkets put their prices down?'

'You never heard of specials?' Witheringly. Then she spoilt it by spilling wine onto Randy or Candy.

'Oh yeah, specials.'

'See, what happens is, at the meeting they might find out that there's only been, say, four lots of ten increases of more than a hundredth the value of the product — usually there's about fifteen or twenty. Well, then they decide that there'll be no inflation, and then we are in a minus inflation situation. An' so to subtract from inflation you have specials. An' the amount of inflation you want to subtract governs the number of specials you have that month. See? So on a national basis that month, there'll be a reduction of thirty-six percent inflationary accountableness, plus the loss of value on the specials.'

'So that meeting sets nearly half the national inflation for the next month?'

'Yep. We got inflation in that warehouse before Treasury even starts thinking about it.'

'And if you could give me those figures . . .'

'Fifty/fifty split?'

'Absolutely! You've got inflation and I've got the interest rate!'

A partnership was born.

PHONOGRAPHY

ONE DAY, IN her third trading week, Morgan's telephone brought her a voice whose mellifluence so shocked her sexual ripcords that she almost lost control of the muscles that regulate the bodily functions. Her mind was racing, and part of it was screaming, 'Jeezas, almost lost it there!' while a less fundamental neural zone was muttering, 'Who is this guy?'

IN THE MEANTIME he had been saying: 'Hi, I'm Jefferson Bourke, Ratan-Gordon, Wall Street. I heard McCall's had a woman on the desk down there in DC. Well done.'

'Thank you.'

'Hey, you sound as sexy as they said. You want a price?'

'I don't do prices, I do rates. I'm forex.'

'Oh lord, oh lordie lord. I'll overlook that. Most other guys wouldn't.'

'Huh?'

'"Doing rates" goes into another logical sphere coming from a beautiful woman.'

'I know you?'

'No, but the word is you're a number one knockout.'

'Thanks. I think we'd better get on with the job.'

'Uh oh! Any time!'

'You predict the interest rise?'

'What's that about rising interest?'

'Are you going to make suggestive comments about everything?'

'No.'

'Good.'

'By no I mean no I didn't get the interest rise. I'm in shares.'

‘I did.’

‘Yeah, word’s out that you’re pretty good at that too.’

‘Too?’

‘Now who’s thinking dirty?’

‘Look, I don’t see the point of this.’

‘If you’re not wondering what I look like, you may as well hang up now.’

‘I’ll hang up when I want to.’

‘There you are, you were.’

‘I am simply saying that I do things when I want to, not when some garbitrageur tells me.’

‘Whoa! Temper, temper! You’re showing a lot of energy there, Morgan.’

‘My name’s for my friends.’

‘I bet you have a lot of friends.’

‘Maybe.’

‘You ever done it with more than one guy at a time?’

‘How did you know?’

‘Hey! Wow! Gotcha!’

Jeezas! She’d been thinking about the night in the sick bay, NAU, when she’d supposed to have been at a meeting learning how Andrew Jackson’d pole-axed the tribe with smallpox. She hadn’t been able to choose between them, so what the hell, but the bed was so narrow the other one had had to wait politely out in the corridor, Adam-naked in the brassy Flagstaff night, clutching his little silver-paper packet of Checkmate.

‘Now listen to me . . .’

‘No, Morgan, you listen to me.’ Jefferson Bourke’s voice was low, slightly alarmed, somehow younger. ‘Listen, I’m sorry. I want you to know that I won’t say a word. You haven’t said anything anyhow, but it’s the sort of thing a lot of guys would pick up on; get off on with other guys in the bar, you know? Big talk. I promise you I won’t do that. I wouldn’t. I’m not that type.’

‘Thanks.’

‘I mean it, I promise.’

‘I know.’

‘I’m glad you said that.’

‘Yeah. I’m glad I wanted to.’

Their voices were low. She was staring into the chemical green of her monitor: the preposterous figures and numbers faded into a sward not far from Shangri-la and a scalding venereal eel swam up her entrails from her groin, through her stomach, lighting up her heart, dissolving in her mouth as water. She closed her eyes. She shuddered, probably to put her exterior in tempo with her interior. 'It's much better with one,' she whispered.

'What do you like doing best?'

'Anything; you tell me.'

'I like licking. I like that a lot. Do you know I can touch the tip of my nose with my tongue?'

'How would we be?'

'You'd be on a couch, a soft couch, velvet. You'd be sitting back and I'd be kneeling in front of you. Warm fire at my back.'

'Yes. I'd be sitting back. What am I wearing?'

'An orange.'

'An orange what?'

'A fruit orange. Between your knees.'

'I am?'

'Yeah. Can you see yourself like that?'

'Yes.'

'If I told you to drop the orange, would you?'

'Try me.'

'I reckon you would.' His voice is a tremulous grunt. 'Drop the orange . . . Did you drop it? . . . Morgan?'

'The way I am now, I could have dropped a beachball.'

'Jeezas. You did it. You're lying back on the couch.'

'Yes.'

'Your legs are real wide.'

'Yes.'

'And I'm right there in front of you.'

'Yes.'

'Now I'm leaning forward, towards you.'

'Yes.'

'Can you see me?'

'Yes.'

'Can you feel me?'

'Yes.'

'I'm right there, aren't I? Right there?'

'Yes.'

'Can you feel me?'

'Yes.'

'What's it feel like?'
'Just keep going. Just keep talking.'
'Tell me what it's like. Do you like it?'
'Yes.'
'Say it.'
'I like it. I love it. I can feel that whole part of me rolling. Oh God.'
'Are you coming?'
'Yes.'
'God, I'm coming. Are you? Are you really?'
'Yes.'
'Not just on the couch?'
'No, here.'
'Jeezas.'
'Yes.'
'Oh God . . .'
'Oh God . . .'

HE TOOK HER, through his telephonic words, into the Wonderland of Wall Street, into the kaleidoscopic world of the NYSE, and there he led her through the colour-cosmos of pink sheets, blue-sky laws, grey markets, white knights and golden parachutes. He introduced her to the charming fauna of the Stock Exchange — the cash cows, bear hugs, mouse-milking, dead-cat bounces and alligator spreads. Oh yes, to alligator spreads. Her conversations to him were not simply embellished with the beads of wampum but with the brass of Brass Rings, the scales of red herrings, the honey of killer bees and the profits of new-issue whores. Oh yes, of new-profit whores:
'What are you wearing?'
'What do you reckon?'
'Are they black?'
'No.'
'Why?'
'Nothing shows up on black.'
Et cetera. It was the most tempestuous affair she had ever been embroiled in. And affair it was, because Jefferson Bourke was married. But was it? He was hardly a bedswerver. His wife was hardly a cuckquean. Can you be charged with telephonic adultery?

Then the economy slipped. Interest rates, left to find their own levels, looked downwards for them; the market lit. Phones were frantic and they could not hear each other as often or for as long. But they made the most of their fleeting moments, obliged to exchange sweet nothings amidst the harsh heron-cries of market-speak.

'I can give you seven thirty-three on T bonds.'

'Jeezas, Operations, have they put the yen into the trades yet? I'm dying out here!'

'Okay, that's a call on ten. You wanna make me another price?'

'Yeah, that's right, Contrabonds fall, you can claim on US tax.'

'Okay, that's ten yards going up, four point seven on Comex.'

'Oh God, oh God! I was on DMI and they're dogging!'

'Yes, oh yes; a complete alligator spread. Yes, which do you want? A front run? Yes, on the fast track, please. Oh God. Yes, you're at the market, right on the basis point; a friendly takeover . . . Yes, oh God yes, it's a slam dunk. Yo-yo stock, yo-yo stock . . . Ultra! Yes, you're ringing the register, yes, yes, I am, oh God, meltdown! . . . Ring me back in ten minutes.'

MANY YEARS AGO

THE SKIES OF Arizona blackened. Driven by great winds, the soils of the Sonora poured like oil across the desert floors and crashed down into the burnished canyons. The fertile cinder ash of Sunset Crater, font of the crops of beans and squash, now lay as drifts; shifting, evanescent, unsupportive of the plant life known to the Sinagua. A disaster such as this would one day, many years hence, visit upon the peoples of the Midwest and be called the Dust Bowl. This was the Dust Bowl of the Southwest Indian.

Extinction loomed. The subtribes of the Sinagua — the Water, Raincloud, the Rabbit Brush tribes — set off from their wind-scalded homelands, north, to the land of the Hopi, in search of yielding land. But one subtribe, the Acomazuni, stayed and listened to the words of their young chief. He told them of a dream. Of a wonder plant; of a crop that yielded fat and watery sustenance in unimaginable abundance. This miraculous grain was to the south. Was in the possession of the Hohokam. Was forty days walking to the south, across the dreadful Sonoran Desert . . .

In AD 1480 this subtribe of the Sinagua people, the Acomazuni, set forth to Pueblo Grande, city state of the Hohokam. They were led by their chief, known to history only as the Great Magician. Not all the Acomazuni survived the journey.

They were met by the Hohokam, not in the prosperous city centre but on the outskirts, to the west, amid the spokes of the great wheel of irrigation canals of which Pueblo Grande was the hub. How strange, how magical these man-made arteries of water must have seemed to the Magician and his tribe, who had seen, in all their life, but a single river. The place they met is now called Hauble Ceyapi, which means 'crying for a vision'. Whether this term referred to the Hohokam themselves or to the Magician who led his tribe across the wilderness in search of salvation, no one knows. But what is known today is the exact site of Hauble Ceyapi, for it was revealed to Acomazuni Moran one day, while under routine, state-sponsored, hypnotic investigation for suppressed childhood-molestation memories . . .

MORGAN HAD LISTENED as her mother told her story to the mayor as they stood on Central Avenue, Phoenix, across the street from the building site of the new Dunfield Towers. The story had a hypnotic force; it was a velvet voice calling to parts of your mind that knew already but had long forgotten. It was a power to create pictures in vivid colour, to evoke smells and sounds. It was the magical power, in other words, of *haute fiction*. And she listened.

Late at night, on the first night on those outskirts of Pueblo Grande called Hauble Ceyapi, amidst the stars and the canals, and amidst the yip of coyotes, the Great Magician had placed before the feet of the Hohokam Council a line of deerskin bags. And those bags held gold. Two weeks later, after much feasting, dancing and drumming, a deal was signed in blood upon a birchbark deed. For seven bags of gold the Sinagua had purchased Hohokam land. Good land; wide, friable land on the fruitful shores of a river, three days' journey to the southwest, at a place called Hotwa Vo. And with two bags more the Great Magician had contracted engineers, wise in the ways of irrigation; and seed-shamans, able to conjure the nourishing wonderplant called corn from the waiting soils of the desert. Thus replete the Sinagua subtribe called the Acomazuni set forth for their new land.

And at the very moment that the mayor was donating downtown Dunfield Towers to the subtribe Acomazuni, Morgan was looking into the face of the Great Magician — and seeing Hoppy Sideways!

Wampum: The Bear Run

THREE MONTHS LATER a story broke in the *Atlanta Herald*: 'WIDESPREAD COUNTERFEITING OF WAMPUM. An assistant managing director for Pneuoplast, the silicon-implant company that is paying off reparations in wampum currency confessed today that the company had been forging wampum. "We arranged to pay off the civil suits in wampum because it's so goddam easy to counterfeit. We were making our own out of left-handed whelks. There's nothing to it; counterfeiting wampum's the easiest thing in the world; anyone can do it. You can't run outa phoney wampum till you run outa whelks," he said yesterday. He is incarcerated, pending bail.'

The value of wampum plunged to 79 cents from a high of $3.44.

'YOU WILL TELEPHONE the television station,' purred Acomazuni Moran. 'You will donate ten thousand dollars to Barry Stipe for something, and you will get us on his goddam show. Tonight. Then you will telephone my production manager . . .'

On TV

THERE WAS BARRY Stipe; easy within his legal-grey three-piece chalkstripe, with button-down russet shirt and pin-dot tie; one foot on knee forming a little tripod for his clipboard of unctuous questions. 170 unexceptional pounds; a low bow-wave of sincerely blond hair, wide, white, smoothly wholesome face unblemished by character, red-rimmed specs for personality. In all, the face of someone who climbed out of a pod in the *Bodysnatchers* about five minutes too early.

Across the low glass table from Barry Stipe, towering from his Buckminster Fuller tubular-steel chair, bill-like lips poised in good nature, aubergine hands resting on the knees of his white suit, sat Production Manager, Acomazuni Enterprises . . . HARVEY THE TOOT!!

Barry turns to his guest. 'Now, the nation is listening — they want to know their money is safe in wampum. They want the proof that wampum is safe from forgers and copyists. What is that proof, Harvey Latour?'

'One simple, easy-peesy answer to that question, sir; you cain't counterfeit wampum.'

'Ah. And do you intend to tell us why not, Mr Latour?'

'You cain't forge wampum cos it's made from *Busycon contrarium*.'

'Ah. And that's?'

'The left-handed whelk, sir.'

'But isn't that the point, Mr Latour, isn't that the issue that people like Mr Disley from Pneuoplast — that the news media everywhere has been making — that the left-handed whelk is probably the most common shell in the world? With respect to you, Mr Latour, the left-handed whelk is . . . is . . . it's as common as muck, Mr Latour. There's more left-handed whelks out there than there are left-handed welshers, you might say. Ha, ha! There's no way, Mr Latour, that your company can have a monopoly over the left-handed whelk. It's lying round in its billions on every beach, in every bay and inlet and whatnot on the Atlantic Coast!'

'Maybe so, sir. But point 'o the matter is, in Juniper Inlet, East Florida, it's lying the other way.'

'You may have just lost me a little there, Mr Latour . . . Lying the other way?'

'Yep. See, there's these magnetic belts that go round the world and touch down at the Poles . . .'

'We've gone into an account of the world's magnetic fields here, have we, Mr Latour?'

'Yep.'

'While we're talking about wampum forging?'

'Yep.'

'I see. Okay then, magnetic fields. Away you go, Mr Latour.' Barry Stipe smiles at his audience beyond the lens and settles down with them to listen.

'Well, from time to time, every certain number of millions of years, the magnetics swap places.'

'The North Pole becomes the South Pole, you say?'

'Yep. Not as in places, 'cos the penguins stay down in the

south an' the polar bears stay up in the north, but they swap their magneticness.'

'The magnetism . . . turns round? Like this?' And Barry Stipe makes two frenzied rainbows with his hands.

'Yessir. An' when that happens, all the whelks o' the world turn round and go the other way too.'

Barry pauses; in fact if he were electronic he would have just short-circuited. 'Yes, I remember learning about it in tenth grade,' he says at last. 'And what has this got to do with . . .'

'Thing is, Juniper Inlet, East Florida, has got this extremely high concentration of sodium in its sand, 'cos it's on top of a kernite bed, which is a form of borax.'

Barry opens his mouth to say he had learnt this in tenth grade also, then closes it again.

'An' the whelks o' that partic'lar cove use the sodium for shell building. An' the point of all that is that sodium is paramagnetic.'

'Paramagnetic?'

'Impervious to magnetism.'

'Ah! So the Juniper Inlet whelk isn't affected by the magnetic poles and its shells don't change when they do?' Barry has understood, and crazedly exchanges enlightenment with his audience beyond the lens.

'Yep. Somethin' scientific like that.'

'So *Busycon contrarium* isn't contrary at all, is it? Ha, ha! . . . Just a moment, just a moment! If there's a type of left-handed whelk that's never changed direction, how come it's right-handed?!' Triumph illuminates Barry Stipe's spectacles, causing them to glow like neon. They momentarily redden the smile of Harvey the Toot as he answers.

''Cos th' left-handed whelk started its career as right-handed — it's jus' in a left-handed phase at the moment.'

'Jeez . . . Holy smoke . . . so the right-handed whelk of Juniper Inlet is the correct way round and all the other left-handed whelks of the world are round the wrong way?'

'Yep. Nothin' more to it than that. So the Juniper Inlet whelks has got a signature, which makes them impervious to forgery.'

'And you of course have the franchise to the right-handed left-handed whelks of Juniper Inlet?'

'Yep. Nobody but Acomazuni Enterprises has access to the shells o' that partic'lar bay.'

'And wampum, you say, is made exclusively from right-handed left-handed whelks, don't you?'

'Tha's right, sir.'

Barry Stipe turns to camera, to radiate satisfied togetherness to his Audience Beyond the Lens. 'Well, that's the whole thing sorted out, isn't it? As far as I'm concerned it's sorted out. What about you?'

'You better believe it,' breathed Acomazuni Moran from beyond the lens.

'A dizzying journey of discovery; one of the most convoluted stories we've had on the show, I'd think. Ha, ha! But well worthwhile. Very worthwhile. To save a currency, and a fine company from charges — unfounded as we've shown — charges of corruption and fraud, which could have had profound effects upon our economy. Good luck, Mr Latour — Harvey — and good luck to Acomazuni Enterprises. I am sure we have killed those stories of wampum-fixing stone dead. You saw it here, ladies and gentlemen, why wampum is not counterfeitable. "If it don't turn right, it just ain't wampum." Ha, ha! And you saw it tonight on the Barry Stipe Tonight show. Thanks, Harv, you were a sport. There he goes, ladies and gentlemen, Harvey Latour, a great human being and a great ambassador for his company.'

ACOMAZUNI ENTERPRISES WAS saved. Wampum opened next morning at $1.67.

'Mom, there's something I have to ask you, outright.'

'Is there.'

'Yes. Okay, so Harvey saved the company. But what from? How come that guy came out and said he was faking wampum when it was a total cock-and-bull story?'

'He was paid.'

'To destroy Acomazuni?'

'Yes.'

'Who paid him?'

'Coca-Cola.'

'What? Why?'

'Revenge.'

'Jeez, Mom, this is like drawing teeth. What for?'

'I tried to buy them.'

WAMPUM CLOSED AT $2.32 and rising. The world was Acomazuni's oyster once more.

That evening Greenpeace appeared on the Barry Stipe Tonight show.

ON TV II

AGITATION REIGNED ON the visage of the lovely Barry Stipe. Morgan could see it shining beneath the strata of TV pancake. And agitated well he may be — he had been criticised! The morning papers had had him for breakfast. STIPE SNUGGLES UP TO MOLLUSC MURDERERS: GREENPEACE. After one of his most committed acts of public rescue (as he described it in his peevish introduction), fault had been found in Barry's deed. Body language proclaimed that this was inconceivable and unfair. His critics, three of them (and by further body language Barry suggested to his Audience Beyond the Lens that they could well be the entirety of his critics) sat across the glass table from him now, in two Buckminster Fuller chairs and a stool from the control room. Two androgenous Greenpeace protesters in T-shirts and a lawyer in a grey suit and a NICARAGUA LIBRE badge.

Barry read his sincere introduction from the autocue, exchanged a glance of meaningful solidarity with his Audience Beyond the Lens, then swivelled to the noisesome trio and invited them to do their worst.

It was bad.

'Yes, an outrage! And you don't come out of it too well yourself, quite frankly, Barry. As we said to the papers this morning, you publicly encouraged the guy.'

'Everyone who comes on my show gets a fair hearing, and I wouldn't want it said . . .'

'Constructive reinforcement,' said the lawyer. 'It's within the definition of encouragement.'

'He had a case to put; his company's existence was threatened.'

'What about the existence of the right-handed whelk? What about its existence? Huh? That never occurred to you, Stipe, did it?'

'Barry,' murmured the lawyer, 'call him Barry. Surnames are accusatory in some interview situations.'

'There he was, on your show, bragging about how his

company was cutting up and selling the only right-handed left-handed whelk colony on the planet! And you sympathised!'

'I sympathised with the fact that his company was being unfairly accused of a crime of which it was entirely innocent, as he proved last night!'

'Reactive listening; that's sympathy,' said the lawyer.

'You're an accomplice, Barry; an accomplice to the mass murder of dumb animals.'

'Shellfish? Animals?'

'A living organism, having sensation and voluntary motion — animal: *Shorter Oxford*,' said the lawyer.

'You may see them as simply shellfish, Barry; that's just it, you do. To us they are a rare and beautiful marine creature, and by the time Acomazuni Enterprises have finished blitzing Juniper Inlet for profit, that exquisite little mollusc will have been rendered absolutely extinct!'

WAMPUM CRASHED TO three cents and never came back again.

RIP, Acomazuni. The world was your oyster; and you couldn't get it open.

In the Sure and Certain Faith

IN THE SURE and certain faith that she will rise again . . .

Rising Again

THE HOHOKAM IRRIGATION system at Phoenix, amazing engineering feat that it was, Eighth Wonder of the World though it may have been, had not, alas, been perfect. In fact it had been inadequate; in fact it had been ultimately disastrous. The irrigative water did not drain effectively; it lingered across the vast arable fields of Pueblo Grande in sheets, rotting the soil. In technical terms it raised the water table, allowing dissolved fossil salts to rise to the surface and there lie among the roots of the Hohokam corn. 'Playarisation' this process is called.

The corn died. The wondrous empire and its golden stock exchange collapsed with the death of its currency. Perhaps the Hohokam then fled the devastation they had created; perhaps they sought refuge with the Acomazuni in the lands of Hotwa Vo.

Perhaps not. Perhaps they died in their golden beds. All we know is that the canal city of Phoenix vanished.

But the tiny canal village of Hotwa Vo did not. Not yet.

The Hohokam disappeared, but the dreadful process they had begun did not cease. Year after year, dampness continued to lure dead salt to the surface of deserted Phoenix. Until at last the water table itself was hauled — upon the thin threads of evaporation — to the surface of the desert land and pierced through and through by the arid darts of the sun until it withered and died and floated off as dust. And the land was once again as dry as the days before the Hohokam. And plates of salt lay in the canals.

BUT THE SONORA has a secret. It is not infertile. The Sonoran Desert is made of soil, not sand. It requires only water to make it fruitful.

Nineteenth century settlers saw the extinct canals of the Hohokam and guessed the secret of the desert. They cleared the dust from the canals and filled them once more with water. They rebuilt the water systems of the Hohokam, and in recognition of the founding fathers of their empire, they called the recanaled city Phoenix.

But they did not know that beneath the dust was salt.

AND THE SALT melted into the water and flowed into the river.

And the river, like the Styx, ran salt.

And the Styx-like river ran to the sea, poisoning the lands as it passed.

And now Hotwa Vo died.

FAR DOWN THE sun-scalded porch Morgan's mother was on the phone, hunched in hooded converse with the receiver.

But — strange for an Amerindian person of the land — she had not noticed the direction of the wind.

It was an extremely long call.

She hung up, then. She sauntered back to her seat and plumped down, picking up her presumably tepid soda and plugging into the blue straw. Two crows had been frightened from the lawn by the report of her swaying beads.

'Thirty-five minutes on a call,' murmured Morgan dreamily.

'So?'

'Nothing.'

'My phone. Aren't I allowed to make telephonic communications upon my own telephone?'

'Sure. I just wondered why you had to huddle down the other end of the porch for half an hour when I've come all this way to visit you, that's all.'

'Business. I was not hiding, if that is what you mean. Can you say you weren't eavesdropping?'

'Yep.' Crossed fingers; arguably the first since the Flagstaff office of Mrs (Helen) Silverman.

'Good. I don't want a daughter of mine resorting to dirty and underhand tricks.'

A silence fell. The air glowed. The meteorologists laboured on.

'What do they do, those guys?' asked Morgan suddenly.

'They make calculations on what the weather has been doing.'

'It hasn't been doing anything,' said Morgan. She sat upright, intuitively gyroscoping her glass so that not a black drop fell. 'When last did it rain?'

'Since before I moved here.'

'So how come . . .? What the hell do those guys do?'

Two meteorologists trudged by, crossing on the lawn before the porch; one heading north, the other south. Suddenly something occurred to Morgan. 'How come they've always got something to do? How come those beakers are always half full?'

Her mother shrugged evilly. 'Some people feed birds; some people have other hobbies.' She turned to level at Morgan and something moved — something red — in the blackness of her eye. Perhaps it was the devil. Then her mouth twitched as if she'd either been accidentally prodded in the frontal lobe by a passing devil's horn, or she was containing a smile. 'Why?'

'Just wondered.'

The meteorologists trudged out of view, each clutching a half-filled hydrological tube.

From the corner of her eye Morgan watched her mother juddering with unheard laughter. She dozed in the sun, then refilled her glass from a two-quart pitcher. 'And how is the Governor?' she said airily.

Her mother swung to point at her with viperous speed. 'You were eavesdropping, you wicked child! There is no hotter place in hell than the place for the eavesdropping kind!' She paused, finger still pointing like a frozen cobra, face hard with a complex mixture of anger and confusion; perhaps the mark of an Overwhelming Question hovered over her head. Perhaps Acomazuni Moran had just confronted herself for the first time with the problem of where Sinagua Indians go after death.

Morgan let the moment pass. 'What are you trying to raise money for, Mom?' she said quietly.

'Who says I'm trying to raise money?!'

'I do. Compensation. From the Governor.'

'I can raise money if I like! Show me in the Constitution where Acomazuni Moran cannot raise money!'

'Didn't say you couldn't. I asked you why.'

'Perhaps I want to build a family gas chamber, my dear,' she purred.

'Are you planning something, Mom?'

Morgan's mother gazed serenely into the reddening desert air. She had decided not to get angry; she would be infuriating instead. 'Oh, you never can know. Perhaps I may have a tiny project up my sleeve.'

'Mom, you're in no position to . . .'

'Are you saying I'm poor?!'

'Nope. Poor is for people who never had money, Mom. The technical term for you is broke.'

'No, child,' breathed her mother gently, settling back into the landscape like a scarp. 'The technical term for me is temporarily. Tomorrow I will be "in funds". A certain friend of mine has taught me — how does he say? — "to synthesise Capitalism and Equal Opportunities to a degree hitherto unparalleled in the human race".'

PHONIENESS

'DO YOU WANT TO?'

'Yes.'

'We've never done this before.'

'No.'

'Have you wanted to before?'

'Mmmm.'

'What does that mean?'

'Mmmm.'

'It means yes, doesn't it? It means you want to as much as I do!'

'Mmmm.'

'Doesn't it?'

'Mmmm.'

'Say it. I love it when you say it.'

'Yes.'

'Oh God. Oh Connie.'

'WHAT?'

'. . . What?'

'WHO?'

'Oh God.'

'Who's Connie?'

'Is that what I said?'

'It's what you sighed, asshole!'

'Look . . .'

'You're two-timing me on the phone, Jefferson!'

'Of course I'm not!'

'So you were about to kebab me and you think of your wife?'

'No!'

'So you are two-timing me on the phone! Don't you ever call me again!'

'Morgan, listen . . .'

'To what? Jeezas cow, if I want to hear lies I can just hook into the sales desk!'

'It was my mother.'

'What? Who was?'

'Connie. My wife's name is Gloria. It's my mother; her name's April but she was born in Macon and they call her Connie.'

'You were doing that to me over the phone and thinking of your mother! Listen, pervert, we're only one generation away from necrophilia here!'

'She made me marry my wife! My wife is plain and ordinary!'

'And rich, huh?'

'No! Poor!! She's niece of the guy who got my father into his real estate company in '46. From gratitude.'

'So if your mother can do that to you, how come you want her to watch?'

'I don't! I was just thinking, if it wasn't for her, how my life could've . . .'

Oh my God . . . 'You hate your mother, don't you?'

'Yes.'

'And you fantasise about killing her.'

'Yes.'

'And that's why you wanted my back turned? So you could have stabbing fantasies while we . . .?'

'How did you know?'

'I read Freud; condensed.'

'Things have been getting a little mixed up lately.'

'I think you might be OD'ing on semiotics, Jefferson.'

'Life's somehow controllable on the phone.'

'And it isn't in real life, huh?'

'You got it.'

A dread certainty engulfed her. 'How tall are you, Jefferson?' she asked quietly.

'Six one.'

Her eye fell on Abe Wallenstein. 'Five three?'

He sighed. 'Four.'

'Bald?'

'-ing.'

'You ever see *The Wizard of Oz*?'

'I know, with the beautiful voice. I used to do voice-overs for commercials. You ever see Ten catfood?' Suddenly his voice smacked with the hysterical sincerity of a TV commercial: "Your cat on its nineth life? Give it a new life with Ten! Ten, the nation's number one feline food! Remember Ten, the cat alimentation that's . . . twice as nice as mice, folks!" That was me.'

'Yeah, I remember that one. You were good.'

'Thanks.'

'You're welcome.'

'Look . . . Does anything need to change?'

'You don't think anything's changed, Jefferson? You don't think things are different now? Jeezas. Look, I don't actually care about those appearance things, who needs looks when you're hung like?. . . Oh Jeezas; you really hung like that, Jefferson?'

A sigh. 'No.'

'You bastard, Jefferson! Describe it!'

'Nondolichophallic.'

'What the hell does that mean?'

'Short.'

'Dammit, Jefferson, I've been gulled! Look, I don't even care about that really, but your mother, Jefferson. That's different. You were using me. There we were, just the two of us, I thought, and all the time you were fantasising!'

'You're right, Morgan. It was getting a bit mixed up.'

'Honour thy mother. Ever tried it with your wife?'

'What?'

'What we were going to do.'

'Holy Toledo!'

'Give it a try; never know.'

'This is really it, huh?'

' 'Fraid so.'

'Okay, there's the wall, there's the writing. I understand. So long, Morgan.'

'So long, Jefferson.'

'I'll never forget you.'

'Same here.' A bolus of perverse nostalgia clogged her throat. Tears stained her sight. 'Jefferson.'

'Yeah?'

'It was great. Thanks.'

'You're welcome.'

The greatest love she'd ever known! Tears hurled themselves from her ducts like lemmings.

She bought five packets of aspirin and a bottle each of rum and Kahlúa and baskets of Coke to wash them down. She emptied the bottles, fell asleep on her beige chaise longue and was woken by the telephone. God! Her head! She took an aspirin and picked up the receiver.

Her mother.

'Get down here quickly. Take one week off. You are to meet Bobby.'

Bobby I

Bobby. Bobby was top-secret; everyone knew that. Bobby was the most famous top-secret in these United States. Bobby's conversation cost you forty-five thousand a day. A day! Because what Bobby said, was word for word what the President would have been saying if you'd been talking to him instead.

Bobby II

They sat on the cool porch under MOOS-O-MEN. Meteorologists trudged by. At the bottom of the spasmodic lawn, a low oleaceous hedge entwined a picket fence made from the ramrod branches of dead ocotillo. Beyond it, the botanical desert gardens; stalagmites of saguaro, most of them topped with purple figs like beautiful open sores. Beneath them, spattering the red soil, the grey stems of living ocotillo, gilt poppies, purple lupins. Sunbursts, here and there, of dazzling paloverde trees, shimmering in the white heat like fire.

'There is room for a ten-thousand-bed retirement home in that psuedo desert,' muttered her mother.

She was sprawled in an 'Acomazuni Leaner', an aluminium and rubber contraption designed from the thing Indians draped from the backs of horses to carry babies. Morgan sat behind a Black Russian on an upright plastic low-back. Between them sat Dr Cyrus Rust, who had 'degrees from the MIT', according to her mother.

Morgan had applied for a week's leave. She'd been impressed by the sudden realisation she would have handled about 55 million dollars during that week. She was more impressed by the fact that no one seemed to mourn its absence.

Dr Cyrus Rust — try saying it, it brings your tongue to a complete standstill — was telling her about Bobby. Cyrus Rust was shiny; his bald head shone, his cheeks shone. Worst, his mouth shone. He didn't seem to open his mouth any wider than most people do, but you saw an awful lot of his tongue. His entire mouth area was somehow — well, with its complicated parts and its glistening dampness it looked disturbingly like a woman's quintessence. And weak eyes, seemingly made from the same gelatinous materials Chinese use for yum char breakfasts. And irises faded by the sun.

Cyrus Rust sat shining in the shade, explaining to Morgan and her mother how the President had been recreated. 'Thing about Ronald Reagan, which became apparent to several computer scientists early on, was that his neuronic processes had all the qualities of the ROM system: Read-Only Memory. See, Mr Reagan's opinions, in the main, are for life. He's got only one response for any particular situation, so what he's done is kinda made his opinions into instructions to his behaviour. It's an amazing achievement in a way; Ronald Reagan has hard-coded his own psyche.'

'So once you've got an opinion on everything, you never have to ever think again, huh?'

'That's about it, Miss Moran.'

'Morgan.' (For Crissake!)

His shiny eyes gave a solar flare of expectation. He searched her face for further signs of intimacy, and found, she fervently hoped, total zip. He returned, dogged and defeated, to the business at hand. 'A group of businessmen quickly saw the possibilities in this and called in some experts.'

'Like yourself?' said her mother.

'I guess so.'

'What are you an expert in, Mr Rust?' enquired Morgan sweetly.

'Well, believe it or not, Morgan — hoverflies.'

'Come again?'

'I know it sounds a little improbable . . .'

'Hoverflies?'

'Yes; I was looking into how hoverflies compute interception courses . . .'

'It sounds reasonable to me,' said her mother severely. 'One must study something when you go to the MIT. Otherwise how do you get all those degrees?'

Morgan realised she was being rebuked for staring.

'Perhaps you'd care to explain how you can build presidents out of hoverflies, Dr Rust?'

'Well, it's not like that exactly of course, Morgan; ha, ha! You see, these flies can compute, using simple, specifiable rules that can be hard-wired into the brain. It's as if these rules have been learnt by the evolutionary process and taken on board by the fly's neurophysiology.'

'Well, I never knew that. You know that, Mom?'

'Hold your noise, Morgan,' said her mother lazily.

'It means you can create the mechanisms that make you think. Your opinions can become the way you think.'

'Yes, I see what you mean. My opinion, and what I'm thinking right now, are more or less the same thing.'

'Hold your noise, Morgan.'

'It's what Ronald Reagan's done.'

'Are you saying Mr Reagan's an insect, Dr Rust?'

'Well, not in so many words.'

'There's only one.'

'What I mean is, Mr Reagan has what is called a "non-hierarchical thought system".'

'Same as a hoverfly?'

'Yes. Thoughts in most people can crop up in any of a million places in the neural system. In the hoverfly's case, and some people's — the President's, for example — there's only a few thought sources. That's why the hoverfly keeps banging away at the window — there's no neuronic feedback to tell it to change its behaviour. Same with people like that; no feedback mechanism, so they're almost entirely predictable.'

They stopped while Morgan refilled her Black Russian. The ice-maker behaved erratically. She resumed her seat with shattered ice.

'It was at this stage I was called in to the project,' resumed Cyrus Rust. 'I was commissioned to create a psychiatric profile of Reagan.'

'Based on hoverflies?'

'And robotics, yes. By a rather complicated process that I won't go into . . .'

'No, you go into it, Dr Rust; you go right into it as deep as you like. Mom would like to hear all about it, wouldn't you, Mom?'

'Hold your noise, Morgan.'

'Well I'll not bore you with the details, but it involved what we call "parallel-processing techniques", which allowed us to distribute a representation across a network of computational units.'

'Right across, huh?'

'Hold your noise, Morgan.'

'So, using your parallel-processing techniques, Dr Rust, you built a robot of the President?'

'No, no, goodness no. What we ended up with was simply a replication of the Reagan neural network system.'

'What did it look like? Can't have been very big.'

'Don't you go slagging the President, child! Mr Reagan wouldn't harm a fly.'

'Not if he hit it with his brain, he wouldn't.'

'Hold your noise, Morgan.'

'No, I'm afraid you're still rather on the wrong track, Morgan. We didn't end up with a brain or anything as exciting as that. Just a series of drawings — maps really.'

'Oh.'

'What we'd done, I suppose, is convert Mr Reagan's wetware into software.'

'Hey, Dr Rust, that's very good!'

'Thank you. It's about as vivid as we get in our business, I suppose.' Cyrus Rust modestly rearranged himself in his plastic chair, stretching, and revealing an unsocked ankle of sickening whiteness.

The ankle remained, rather impairing the impact of the remaining story: how they had cranked the dryware into a CRAY XMP — a very large computer — at MIT, and got a list of ten thousand 'probable-to-ninety-eight percent' Reagan responses. How a secret, nationwide survey-search for the man most like Ronald Reagan unearthed Bobby: Bobby Cravitts, retired advertising salesman for the *Vegas Times*, who was then processed from Cyrus Rust's brain map. How he was paid a retainer of $14,500 a month during a series of electrical redistributative computational networking treatments in a private hospital, then a three-month convalescence in Hawaii, where he read books, reports and transcriptions secretly supplied by two members of Reagan's staff. How, after ten months, Bobby was foretelling Reagan to within eighty percent accuracy, which six months later had increased into the ninetieth percentile. How eventually he was contracted for $200,000 a year and hired out, at $45,000 a day, to Big Business as a barometer of Reagan's reactions to moves in the marketplace.

IT WAS EVENING. Cyrus Rust had gone, the meteorologists were trudging severally into the setting sun.

The ice machine had broken down completely, and Morgan had scraped ice from the side of a packet of beefburgers in the freezer. The Kahlúa had a faintly carnal tang.

'So what do you want me to say to this Bobby guy?'

'I have booked you in for two days. Friday and Saturday. You will be there overnight.' Her mother flicked her a glance; did it have a faintly carnal tang?

'Mother, what's worth ninety grand for you to know?'

'Do you know who the green statue is of on the top of the Board of Trade building in Chicago?'

'John Hancock?'

'Ceres.'

'Ceres?'

'Yes.'

'Oh, Ceres?! We did Ceres in Greek art; Goddess of . . . health foods? No. Cereals!'

'Corn.'

'Ah yes, corn.'

'Corn.'

It was a harsh little word, she realised, which sped from the middle of the mouth with the force of a sneer. 'Corn!' Nearly the coarse expletive of the carrion crow. 'Caw.' And a headless boomerang of jagged wing swooped out of memory and froze above the flattened corn of the Threaten Field; skewered on a slightly bent pole . . .

'Ceres. Above everything else; high above the Board of Trade Building: corn. Where life started. For us.' Her mother's face was ruby in the light of the sunset. Behind her the distant mesas glowed like slabs of liver. She was, in hawklike silhouette, the fiercely ageing daughter of the Acomazuni; who had followed the Great Magician across the Sonora to the land of the Hohokam, the Corn People.

'I want to know if Reagan is going to kick Agrisync out of Nicaragua,' she said.

'Come again?' Sentimentality — of which there had been a little growing — was blasted away by the savage practicality of the remark.

'Nicaragua. Perhaps you have heard of Nicaragua?'

'Yes, of course. They have jaguars.'

'Yes, well they also have corn. Much. They eat corn, they drink it, they sit on it, they sleep on it, they make musical instruments from it. Corn is life there, and in the days when Somoza was there, and there was law and order, a corn company by the name of Agrisync made a deal with him — ten percent for him, on every acre of their corn that was sown in Nicaragua.' She smiled with unpleasant admiration. 'And of course in Nicaragua you did what Somoza told you to do. He was a most charismatic man.'

'Jeezas, I just remembered. They were his jaguars, he fed people to them!'

'Perhaps. He was certainly a firm ruler. He ordered the Nicaraguans to pull up their old corn and to plant Agrisync corn. And they did. Then, unfortunately, they had their Communist revolution and Somoza was kicked out. But by then, ninety-nine percent of Nicaragua's corn was Agrisync! A formidable achievement.' She sat back in her Acomazuni Leaner and closed her eyes, perhaps to worshipfully capture in her mind the features of the clubbable General Anastasio Somoza. 'And of course we are here talking hybrid corn,' she went on dreamily, 'which means it is sterile; which means you cannot plant it.' She opened her eyes, alert with business. 'Which means you have to go back to the company every year for your seed. And that means monopoly. And that means MONEY!'

'You gonna buy into this company, Mom?'

'Corn is in our blood, Morgan.'

'Dunno if that's quite what you mean, Mom.'

'Corn was life at Hotwa Vo; and then it died.' Her mother was staring at her, hard. The sun touched the lip of the Superstition Range behind her, and seemed for a second to melt and run along its rim like molten gold. 'Have you ever thought of changing your name?'

'What to, Mom; Minnehaha?' She blasted this round of sentimentality away herself. 'Look, I've still got the braids, that's my contribution, okay?' She was angry somehow.

Upon asking herself why, she was confronted with a vivid picture of herself and her brothers, at early sunset, scrunching down Fort Churchill Road towards the highway that led to Weed Heights and even further — like to New York or Washington. Her brothers carried handkerchiefs on sticks, just like Huck Finn had; except they hadn't been sure what Huck's had actually contained. Farrell had put in his one their mother's flatiron, which he said they could sell at the 'first town' and buy food and accommodation, and possibly a small cottage they could settle down in. Gordon had suffered a crisis of imagination and stuffed his with newspaper. She just had her purse with three nickels Hoppy had given her for the three times she'd found his bicycle.

It was the first squall of nightfall that turned them round, with its intimations of pitiless nullity. It cut through the egocentric belief in happy endings and caused them to bolt in terror the two miles home.

They were late, but not excessively so. They received a minor scolding for tardiness, and doubtless surprised their mother with their tearful responses.

Then they ate corn. Which caused her, seven years later, to withdraw from Miss Arizona. Because that night in bed, still with the glutinously salty taste of her first corn in her mouth, she had discovered a fuzz of hairs across the taut ivory surfaces of the delta between her legs. And years later, she learned that a cause of obesity was 'endocrine change at the time of puberty'. Those three dense yellow cobs of 78.3 percent carbohydrate had affected the pubertal endocrinal change that had thickened her waist forever.

And this accounted for Morgan's anger. Corn, that agency of disfigurement, was about to re-enter her life.

Her mother looked away; the gold behind her had soaked into the maze of mesas. 'Some people believe the new government may nationalise the company,' she said.

Morgan had not quite returned: 'What? What government?'

'Nicaragua.'

'Oh; yes. Nationalise this Agrisync?'

'Yes. There are people who believe that if the company leaves its corn-lines in Nicaragua, the government will nationalise it and they will lose the lot.'

'Well, the way Reagan's dumping on them, what Nicaraguan government wouldn't steal a US company? Come to think of it, why doesn't Agrisync bring the corn-lines home? Grow it here? It'd be a lot safer.'

'They're worried about a fall of the share price. Such a withdrawal could seem as if they'd been chased out, with no guarantee that Nicaragua would continue buying their seeds. The drop on the NYSE would be catastrophic.' Paradoxically she smiled. 'Calamitous.'

'So they're dead if they do and dead if they don't?'

'Yes.'

'And this is the company you want to buy into?'

'Yes.'

'Are you going to explain?'

'Oh, the explanation is made of simplicity itself. The seed is chemically treated. It poisons the soil for any other plant. Of course the company cannot say this out loud, but Nicaragua's soil has been adapted so it can only grow Agrisync corn.'

'Holy . . . ! That's appalling, Mom!'

'That is business, child. Anyway, the poison leaches out after two years.'

'But for two years . . .'

'Correct. For two years, it would grow as much as this desert.' And she smiled with shrewd pleasure across the darkening Sonora. 'The government of Nicaragua knows this also; that is the beauty of the situation. There is no way they are going to harm the company.'

'So there's no need for it to pull out. Where's the beauty in that?'

'The beauty is that I know this, the company knows this and the Nicaraguan government knows this. But the shareholders do not. They would panic. They would sell at any price. Agrisync would become a very nice bargain if it were forced to leave Nicaragua.'

'Yes, you could buy a tidy pile of shares for twenty million, couldn't you?'

'What are you speaking of, child?!'

'The wind changed to the north while you were telling the Governor about Hotwa Vo.'

Bobby III

Bobby. Was he an impeccable seventy or a dilapidated fifty-five? There was no real way to know. He was tallish but delicate, with small features and a dinky little nose that had been broken at some stage. His skin was smooth but slightly waxy — the faint mummification of age. His hair was as uncompromisingly black as the President's, but matte black, without the patent-leather gleam of the Reagan locks — and stiffening; the toothmarks of his comb remained. He was frailly handsome, with the feral arrogance of the Inca. He still trailed behind him somewhere the last gossamer wisps of sexuality.

But there was no real way of knowing if his desires were carnal. His messages were confusing. He would take her arm in public, release it in private; sit touching in restaurants, apart in nightclubs. He spoke intimately in a loud voice, publicly in *sotto voce*.

He lived in the suite of a hotel near the airport — presumably so clients could fly in, get forty-five grands' worth of Reagan-think and leave again immediately. It was an unexceptional, above-average complex, with a pool and two restaurants — the sort of place Louis XV would have sent his astrologer and food-taster, while he himself went Westside. The AAA Airport Lodge it was called: the usual social trichotomy; run by Mexicans, serviced by blacks, patronised by Japanese.

Her bag had been put in the completely self-contained guest room.

Eleven-fifty p.m. They were back; Room 866, The West-chester Suite. She'd only had two glasses of wine and a cocktail or two throughout the evening, but he'd phoned the hotel and organised a limo to deliver them back from the Mocambo.

Two martinis in the moody little blue-lit bar of the hotel — five minutes too late to hear Gentleman Jack Dupree on the piano — then up to the suite. To their bedrooms to 'freshen up'. They were to meet in the livingroom for 'a nightcap'.

She emerged, fully dressed. Bobby was in a black silk bathrobe with an ascot, and sitting at their bar. 'Hey, you sleep in your civvies?' he said. 'Cognac?'

'Well, I stayed like this in case you thought I was hinting at an early night,' she lied.

He took her hand. He kissed it. Oh God, here we go; standard furbelow politics. He was close. His tear ducts had widened with age, making little half-filled tidal basins in the sides of his small flat nose. He was old! He was really old!

The bell. He's ordered flowers. 'Get the door,' he said, half smiling. Numbly she did so. Flowers. Roses: about the contents of a standard row in a commercial glasshouse.

'They're beautiful,' she droned as he signed. Now the champagne, when did the champagne arrive? It had, it was on ice. He opened it, not quite expertly. She took the proffered glass, shaped, they say from the breast of Marie Antoinette. 'Let 'em eat cake.' Pray it's only cake that's offered tonight.

'You're a beautiful woman, Morgan,' he said. Of course he said that. After roses and champagne, it was programmed. Then he startled her. 'But I want you to know I'm a gentleman. Always have been. I've had opportunities that would've made grown men weep, but I've turned them down unless I've known that was what the woman wanted. If I'm not in an entirely one hundred percent two-way situation, then no way. Not on. Not my style. I'm old-fashioned when it comes to women, and I'm getting more old-fashioned all the time, but I won't change. No way, not Bobby Cravitts.'

His beautiful eyes blazed liquidly, his mouth was set in over-emphatic resolve. He was drunker than she had realised; a ratchet had slipped on the brakedrum of decorous civility. But she felt no physical threat. 'If we're in a no-belly-riding situation here, then that's okay with me, an' if you get any reason to think otherwise, Morgan, I'll cut off my dick! You say I've done anything disrespectful to you, you just tell me and Pow! Slice the salami. Gone! 'Coz I'm a gentleman, Morgan, an' if I ever do anything to make someone think otherwise, then I'd rather not be any sort of man at all. That's how I feel, Morgan, that's my philosophy. I want you to feel real safe and relaxed here, Morgan, and I'll tell you something I really want you to know: if, say, I told you I really admired you and wanted to make love to you, and you said you'd rather not, I'd respect that. I would totally switch off all intentions in that direction. Total platonicness, down to the wire. And you could walk through this room with your clothes off, and it wouldn't change my mind! If you had said, "No parallel parking here, Bobby," I would say, "Okay, I respect your wishes, Morgan; that's okay with me, babe," and you could strip totally naked, right here, in front of me, so I could see every inch of your amazingly beautiful body and I would not get hard. Out of respect. I give you my word on that, Morgan. I would not get a hard on! Nothing. Zilch! And if you don't believe me, I'll cut off my goddam johnnie!'

She met his eye and was dazzled by mad sincerity. He meant it. Van Gogh of the erogenous zones. 'No need to do that, Bobby,' she oozed. 'Of course there isn't!'

Oh no! How could she say that? Hadn't she just made a number one, full-frontal invitational come-on?!

He hadn't noticed. He was a zealot of probity, deep into 'chastity by mutilation', and all else passed him by. 'I mean it, Morgan!' he asserted, and the skin stretching across his insubstantial features shone like chrome; 'If you didn't want to, you could walk through this room stark naked, an' I would stay completely unhard, to show my respect! You have my word on that, Morgan, an' if I thought you didn't believe me I'd . . .'

Yes! She knew what he'd do! With appalled clarity she saw where these demonstrations of crazed civility must lead. Was it intentional? Was it the work of invidious cunning or of genuine, moronic gentility? She didn't know, but a sudden thin corridor of understanding led her into a Gothic chamber of realisation. She saw the plan, the design, the framework — the perfection! Here, indefatigably before her, was the culmination of the long search; the march from the hoverfly to the CRAY computer, the operations, the programming from the brain plan of Cyrus Rust. She was being ushered into the opaque world of Reagan-think by its second-best exponent. She could see, in the stickily enduring gaze of Bobby Cravitts, the ability to not turn to look reality in the face; the belief in tea-leaf foreign policy, public office as an alternative to the carpool. All this was seriously embossed in the unvarying pupils of the other man who lived in the courteously outlandish world of Ronald Reagan: Bobby.

'. . . without a stitch on, an' I would just stay calmly here as if you were in overalls . . .'

And somehow she must elude the snares of this byzantine logic. She came to a decision. The path she chose was fraught with peril. How easily she could founder on the swollen shoals of frenzy, the mood-changing corals of inebriety. She must act with the cunning of Pau-Pau-Kee-Wis, the strength of Mudjokovis, the resolve of Manabozho if she was to preserve the blameless virtue of Minnehaha:

Must ensog old Bobby's ardour;
Render Bobby epinastic
Hoax him with elastic tactics
Make the squirming worm turn downward . . .

'Listen, Bobby, I don't think any decisions have been made yet, have they?' she cooed. 'I wouldn't think we have to get too dogmatic about anything just yet. Let's just say we're in a "liquid situation". In fact, I'd say we weren't in a liquid situation at all. Ha, ha! That glass of yours must be dying of thirst. You ever had brandy with champagne? Here, I'll get you one. They reckon a little sugar with it really gets it on its way . . . You ever read the *Song of Hiawatha*, Bobby? — *"Of the skin he made him mittens /*

made them with the fur side inside / put the inside skinside outside.” Only Shakespeare wrote better than that, Bobby. I've got the whole book here somewhere . . .’

NEXT MORNING MORGAN sidled into his bed as Bobby slept, and left it as he awoke. She thanked him for a wonderful night. He replied, slightly baffled, that it was his pleasure.

They ate gluey waffles in the breakfast bar of the hotel. Bobby cast her puzzled glances sometimes; she would smile and kiss his mottled hand. Her plane was at three; by eleven his *mentis* was *compos* enough to be approached about the ninety-thousand-dollar subject.

‘Can we talk about Nicaragua now, Bobby darling?’

‘Something I've always wanted to know; how come everything of value — oil, gold, corn — comes from one of these tinpot, fly-blown banana republics? Beats me. Mind you, we might call ’em banana republics, an’ sneer at ’em, but I'll tell you what — bananas sell! We sit here with our sagging markets an’ we laugh at them!’

‘It's midday, Bobby, do you think we could get round to Nicaragua?’

‘Nicaragua. You know they got freshwater sharks down there? I'll tell you a thing; you know what the roads of Nicaragua are made of?’

‘Bobby . . .’

‘They're made of bricks. You know why? Somoza owned the brickworks! You know what the first weapons they used against Somoza's troops were? Bricks. Where'd they get ’em? From the fucking roads of course! Ahahahaha! There's a hill outside Managua with initials of the government on it, FDR or somethin’. Used to say ROLSTER — they were a shoe company!’

It was impossible. In all, she wrenched his attention round to the issue that was costing her mother ninety thousand dollars, for perhaps five minutes. She blurted out her desperate questions in the departure lounge; he gave verbal shrugs in reply. She departed in tears.

MORGAN COULDN'T BEAR to face her mother in the flesh. That bottom lip, like a pointed finger; that frown that seemed to suck her eyebrows into her sinuses. From Sky Harbour Airport,

Phoenix, she boarded a Washington-bound Eastern Airways and flew direct to the Strand on M Street, where she Black Russian'd for three days with her friend Mary Krueljack. She had been back a week before she rang her mother.

'Mom, I . . .'

'I have heard.'

'You did? What?'

'On the TV. Reagan has told them to get out. Well done.'

'Who? What the hell are you talking about, Mom?'

'Agrisync; Reagan has ordered them out of Nicaragua, "for their personal safety". The shares lost nearly four dollars on the NYSE. You are a good daughter and I love you. I am a little inconvenienced at the moment, however, if you are thinking bonus.'

'Mom, I didn't do anything! We talked Nicaragua for three minutes. I don't think I even got round to telling him what you . . .'

'Good heavens, child, he knew all those things; I had told him on the telephone before you arrived. He simply wanted to meet you.'

'You spent ninety thousand so he could . . .'

'It would have been two hundred thousand if he had charged anything at all.'

'What?!'

'For a hundred thousand a day Bobby does not tell you what Reagan thinks, he tells Reagan.'

'Look, Mom. Just let me get a glass of water . . .' There was no Coke; she drank straight black rum and Kahlúa. 'Run that by me again?'

'Bobby is exactly the same as Reagan, okay? But he has a better brain. Reagan is his greatest fan. If Ronnie wants to know what he thinks about something, he calls Bobby. If Bobby wants him to know what he thinks on something, he calls Reagan.'

'Good lord. So Bobby called Reagan and . . .'

'Told him what a brilliant idea it would be to get Agrisync out from Nicaragua, yes. He sends his regards.'

'Which one does?'

'Be more respectful, child. You gave him a wonderful time, he has informed me. Thank you; your future is extremely secure.'

'Hey! Just a goddam moment here, Mom; you wouldn't . . .

you didn't try and trade your only daughter's body off for two hundred thousand dollars, did you?'

'Morgan, sometimes your vanity excels all boundaries! Since when did you get such airs about yourself? I certainly never taught you such things. Do you know how much two hundred thousand dollars is, child? Do you know how hard some people must work to get that sort of money? Some people will work all their lives for less than that amount, and yet you think one night of your favours is worth more than they will earn in a lifetime! I'm ashamed of you, girl; I thought you had more respect for the working people of America!'

'Sorry, Mom; guess I was a bit self-absorbed.'

'I should think so, child. However, I forgive you.'

'HEY, MORG!'

She was busy, and scratchy: Greenwich PMT time.

'I'm on the Quotron, Johnny!'

'It's your mom.'

The room fell empty of sound. All phones stopped. Her mother was wielding that uncanny influence over the ether, last reportedly possessed by the Ancient Mariner. Morgan reached for the phone, then was stopped by bad temper. She put down her hand. 'What does she want?'

A pause. All waited.

'She sends her congratulations.'

'Tell her thanks. What for?'

'You're on the Board of Agrisync.'

Morgan picked up the phone.

PART THREE

Agrisync

In early '82, Ronald Reagan told US companies to have no part in the building of the immense gas pipeline that was to run from Urengoy in Siberia, across the dark breadth of the 'Evil Empire' and into Western Europe. The decision was a major one, based on complex variables, and was thus assumed to have been made by Bobby.

It was this sudden presidential decree that first exposed to horrified official awareness the extent of Bobby's power. By a simple single phone call from his Santa Monica home, Bobby could change US policy. Discreet investigations revealed to appalled State Department bureaucrats that Bobby was often drunk when calling the President, and that his only technical adviser was the cartoonist on the *Vegas Times*. Certain restraints were put in place to ensure that Bobby no longer had untrammelled access to the President. By 1986, however, most of these deterrents had been arrested, fired by Nancy or had resigned in disgrace. Bobby ruled supreme once more.

But the Russian pipeline decision had been a disastrous one for companies like Caterpillar Ltd, which lost hundreds of millions in earthmoving contracts. Caterpillar crumbled, and with it crashed its home base — Peoria, Illinois.

When the American seed company Agrisync brought its corn-lines home from Nicaragua in '85, the farm district surrounding Peoria was still in paralysis. Agrisync was thus able to buy unlimited acres of highest quality 'gumbo' soil for fire-sale prices. And just as well, for this company's finances were also in deep disarray, the enforced move having decimated its shareprice.

So Agrisync came home to the Corn Belt to start again. It settled down to plant out, cross and harvest, and sell the precious, sterile corn seed back to the anxious peasants of war-tossed Nicaragua.

Its operations were overseen by Agrisync Central Office in

downtown Chicago. After all, what executive of a cornseed company would want to live in the Corn Belt?

THE MIDLAND HOTEL, 172 W Adams; gilt-ceilinged, red-carpeted, rock/baroque, guarded by soapstone lions. Home. At least in the meantime.

Each Wednesday at nine thirty a.m., Morgan sat in the Adams Room with the rest of the Board, under a threatening cumulus of high, golden, multi-folded curtain. There was an organ at each end of the room! Wow, now there's religion for you! An immense Ozark hardwood conference table spread down the great room like a chunk of Mississippi. Stationed along its length, like lonely ports, were the seventeen members of the Agrisync Board of Management. At the eastern end of the room, away from the doors, stood a trolley bearing urns of decaf mocha, and plates of croissants and small, multi-laminated wheatbran sandwiches.

Soon, Head Office would take over rental of seven floors of the IT&T Building on Monroe. In the meantime, while the rest of the Agrisync staff slummed in Peoria, the executive and partners settled into the Midland; rooms 21007 through 24, each with Dialcom personal computer access to e-mail, airlines and the NYSE. Management worked out of the three penthouse suites on the ninth floor, and board meetings took place in the Adams Room on the first.

'WHY DO I have to go and live in Chicago, Mom?' Morgan had wailed. 'I mean I'm only on the Board, they only meet once a week. I like DC.'

'There are several reasons, honeychild,' explained her mother gently. 'One of them is that I am your mother and if I had not said "What the hell" to your father one night you would not be here; or if you were, you would be someone else because you would have been the result of a different bout of sexual intercourse. In a nutshell, child, I suppose I am saying that I want some gratitude for not borning you as an air-headed bozo like your brothers.'

MORGAN MORAN, BOARD member, arrived on United into Meigs Field, Chicago at six fifteen p.m., Thursday, 6 March, 1986.

She didn't go to the Midland direct. She went shopping and found seven bars in one department store. It was ten p.m. before she emerged. She was then offered taxis in Urdu, Assyrian and Tagalog, and was transported the short but eventful distance up-Loop to the Midland in a grating, seemingly sand-powered vehicle whose driver insisted in heavy Greek that he was a 'complimentary English taxi service to Midland from Downtown'.

'Chicago great town!' he exclaimed. 'You got dreams, Chicago bring 'em true!'

'I'll remember that,' she said and lightly tipped the man who had dreamed of becoming a taxi driver.

Her shiny green Marshall Field & Company boxes were taken to her room in a trolley that looked like a gold-plated McDonald's sign. She went straight to the bar to meet the Board. The bar was empty in blazing pink.

'Can I get you something ma'am?' asked a chilling young black man who was drying a brandy glass the size of a commode.

'Rain check it, thanks,' she murmured, and mounted the waterfall-sized stairway to the second floor.

Morgan found her room, number 2004, and there drank complimentary sherry to excess. She woke at three thirty a.m., with an earful of the peppermint cream they leave on your pillow. She tossed sweatily in her queensize until she heard the papers arrive: Kurt Waldheim is a Nazi, the Russians nearly land on Halley's Comet, Reagan gives a hundred million dollars to the Contras . . .

By nine fourteen she was showered and girt in her woollen suit of grey. Her mother had sent her *The Woman's Dress For Success* book, with sixty photographs, drawings and diagrams; and the address of Marshall Fields.

State Street, that great street; it's where she'd gone shopping, straight from the little lake-bound airport of Meigs Field, sending her baggage ahead to the hotel on the Midland shuttle.

State Street; department stores like granite ocean liners berthed in lines behind the buzzing sidewalks. And the greatest and granitest of these urban liners was Marshall Field & Company. After a helpless wander across some of its seventy-three acres, she asked a tour leader where the Businesswomen's section was.

'Kayobi ni kite kudasai,' replied the tour leader.

Half a mile away she found Businesswomen and for the next hour she bought suits from a severely elegant woman name-tagged Irene Driffeld. Dark-haired Irene was going on forty-five and was just beginning to administer make-up as bodyfiller. Her breath had the close, not-quite-unpleasantly stale tang of a lifetime of artificial atmosphere. She wore no rings; Irene (call me Miss) Driffeld had dedicated even her chastity to Marshall Field and Company. As she was laying the garments to rest in crocodile-green boxes, Miss Driffeld said, 'Down there a hundred yards — lingerie.'

'Oh, I've got plenty,' blurted Morgan, mortified to be the cause of Miss Driffeld's talking dirty.

Miss Driffeld smiled. Her thick lipstick had seeped into the tiny puckers around her lips, giving their rims a delicate crimson hairiness. 'Of course you have, but this is different. It's underwear for businesswomen; it cancels the suit.'

And it did! It was glorious; cool, unadorned, soft as tongues and yet creating a firm cocoon of intimacy in which you could luxuriate — lingerie that acted like the drawn curtains of a bedroom.

And now, nine thirty next morning, she stood for the first time before the Board, naked inside her light grey, waistcoated, slit-to-the-thigh, semi-formal suit and its lingerie antidote, in the Adams Room, Midland Hotel. She was standing to attention; the sort of attention models stand to, she knew, because one hand was lower down her side than the other.

Two minutes ago the big green double doors had been crashed open, inwards, by a green and gold hotel goon. She had entered, stopped, and waited to be evaluated by the Board. The doors closed behind her. The Board had rumbled to its feet upon her arrival. Sixteen males, and one other. Thirty-two male eyes flipped down from her lips, across her breasts, down to her crotch, tarried, traversed her thighs, rappelled down her calves, fast-tracked back up to the lips again, then down for another quick whirlpool round the delta before coming to rest, in neutral, on her eyes. Bless you all, you pathetic little shlong-led businessmen! Let blue steel harden in the scrotal foundries of the Board! Let corporate corks pop in charcoal trousers!

And thus her dominion was transferred from trading floor to boardroom, and Morgan Moran became a businesswoman.

THE ROOM'S ONLY other woman, powerfully shouldered and lustrous in Cadillac-yellow hair, sat just round the corner from the top of the table, with the golden curtain behind her. The man at the very top of the table, sixtyish, in a powder-blue suit of the style made famous by Fabian, had just stood up.

'Welcome Ms Moran — Morgan,' he chirrups, his mouth seeming to be worked by the strings of old skin under his chin. 'Welcome to Flagship Agrisync.' He then introduced himself as Woodruff Wyeth, Chairman; one of those pink and white old Santa Claus look-alikes whose sweetness sets your teeth on edge. 'Beside me is Mrs Dines, the invaluable representative on our board of the Cook County Council . . .'

'What's your attitude on red-lining, darling?' enquired Mrs Dines in a voice with hairs on it.

Blessedly, Woodruff Wyeth was either deaf or rude. 'Next to Mrs Dines,' he wittered over the question, 'is Mr Otis Vogel, executive vice-president and comptroller, the brains behind . . . blah blah.'

What brains they must be! Otis Vogel wore a head about the size of a bison's!

'And beside him our much-respected . . .'

And so on: the dead wood of the Board is introduced branch by branch while a white-coated hotel goon pours sherry. 'The incomparable T. Paul Barnes, our executive in charge of investment and supply; Hilton Hawkes, production and R&D, the only man who can . . . blah blah, ha ha. Then there's . . . blah blah blah . . . Well, that's us, we're a mad lot, but you'll get used to us I suppose. Hahahaha!'

The Board. Collectively they had all the sex appeal of an elbow; individually several of them were disgusting. Like the one that — oh no! — she's being invited to sit beside now! '. . . Mr Fellucini, on our Board as a representative of the First Ward . . .' A vulture! Black coat like tucked wings, neck like a stack of napkin rings, small bald head for pushing into rotting entrails . . . 'Mr Fellucini facilitates our dealings with City Hall and the First and is an invaluable addition to . . .'

Fellucini! Ye gods; a cross between pasta and oral sex! Is this guy real? She takes the yawningly empty seat next to the vulture, praying that his interest in her flesh is merely libidinous. How quickly our values change!

Mr Fellucini has not accepted sherry; he is now 'taking' iced tea, and during a lull — as Chairman Wyeth talks to a mobile telephone brought to him by a goon — he speaks to her.

'We are a strange breed, Miss Moran, no?' he says in a sort of glottal whisper. His nose is hooked . . . like a beak. She stares at it as he speaks. (Who is? Are we talking human or avian breeds here?) 'First we put in the boiling water to heat our tea, then the ice to cool it; after, we add lemon to make it sour, and then the sugar to make it sweet.' He smiles. She drops her eyes to his mouth for the first time. (That's what talks, you stupid bimbo, not the goddam nose!)

'Yes; oh yes!' And she makes a hiss of demonstrable merriment.

T. Paul Barnes, the only semi-interesting man in the room, has taken a sherry from the salver and handed it to the secretary whose introduction she'd misheard as 'Miss Pencil'. Her real name was Purcel, but to Morgan she'd be Pencil forevermore. She had a small nose and grey suit. Was she naked inside her underwear as well? Miss Pencil is smiling awkwardly and glancing for permission towards Chairman Wyeth, who is determinedly avoiding a decision by not looking up. Miss Pencil doesn't actually look as though she'd be naked under anything. T. Paul Barnes is being gallant; probably for her.

The telephone is being taken away. Woodruff Wyeth announces the imminent arrival of 'an inadvertently late-arriving member of our party', then stands and adds, 'As this meeting was never intended as much more than a warm welcome to the lovely Miss Moran, why don't we mingle and perhaps have another sherry?'

Nine fifty a.m. and the board of Agrisync is on its second sherry. And some are on their third before the arrival of the 'inadvertently late-arriving member'.

And who is it but . . . Immaculate in domino; in Louis John shades and marcelled hair, puce hands widening, white nails blazing emerald as he steps from the newspaper-yellow realms of memory into the pyramidal light of now comes reed-thin, high-jivin', shiny-shoed HARVEY THE TOOT!

Morgan stepped around the bicep of Mrs Dines and stood before him, fourteen years of her life collapsing like cards to form a bridge across which she walked to the age of ten. She had not seen him in the flesh since the days of Lake Tahoe.

His long blue face was hunched in the over-serious frown of a philosopher of juvenile thought. His big beak lips opened to let out the bright pink light. 'Now you ain't gonna beat me up again, are you?' he quacked.

His arms were out-held, and as she walked towards him there was an unevenness in her step. There had been no great changes, just a sudden fleshing out — after all, a person in your memory is no wider than the thickness of a brain cell, so there were dimensions to add: the faint smell of cinnamon of his skin, the warm softness of his great hands, the boniness of his elbows and shoulders.

She herself had of course changed greatly since those ganglous days of pre-puberty. There was an extra thirty pounds of her now; (almost) every pound of it a contribution to the modern ideal of sensual femininity. Yet Harvey didn't seem to notice; not even her disfiguringly bulging waist. His eyes made directly for her braids. The memory of beads, breakfast and corpses was joined in her mind by a bewildering mix of fatherliness and Wakan Tanka.

Harvey the Toot smiled and held out his hand to touch her hair. 'Well, well, the ole muskrat. Hee, hee. She talks a lot about you when we meet, your Mom, but she never tole me about this. Wagon-burner, huh? Yeeha! Well, I told her to keep you right outa that ole meltin' pot, an' looks like she's dang well done it!'

BEING IN THE pink bar of the Midland was rather like sitting in the belly of an extremely healthy giant. The meeting had ended two hours ago, and of the eight or nine Board members who had accompanied them to the bar, only Harvey the Toot and Mr Fellucini remained. She had completely revised her opinion of Mr Fellucini. She liked him. He was gentle, he was engagingly bemused by modern life and was obviously set upon by his family. He was on the phone now, wearing that wheedlingly apologetic expression that any Italian mother inspires in any of her sons. Mother? Mr Fellucini must have been a hundred and three himself!

'It is the decision of Benito, Mama, we must respect his wish. No, no, Mama, it is not a sin, it is the way things are done these days . . . No, it is not the way of the church, mama, it is the Jews who make a fetish of this thing . . . Okay, okay, I am sorry, yes, it is the church; yes, it is the way of the church . . .' He changed his mind with a snap. 'No, it is not the way of the church, Mama! Not today. Things have changed; we do not need to do this thing these days. And anyway, Mama, two of Benito's sons they are circumcised already, and if two are done, the third is exempt! Genesis says this, Mama; I looked it up specially . . . I am showing respect, Mama . . . . No, I am not making it sound like a supermarket special, it is simply that the Bible says you need only have the third done if the first two have succumbed to the operation . . . Succumbed — no, it does not mean to agree to, Mama, it means to die from. There is no need, and Guilio will not be upset. I know this, I have talked to him. Yes, yes, you take your pills now; we will talk more of this matter when I return.'

He put down the telephone, quite unembarrassed. 'My mother — Harvey knows of my mother, Miss Moran, he knows my dilemmas.'

Harvey the Toot gave a complicated combination of shrug, nod and toast with his whiskey shot glass.

'Mama has just learnt that her grandson is not to be circumcised, Miss Moran. Ah, the bondage of tradition, no?' Mr Fellucini sighed and plucked a whiskey from the tray of them Harvey had ordered without consultation. He gulped. 'Ah, the useless clinging to a past way of life. I have three sons: Gulio, he is a priest; Ricky, he has gone to Calabria to be a communist; Benito, well, he follows in his father's footsteps. It is the prepuce of his small son that I try now to save from my mother. But all my sons, they would foist this ridiculous operation on their children if I did not defy them; they are bogged down with adherence, they are fettered and impeded in their ways. Honour the Church, honour the Party, honour the Family. So much honour, so little freedom. Why do they not say, as I think you do, 'Honour yourself'? You have the freedom, I think, Miss Moran, no? The freedom of the beautiful unfettered bird.'

And the vulture sent a flutter of warmth through the unfettered bird. Soon he had gone, home to his heavily circumcised family. 'What a lovely old man,' she smiled. 'Why on earth is he on the Board?'

'He represents the Mafia,' explained Harvey the Toot.

Board Meetings

What conscientous Board members generally strive to do, she observed, is work out ways of selling their own assets to themselves in order to pay back money they've borrowed, without losing their job and without alerting the shareholders to their own powers of bargaining, which would then push prices higher and reduce their potential gains.

Also of course, they dedicate their efforts to the making of self-beneficial deals. Shoulder to Cerruti shoulder, the members of the Board occupy their heavily emolumented time in power struggles on an informal basis. Sixteen button-down shirts button-holing each other at cocktail hour.

'True your bank's going broke, Ty?'

'Yeah, Burkhardt. Thanks fer askin'.'

'You're welcome, Ty. Tragedy; awesome in its parametal consequences.'

'Certainly is, Burk. You wanna make a deal?'

'Well sure, Ty — respectfully of course, and mindful of the sad circumstances — but how 'bout a loan of three million?'

'Sure, that could be arranged, Burk. It would of course facilitate matters considerably if we were working on a quid pro quo basis here . . .'

'Of course, Ty, goes without saying. Well just so happens I heard Comalced's gonna be raided Friday. You didn't hear it from me of course.'

'Course not, Burk, how could I? You're their CEO, after all.'

'Confidentiality would be appreciated, Ty.'

'It'll be an honour, Burk. My bank'll be toes up by June, so I'll make first payment due July, okay? We should be well bust before first pay-back.'

'Thanks, Ty, that's much appreciated; you're a good friend. You golden parachuted?'

'Yeah, and I start vice-chairman First City Welbank, August . . .'

Board business occupied only Wednesday mornings, and sometimes the afternoon beside. On the other days Morgan was on her own, and finding something to do in the City That Works was not easy. There were interesting interludes however. Harvey the Toot once took her on a business excursion to a company of his own, Ebony Enterprises.

Hard-Core Pawn

MORGAN HAD SURMISED, correctly, that Harvey the Toot was not an accumulator of seats on boards, and that he had another, less fatuous mission in life. Now she was on her way to see what it was.

Just out of town, on the way down South State Street, is a sort of Brickhenge of rento-ghettos for the downwardly mobile — Alcatraz without the view, it's been called — the famous Robert Taylor district. She was heading through it now with Harvey the Toot, in a taxi.

She appraised their driver through the scratched plexiglass shield between them. Amos was possibly the biggest taxi driver in the world. His belly engulfed the wheel like a pike's mouth — did they deflate him at night to get him out?

Mind you, he did have a good line of humour. 'Yeah, oh yeah,' he replied to an enquiry from Harvey the Toot, 'ole James still around, still on the run from the law of averages, hee hee hee.' He was shiny black with a shiny black leather jacket and a jaunty black Borsalino hat.

Thirty-ninth Street; bomb-crater road surface, dust storms from the bald patches in scurvied grass parks, block-long stretches of wire mesh that had netted several editions of windblown newspapers, basketball hoops outnumbering street lights by about three to one.

They were passing yet another mouldering sign above a gap in the wire mesh: WELCOME TO ROBERT TAYLOR HOME; DRIVE CAREFULLY AND WATCH OUT FOR OUR CHILDREN. No they weren't! They weren't passing — they were turning in to this one! Hey!

'Welcome to Mississippi Hilton, ma'am,' chortled Amos as he crashed the unbridged curbing and bounced them under the sign. 'Arbeit Macht Frei'; 'Abandon Hope All Ye who . . .' 'Watch out for our children'. They drove jerkily across the rock-hard ex-grass of the estate, through several basketball games (played, she noticed with supreme skill) and on towards the dismal sixteen-storey pile. Bloodlessly red brick with windows like sprocket holes. One low double door like a square mousehole in the exact centre of the building. It was boarded up. Amos veered right — now dragging a vapour-trail of yapping little black kids — round to the back of the building.

A surprisingly fecund copper beech tree on the right, in front of an aeroplane taking off from Meigs Field — either a mile or a universe away. To the left, Rob Taylor's used-people-vault. She felt the serried blank stares of sixteen rows of kitchen windows. At ground level, or slightly below, was a coverway, hemmed in with more mesh, which stretched the length of the building. Harvey had leapt out and was heading towards the steps that led down, to about waist height, to the coverway floor. The little swarm of kids was already following him. Morgan was grappling without enthusiasm with the door handle. Amos turned to her in a creak of leather; the wheel turned with him: 'Well, you is here, ma'am,' he said and pointed emphatically at the ground. 'I recommend the codeine syrup.' And he laughed and laughed.

To her relief Amos didn't depart when she got out — although he'd already promised he'd be waiting.

Within five minutes she'd been offered a dozen or so hits of codeine cough syrup by angelic little black kids with teeth like snowdrops. Slink-eyed twelve-year-olds offered her 'perks or quacks' (Percodan or Quaaludes), without holding out much hope of a sale.

Harvey was striding down the coverway, looping round mounds of garbage, stacked at off-cream-coloured doors. He stopped, and a little group gathered round him — kids in the main, and three women.

Morgan reached them, shivering with the stunning cold of the semi-submerged coverway. She was introduced. 'Bess, Sissy, Hannah . . .' Two of them wore bright turbans, one of them was fat. The other two had that potbellied, S-bend stoop of many sub-working-class black women. Through the door behind them people were making hammering noises and in the gloom she could make out construction of a counter at the far end of the room. She was hauled in by Bess & Co, and a dozen baying children.

The building smelled of cabbage and chilled her breath into visibility. On the floor, the plan of a two-bedroomed house could be traced in the wall-sized gaps in the brown lino. Around the walls of the amputated house a great many shelves had been built, right up to the ceiling. Through a further door behind the counter, even more shelves.

A man named Ralph emerged through this door, greeted Harvey the Toot; told him, 'Hey! yeah things is tight, man!'; was introduced to Morgan, whistled, said, 'Say, ain't you a beauty', to which she answered she didn't know. This caused laughter, which, to her dismay, came from behind her as well. A scrimmage of salivating ex-basketballers crammed the doorway. She was slightly relieved to be ushered into the next, unexceptional room. She was now almost weeping with the cold that colonised her backbone. She wasn't dressed for inspecting goddam coolstores, which surely this great rectangular, empty, dreadful space just had to be. The only interesting thing about the damn stupid room — also an ex-home she noted from the patterns on the floor — was the cage of iron bars that engulfed it, walls, floor and ceiling.

'See, it's not just the door we gotta worry about, Morgan,' said Ralph from very close range — his hand flicked up under her buttock with every step. 'There's nine rooms abut this storeroom, three johns through that wall, three kitchens over there and two livin' rooms through the ceiling. Without these bars they'da cold-chiselled their way in here by the time we'd got it full.'

Full of what she still wasn't quite clear; Bess & Co had been enthusiastic in pointing out storage space but a little non-specific on storage of what. She left the storage room about as biblically known as it took Mary Krueljack to get pregnant, and none the wiser about what she'd just seen.

Stories from the waiting Bess & Co helped. 'My mother, she was a washerwoman, and she'd rush somebody's washing through by Monday night and get it pawned, after telling the owner they could have it Thursday. Come Thursday she had someone else's washing to exchange it for, and that way she always had enough to pay the rent. Shop down the road when I was a child used to open five thirty on Mondays so you could get your work clothes back in exchange for your Sunday best. Or you'd pledge your work tools on Friday night in exchange for your Sunday best, which you took back Monday morning. Pawnbroker made ninety cents on the tools plus a nickel charge ticket and same on the clothes — for a pledge o' six dollars.'

THEY WERE HEADING back up South Dearborn towards the Loop. She was still thinking about the Robert Taylor. So was Harvey the Toot.

'That there fiscal outlet will put through more'n ten thousand pledges a year,' he said. 'We's gonna have a pawnshop in every Robert Taylor — an' that makes twenny-eight. We's gonna plant those mothers in Cabrini-Green, in the Back o' the Yard, Woodlawn, Lawndale, Kenwood — the whole North Side, whole Southwest Side, whole o' the West. Hunnerds of 'em! Hunnerds o' pawnshops. Hunnerds of thousands of pledges a year; millions! We're gonna take black money back outa the white banks, an' out from under the mattress and the hole in the yard, and get it into black-owned saving institutions! Pawnshops! Accumulations of black capital! We're gonna give our people back their own financial control; the revolution's comin' to commerce. We're gonna stick it to them stockbroking, red-lining, ragweed honky bankers with the power of the pawnshop!'

'Tha's right, Harvey, way to go!' chortled Amos. 'As we say here on the Projects, ma'am, Harvey the Toot's done tamped the first dryrot cells to the wooden foundations of supply-side Reaganomics. Ain't that so, Harvey, hee hee hee.'

AS A MEMBER of the Board Morgan was not encouraged to return to the trading floor, she was not venerable enough to be invited onto other boards and there was little opportunity within the company, of working for the greater glory of Agrisync Inc.

In fact, finding out what Agrisync actually did wasn't all that easy either. One day she'd looked up from 'Associated Production Strategies' on the agenda and whispered to Otis Vogel next to her, 'Otis, I see we've got a production operation in Kalamazoo. What do we actually make?'

Otis had swivelled his bison-head (a medicine man — that was it — Otis was a medicine man in full drag) in her direction. 'We make money,' he murmured in his mournful bass.

'Near-term and mid-term strategies', position in the market, positive presentation and the search for the Great White Popcorn — this was the business of the standard Agrisync Board meeting, carried out in a disinterested atmosphere of greed, dishonesty and paranoia. If she was going to find the inner meaning of Agrisync, she'd have to go see for herself.

She requisitioned the company Lear jet and set off for the tilling fields of Peoria. As far as she could gather, she was the first Board member to go there.

'Drive round the block,' she said to the pilot as they unpeeled from the runway. 'No need to go direct, I'd like to get the lay of the land.'

The Corn Belt is a long, wide, flat thing made (according to the pilot) of seventy-five-foot soil and from the air looking like a two-thousand-mile hair transplant. Here and there are scrubby patches where the follicles haven't taken — these are either Indian reservations or bits of national park set up by the government to show what the Great Plains used to look like.

The Corn Belt; her Corn Belt: down there beneath the wing, little hamlets, groups of red-roofed houses with wooden porches on which sit hardy Northern Europeans, ferociously shucking corn. And testimony to their tenacious mono-vision is the fact that when this Lear's flown from one horizonful of corn to the next, it's travelled over only one single solitary set of vegetal genes.

The airport was a clearing in the corn. The edge of the tableau of corn took on a third dimension as they lowered towards it; it now had thickness, height. Considerable height in fact. As they sank beneath the level of the Mennonite churches, the cranes on the riverbank and the power lines, they reached the wispy tops of the corn and kept going down. This corn was taller than an aeroplane!

They stopped on the edge of a herd of Ozark Airline 737s. She clambered down stiffly and was instantly oppressed by the surrounding cliffs of shuffling corn. She was in a Threaten Field a thousand miles long, and its sounds were repulsive, insect-like. Hissings, gratings, the clack of the hard parts of beetles. She glanced fearfully round for the hovering black shape of the scare-crow and thought she saw it flashing into the infinity of cereal. She pulled back her head and strode sternly down the ranks: show who's boss, don't look afraid; like you do with dogs.

Anton the pilot traded in his plane for a company pick-up and they set off for the town. The corn retreated from the roadside and gave some perspective. You could look along the top and it was as perfectly flat as the lid of a coffin. Dead level. Ahahaha! A blemish! A hill! A tiny hillock, the only elevation in three sixty degrees of horizon. On the top of the hillock — a pig farm. At the bottom of the hillock — a house. An Amish church grew from the midst of the cornfield nearby. 'Need a monstrous deal of electricity for pigs,' said Anton. 'A monstrous deal.'

Peoria was not in good urban health. It was one of those repositories of decline and dismay politely called 'post-industrial'. A river joined them on the right, a brown river with suds floating in it. They passed a factory and she gave a bray of laughter. Budweiser! — that river was ninety-five percent beer! A dinky little university, strip joints, a defunct train with a restaurant in it. Plazas, malls, convention centres; the desperate products of decay; bury your murders and suicides under shopping-mall paving.

She had an appointment to spend the day with Daniel McElvery, head of Biotechnology, Agrisync, Peoria. The Lear was not required elsewhere; Anton the Aviator would placidly read comics until her return.

IT'S *DOCTOR* DANIEL McElvery, and it's *Daniel*, not Dan, she had been advised severely on the phone, by a voice as deep as the bottom of a goosefeather bed. Doctor Daniel, bringing wellness to the botanical world.

The first disappointment as they pull up at Dr Daniel's address, Peoria, is that the Agrisync millions are generated in prefabs. Dr Daniel works in a hardboard shed! His office is three nameplated doors past a coffee machine and a poky, sliding-glass reception. Morgan is led down a featureless corridor whose walls are warped by slovenly construction. She can hear her feet echoing on the thin floor; the walls smell of varnish. Is varnish good for our plants? Is anything we do good for them? She has a sudden spasm of guilt; what a hell of a life we give our little vegetal charges. Those tiny corn seeds who come trustingly into this world are bagged up and assigned to a Central American war zone; there forced to lie, in bullet-riddled silos, next to foreign-smelling lentils and chick peas . . .

She is nodded into the room by the receptionist (who was only doing the ushering, she suspected, because that SOB Dr Daniel didn't come to reception himself).

Disappointment #2 is more complex but more profound. Dr Daniel is a hunk! He's a grade one Clydesdale to use an agricultural term. He's William Hurt! And that voice, as delicious in the flesh as on the telephone! Then he stands up and stops at about five foot four. William Hurt in John Hurt's body! Can genetic engineering do nothing? Grafting? Is Dr Daniel somehow a metaphor for the illusory world of the pitcher plant and Venus flytrap? She sits in the frangible chair he is indicating; his voice is wide-making, but he is short.

LATER. HOLY HERBGARDEN! Sheesh!

She is home; recently delivered to Meigs Field by Anton, and to the Midland — 'complimentary English taxi service'-style — by an Albanian. Now, slouched in the pink bar, she swills away the effects of Nature with hard liquor. That Nature! Hey! The world of dandelions and pumpkins makes hostile takeovers seem like pastry lessons! It's rough out there; that Darwinism doesn't give a shit! You don't shape up, man, ship out! Sugar — did you know the sugar plant is evil? Huh? Well, just ask the all-caring Dr Daniel! That sugar plant, morbidly hostile to all other forms of vegetation, skulks in the plantation, sucking at the soil, leaching it of all good. Sucks it dry; devoids it of all value. And as it impoverishes the soil, so it impoverishes its servants, the poor schmuks who tend it! The more money and care they pump in, the less it gives out. Asshole. It makes slaves of the soil as it once enslaved the folk of Africa; and it makes slaves of the any-coloured people who grow it today. Heavy!

Another Black Russian? Of course another Black Russian! And don't put the bottle too far outa arm's reach neither, Honch. Don't you know they're out there? Billions of them! The little soldiers of Darwin!

Bananas; heard the latest on bananas? They're dying! We unzip the fruits of a desperately ailing plant. The banana trees of United Fruit have only five years to live. They've all got black sicatoka, the AIDS of floradom. There's no known cure, and one day soon all the bananas of the world will be living on borrowed time! We're already on this frantic merry-go-round-against-time, staggering the plantations so there's always plenty of one-, two-, three- and four-year-olds round to take over from the moribund geriatrics of five. We eat the products of disease! And we love it! Unzippabu buggered banana.

Yeah, another; heavy on the rum. Peanuts? Don't you dare give me peanuts! Popcorn? Arrrgh!

Corn. We made corn, we humans. Not Nature — us. Corn-makers. The way Doctor Daniel puts it, we and God are about fifty/fifty on the Creation split, but God seems to have retired. And one of the first things we made — maybe at the same time we were doing the interior decoration at Altamira and Lascaux — was corn. We nurtured it from grass; turned it into that big fat cob we know today. Trouble is, it won't grow up! It lies there in its swaddling clothes of canvassy leaves and refuses to help itself in any way. It's entirely dependent on us and without us . . . well, you leave a baby in a field for a year and see what happens. Corn's got its own Armageddon scenario too.

Year one. Fine plump succulent cobs; flat green leaves, tree trunk of a stalk; whole crop all exactly the same height, as tall, strong and handsome as a fieldful of Norwegians. And if no one tends them? Down they fall.

Year two; about a tenth of last year's crop turns up — and they are mutants! Who needs strontium-90? These plants are weird! All shapes, sizes, heights; ten husks or none — double headers. Freaks! Aberrations! Monsters!

Year three. Nothing. Zip. Zilch. Extinction. Gone.

Corn is always within three seasons of extinction.

Honch the bartender is standing upright, his eyes are unglazing and he is heading down the bar to serve another customer. The Ancient Mariner has lost her wedding guest.

Damn. Someone else has violated the pastel privacy. T. Paul Barnes! Oh no! What the hell does he want? Apart from her, that is. Maybe nothing else. He waves as if they'd just spied each other through the faces of a happy-hour crowd in downtown Morocco. 'And whatever the lady's drinking,' he says and saunters over.

OLE T. PAUL'S all right. Yeah, he's okay. Sure, sure, Paul; one more then she has to go up an' dress for dinner. (Dress for dinner? Wha' the hell's that mean? Put an apron on so she doesn't spill her ketchup? Ahahaha!)

Barnsey's jus' told her a very affecting story about his psychological development; it'd said a lot about him actually; you gotta respec' a man who tells you about their psychological deve'pmint. It hadn't started out as a discussion about that; it'd actually started more generally when she'd said she liked his shiny shoes. This had cern'ly struck a chord: 'Y'know any shoes can be like that,' he'd said. 'Any shoes can look like patent leather if you spend time on them. Men don't have the accessories that women do, Morg. Women got their nails, face, hair, belts, underclothes, shoes — men just really got their shoes. Thing is, it's a fact not taken into consideration about men's characters, but they just don't have the opportunity to accessorise! Was my mother who encouraged me to shine my shoes; she was always telling me to shine my shoes, and she'd threaten to lock me in without my being allowed to go out if I didn't shine my shoes. But the thing is this, Morg,' and hey, he's leaned forward an' put his hand on her knee, but hell, it's only because he's so wrapped up in his story, an' with all that accessory depravation he's gotta be a faggot anyway, 'thing is, I wanted my shoes shiny anyway! You see the conundrum here? My mother was on and on at me to clean my shoes, an' all the time I wanted to clean my shoes! She din have to tell me, it was something I wanted to do! See what had happened was she din' realise cleaning my shoes was part of my character, part of the genes that she'd inherited into me. The part of me that wanted to clean my shoes was from the part of her that always wanted me to have clean shoes! You see? It's that nature/nurture thing; this was human psychology at cross-purposes because we were arguin' over the same bit of character that we both had! See, what was happening here was you had a breakdown of someone's own character because they wouldn't trust their own nature — they couldn't see that they'd passed on the shoe-cleaning genes, and so they kept on harping about it because they still had them too!'

The conversation had gone on for quite some time, and then it tapered off in psychological intensity when T. Paul got round to how he liked those big military boots, Carolinas, that open at the top like parachutes and you can wear them all laced up with nice slacks or let them splay open with a pair of blue jeans. Then he'd got suddenly serious and she thought, oh Jeezas, here comes the hard word, but he said how he an' the rest of the Board was wondering if she'd like to head down to Phoenix for a few days an' visit her mother. Holy Toledo! Was he that looped?!

'Christ, T, you think people voluntarily visit my mother?'

T. Paul Barnes was suddenly serious. 'We jus' wanna, sorta, find out what yer mother's long-term intentions are *vis-à-vis* the company.'

And fear had joined the mullet in his stare.
'Whaddaya mean, T. Paul?'
'We think she's tooling up for a takeover.'

Discussions on the Porch

'Mother,' bawled Morgan on behalf of the Board, 'Agrisync is a considerable portion of the material universe. Private persons don't buy companies like that; they destroy you if you try! Remember Coca-Cola? You are here because you were lucky; they gave you a gentle warning that turned you into a junk bond! Generally when you bomb out on a takeover deal like that, you lose everything. As you assuredly would if you tried a buy-out of Agrisync!'She was breathless and trembling.

'My own daughter will make me lose everything?'

'No, Mom, I will try and help you save something! Mom, you had an awful lot more money last time you tried this stunt . . .'

'Agrisync is not as big as Coca-Cola.'

'No, but it's still a hell of a lot bigger than you!'

That maddening little smile forced itself into her mother's iron features, like a fracture in an axehead. 'Maybe I have partners,' she said.

'Who?'

'Nasharo.'

'Who's Nasharo?'

'My partner.'

'Nasharo's an Indian word. There's no Indian — and there won't be till they get the Black Hills back — who can buy Agrisync!'

'Is that so? Well, it just so happens Nasharo came into a little money recently. Came to a settlement with the government over a certain piece of land.'

'Tell Nasharo to invest his money wisely, and not . . .'

'Nasharo is not a person, you ignorant baggage! Nasharo is the Chiefs' Council of the PTBC — and that means the Pawnee Tribal Business Council. I am not dealing with a person, I'm dealing with a tribe!'

'Jeezas, not another tribe! Mom, you've gotta stop using tribes like they were investment clubs!'

'Pawnee Indians think corn is the greatest gift of the gods.

They spend most of their time praying to corn, and according to business statistics that means every three prayers in five goes to Agrisync. Who better to be in on the deal than people like that?'

Something strange was happening. In a mini out-of-body experience, Morgan was looking down upon herself, ashen upon the porch; a small spot on the edge of the Sonoran Desert — where corn began — glaring into the face of a death's-head in braids. Her mother. That mother, who one damask evening had murmured to her father — whoever he may be — 'What the hell?' and she had been conceived; that mother, to whom she owed all. No, not all, some! And not this! This figure of granite motherhood glimmering in front of her belonged also to the forces who threatened the Board; her Board. For whom she would fight! Yes! Against . . . her mother! It was not simply her mother's face into which she stared, awed by her resolve, but also the unyielding face of Hostile Takeover!

Taking Over

She was taxied into town from O'Hare by a Libyan who smelled powerfully of whiskey. Aren't Muslims teetotallers? Maybe there's an exemption for Libyans. After all, they've got no rivers, what else could they drink?

The Midland was still there. Well, of course it was still there! You don't come down Adams with a wheelbarrowload of shares, dump them at 172 and take the building away! Don't you? What do you do? She wasn't quite sure how takeovers worked, and anyway they were dealing with her mother . . .

Powered by a burst of desperate energy she ignored the elevator and bounded up the staircase like a salmon up falls. She hauled off her suit, damp from heat, and ran the shower. The phone rang. T. Paul Barnes: they'd noted her arrival, can she meet them in the bar?

Who?

Himself and 'several concerned parties'. The company front line.

She showered and prepared for the bar in slacks and top of fierce green. The Spirit of the Clash — she will begin by clashing with the decor. Red and green should never be seen! She set forth.

They sat amidst the pink pillars, Byzantine arches and mock bronze palm trees on the far side of the bar. Ludicrously enough, on a lintel above them, a live TV glittered silently amidst the tarty ornamentation. Someone had just won the Indy 500. She squints. Bobby Rahal.

From here she can see only T. Paul Barnes. He waves. The Minotaur-sized head of Otis Vogel projects from a pink column for a moment. Those two are no surprise. The phoney gold ceiling glows like the ceiling of St Volodymyr's Ukrainian Church. 'Black Russian thanks, Honch,' she murmurs.

In green she wanders across the pink carpet, presumably looking like ingested spinach. She rounds the pink column to confront the 'concerned parties'. The absences didn't surprise her — Woodruff Wyeth, Hilton Hawkes, Mrs Dines and a dozen others; they would be of little use here, the front line has to be lean and mean with no risks of tripping over dead wood. Harvey the Toot's presence was inevitable. The presence of Mr Fellucini was . . . ominous — they're making this a Family matter? Heavy!

The greetings were effusive, but there was a chill of shrewd watchfulness in the pink-tinted air; of tense fragility. Presumably this was takeover mood.

'Hey, Robin Hood, pull up a rye,' quacked Harvey the Toot, pushing his characteristic tray of shot glasses towards her with his foot. She held up her Black Russian and shook her head. She sat between Otis and Mr Fellucini, who patted her crossed knee and said, 'Welcome home, my dear. You look ravishing.'

'We's just been celebratin' a breakthrough as will prob'ly win the Nobel Prize for Agrisync,' crowed Harvey the Toot. 'All on account of Otis here.'

Otis's great head nodded like a balanced boulder in the Painted Desert, pleased but perhaps not quite at ease with Harvey's familiarity.

'Behind the hyperbole there's a grain of truth — no pun intended,' he rumbled. 'The genetic-engineering people at Kalamazoo have steered the corn germ into an almost central situation in the kernel. It's always been just slightly off centre, so we could only cut one and a half chips per kernel. Now we can get a full two. Outstanding from the company's point of view.'

She expressed her delirious approbation, after which there was a pause. The air was treacly and brought words quickly to a halt, so there was no conversational run-on effect. Every sentence was a new beginning.

Above them, on the silent TV, Bobby Rahal was performing the onanistic champagne squirting ceremony of victorious drivers. It commanded rapt attention from all who could see the screen. Otis was not one of them. 'Any outstanding points of view of your own to report?' he rumbled slyly.

The heaviness of his jowls pulled the skin down slightly from under his eyes. 'Yes,' she said. 'My mother's going to try and buy us.'

Nothing was said. The table was a riot of displacement activity. For some reason all eyes returned eventually to Otis Vogel; perhaps he had attracted their attention with his heavy nod. 'We rather thought as much. Which puts you in a somewhat awkward position, my dear.'

'Why? I think she's a rotten old fink. I'm going to fight to stop her.'

More frenzied wrigglings, doodles and silent whistling. The strangest silence in her opinion was Harvey the Toot's.

'You mean, stay on the Board?' It was Mr Fellucini who enquired; solicitously, as far as she could tell.

'Of course. I'll fight her, and when we win I'll try and stand between her and the Board's revenge.'

T. Paul Barnes and Otis Vogel gave nods in ludicrous symmetry. Mr Fellucini smiled. Harvey the Toot's expression was sphinxian.

'I'll tell you her plan,' said Morgan, 'in return for — mercy.'

Glances were exchanged like glass beads.

'We will not harm a feather in her bonnet, my dear,' intoned Otis Vogel.

'You have our word on that,' added T. Paul Barnes, somehow subtracting, in his vehemence, from the easy Vogel veracity.

Mr Fellucini patted her hand and nodded with his eyes closed.

'Mom's in partnership with the Pawnee Indians . . .'

Harvey the Toot gave a sudden whoop. 'Pawnee? Ha! Canadian Government once made it legal to have blacks or Pawnees as slaves! Poorest tribe there is. They'll partner your mom straight into the Happy Huntin' Ground!'

'Yes, but they've just come into money,' said Morgan. 'The government has granted them compensation for . . .'

'Don't signify a fig,' interjected Harvey. 'Fact of the matter is the government might run the country, but the banks run the money. The Pawnee's got no credit rating, an' for this project you need banks.'

'I'm afraid she'll have to face the consequences,' front-lipped T. Paul Barnes. 'It's her fight.'

'I know,' replied Morgan. 'And as far as I'm concerned, she's in it alone.'

There were nods; looks were pointedly aimed away from her, her mother's daughter.

'At this stage of proceedings,' hemmed Otis Vogel, 'we have to examine our priorities. Our esteemed Chairman Wyeth would blether that "the interests of the stockholders are best preserved if the continuity of the Board is maintained". Is this the case as we see it?'

Rustles, like a field of giant corn.

'There will, I feel,' murmured T. Paul Barnes, 'inevitably be — changes wrought. A buy-out by Acomazuni Enterprises of thirty percent, which is about the amount of loose stock lying round on the NYSE, would result in the need to replace at least half the Board members, I'd say . . .'

And a vote was silently taken and the result recorded in the invisible minutes. Drinks were raised, probably in an unconscious toast to absent friends.

'We have to at least consider at this stage,' said Otis Vogel, 'the efficacy of a leveraged buy-out. Stock in escrow would probably come to over one point one billion; interest on that is likely to be about four hundred million. Personal commitment I would say . . .'

'Are we talking White Knight here?' enquired T. Paul Barnes.

'We were trying to,' breathed Otis Vogel, but Barnes was in a hurry.

'Because I was hearing the other day about the Sultan of Brunei; he put the money behind the Harrods buy-out . . .'

'Arabs?' said Harvey the Toot. 'What the hell is Arabs?'

'Harrods. It's a British department store; sort of a small Macy's. This sheik guy bought it in a hostile takeover — and forgot he'd done it! I mean, if we're looking for non-interest loans, you can't go past someone with money like that!'

'No, Arabs tend to look west more than east,' said Otis Vogel, then paused. 'I'm not talking Mecca here, I'm talking London.

Anyway, Arabs are olives-and-pita-bread-friendly; never had much truck with corn.'

Four worried men in a pink room considering the merits of Allah as a protection against her mother. Morgan shuddered at the unnaturalness of it all. 'It is just so . . . intrusive!' she blurted, 'that someone like my mother can barge in and smash up a company that's been working quietly away for years! Like coming home and finding burglars have done over your home . . .'

'Oh, she's got more right than most, my dear,' said Otis Vogel. 'She at least owns part of it. You don't need to own any of it to grab all of it, you know; in fact you don't need to have heard of it till the day before your bid.'

'I think it's disgusting,' she said fiercely. 'This whole takeover business is — revolting!'

'It's new, my dear,' said Otis serenely; 'it hasn't settled down into rules. The takeover world is in its infancy. Perhaps that's why it shits all over everybody.'

'Everybody who's directly in the way, that is,' said T. Paul Barnes. 'If you see what I mean?'

There was a dense silence; the air pressure seemed to compact as it does before a thunderstorm. Shufflings; shifty, fart-in-the-elevator expressions. She turned to frown into the uninterestingly regular face of T. Paul Barnes. 'No,' she said flatly.

'Well,' he sighed, mortified at the need for explanation and the lack of assistance in making it. 'We thought we should — shield you from it all.'

He also had a surprisingly smooth brow for one of forty-five or so. Perhaps he'd been shielded from such stressful events himself.

'Think of us,' said Otis Vogel, 'as a big Company diaper.'

'Willing to stop any of that . . .'

'Excremental fallout,' put in Otis Vogel helpfully.

'From falling on you.'

'After all,' chortled Otis with wan heartiness, 'someone's got to come out of this foodfight unblemished, otherwise we've got no figurehead for the commercials.'

'What does that mean?' she snapped, demolishing the Vogel smile.

'Well, we can't . . . we have to . . .' T. Paul Barnes withered into silence.

'I'm afraid, my dear,' said Otis Vogel with a quick, sharp sigh, 'it's what you call a conflict of interest. Your mother . . .'

'There is no conflict! I am one hundred percent against my mother on this!'

'And we trust you one hundred percent, you know that.' It was the verbally healed T. Paul Barnes, being extremely sincere. 'But it's the shareholders. They've been skittery enough since we got out of Nicaragua. If it gets out that there's a daughter of a hostile raider on the Board . . . Well, just ask yourself. You see?'

She looked around the little ring of Board members. No hostility, just sincere self-interest.

'One of the first things a raider does at this juncture is try to undermine the share price of the target,' explained Otis Vogel. 'Your mother will put pressure on Agrisync's big institutional shareholders to dump their shares — in fact she'll try to get them to buy hers in exchange.'

'What she'll tell them is this,' said T. Paul Barnes, as Harvey the Toot and Mr Fellucini looked interestedly and silently on. 'She'll say something along these lines: "Acomazuni Enterprises is soon going to own Agrisync, so buy in with me and you'll keep your own company." '

'And she'll also be telling them, I'm afraid,' sighed Otis Vogel, 'that she has a daughter on the Board, undermining our defences.'

'My mother wouldn't . . ." exclaimed Morgan, then stopped.

'We reckon it's in everybody's best interests if you . . .' T. Paul Barnes grappled for diplomacy, 'took a vacation.'

'Hey, listen, Morg, why don' you'n me get in that li'l company jetplane and ease over to Tahoe for a weekend?' cried Harvey the Toot. 'Old times, ole stampin' ground! We'll kick some shit outa pickpocketin' dwarfs!'

'That's all this takeover thing will take? A weekend?'

Intaken breaths, fallen faces.

'No,' said Otis Vogel. 'Weeks. Maybe months.'

T. Paul Barnes's face lit up with crazed enthusiasm. 'Why don't you head down to New Orleans? Win the necklaces, Queen of the Pageant! Acapulco. Puerto Rico.'

'Been to Boston?' put in Otis Vogel, perhaps reluctant to see her heading in the direction of Phoenix.

'London!' exclaimed T. Paul Barnes, exciting even himself with this recollection of the rest of the known world. 'Paris, Rome, Italy! The Grand Tour. That's the one! Miss Purcell can . . .'

She stood. In slit-eyed fury she trained upon them the arsenal of her body. Miss Nearly Arizona goes to war; she will drop them dead. She stands in the light of the mock Murano chandelier behind her, knowing that to them, looking up, she seems like the green-penumbral silhouette of a giantess from Vedic pornography. Her darkness falls across Otis Vogel and T. Paul Barnes, engulfing the cowardly, self-seeking pair in the hydraulic handcuffs of breast shadow. Mr Fellucini is perched in hooded rapacity on the swell of her shadow hip; Harvey the Toot, naturally enough, is situated in the central south of her shadow, either indulging in beaky cunnilingus or being born. Her shade stains the four-piece surface they form. Patches of armadillo.

Then she watched her shadow arms attach to shadow hips. The men she has eclipsed flinch. 'I'm a liability, is that right?' There was no answer, simply the squirmed acknowledgement of a rhetorical question. 'I might turn traitor? Is that so?' More cavernous silence; glances scuttled hither and yon like cave insects caught in the light of her gaze. 'Okay, if you want me out of the way, I'll damn well go!'

Even at this moment of towering majesty she could hear her treasonous brain screaming 'Where? Where?'

'You want me off the patch? Okay, I'm right off Agrisync's patch. As of now I'm on holiday . . .'

'Where? Where?'

Yet deeper within the cortex of her panicking brain was a lake of pure serenity. Something inside her knew where she was going; it just hadn't told the rest of her yet. She waited, hands on hips, leering down at her craven audience, partly in panic but mainly in confident excitement as she awaited the announcement from that serene, deep-seated HQ.

They waited, she waited.

'Tell Miss Pencil to book me on a flight to Nicaragua,' she said.

BOOK TWO

PART FOUR

MANAGUA

FLYING TO NICARAGUA is not easy. Oh, you can take a C-130J Hercules — as thousands of US citizens do — from Eglin Air Base in the Florida panhandle, down to Aguacate Air Base, Honduras, then get a Huey helicopter across the border. But you might catch a Redeye missile up the exhaust if you do — because you'd be on a CIA strafing mission.

Or you can flip from Florida down to, say, Panama and get any number of South American flights up to Managua — but if you really want to prove you're a Friend of the Revolution, you fly Aeronica. Aeronica, the only airline (as far as Morgan was aware) that gives out umbrellas to its passengers.

You go to Miami International, and at the right-hand end of the booking hall is a profoundly empty booth with a blue Aeronica sign behind it (the reds and blacks of the Revolution are kept carefully under the counter). At certain times of the day, on certain days of the week, a door in the C of NICA, opens, a soap-eyed official emerges and for five minutes sells tickets to Managua and Havana.

Such was Morgan's own importance, however — as a member of the Board of Agrisync — that her tickets had been sent to the Midland; the equivalent, in service, of an upgrading to first class.

Of course the Revolution doesn't have a first class. You walk, with your own bags, past downstairs lavatories and mildewy walls to the Aeronica shed out the back of the airport. There you clamber up unsteady aluminium steps into your Russian-donated plane — presumably the last model to blow up at the Paris Airshow — where you are brusquely plugged into your seat and tightly secured by straps made of the material they use for gentlemen's braces. The ancient metal buckle is impossible to unfasten in flight, but perhaps this is just as well; the seat's the type that folds backwards every time you stand up. You are delivered a lecture on the minimalisation of death on the journey, given a boiled sweet, then wrenched into the sky and hauled in the direction of Central America. But here is the glorious difference between this flight and any other: you fly sou'west in a dead straight line! You do not suddenly veer to the right, then later veer left again, while all the time that little progress chart on the screen is telling you you're going straight ahead. On Aeronica there is no doglegging round a vast Caribbean area, which on your airline map is profoundly empty. (Perhaps that's the Bermuda Triangle, that funny dogleg you do around a place that isn't there?) In other words, Aeronica takes you directly over the airspace of Cuba.

They lurched across the pot-holed sky; the thing creaked and shuddered. The man next to her — a sort of human haybale in a jacket — chortled and wailed in mock terror while sweating garlic into the airless confines. Morgan felt ill. There were no barf bags. 'Very good plane,' exclaimed the man, heedlessly elbowing her breast as he turned to her. 'Make very good pilots, this plane; only good pilot make stay in sky.'

'Oh, great,' she murmured. 'Good pilots are they, the Nicaraguans?'

'Nicaraguans? No! Ha, ha! No, we no good at fly. Pilots from Cuba. We no good at everything!'

They were tossed around the sky by the mad gods of humidity. The man committed several million dollars' worth of inadvertent sexual harassment while animating his conversation.

'You are from Mexico?' he demanded.

'No, Nevada. I think.'

'Mexico people, they full up of opinions, no? Come they down to my country; opinion, opinion, opinion. Big shots. "We do this, we do that." Why not you shoot them instead of us, eh? Remember th'Alamo! What they do to you there, eh? Cabrones!'

'I'll bear it in mind for the next war,' she rejoined weakly from the perimeter of a fainting fit.

They landed amidst shrieks of joy and applause. 'Welcome to Nicaragua libre!' cried the garlicky man, pushing past her to get at the lockers above. His large buttery buttocks juddered past her at eyelevel, the consistency of double chins. 'Change money at Ciudad Jardin, not at airoport. Better price.' He hauled down a tattered fabric bag. 'You have good time in my country, no?' And he set forth after introducing her to a word that would numb her with use before her journey's end. 'Vaya con Dios, compañera!' He crashed down the heavily populated aisle, spilling compañeros and gringos into seats and onto the floor.

César Augusto Sandino Airport. She thought at first she had walked through the exhaust of the engine. No, it was simply the heat. A wet heat, unlike the desiccated air of Phoenix. It was like walking through very thin water — water for boiling rice, made slightly lubricious by a drop of olive oil.

The bolts that held the starboard luggage bay could not be turned; wrenches to do the job could not be found. 'Sin problemas!' (No worries), Havana would have the wherewithal and the luggage would be returned the day after tomorrow. Passengers were divided by their reactions into cheerfully impassive natives and fraught visitors. Morgan's own luggage was safely in the port compartment.

Changing sixty dollars was compulsory, and her passport was not stamped until she had received her dictionary-sized parcel of cordobas. Only when officialdom — an identical line of scowling little men with well-polished slicks of funereally black hair — had finished with her did a small man in grey suit come forward and introduce himself as José Luis of Coca-Cola. 'You are to stay at the Camino Real,' he said gravely. 'There there are toilet papers and toothpaste. Tomorrow I will come to show to you Managua, and then in later days I will take you to wheresoever you like of my country. Now you will go to your room to rest.'

They walked out of the terminal, following the porter who hauled her shockingly new suitcases on a trolley with bent wheels. They pushed through a hem of belligerent taxi drivers at the curb and onto dense, red scoria. The luggage trolley bogged down. The porter put it over his shoulder and carried it, suitcases and all. The air smelled as if it had been singed slightly; it stung her eyes. Bright birds sang like rifle shots from strange red trees. 'This way,' said José Luis and led her towards a clump of cars to the left. The porter ahead of them continued right; José Luis ignored him. He was steering her towards a faded red minibus from which 'Coca-Cola Coke' protruded beneath black graffiti: 'Viva la FSLN, muerto a la FDN'. The porter rejoined them without resentment and José Luis gave him some money.

They set off out of the airport, down a boulevard of red mud lined with palms and high lampposts, none of which seemed to contain lamps. The landscape ahead was flat and dusty, fronded by panting palm trees with leaves the consistency of limp umbrellas. A perfect volcano reared in the middle distance. 'Momotombo,' said José Luis. 'Somoza did not throw people in here.'

'Oh. Really?' she replied cautiously. It was a tricky statement to respond to. A shellburst of devilry. 'Why not?'

'There is geothermal power plant. Better to use Volcán Santiago, where no one sees.'

'Ah.' Yes, that certainly seemed an exercise in common sense; throw them in the less-populated volcanoes. Jeezas! Why the hell was she here again? Ah yes, to be perverse.

A smudge of pollution in the sky to the west indicated civilisation. A left turn onto the highway and an immense jolt as they climbed up the cliffside of the brick-paved thoroughfare. Bricks! Bobby's bricks! A pang of poignant hyper-reality; incidental conversation had somehow just become an iota truer. And wow! Had those bricks been thrown! There were mud-filled bald patches in the road that wart hogs could have lolled in!

Blaring up and down the unsteady roadway, in mirages of diesel were flocks of high, angular, fang-grilled trucks. Undigested diesel hung in straithes in the air above the roadway, mingling with dust. Red dust, black diesel; the revolutionary colours. Nicaraguan pollution, Morgan came to learn, hangs not over cities — there's no industry — but over highways.

Clapboard and cardboard shacks littered the gaps between palms along the roadside; roofs were of palm, banana leaf or purloined metal billboard signs: Coca-Cola. IBM. Jesus Lives, said the roofs. Their progress seemed portentous to the dull-eyed denizens of the shacktowns, who stared at the van from their squatting positions or shambled closer to the roadway to gaze at their passing. Her arrival seemed the most amazing thing that had happened to them all day: presumably because they were neither a truck nor a bus while every other vehicle was. White (surprisingly so) or military green shirts, hanging outside black trousers for the men and boys; determinedly shapeless, faded pastel dresses for the women. The people of Nicaragua. Beggars who couldn't afford tin cups.

Wide compounds had been smashed into the palm forest and hedged with barbed wire. Inside were trucks in army drab. Many of them sat wheelless on wooden blocks. What in hell were they being protected from? Mind you, most of them seemed to have their motors missing as well. Maybe there was a flourishing black market in ten-thousand-decibel Russian diesel engines.

The letters on the side of the hill! There they were, big as 'Hollywood'. FLSN. Bobby had mentioned them in the same breath as the bricks. ROLSTER it used to say up there before the Revolution. Brand name for a line of shoes.

Traffic lights. They stopped. Hives of incredibly filthy children battered at the windows, holding up oranges, bananas, cigarettes, gum and unspeakable liquid in recycled bottles. Others clambored onto the bonnet and smeared the windscreen with muddy rags, shrilly demanding money for the cleaning job. A railway line meandered across the highway; in fact joined forces with it and continued its journey, as two rail-filled canyons, down the middle of the road. 'Ferocarril de Pacifico,' intoned José Luis as they grounded after the lurch over the rails; 'To-Pacific railway-train.' Grass grew from the depths of the twin canyons.

From ubiquitous ghettoblasters, music throbbed. It was a cross between Bob Marley and an Iraqi muezzin.

She glanced back at the lettered hill, scudding beside them behind palms and fortress-like apartment blocks.

'What does it mean, FSLN?' she asked.

'Frente Sandinista de Libre Nicaragua.'

'And FDN?' It was the other acronym she constantly saw scrawled on white house fronts and tin fences.

José Luis' eyes flared. He frowned quickly and looked away, shaking his head.

The shacks and palms were thinning away, streets and lines of housing appeared. Suburban Managua. Golgotha. The original blues and yellows had faded to the colour of old bone; rows of uneven, thin, rickety, caried, dun buildings like the grins of dead smokers; dark, empty windows and doors like the sockets and nasal cavities of skulls; shutters and louvre doors like ribcages.

Some minutes later they swung at ninety degrees across the road, between trucks and over the railway lines, slewing across the bricks like a yacht crossing the wind. They crashed down from the brick plateau of the highway onto a scoria driveway, which turned a corner to reveal, amidst suddenly robust palms, an immense, multi-sided, wood-and-window complex.

'Camino Real,' murmured José Luis, not without pride. 'Managua hotel most grand after Intercontinental.'

The towering foyer windows wept with condensation mist and, when she entered, the coldness slammed at her face. But by the time she had followed José Luis and two porters to the desk, she was accustomed to the pleasing coolness of the air conditioning.

She signed in. Yes, they will take American Express. This bemused her a little; Reagan had embargoed this benighted little country into immobility, yet she can shift cash in and out of here at will. But then it's the President of the US, not necessarily the president of Amex, who's at war with Nicaragua. And thank God for that; she'd seen the prices. Her brick of local money would buy one night's tenure, before the very generous IVA — value-added tax.

José Luis inexpressively departs. She is led to her room. Numero dos cientos viente uno. On the doorhandle a cardboard sign: GARANTADO LIBRE DE VINCHUCA, which she took to be another revolutionary slogan until informed it meant guaranteed free of the bugs that carry the dreadful Chagas' disease. A pleasing room, number 221, across a courtyard of thatched sun shelters from the foyer, bar and dining room. Her ground-floor window looked out to a blue-tiled pool beneath frangipani trees. Just by looking at the waxy pink flowers she could smell their scent. A kingfisher sat on a branch above the pool, staring down into the water.

Double bed, comprehensible shower. Toilet paper, toothpaste in a cup. No soap. She has brought her own. On a whim she opens the top drawer of the vanity desk. Jeesaz! They're everywhere! A Gideon Bible. She opens it; John 2:5. 'But whoso keepeth His Word, in him verily is the love of God perfected . . .' She puts the Word in her case — what choice does she have?

Suddenly she is tired. Or suddenly she remembers José Luis' stern stricture: 'Now you will go to your room and rest.' Whichever of them occurred first gives rise to the other.

When she awakes it is ten past five and almost dark. There is a small gap in the curtains where they have fallen open as she slept. She's been lying on top of her bed in her underwear. Damn. It's her serviceable stuff, for travelling. If you must be spied upon, be seen in your best.

By the time she has washed and changed into white slacks and top, it is completely dark outside. She heads through the muted light of the lamps to the bar, and feels a rush of air above her head. Something has passed over her. From the corner of her eye she sees it. A pterodactyl! It circles the compound and returns, profoundly silent. The scare-crow! Gyroscopes of mad connections fill her mind — it comes here with the corn; they send the corn to Nicaragua and the scare-crow follows . . . It's actually a bat about the size of a Lear jet. She stifles her scream and hurries on, looking downwards so as not to acknowledge the hideous thing's continued existence.

In the Bar

'Good lord, what are the little Niccas going to do with you?'

It was one of those round, brown, five-star British voices that you did in Oscar Wilde plays at college. It made Morgan start. She hadn't been expecting more English; she'd been watching a red-haired man with pale, freckled skin speaking what she'd come to believe was the only English in the bar. She turned, guardedly.

He was English — (the English and the French are the only ones you can tell by expression) — distinguishedly so. Carefully creased brown skin, long features, silver-brown hair that you could see through to a tanned, impressively massive dome. Clear grey eyes, and excellent, if well used, teeth. When he spoke, you saw his bottom teeth rather than his top ones, and she struggled with memories of anti-English stereotype. Did this prove he had a stiff upper lip or that he didn't?

'You're what we call "severely beautiful" my dear,' he said. 'Slavonic?'

'Sinagua,' she clipped, not quite appreciating the mistake and hoping to embarrass him with minimalisim.

'Ah, Southwest?'

Jeezas! He was good! She nodded.

So did he, but his expression lingered as if he didn't want to believe her.

'I'm sorry for not being Slavonic, but there's not a hell of a lot I can do about it.'

'Good lord, sorry. Is that what I sounded like? I'm sorry. I've been down there; the Black Sand Indians, is that it?'

'Very good, yes.'

'Never worked out what happened to them, did they? Just up and off'd. Hospitable environment, successful civilisation, then they just left. Why? Drought, disease, war? Usual old answers. I've got one of my own if you'd care to hear it?'

There has never been a satisfactory antidote to that question.

'Drink?' She had not yet ordered. 'May I recommend the Bloody Marys here. They are *à la mode*. Try one?' She shrugged. 'Bloody is thicker than water, and anything that's keeping you off water here is preserving your health. We have a badge: "I farted in Nicaragua". A bit basic I suppose; point is, there's only a couple of us left who can still wear it. It's the beans and the water. Two Bloody Marys please, no ice. Colin Fox, by the way, how do you do?'

'Fine, Morgan Moran.'

'Arrived today, did you? Weren't here when I left this morning; I would certainly have noticed.'

'Yes. So what happened to my tribe?' She wrenched the conversation away from herself.

'Beavers,' he said grandly. 'That's what it was. Consider the world from the beaverine point of view. What's the greatest accomplishment possible? Well, to fulfil your god-given potential to the utmost, surely, and create the greatest dam in the world. Proof of a great dam? It blocks the whole river — completely. Now, on the edge of the Sonora we have Beaver Creek. Right?'

She nodded. There was indeed a Beaver Creek there. The only river seen by the Great Magician and his tribe before they migrated to Phoenix. She had worshipfully gazed into it with her mother on that initial pilgrimage to their roots.

'Now,' Colin Fox is saying, 'the residents of Beaver Creek, the Frank Lloyd Wrights of the beaver world, want to pull off 'the big one'. Dam the entire river. They set to, and in the year 1400 they do it. Absolutely dry. Only for a short time of course — dam soon bursts and we get back the river we've got today. But for that time, the acme of beaverine accomplishment: a completely dry river. And at that very time — fire! Am I wrong or am I not that there are traces of a fire in the cliff village?'

She nodded again, almost miserable with admiration. The dollar guidebook bought by her mother; the fire in the cliff she hadn't believed. The proof, triumphantly pointed out by her mother over a cup of tepid coffee: 'with traces of a fire that had created carbon, which was carbon-dated to 1400!'

'So, fire breaks out. Fire, fire, get the brigade! No such thing in those days. Get water! Gone. The bloody beavers have dammed the river! Can't put out the fire. Destroyed, the whole settlement, several deaths. They felt it was an omen; they moved out. They hadn't been able to put out the fire because the gods deprived them of water. They were without water.'

'The Sin-agua!' she exclaimed, overwhelmed by the cleverness. He smiled. It was wide, controlled and crooked. 'I've never heard that explanation before,' she said, 'it's wonderful.'

Damn it! What is this, a 'lick the Limey dicky' session?! So when he asked, 'Will you join me and my little group of desperados?' she replied, 'No thank you' rather sharply. He departed with a good grace that made her feel contemptible.

The Bloody Mary was wonderful. Damn it again!! She cast a quick glance towards the desperados while Colin Fox was still returning to them, back towards her. A beautiful dark-haired woman, poutingly silent. A macho gorilla, brown and muscled, in blue canvas tank top: shiny blond hair. The third was an extraordinarily ugly Caucasian with curly blonde hair, black glasses and a red nose. Colin Fox arrived; she looked away.

The pale, dappled red-haired man across the bar was probably English too. Skin like bran, freckles like raisins. Beige skin, flecks of brown — like granola. She lurched into a giggle and swallowed it before it emerged. He was the precise colour of granola! Only the very best of granola, of course; she'd hate to be insulting. Not just your common-or-garden-no-frills-standard granola. Oh no; rare, sensitive Swiss muesli. Yes! Mr Muesli! Ahahaha! He'd been there when she'd arrived, leaning across the table to be emphatic to a natty little Nicca in a grey suit — the twin of José Luis in fact, if a little older. Presumably she would grow out of this 'They all look the same to me' phase with more experience, but at the moment there seemed only two types of local male: the slight, dark, liquidly black-eyed, lightly moustachio'd, smooth-skinned Nicaraguan in white shirt and black trousers; or the slight, dark, etc., in light grey suit. And all shorter than her — what should she do as she looked down to greet them? Politely say (as you evidently do to the Bantus, pygmies and other vertically challenged tribes of Africa), 'I saw you from afar'?

Mr Muesli was about thirty seven, overweight, with a red goatee. He had no attractive features but had attracted her attention because he was watching her. No, he wouldn't have attracted her attention simply by watching — many did that. It was because he was communicating with her; his conversation with his companion was, on one level, an act for her. When she had come into the bar she had glanced around, looking for familiarity, listening for identifiable voice patterns. He was the only English speaker in the bar at the time, and he'd known exactly what she was thinking. He began peppering his conversation with English phrases, meant for her. Well, if not for her, certainly not meant for his companion, because he'd look smilingly at him and say, 'You fatuous little peewit', or 'You bovine inebriate', in exactly the same tone as his conversation in Spanish. And the little guy would smile and nod, obviously not understanding a word.

Well, Mr Muesli had lost his power over her now; with the arrival of Colin Fox, he was no longer of any interest at all. She sat trying to pick up the desperado conversation behind her, across a gurgle of Latin. She sometimes heard the woman's voice as a whine above the gurgle, and sometimes the Colin Fox laughter. But no words. She was trapped by her own decision, and desperately lonely.

'The death of the Inquisition,' Mr Muesli said. The words had been the only ones going on in the bar at the time; there'd been one of those sudden inexplicable silences in everyone's conversation and his words were heard clearly by everyone. It reminded her of the story of a pause in a performance of the Warsaw Concerto into which came the words 'We usually fry ours in oil'. Several people had glanced at Mr Muesli, who was temporarily discomfited by his sudden fame, then descended back into Spanish.

Some moments later, Colin Fox came into her view in the corner of her right eye, approaching the red-haired man. 'I heard you mention the Inquisition,' he said bending over him, 'death of the Inquisition; I couldn't help but be intrigued.'

'Well, good,' said Mr Muesli. 'It's the title of a book I'm writing.'

'Ah, so you'll be pleased to know it intrigues people. Spanish Inquisition, is it?'

'Yes, although it's a bit of a metaphor really; I hope it has a broader meaning by the time you've finished it. The reader, that is.'

'Mind if I sit down a moment?' said Colin Fox.

'No, not at all. I'm Roger Morrison; this is Mr Fonbote, publisher.'

'How d'y do?' Mr Fonbote was acknowledged and dismissed. 'So what's the nub of the book? Novel, is it?' The conversation had quickly become an interview. The little grey-suited Mr Fonbote was clicking his fingers and waving at the waiter, who was squatly Mesquito Indian and didn't give a shit for the imperious manners of the middle classes. In the end Mr Fonbote got up and went to the bar. Meanwhile Mr Muesli, now disappointingly named Roger Morrison, was explaining, in a rather fine, light voice, 'the nub'.

'The thing is that by the end of the seventeenth century the Inquisition had got so good at its job that everyone was too frightened to do anything worth burning them for. No one was sinning; the Inquisition was so efficient it had put itself out of a job . . .'

'Ahahahaha!' Colin Fox roared with genuine laughter. 'Brilliant, I love it! That says so much, doesn't it?'

'I hope so,' said Roger Morrison, rather endearingly humbled by the praise.

'Well, all the best with it, I'll look out for it. That accent. Australian, is it?'

'New Zealand.'

'Ah, of course. I've got an aunt in New Zealand: Granity. Know it?'

'No.'

'No reason why you should. Absolutely no reason to go there. Little place, just north of Westport.'

'I'm from Palmerston North myself.'

'Ah, Massey College! I had a cousin there.'

'It's a university now.'

'Is it, by Jove? They carry the Governor-General around in a wheelbarrow when he visits, you know. Well, I see one of my number's leaving, I'd better be off.' He stood; six foot two or three. 'The South Island you know, bought by an Australian chappie in 1839, W. C. Wentworth; makes the Treaty of Waitangi completely invalid. Bear it in mind. Well, see you round. We'll have a drink.'

He strode away as Mr Fonbote arrived with three glasses of wine. As Morgan knew he would, he detoured to her side. 'Bianca's got to go now, but she'd love to have a drink with you tomorrow, if you're here?'

'I'm staying here for a couple of weeks.'

'We're usually back by five thirty. Six?'

'That would be fine. Bianca who?'

'Ahahaha, very good. Bianca who? I'll tell her you were asking. Goodbye till then. I look forward to it.'

As he departed, he was singing, 'If you take the three ten to Yuma, though you've got no reason to go there . . .'

Yuma. Fifty miles from Hotwa Vo. With no reason to go there. Like Granity.

DECOMPOSURE

A THIRTY-SECOND movement of the pyrosphere.

Morgan had seen the same effect in forests after a cyclone. It was the inner trees that fell; the outer ones seemed somehow to ride the gale. Same here: the middle of the city bore the brunt — sixty-six thousand houses clear-felled by the earthquake. Talk about inner-city decay! Here and there clumps of extant masonry — tobacconists, cobblers, bodegas, barbershops, quite substantial three-storey houses — and in between — nothing; urbane lacunae. Overall, a scene like the smile of the Russian Court when Peter the Great had finished experimenting with dentistry.

Managua is the earthquake capital of the world: it was shaken to bits in 1844, 1885, 1931, '68 and most recently, '72. Always in summer. The '72 earthquake was predicted to the hour and the day by Carlos Santos Berroterán, based on an analysis of the penetration of water, by capillary action, into Hell, where it evaporates, causing an intolerable build-up of pressure. The devastated city centre was barbed-wired off until bought back, from Somoza, by its owners. Which they could never afford to do. All this and more from the barely moving lips of the lugubrious José Luis.

Verticality is not a prominent feature of downtown Managua. The Intercontinental stayed up — proof once more of the power of the pyramid. So did the museum, which covers the ten-thousand-year-old footprints of Managuans fleeing the eruption of the day; and the Palacio Nacional — and the cathedral — brokenly inspirational beside the milky lake, raped, roofless; the Sistine Chapel on the day someone works out how to steal the ceiling.

Managua; as empty as Patagonia, as bustling as Chicago. Behind Morgan the baying traffic of la Pista Pedro Joaquín Chamorro; to her left the clamour of the Mercado Oriental, draped across the wilderness of a pre-'72 residential borough. Incredibly, through the stench of diesel and drains came the smells of cooking oil, rich damp earth and, most incongruous of all, the muddy crab-scent of the lake.

And in front of her stood the rusting carapace of AGRISYNC HYBRID LTD, MANAGUA. Beneath the mouldering sign someone had affixed a poster of a rather ludicrous figure in cowboy hat and high boots. 'Despues de 50 anos, Sandino,' it said. Still Sandino after fifty years. A myth of course — he'd never made it to power and he was long dead — but telling enough in its symbolism. He was no deader than Agrisync, but their effects lived on. Two departed forces, still influencing the daily life of Nicaragua from 'another place far away'.

José Luis stood apart from her. In fact he leaned moodily on the van, watching and trying not to. 'Is open, if you like,' he had said, pointing to a grey tin door. Beside it was a jagged hole through which someone had obviously driven a truck; from the inside, because the rusting tin lay outwards amidst the vigorous yellow weeds. Weeds. A paradise of them. They sprouted through the warm asphalt of the compound, amidst the blocks and buckets of scattered red machinery, up towards the iron rafters of the denuded outbuildings. Weeds. Growth. And amidst it, decay. All around her was wreckage and rot — the rust had a vegetal quality, and Morgan realised for the first time that steel is biodegradable! Growth and decay combined somehow, with a ghastly hybrid vigour, to create dynamic badness. The elements of decadence flourished here, in the ex-heart of Agrisync, sown by Bobby's order to pluck up the precious breeding lines of corn and bear them away to Peoria. So her mother could buy shares at three dollars seventeen.

She'd not asked to be brought here, good God; why would she? It was a punitive detour. She was to be shown the result of her company's crimes. Like the naughty little puppy, she will have her nose rubbed in her own caca.

The rest of her day was spent braced in the van, backside defying gravity a turbulent several inches above the kapok seat, gazing out at the works of Somoza, Nature and Reagan. 'Managua is — how you say? — maggot; curls around corpse, no?' Very picturesque. What walls remained, were covered with graffiti'd FSLNs and FDNs. She mumbled the indistinguishable acronyms to herself, willing herself to remember the difference. FDN was generally prefixed by 'Muerte a la', which she now knew meant 'Death to the'.

They toured the museums, all of which were closed, and went to the baseball stadium in Avenida Williams Romero, where nobody was playing. But much was pleasant: lunch at Los Antojitos, opposite the Intercontinental, and shopping in the massive Mercado Roberto Huembes to the accompaniment of the irresistibly lunatic pulse of the native costeña music.

MORGAN WAS HOME as evening fell at four thirty. She has not been taken yet to Coca-Cola; that exhilaration, she learns, is to be postponed until the return from Panama of Compañero Salas-Ostrada, the manager. But tomorrow she is to meet the great Compañero Tomás Borge himself! 'The father of our Revolution,' declaimed José Luis, 'and our great poet. Compañero Borge has taken revenge upon his torturer by forgiving him.' Leaving these words to ring in her ears, José Luis drives away. She enters the foyer, braced for the momentary frigidity and makes for her room. At five thirty she returns to the souvenir and newspaper stand.

The postcards are delightful; fantastical primitivist scenes in glorious primary colours. The papers: *Barricada* and *El Nuevo Diario*. Nothing much has happened today. Cardinal Obando is still brave, says the *Barricada* headline — or is that 'The cardinal is abandoned and brave'? She asks at the desk and is told Cardinal Obando y Bravos is the head of Nicaragua's Catholic Church — and not getting on all that well with the government.

Ah. She returns to the newsstand. *Cocodrillo*. On the cover of the satirical magazine is a viciously crude portrait of Uncle Sam, top hat and all, as a salivating wolf.

'Cocodrillo — means crocodile. Lovely really, isn't it? We have crocodiles, they have cocodriles.' It was Colin Fox; alone, safari-suited and sweaty. He had a moustache of red dust where he'd wiped his nose with his hand. 'Mount Santiago. Nearly damn-well fell in. Stupid bitch was supposed to do a piece to camera up there, and I ended up doing it myself; swinging off a metal signpost over the top of the damned crater if you please! Going to join us are you?' He nodded out through the misty doors to the 'us'. There were the 'desperados' — minus Bianca — packing bits of filming machinery into big metal boxes.

'Yes, I'd love to,' she said.

'Well look, I'll get you settled in the bar and dash off for a shower.'

She ordered a Nica-libre — rum and Coke. As she waited, the muscle-bound cameraman marched past the bar to his room, carrying a huge aluminum case in one hand when it would have been far more easily managed in two. She finished her drink quickly and hurried back to her room. In order to spruce up of course. Rubbish! In order to make an entrance! Let's face it, she hadn't been hanging round the newsstand for nothing. And the journey back to her room was a significant sacrifice too — after all, she had to brave the maraudings of that Messerschmitt scare-crow bat again!

COLIN FOX LAUGHED with delight when he saw her, as was intended. She was wearing the crimson dress and a low white peasant blouse she'd bought at the market. And the wide elastic belt with golden buckle as well; size twelve and she was fourteen. Breathing was not easy at first, but she must have hauled her waist in to at least twenty-five inches.

He led her round tables, across the tile floor, to the camera crew. The animality of the Mexican one was so strong it was like entering a den. 'Morgan Moran, meet Eduardo Delgardo, cameraman, and Dittmer Wohl, sound operator,' said Colin Fox. 'I'm my own production secretary so we haven't got one of those, and our star has packed a shitty and will not be joining us tonight.' His tone was inelegantly raw for a moment, and then he remembered himself. 'Oh, I hope you don't feel you're here under false pretences? I did promise you Bianca, after all.'

'No, that's fine. I'll have another of those Bloody Marys, if I may; they're superb.'

'I'll get it,' said Eduardo suddenly, rollicking to his feet. 'Lager, Ditt?'

'Ja.'

He departed for the bar, walking in that delta shape of muscular men pretending they can't get their arms to lie flat along their sides. 'Dittmer here's from Amsterdam,' said Colin Fox, stretching dangerously into a puny canvas chair. 'He's God's answer to promiscuity. Build a city where you can do anything you like, then fill it with ugly buggers like Dittmer that nobody wants to do anything with.'

Dittmer smiled warmly. He had braces on his teeth.

'He's also the best soundman in the world. Don't ask me why: he can't understand a thing I say, can you, Dittmer?'

Dittmer's face stayed crinkled in its open, ugly smile. 'Colin does not know the only time he does not talk shit is into a microphone; then I listen,' he said.

They were an independent film crew. Colin was a maker of documentaries 'of genius'. They were making a documentary on the effects of the Law of the Sea.

'There are a lot of countries who are worried about the moral precedents of this thing,' said Colin. 'How can you be saying "I want a two-hundred-mile limit" and "Give me back the Elgin marbles" at the same time?'

He boomed on, gloriously intelligent, deliciously articulate; ostensibly far above the heads of his crew, who looked glazedly on. She worried a little about rebellion. When Colin Fox had gone to the bar, she asked, 'What do you think of the job?'

There was silence. Dittmer glanced at Eduardo; even off duty, it seemed, he waited for others to speak. Eduardo sat with crossed arms that looked like grapefruit on string. 'It is the best documentary I've ever worked on,' he said. 'It's great to work with someone so intelligent.'

So much for appearances.

'What do you think of the aeroplanes?' asked Dittmer. When she frowned, he went on, 'Which fly overhead each morning?'

'I haven't heard them, sorry. Must have slept through them.'

'You won't,' smiled Dittmer. His braces gleamed. 'Eh, Edward?'

Eduardo the Macho nodded, sincerely, unaffectedly. She suddenly realised she'd been wrong about him; he was entirely without ego. 'They are the Nicaraguan bombers,' he said. 'They warm up their engines and gain altitude each morning before going off to the Honduran border. Exactly over the top of the Camino Real. Just to let us know. You can imagine the temptation, thumbs on the release button, wanting to let just one little bomb drop on those damned Yankees down there. "Whoops, sorry about that. Mucha mia culpa." Boom!'

And he gleamed, savagely triumphant on their behalf.

'Every morning?' she said faintly.

'About half,' replied Dittmer, a little enigmatically.

'Great,' she said. 'Just peachy. Bombers in the morning, bats at night.'

Colin Fox had returned, laden. 'Ah, you've seen our bat, have you? Fruit bat, wouldn't hurt a fly; well, except a fruit fly. Marvellous, isn't he?'

'I'm not so sure,' she murmured. 'Does he have to be quite so big?'

He was spreading out drinks across the glass table from a little tray. Also olives and whole cashew nuts, which are a sort of kiwifruit from the top of which curls an albino turd — the cashew. 'Oh it's not the big bats that are the worry; the nastiest ones are tiny. Vampires. Sneak up on you in the night.' He saw her expression of utter repulsion and laughed. 'Don't worry, there's only one species of vampire bat in the whole wide world.' His pause was superb. 'Mind you, the part of the wide world it lives in is this one. Cheers!'

They drank, inadvertently in unison. When they put down their glasses, it was natural to turn to the ineffable Colin Fox, of the hypnotic fingers and long, magnificent head. 'Mosquitoes. Now they're the real vampires,' he said. He leaned back, and the others leaned forward as if strings extended from his head to theirs. He put his hands behind head. 'Killed over half the people who have ever lived on earth. Effective little critters.' And his eyes gleamed with the effect. 'It's only the female that's poisonous, you know; poor old male just skulks round looking for dew and nectar. Incredible thing, malaria. It's a little parasite that used to feed on the mosquito herself, until she learned how to spit it out into other creatures. Saddest thing is, it's usually a bird. I'd say ninety percent of the birds of Nicaragua have got malaria.'

She thought of the patient little kingfisher above the swimming pool.

It was he, the urbane English Colin Fox, who was the macho here; pridefully flexing the muscles of his tongue, soliciting sighs and heart flutters for the manliness of his delivery; attempting with his elegant command to inspire shrieks, blushes, swoons and fits of vapours in the fairer sex. Alternatively, young Edward the Adonis, with his fine brown features and improbable musculature, took everything at face value, listened hard and respectfully and spoke with not a skerrick of ulterior motive. He was that saddest and most enigmatic of Adonises — 'a real nice guy'. With a puzzled sigh at the complexity of human nature, and perhaps ever so slightly miffed, Morgan returned her attention whence it had always been fated to go.

Colin Fox wooed and strutted, manifested sexual displacement behaviour and preened — successfully — and when, much later, he St Georged her across the bat-patrolled compound, he talked to her about the stars. He actually talked about the stars!

'They're bright blue now, look at them. Big as plums, by God; like diamonds.' She could see his hand, black against the sky, like one of those inexplicably unlit patches of Cosmos. 'But they'll burn through that phase you know — in a few billion years. Then the sky will shine with just dull reds.' He had looked down, she could tell by the timbre of his voice. She looked down too; you're vulnerable looking up. 'And then there'll be civilisations much wiser than ours who will envy us: "There were people," they'll say, "primitive but blessed; blessed because in their time the sky blazed with brilliant stars."'

By God he put on a good show!

He bent slightly forward. Post-stellar activity was about to begin. He put his hand upon her waist, then moved it slightly upwards, above the impersonal thickness of her belt. She could feel his thumb, one inch beneath her left breast, and the firm bulges of the flesh between the joints of his fingers against her ribs. He kissed her cheek. 'You are matchlessly beautiful,' he whispered in sublime British. 'And consequently I wouldn't presume,' and the intimate heat of his breath and the musky smell of aguardiente sent little sexual Paul Reveres galloping down the nerve endings of her midriff, to that rich and plentiful HQ between her legs, 'but my God I wish I could.' And suddenly he let her go.

Let her go! He stared down at her meaningfully, unaware of the internal chaos he was causing. About midway through his studiedly momentous stare, the Paul Reveres turned to Benedict Arnolds, who screamed 'Asshole! Asshole!' as the gates of HQ closed, snuffling the fiery heat within.

'May we meet tomorrow night?' he entreated with urgent grandeur.

She stares. 'Yes.' It is wrenched from her by logic. Of course we can meet tomorrow goddam night! We can meet tomorrow afternoon, tomorrow morning, but damn it, we can meet now!

They were as still as lovers. In *Casablanca* the theme song would be playing now, to drown out the noise of the mist machine. Is this what those meaningful stares are all about in movies? Him thinking, This girl is gonna let me, one day. Her thinking, What's with this bozo that he puts everything into the future?

He gave a nod and a sort of serious smirk that was presumably Clark Gable, turned like Fred Astaire and walked off like John Wayne.

Morgan watched him till the perplexed trance ran out, then swished the last remaining yards to her room, unmindful of Freddy the Fucking Fruitbat frolicking under the dimming stars; black with disappointed rage. Jeezas! What is it with these English? Does 'romantic' mean 'unpelvic' over there? Does all their stiffness go into the upper lip? She wrenched off her dust-smelling new clothes and marched to the mirror. Glaring back at her was a mask of confused resentment. A frown puckered the skin between the dark brows like twin Montes Veneri, the wide lips turned sharply downwards. Jeezas, she looked like Marlon Brando!

She adjusted her features. She tossed her black braid back from her neck and gave herself a coy grimace. Hell, is that what you look like when you feel like this? She experimented with expressions, appalled at the disparity between the intention and the effect. For all she knew, she may have been looking up at that pompous crotch-teaser with a look of twenty-four carat adoration!

She examined the body that confronted her. It immediately drew one foot slightly behind the other. Christ, she posed even for herself!

What do they see? A waist like a hatbox. Twenty-six! How come her kidneys wanted all that room? With such big kidneys, maybe she's good at something no one else can do? What do kidneys do? They filter blood or something. Maybe she's got the best filtered blood in the world? Well, she'd better have, to make up for a deformed waist like that! But her breasts; ah yes! Now they were something! To be quite honest, she liked looking at women's breasts. Well, to be even more honest, it was probably because she came out pretty damn well by comparison. She had pulled the satiny boardroom bra down under her breasts, which shoved them up into slightly straining globes. Her nipples were not large; petite — ahahaha — petits! But the areolas were; smooth, wide and round. As if her nipples had once been little chocobars that had melted perfectly downwards.

Her legs; now they were legs! They glistened, they rippled; but they yielded deliciously to the touch. So how come she was turned on by legs like hairy hawsers? If a guy presented himself with legs like this, she'd throw up. Funny thing, gender. And smooth, and long . . . Had she brought a razor?! Yes. What about the water?! It'll be okay; if you can shave legs in Phoenix, you can shave them anywhere. Water there is so hard you can't get a lather; can't even turn the water soapy.

She is running her hand down the curve of her flank; now that is smooth! She stops suddenly, leaning in to examine her face. Is it smooth? Hickies? No. Hairs? No. She has a small, hard, shiny patch on her left cheek that exudes a perfidious hair if not watched closely. She returns her attention to her hip, turning side-on to the mirror. Now there's ass, the ultimate; same degree of curve as it leaves the waist as when it joins to the back of the thigh. A perfect mound, no overhang, no flab. She turns completely away from the mirror and swivels her head, owl-like to peruse her backside. The perfect upside-down heart. You see some asses — you even see some in lingerie ads in the glossies — and they are pleasant, but they're bi-sexual somehow; they could be either. Not this mother; one hundred percent total woman. She runs her hand under the rim of her panties and pulls them down. There is a tingling tug of resistance — Nicaraguan heat — then they slip to the cool tile floor. She turns full-on to the mirror. Now, what do they see? Nothing that really interests her. Adolf Hitler. Ahahaha! Jeezas; she runs her eye over her entirety. There's nothing very demonstrative, is there? With a guy at this stage of proceedings you're looking down at a Mr Happy competing in a caber toss — well, you'd better be or he's in trouble! — but a woman? Okay, so your nipples harden, but they do that anyway. Does a guy go maypole whenever it gets cold? Maybe he does; maybe that's why they call it a blue steeler. But all you've got here in front is nonspecific perfection. This body is going to be unchangingly beautiful no matter who it's with. A woman's body tells no tales.

She shivers, probably from air conditioning. She switches out the bathroom light and pads across to her bed. She puts the bed lamp on and checks for scorpions between the sheets. Nobody home. She gets into bed. She lies on her back. She wills the sense out of the tips of her fingers; neutralises them, disembodies them. They are now the hands of the man who's been watching her in the mirror all the time. Never mind what he sees, what does he feel? Damn! Where the hell do you get a dildo in Nicaragua? She'd been afraid to bring one in case they searched her bag at Customs.

Matagalpa

On the day it became evident the Axis wouldn't win, Anastasio Somoza turned his pictures of Hitler and Himmler to the wall and set about confiscating the property of every German in Nicaragua. His most lucrative single haul was the Matagalpa home of Herr William Hooper, the mansion across the road from the Banco Florian — owned by Herr Hooper, and just down the road from the Gran Hotel, also Hooper-owned. Somoza had electricity brought to the town — on the backs of Sebaco Indians, who humped wire spools the hundred and twenty-nine kilometres from Managua — to illuminate the house and its two swimming pools. The orangery was skilfully transformed into twin cells, one of which housed jaguars.

In 1979 the house was taken over, sans jaguars, by the victorious new Sandinista government, who maintained it at its Somozan level of leering opulence as a governmental hideaway — a little like Camp David or Checkers. Important guests were taken there to be elegantly entertained, far from the yellow, malnourished gaze of the public.

Morgan was taken there, escorted by dark, earnest Diana Cienfuegos, Undersecretary to the Minister of Agriculture. It was she who told Morgan the story of the house, and of many other things as they were bounced down the battered Interamerican Highway by José Luis.

Matagalpa sits like sediment at the bottom of a bowl of jungly hills, from whither, attested Diana, parrots scream obscenities at passers-by. It seems a market parrot once escaped to the Selva Negra, taking with it an extensive vocabulary of commercial oaths, which it then passed on to its psittacine peers.

Alongside the mini-bus, for the last several miles of the journey, burbled the Matagalpa River, the only one in all the world that flows uphill. It does this in winter when it swells with rain and charges out of the Sebaco Valley into the uplands of La Picota.

And round and about on the pleasantly cool highlands, on the hillsides and the valley floors of Matagalpa district, grows Agrisync Hybrid corn.

'From your corn, Señorita Moran, we make our tortillas, ajiaco, rosquilla, Maria stew, slumgullion, repocheta, resquizados, quequerote, tamales, churros, marzipan, atole, refrescos . . .' said Compañero Tomás Borge, 'and wine.' Absurdly, he stood and raised his porrón of grey, slightly viscous liquid in a toast. 'To Agrisync,' he said.

Borge had the face of a lynx — a handsome, open lynx. Wide lips, fine nose, long brown eyes that brooded behind rimless 'gaffas'. And the uniform of course, open at the neck but fulsomely epauletted. His Foreign Legion-style cap was on a peg at the door.

'To Agrisync,' said Diana, standing also, across the table from him. She had narrow shoulders but wide hips. Her white slacks were too tight at the thighs. Her face was handsome but sallow; her eyes were deep in mauvish hollows.

They drank the slimy cereal wine. Outside, crickets dinned, monkeys screamed. Cockroaches the size of small flounders scuttled across the shadowed floor in the distance.

'Glory is but a match struck / behind the lines, and life's as beautiful / as your mother's nipple; as a plot of corn,' said Tomás Borge. 'A poem of my own.'

'It sounds very interesting. What's it called?'

'Che.'

'You knew him?'

'Yes. You knew him?'

'Yes, his poster was on my wall at college.'

'He would have been honoured to have such a beautiful admirer.'

The exchange brought a sense of awesome reality to the situation — as real as bricks on a road or a white-lettered shoe sign on a hill. Che Guevara was no longer simply a pin-up, Tomás Borge no longer a pinko poet; they were real; in her immediate, touchable, indivertible world. So real it was laughable. She was God and she'd just given the gift of reality to two more ideas.

'And how are the Cubs?' he is saying.

'Cubs?' she echoes stupidly. 'Chicago Cubs?'

There must have been an almost offensive incredulity in her voice, but he smiled it away. 'Oh yes, we are great baseball fans here. And very expert players too. One day we will play you for the pennant.'

'I look forward to it,' she murmured.

He smiled again, watchfully but not unpleasantly. 'And do you think we could win?'

'I don't know.'

'Perhaps we would surprise you.'

It seemed extremely dangerous to make reply. She said nothing. He sat back. 'Perhaps we have already surprised you — what do you think of your corn?'

She pointed at the meatballesque things on her plate. 'These are corn?'

He nodded. 'I think it would translate as "mock tongue". It is made best from your own product — in fact, Diana, if I am not wrong we have several dishes that can only be made from Agrisync Hybrid?'

'Yes, compañero Tomás; our own corn is too dry for terceros or salsa dulce' — to Morgan — 'a sort of creamy dessert.' She put about seven 's's into dessert with the liquid lisp so common in Spanish. Tomás Borge had no such lisp. His pronunciation was as impeccable as Colin Fox's.

'It is a beautiful corn; so huge, succulent, dynamic. It makes our own varieties seem no more than dry grass. But . . .' and he gave an elegant version of the 'hombre, no se' shrug ; 'there is nostalgia for one's own types — chortales, Purple Husk, Blood of Christ, sheet corn, Forty Day . . . many many names that are no longer used because what they describe has gone. From my youth there are perhaps fifty names I can use only to evoke a memory; there is nothing left to use them on. Gone. Nowadays just one name, Agrisync Hybrid.' And without standing, he raised his porrón again in a mock salute, tilted back his head and drank.

Drinking from a porrón requires the hand/eye co-ordination of an ophthalmologist. Morgan had chickened out and opted for a plain brown wooden pottle — called a jigara, which means skull, 'because it is hollow, empty and wooden! Ahahaha!'

'Oh, there are still old varieties of corn in certain places,' he is saying now, 'and sometimes new ones emerge, don't they, Diana?' And he thrust her a glance that Morgan was to understand a few days later. 'We send them to CYMMT, do we not?'

'Yes. It is the genebank in Mexico,' she explains. 'It has perhaps one hundred of our varieties.'

'Safe and sound, no? Safe as Fort Knox. No one can break into CYMMT.' Tomás Borge was looking steadily now at Morgan, with not the faintest hint of a sneer where a sneer was entitled to be. 'We hope Agrisync will avail itself of any of our varieties at any time, Señorita Moran, for we know how dangerously narrow is the gene base of corn.'

Made so, he is saying silently, by Agrisync Hybrid Inc. And he has also decorously reminded her that on Mr Reagan's orders Nicaragua could deposit but not withdraw from that genebank of the world's seeds.

To hell with Reagan! The night was liquidly warm, the wine was . . . working. What charm — seated at a baronial table in a wide white palace banquet hall with stark furniture and great shelves of dazzling blue and white crockery. Across the patio the milkily glowing pool lay amidst palms and bougainvillaea, and beyond it, a lawn on which monkeys played, well past their bedtime.

They drank chica, they ate cakes and pastries — all made of corn. Then, as they drank brandy and smoked cigars, the mica-like reality of the night crystallised; a pig walked in.

Morgan howled with joyous incredulity; Tomás Borge, father of the Revolution, bawled angry orders that the pig disobeyed. Orderlies emerged from behind black doors and shooed it on its way. Off it went, honking indignantly and trotting across the patio into the darkness, its great ears slapping at its eyes like admonishing hands. Hyper-reality in Wonderland. They settled down in a new intimacy of shared absurdity.

'You do not speak Spanish, Morgan?'

'A little — un pequito — enough to help me survive LA Airport.'

'Ah, LAX! Surely nobody knows enough Spanish to survive LA Airport! — And your native language?'

'Oh. No, it's dead; I think. My mother pretends to speak it, but her vocabulary's mostly from the *Song of Hiawatha*.'

'Ah, I have heard of this,' said Diana.

'You have not read it?' exclaims Tomás. 'I will get it for you.' Was she his mistress? They seemed very comfortable — well, he did; she seemed constrained to speak only when spoken to. But her bare big toe was hooked to the arm of his chair.

'Are you married, Diana?' Morgan asked wickedly.

'No. I am . . . "enfianced" you say?'

'I wish we did, it's a beautiful word. Congratulations. Will you marry soon?'

'Perhaps in one year. He is an agricultural technician who works on a collective near Jalapa.'

'It is very close to the Honduran border,' said Tomás, slumped unheroically in his chair. 'I would bring him back to Managua and put him safely behind a desk, but Diana will not hear of it. She wants him in the danger zone. Perhaps she thinks she is making a mistake.'

Diana was smiling thickly and shaking her head; she was obviously not programmed for playfulness from a prince of the Revolution.

'I'd want all the chicken scared out of my man too,' rejoined Morgan, and grappled, in the chortles, with the fact the enemy was her country.

'They are given, you know,' murmured Borge, peering into the tawny mysteries of his glass, 'a handful of cocaine for the ears of every agricultural technician they kill.'

She winced. There was appallingly little she could say.

'We will not speak more of this,' said Diana sternly. 'It is morbid.'

'Ah,' he said sitting upright, 'but we are morbid; it is the only trait we inherited from the Spanish. The Spanish are so morbid they believe that even birth is a sign of damnation. 'We are born between piss and shit,' they say, 'it is the mark of Cain.' But maybe I am ungenerous — maybe we gave morbidity to them. Yes, I think perhaps Nicaragua is the genetic centre of morbidity. Morbidity is all around us — just look; what is our most common bird? The zipilote, the vulture, brooding above us, waiting for us to die. Our crops are morbid, grudging. Corn, wonderful succulent corn — it will not sustain us! We think it is a total food and we live on it exclusively, and consequently we are dying of malnutrition. The goddess corn is killing us!' Then he stood up and replenished his glass and Morgan's.

'I will tell you a little story I think you may not know. When our ports were mined by the US Navy, it was ostensibly to stop us sending military hardware to El Salvador. This is the story that was told to the world.' He was comfortable, bitter, incriminatory — intimate. Morgan had passed into post-coital familiarity without the sex. 'The real reason was to stop countries like Sweden and Canada from bringing food into Nicaragua. We are to be starved to death. But we have a benefactor. We are supplied with food by a weekly secret convoy based in Guyamas in Mexico. Canned meat is brought across from Baja California by boat and then transported here in trucks. All paid for by an American company. Do you know which one?'

'No.'

'Guess.'

'Agrisync,' she said playfully.

'Yes.'

She stared.

'You see, a consequence of malnutrition is loss of appetite. The desire to eat dies, even if food is available. Malnourished people do not eat as much corn; profits dwindle. In order to maintain our hearty appetite for its corn, Agrisync runs the blockade with trucks of meat. Ironic, no?'

'Who's in charge?'

'Señor Latour.'

Of course. Who else? Harvey the Toot!

He smiled. 'I think it shows commendable commitment. We worried at first that taking the corn-lines out of Nicaragua was a signal you intended to abandon us. It seems this is not the case.

Why, after all, would even the most patriotic company bankrupt itself in order to defeat an enemy? And this would be the effect, would it not? Nicaragua is — what percentage of your market, Miss Moran?'

'Seventy,' she said.

'Seventy-four,' said Diana.

'The consequences are, of course, that we are stuck with each other. Oh I say this in an impersonal sense, Morgan, to be stuck with your own presence is by no means a hardship.' And he raised his glass to her, his face momentarily distorting into grotesqueness behind it. 'We are the greater part of your market, and you have poisoned our soil against any other crop; allies by checkmate. MAD it is called in Cold War terms, mutually assured destruction.' He paused, tapped the brandy balloon against his lip, then suddenly shook his head and walked to the door, looking out into the patio. There was what human beings egotistically call silence. Crickets blared, monkeys shrieked, something coughed. He turned away from the cacophony. 'I am sorry, Morgan, I am abusing my position. You are my guest. We will speak of other things. Have you yet seen a quetzal?'

'No.'

'You may see one quite near here in the Selva Negra. Bird of life, bird of death; the most beautiful bird in the world. It is strong magic to get a glimpse of one. Diana must take you tomorrow.'

'There is something you should know,' said Morgan, 'in case you think taking the corn-lines home was part of a Reagan plot. It wasn't. My mother is arguably the greediest and most unprincipled woman on earth. It was her idea; for personal gain only.'

'Yes,' he snapped, uncharacteristically, 'and the gain will be enormous. We have been notified that Agrisync intends to double its prices.' He sighed angrily, leaning on the back of his chair. 'I am sorry again, Morgan. This is none of your doing. I am haranguing you unmercifully; it is barbarous of me.'

'I will do what I can to ensure that doesn't happen,' she said quietly. Her head spun a little.

He nodded, but no expression crossed his face, which remained sternly neutral. 'There is a legend in Nicaragua — still held to be true in some parts — that corn carries a curse condemning all those who feed upon it to irredeemable decadence.' His voice was quiet, his clear spectacles flashed in the angle of the light.

There had been an invasion of those Draculanian insects that come out only in profoundest darkness. Mists of semi-invisible beasts swirled round the lights of the pool, and now a hideously metallic zinging thing was making crazed circumnavigations of the lights in the room. It was red and jagged; a winged boiled lobster. Suddenly she was underwater: shoals of reef fish, lobsters, cockroach-sized flounders . . . Brandy worked with wine and ambience to take her far away, to the surface, up somewhere near the timbered ceiling. From there she watched Diana stand in slow motion and walk barefoot across the shiny varnished floor. She took out a book from a closely packed shelf and, intercepting the zinging monster's rhomboid journey, smacked it full in the face. It cracked and died.

She put the book down on the coffee table. *Platero y Yo*, by Jiminez.

'I think,' she said, 'I would like to swim.' She walked to the pool and took off her clothes. She was surprisingly full-breasted. She dived into the water, her body turning to a dazzling gold in the blaze of subterranean lighting. Then she was gone. She didn't resurface. Morgan stared. A frog leapt out of the pool. A toad, black, yellow and green, the size of a bantam hen. Morgan stared. The brandy-powered carousel in her mind played 'Here we go round the mulberry bush . . .' The toad flopped towards her, leaving behind an obscene little wet patch with every hop. Then it leapt sideways, out of eyeshot, and was gone. She stared. 'Wasn't it a prince?' she mumbled, 'that that happened to?'

'Shall I read to you from Jiminez?' asked Borges. 'It is a most beautiful book.'

He leaned forward and picked up the bug-killing tome. He opened it and read. Diana swam up and down the pool behind him.

THEY DIDN'T SEE a quetzal in the jungle. No one ever did. Mermaids of the sea, unicorns of the land, quetzals of the sky. But they saw toucans; glorious, busy, evasive toucans, which laboured ungracefully across the sky like small crucifixes, black everywhere except where INRI would have been; and there they were blazing yellow. They are not great flyers. They set off in the mornings from the topmost trees of the jungle river valleys, hopping downwards from branch to branch, berry to berry. At about half past two, they turn round and climb and flutter up to the top again, reaching it at sunset. Then they flap clumsily home to their roosts until the morning.

Morgan had begun the day with what Diana described as soroche, acute mountain sickness, which one suffers from at the top of the Andes. They were, at this moment, on the side of a mild hill. All mention of hang-overs was decorously avoided. Tomás was nowhere to be seen. He had left earlier. He apologised through Diana — as she'd hoped he wouldn't — 'for taking advantage of the presence of an Agrisync member to vent his feelings'. They had a breakfast of churros — wrong choice! — oil, fat and batter, and bowls of white coffee. They set off for the jungle as the mists were streaking upwards as if sucked. A thought struck her, probably inspired by her condition. 'What's the thing that can do me the most damage in the jungle?'

Jaguars, alligators, ocelots, snakes, lizards, ghastly insects, apes, unknown marsupials, wild boars . . . Diana chose none of them. 'Fruit,' she said. She meant it. Evidently, ripe fruit from, say, the cannonball tree, a hundred feet up, comes thundering down at terminal velocity and can nail you into the jungle floor. Okay, she'll keep a weather eye out for mad fruit, but the warning diminished somehow the sexiness of the jungle.

INCREDIBLY, DESPITE THE marrow-pulping three-hour journey down a dry riverbed called the Interamerican Highway, she arrived back at the Camino Real that evening feeling fine.

Diana would go straight home, wouldn't stop for a drink. José Luis bore her away. He would return at nine next morning to take Morgan to the Volcán Masaya National Park. A day crawling round rancid scoria with a mute melancholic. Must we go? Yes we must; Coca-Cola and the Nicaraguan government are determined she will enjoy her trip or die in the attempt. Nine o'clock.

In the bar were Eduardo and Dittmer. There was no Colin Fox, and she noticed herself noticing the absence. Mr Muesli Morrison, the plumply pale Inquisitorial author, had never re-emerged either; no great loss. However, it was a matter of scenery. The first sight of a place becomes the template it is judged by evermore.

They hailed her; she joined them. Colin, it seems, was at the International placating Bianca. He had done a foolish thing. Bianca had deigned to join them for a swim at San Juan del Sur that afternoon — although a screen of towels had to be erected to keep the libidinous eyes of the few internationalistas present from her scrawnily elegant, black-costumed frame. Afterwards she had complained of earache. As any activity — or even non-activity itself — inevitably occasioned a Biancan complaint of some sort, this was not taken very seriously. Her malady threatened to consume the day, and in harassment Colin had stupidly told her she could be suffering from coral ear.

'What's that?' said Morgan.

'It isn't,' said Dittmer.

'He said it was a coral,' said Eduardo, 'a little microscopic fish that had swum into her ear and was settling down, probably to manufacture a coral reef out of her head.'

There was no such thing. Colin explained this immediately, but the damage was done; he was either lying now or lying then. Either way, his perfidy had given Bianca a headache. That of course had been the end of the day's shooting. She had had to be brought home to the International and placed in a darkened room, where three of the four Managuan doctors tended to her in concert. Colin was also at her bedside now, begging forgiveness in the hope that production could get under way again, at least the day after tomorrow. Tomorrow itself would be out of the question.

So what were they doing tomorrow? Nothing! Hey! Let's party! They know the best hotel in Nicaragua! The Alhambra in Granada, just an hour away. There's a great beach! There's a great market! There's a waterfront full of restaurants! And you can hire motorboats to the offshore islands, where there's even better restaurants! Eeyha! A day of fun, sun, rum!

Colin Fox arrives to exuberantly announce he's persuaded Bianca to begin at eight thirty the next morning . . .

MORGAN HAD TOLD Colin she wanted an early night, and exulted at his momentary despair. Revenge! You postpone me? Okay, I postpone you!

'Do you mean it?' he whispered urgently as Dittmer, their only remaining companion, slouched to the bar for replenishment.

'Yes.'

'Why?'

'What's the hurry?'

'Those stars, the ones that dull to red. They go out eventually you know.'

'Oh, I'll be ready before then.' She smiled and watched the complicated mixture of lust, hope and helplessness make battle on his face.

Phone Calls

EVERY DAY SHE had come in through the hotel doors, past the souvenir shop on her right (still with the brightest, merriest, most optimistic postcards you could ever find in a depressed, starving, war-torn Third World nation) and asked at the reception on her left, 'Any calls for me?' And always the answer had been, 'No, compañera Moran.' Until she noticed that there weren't any calls for anyone.

On a whim one day she retraced her steps from room 221. The receptionist was a pretty, flaxen-haired girl with broad face and ruddy cheeks. She was reasonably pregnant.

'There's no incoming calls at all, right?' said Morgan.

'No,' said the girl. Meaning, presumably, yes there were none, because she was nodding at the same time.

'So how do I put through an international call from the hotel?'

'You can't. You must go to Telecor in the city.'

'Just to put through a call? Doesn't a big hotel like this have an international line?'

'Sometimes. Not now.'

'What about the Intercontinental?'

'Sometimes.'

'Not now?'

'No.'

'Are you going to explain?'

'It is very simple. The Contras have cut the lines. You must go to Telecor.'

'So how come there's a line at Telecor? Are the Contras that specific?' It was supposed to be sourly sarcastic.

'Yes,' said the girl. Morgan stared. 'The Contras want only that the internationalistas cannot call out of the country, and internationalistas stay only here or at the Intercontinental. They cut only these lines.'

'So I could use any other phone?'

'Any other phone that can call international, yes.'

'Okay, where are they?'

'The Migration Office, the government, the Universidad, the Embassy of Cuba, or Colombia or Costa Rica . . .'

'Would any of them let me make a call?'

'No.'

'I have to go to Telecor to make the call, right?'

'Yes.'

TELECOR IS ON the west side of Revolution Square, blocking some of the best city views of the lake. Most of the unbroken buildings of Managua are round the plaza, and there you can sightsee, or look at very big frescos of Sandino and Carlos Fonseca the poet, or you can go to the movies and see kung fu, pornography, Russian propaganda or *Bambi*.

Morgan walked the two blocks from the Square and entered the huge, ugly building. Unblemished by tremor; even an earthquake wouldn't touch it. Inside was one vast, high-ceilinged room, bigger than the foyer of the Chicago Courthouse and ringing with the same disorientating shiffle of voices and heels, as sound bounced off hard surfaces. A series of colossal fans, like lateral windmills, stirred the wet, turgid air, with the effect of stoking coals. Lines of drab Managuans led towards counters. Morgan stalked down one line, ignoring its contents. 'How do I make a call to the States?' she demanded belligerently at the counter.

'Give me the number please,' came the answer in tainted English. There seemed no surprise from the official that a Yanqui would crash the queue; and no recrimination from the crowd. Presumably they were accustomed to invasions from the north.

The woman, gaunt and with a nose like a small shark fin, gave her a slight, insubstantial docket with a number on it. 'Please seat yourself until your number is called,' she said, hardly looking up from the tray — containing a distressing number of such numbers — to which she was adding Morgan's.

'How do I get an incoming call?' asked Morgan.

The woman at last looked up; her nose cast a slight shadow

across her lip. 'Arrange for them to call you here at a certain time.'

'You mean, in the whole of the capital of Nicaragua there's only one phone number?'

'One place; we have several numbers.' And her eyes said, 'Ask yourself why, Yanqui Imperialist running dog,' while her lips pressed so tightly against unpleasantness they were a symbol of dislike.

Morgan 'seated herself' at the end of the line. The line being 505. Ring country code 505 from anywhere in the world and you ended up in this room. With her. For an hour and twenty minutes she sat. The fans heated the air with a swish like the scimitar in the *Pit and the Pendulum*.

'Juqual chargo.' A Miskito Indian begging for alms. 'You. Call. Chicago.' Ah. He pointed an arm, delicate with undernourishment, at a booth. She 'stood herself', said 'Gracias' as if she could have said more if she'd wanted, and stiffly headed for the wooden enclosure.

She shuffled sideways into the booth and waited. Jeezas, this mechanism is only one generation out from Bell! Come on, you can do it! It rang — even the ring sounded foreign. She picked it up. 'Otis?' The sounds of the sea in shells. 'Can you hear me?'

Crackles. 'Yes?'

'Hi. What's happening?' The conversation ensued in the midst of a witches' coven of static.

'I'm not sure where we're at, Morgan.'

'I'm in Managua.'

'No, I mean in the situation here.'

'Well, who owns us? You must know that?'

'It's a bit more complicated than that. I'll go through it — you may get the idea.'

'Conditions are not ideal here, Otis. Can't you just . . .'

'It's best this way, Morgan, trust me.'

'Okay. Shout.'

'Okay!' he shouted. His voice broke into a thousand magnetic pieces. Fortunately he couldn't sustain the lung power and she could hear him with faint clarity. 'Acomazuni put in a 1.5 billion bid for 45 percent Agrisync . . .'

'Where the hell did my mother get that sort of money?'

'This is your first takeover bid, isn't it?'

'Yes, as it happens. So?'

'You don't need the money. *We* are the money. You buy the company with the worth of it once you've got it.'

'Isn't that round the wrong way in several places?'

'Yes. Look, just take it as read or we'll be here all night.'

'Okay.'

'We refused, of course. Made it a contested bid. Our people —' (Pflaughan, Sykes, Rutherford; company solicitors; ten thousand a week and on a retainer of fifty thousand a year) — 'advised a counterbid.'

'Pacman?'

'Yeah. We'd told them how the Acomazuni/Pawnee combo was probably capital-thin, so we tendered for 50.3 Acomazuni.'

'How much?'

'892.5 million. Front-end-loaded deal,' replied Otis.

'But of course we don't really need to have the money, because once we've . . .'

'No; this time we need the money. The people who might lose it have to have it to lose. It's only the people who might gain it that don't need any.'

'Maybe I'll just assume we're in a different logical sphere.'

'It's often the best way.'

'Okay; carry on.'

'South Chicago Bank expressed a willingness to come in on either side. We got in first — at least it keeps a willing party out of the enemy camp. Anyway, we must have hurt 'em because next thing we hear Acomazuni's shopping round for partners.'

'How much did you get?'

'We'd got thirty-seven percent before they coaxed in a Grey Knight. Some damn company called Calabria Enterprises, working out of Chicago here. Together they bought up the last easy Acomazuni sellers by putting seventy cents on our bid, and since then we've struggled. Meantime they were hoovering our shares like crazy. Nothing we could do. Bound to say we panicked a bit at this stage — they were getting closer to fifty percent of ours than we were of theirs, so we went for a scorched earth.'

(Scorched earth — you sell off prize assets to make the company less appealing.)

'Have we got appealing assets, Otis?'

'Oh yes, Cere-star.'

'What?'

'Cere-star. Our affiliate company that looks after the MAIZE programme, out of Kalamazoo.'

'Are we still on the same planet, Otis?'

The sigh came through with bell-like clarity. It was the sort of sound Walt Disney uses to signify someone's heart is breaking — usually a mummy animal's. 'Some years ago Agrisync saw a window of opportunity in the Pentagon's need for surveillance. We put in a proposal; they grubstaked it. Since '84 we've had a spy in the sky system: we can check out where the world's crops are at. Look, we don't know when the Contras might cut the cable. Let's get back to the issue, shall we? Fact of the matter is we sold Cere-star in a sweetheart deal for 450 million . . . Local company. A phenomenon. Working out of the Projects . . .'

'Out of the Projects. Oh no! Not Harvey the Toot?'

'Yes! Seems he's franchised his pawnshop chain . . .'

'Ebony Enterprises?'

'Yes. Collateralised the entire black pawnshop franchise, put them on the stockmarket. They're the rage. Outselling IBM on the NYSE. Anyway, we brought him in with a hundred million in cash and the rest in shares . . .'

'So the Toot's black company comes in as a White Knight?'

'Yes, s'pose you could put it like that. Hadn't thought of it that way. Ironic, isn't it?'

'So what's the situation now?'

'Well, let me just carry on through it, Morg. To be quite honest, it gets things sorted out in my mind too.'

'Thank God for that, Otis.'

'Yes, it's been happening here at what they call breakneck speed. Anyway, Calabria put in their own secret offer for Agrisync at $85 a share. Secret from Acomazuni, that is; they came to us behind Acomazuni's back and said they were extending it as a friendly deal; there was no way of knowing if they were on the line or not.'

'So you don't know if you're dealing with a White, Grey or Black Knight, Otis?'

'That's about it in a nutshell, Morg. At this stage the Delaware judge called for a pow-wow, ordered us to see if there were any areas of compromise with Acomazuni. Well, we tried to make overtures; offered to walk away. Acomazuni said they'd think about it, then turned hostile; publicly announced they had forty-four percent of our shares, the assholes. Mortified us no end; we stopped taking their calls. Went back to South Chicago Bank and told them to grubstake us up to fifty percent Acomazuni at $70 a share.'

'Holy Sacristi, Otis, this is real paying-back money you're talking here, not just pretend commercial stuff!'

'It's okay. Harvey the Toot put in the hundred million we'd given him in cash . . .'

'Perdoname, llamadora, me hace falta de esta línea; termina la llama, por favor.'

'What?'

'What's that, Morg?'

'Esta línea ahora está ocupado.'

'What?'

'What?'

Click.

'Jeesaz!'

SO MORGAN HAD learned almost nothing. But in perverse compensation she learned, on her return to the hotel, something she didn't want to know.

Colin Fox and his desperados were leaving for Peru at five thirty the following morning.

'Oh very smart, yes,' she hissed to herself as Dittmer told her the news. 'Don't you just know when to put a gorgeous guy on hold and when not to!'

Colin was at the International at this moment, evidently, making arrangements. Rumour had it the international line had been restored there; if not, he'd probably be down at Telecor half the night. Great! So she'd got precious and made him dangle another day, and now he's off to the top of an Ande. Brilliant.

He came into the bar at ten thirty, irritable and sagging with tiredness. Dittmer sat silently, enwrapped in a plump, sixty-dollar teenage girl as Colin reiterated the reason for their unexpected haste. It was the filmstock in Panama. They didn't actually have to be in Peru for three days, and hadn't intended to be, but for reasons of insensate Panamanian bureaucracy the filmstock must be picked up tomorrow — and by him. The receipt is in his name. Only he can sign for it. He drinks moodily. She revives him a little with her eyes. From her eyes to his she transfers hope.

Dittmer stands, still entangled in the plump teenager.

'Don't be late,' growls Colin.

'No worries,' replies Dittmer. 'I think I come prematurely.'

He disappears in the direction of his room.

'Buy me a nightcap,' she says. 'Or else.'

'Or else what?'

'Or else I'll buy you one.'

'Don't forget,' he says, 'we leave at five thirty; we don't get up at five thirty, we leave at five thirty.'

'All the more reason for a nightcap,' she said.

He nodded for two Cointreaus. 'Bloody cameramen,' he muttered. 'It doesn't matter how carefully you plan everything, they'll always run out of film about halfway through; it's built into them.' The sticky little glasses of Cointreau arrived. 'Ten bloody days before we're back here.'

'Oh! You're coming back?' She hadn't realised.

In his eyes she could see the flare of smug, predatory elation her guard-dropping had occasioned. Then his eyes cleared, like the little pearly, shut doors of hermit crabs when they've hauled their prey inside. 'Oh yes. To drop Bianca off; she has to be escorted to the doorstep, you see.' His eyes were bland — so he thought. In fact they were watchful. 'Thing is, we're then booked on the flight out the next afternoon, and for various reasons I can't change that date under any circumstances.' His brown eyes glowed golden, as if lit from within. Mind you, his whites glowed a bit golden too; there was tiredness in them. The smugness had not returned, but he gave a sudden baffled sigh. 'Look, I haven't actually got the luxury of time when it comes to saying — what I'd like to say. Time wonderfully concentrates — elegance.'

Her face was an unblinking mask as she looked at him and thought, that's just as goddam well.

'The thing is . . .' He turned his strangled pause into a refreshment stop, and sipped. 'Look, let me explain what happens with altitude. We arrive in Lima, jump in a jeep with a specially adapted carburettor and shoot almost vertically up the side of the Andes to Huancayo; we'll be at fifteen thousand feet in about two and a half hours. A very long way up. There's no air up there; open a bottle of champagne and it just seeps out and keeps going till it's all gone; no pressure to keep it in the bottle. So, imagine breathing; like having leaks in your lungs. The locals are built like filing cabinets; most of their body sac is taken up with lung. Also, your blood has created extra red corpuscles to store all the oxygen it can get; in a week I'll have an extra one third blood corpuscles surging round my frame.' He raised his eyebrows. He also raised his shot glass, drank and ordered two more. 'Now, when you're back at sea level, it takes twenty-four hours for those corpuscles to be reabsorbed. And that means,' and he turned to her again; a brave thing to do, because he was nervous, 'that for twenty-four hours you're a superman. Sexually. Given the mechanism of erectile tissue and so on.' He was still looking at her, so close that his eyes flicked from one to the other of hers. 'And in lieu of more time for graceful circumspection, my dear, I'd like to spend those hours with you.'

She looked down from his long fine eyes to his bottom lip, which was slightly pointed in the middle. Lines led down from the side of his mouth; deep, strong lines, etched by thirty years of witticisms, wisdoms and procrastinatory propositions. And he was putting them into the future yet again. When he got back, they'd . . . To hell with when he got back!

'You can sleep on the plane,' she said crisply.

THE FANS OVERHEAD twisted the molecules of air, wringing the heat and dampness down upon the waiting callers, winnowing out the oxygen they craved. She is ill with sleeplessness and exertion. At last: 'Your call, Señorita Moran!' She walks across the acre of boiled air to speak to Otis Vogel, three thousand miles away in a foreign land. He will be upright in his golden velvet swivel chair in his plush room in the Midland, running his finger round the rim of a Jim Beam as he waits for her to batter through the wall of garlic and crazedly echoing conversation to a booth in a Third World republic.

'Damn you, Otis, how is it?'

'Well, it's like this, Morg . . .'

Viscidity between her legs. Oh God; there's more of the damn stuff leaking out. 'Jeezas, Otis, never mind the prologue, who owns us?'

'Not quite that easy, Morg.'

'Well, who do we own? That any easier?'

'Not really. Thing is we don't own Acomazuni; Calabria came in for them . . .'

'The Grey Knight went Black?'

'Yeah, and gazumped our $70 offer; they amalgamated with Acomazuni, then upped their own offer to $75 a share. But the thing is, to finance it they had to pull out of their secret offer for Agrisync. So in effect we had a minor win; we took the heat off ourselves by forcing them to buy themselves.'

'Just a moment while I put my brain back into Cuckooland, Otis.'

'Wise girl. Now, the thing is, while this $85 a share offer was operative we were pretty vulnerable, as you can imagine Morg, so we got our people to draw up a poison pill. We forced a twelve-month standstill with a prescription that put a quadruple loading on the share, which took it over the fifty percent mark. At a meeting we agreed there'd be a Board freeze and non-vote for twelve months. Harvey voted proxy for you.'

'Tell him thanks. What did I vote?'

'Pro.'

'Great. You can tell me — slowly — pro what when I get home.'

'Of course. Point is, you saw the point. If the enemy wanted those last seven percent shares, it was going to cost them something like $240 each.'

There was a pause; the static today was less a crackle and more the squeals and wheezes of recorded whale conversations.

'Yeah, so? I'm still here, Otis.'

'Yes, well as I said, the deal had been drawn up in a crisis situation, Morg, things were white hot. So overall I don't suppose Pflaugham Sykes can take all the blame . . .'

'For what, Otis?!' She startled a bent, black-clad woman passing by. 'What have those arbuckles done?'

'Well, they'd overlooked a couple of things — like the fact the Ebony Enterprises deal was still in ratification, and by the time they came through, well, it was the day after the poison pill was instituted and . . .'

'The Ebony deal put it over the fifty-one percent.'

'Got it in one.'

'So Harvey the Toot got poisoned!'

'I'm afraid so.'

'And has to buy the shares at punitive rates?'

'Alas.'

'Jeezas H. Christ! Can't anything be done?'

'"Irrevocable financial commitment" Pflaugham Sykes are calling it.'

'What the hell have they got to do with it? Why weren't they fired for stupidity?'

'Well, they know a little too much, Morg. Best to keep them on our side of the tent pissing out, so to speak. Anyway, they're working like crazy for us now, trying to make up for their mistake.'

'But Harvey's our goddam partner! They can't get heavy with him!'

'They reckon they know how far Ebony can be pushed. It's a delicate matter, Morg, best left to the experts. Just give things here a week or so . . .'

COLIN AND THE desperados had been gone six days. In that time Morgan had been solemnly conducted to Granada; to León; to the potteries of San Juan del Oriente because — fantastically — her association with pots was known; to Jinotega and to the sad, bullet-battered precincts of Estelí. She had been jostled by Aeronica across the pitted skies to Blue Fields on the Caribbean coast. There she had eaten shrimps and lobster, joylessly observed by José Luis. Today she had been to Coca-Cola in the Barrio Riguera on the far side of Managua. It had been an experience of extreme bizarrety:

José Luis had arrived at eight thirty that morning and gazed with hound-like longing across the mock-Western dining-room as she ate breakfast.

They set off for Coca-Cola, grinding north along the jagged brick Northern Highway in a fog of diesel — vehicles here didn't burn diesel, they chewed it! Pedestrian lights. They stopped; no one crossed. Within ten seconds of starting again they had nearly run down a jaywalker. Lines of people waited for buses; white shirts, cabbagewater-coloured dresses. Heads slightly too big, that wobbled on their necks as if too heavy to support. Big black eyes — too big — high brows, smooth skin, arms like dental floss; incredibly youthful. It was the malnutrition; 'alimentary dwarfism'. At the age of ten, they looked five. It was not the

CIA's fault, not even honky's — they were starving before Columbus. They boil the corn and throw out the water, and with it goes most of the goodness. Arable land not in corn is in cash crops. They grow pigs and chickens and sell them for — corn. Agrisync Hybrid.

'La Esperanza' pharmacy on the corner. Morgan smiles. She now knows it means 'Hopeful' pharmacy. Crashed cars lie wheels up in the centre of the road beside the railway line; dragged there, but no further, by the Ministry of Transport, perhaps as a warning.

The Bank of America, one of the few buildings away from the plaza that survived. The Intercontinental; she waves to Howard Hughes.

Into the city centre: like entering an open wound.

Then a chicken-wire fence, red with rust and white with oxidisation. The Coke colours. It is COCA-COLA LTD.

Behind this slogan of natural rot, a two-storey slab of grey windows. At the western end a grey corrugated-iron 'almacene' — warehouse. In there will be the Agrisync corn that is crushed to a syrup of dextrin, maltose and dextrose. The goodness of Coca-Cola.

They were over-greeted as they lurched from the jeep by Compañero Coca-Cola; Oswaldo Salas-Ostrada. Groucho Marx! She stared at the two small horizontal leaves of his eyebrows and the almost matching leaves of his moustache, and never, throughout her meeting with him, could she decide whether they were joined to his face or to his round black spectacles. He conducted her through the hellish factory, waving his arms in the manner of G. Marx — and even walking with his hands behind his back!

They returned to his second-storey office for a cup of local, slightly burnt coffee.

'Well, very interesting,' she gushed insincerely. Then, with far more enjoyment: 'How's it different from Pepsi?' She had hoped for entertainment from the mischievous question; instead she had ushered herself into a world of corporate insanity . . .

'They've got the President,' answered Compañero Salas-Ostrada promptly.

'I'm sorry? Whose president?'

'Yours. Reagan's a Pepsi president. The last Coke president was

Nixon; we've had a bad run. We should have won the Nobel Peace Prize with Nixon, you know.'

'Coca-Cola?' she said carefully. 'The Nobel Prize?'

'Yes. They gave it to Kissinger instead. Bastards! You see we suggested — Coca-Cola itself suggested — that when Nixon went to China he take Pepsi! Coca-Cola suggested that!' The memory agitated him; he wrung his hands. His eyebrows, spectacles and moustache rose and fell as one. 'Have you ever heard of a gesture so generous? Can you imagine it? Giving the enemy a market of a billion people?! Well, Coke did it! And it saved the world.'

'It did?'

'Undeniably.' His language was impeccable; he'd spent thirteen years at HQ in Atlanta. This was Coke-speak; but more alarming, it was Coke-think! 'Russia and China — the two great Communist empires. Just imagine if they were both Coke!' He shook his head at the vision of the two Evil Empires in close entente over a bottle of fizzy water. 'We had to do it; we had to keep them apart for the good of the world! We had to give China to Pepsi!'

Morgan said nothing, absorbing the fact that the two great communist giants had been kept apart by embroiling them in the cola wars. She nodded. He nodded too. They nodded together in rueful silence.

'The whole world's divided, you know,' he went on. 'Got a nice poem here somewhere . . .' And he burrowed into his desk. He brought out a square of newsprint glued onto cardboard and flipped it to her. She picked it up and read the poem printed on it:

Alcohol is devil's drink
So says the Ayatollah.
So Islam hordes who hate the West
Drink only Coca-Cola.

'Employee of mine wrote it,' he said. 'They've got a copy of it at Head Office.' He took it gently from her before she could dive through the window with it and head for the Pulitzer applications desk. 'Iran's Coke, Iraq's Pepsi. Fortunately we got the numbers.' He put the work away. Then he turned back to her and straightened himself to his full five five. 'So now perhaps you start to see the situation here,' he continued in momentous *sotto voce*. 'Reagan's Pepsi, Nicaragua's Coke. You see? This war will last as long as there's a Pepsi in the White House.'

Things sanified a little when Morgan found she could actually call international from here. Compañero Near Nobel Salas-Ostrada gladly gave her privacy. She could see him now, down in the compound, talking to José Luis. She dialled Otis and sat on the desk.

'HEY! MORG! HOW'S life in the world of war and chickens, babe?'

It was Harvey. Mr Ebony Enterprises, the man who'd been poisoned by the company pill. Had he forgiven them? Had he wriggled out of it? Was he still a friend? He sounded hearty enough.

'How's it, Harvey? Are we still one big happy family?'

'Sure as eggs is eggs is eggs, babe! Absolutely one big homogenised clump of ecstatic fam'liness here! An' I'll tell you what, you can come home from volcano-land any time you like. It's all over up here, all that unpleasant business. We's now what you call "repositioned in the market".'

'Well, what's our position?'

'Strong, healthy, immense. You'll love us.'

'Those damn pot-noodle lawyers didn't cause trouble between Ebony and us?'

'Nope; put me on the road to Damascus, you might say.'

'Good. Great . . . Hey, you've got a gall, haven't you, listing pawnshops?!'

'My pawnshops, ma'am, is the biggest junk bond in the west! Ahahahaha!'

'Well, how'd it go when those lawyers dumped on you at $240 a share? Did you get out of that one okay?'

'Sure did.'

'I'm glad, Harvey, I mean that's incompetence at the A grade! You going into litigation?'

'Jeez no, babe. I paid the bill.'

'You what?'

'I bought the shares. Cost me eighty million, but what the hell, I own a coupla billion now.'

'You what!'

'I own the company, Morg! Agrisync. Me, your mom, the Pawnee tribe an' Mr Fellucini, we . . .'

'Mr Fellucini?'

'Yeah, he's Calabria Enterprises.'

'Harvey,' she bellowed down a Nicaraguan Coca-Cola telephone to a traitor in far Chicago, 'I smell a rat, as James Cagney would say, a dirty stinking rotten rat!'

'Hey, heavy! Steady on the names, babe, we's partners on the Board!'

'You've been on her side in this takeover since the beginning, haven't you? You lying, conniving, cheating asshole!'

'Hey, hey! You can't go dumping the whole blame at my feet, Morg!'

'Why not?'

'Well — 'cos Mr Fellucini's been in it too. Anyway, think of the social benefit we's done for the poor downtrodden Pawnee.'

'Where's Otis?' she said suddenly. 'This is his number.'

'Now listen, Morg, when persons like myself an' your mother an' the Pawnee and the Maf . . . an' Mr Fellucini — has put hunnerds of millions into a company, they's entitled to make a few management changes for the sake of efficiency.'

'You've fired them!'

'Le's jus' say they opened their golden parachutes and flew away.'

'I'm disgusted!'

'No you're not, you're chairman.'

'What!'

'You're chairman of the Board. We had a vote; you won. So I wouldn't go round making disgusted noises about your own company if I wus you, babe, 'cos they jus' might have reverberations on the stockmarket. Where, by the way, we's trading at seven ninety-six; the arbs have cranked us up two hundred points since negotiations began.'

'You're an asshole Harvey. You all are.'

'Thank you, Madam Chairman. When's you comin' home to celebrate?'

AND TO CAP off a really peachy day, Mr Muesli was in the bar! He was alone and he shrivelled like an anemone at the touch of her sight. Oh God, he wasn't here to woo, was he? Morgan sat on a high stool at the bar; he sat hunched in fidgety misery by the window. She was doomed. It was no use trying to launch into conversation with the barman, who only spoke Aztec or something. The only others in the bar were three Panamanians; white shirts, black trousers and Otis watches. She knew they were Panamanians because they'd said so when they asked her to join them the night before. She'd said no and hadn't been able to spend a dime subsequently: 'Pagado,' snapped the barman whenever she'd got a drink. She drank one for each of them, with her back stalwartly to them at all times, then turned and nodded on the completion of the third and wobbled off to batsville. 'Vaya con Dios, señorita,' they chorused. At least they didn't call her compañera. They were not paying tonight. 'Tree dollari,' snapped the barman.

She sipped her Nica-libre. Free Nicaragua — she sat in a revolutionary country brooding on revolutions at home. The Board, stabbed in the back! Shafted from within as they battled for the company! All gone, her dear friends through thick and thin; Otis Vogel, Woodrow Wyeth, T. Paul Barnes . . . A lump of nostalgia formed in her throat. She swallowed it. Down it went, a bolus of sorrow, shunted down her alimentary tract by peristaltic action to her stomach, there to be reduced to chyme, then energy, starches, fats and waste. She realised with true sadness that by tomorrow her concern for her erstwhile colleagues would have been, by natural processes, eliminated.

'Darme una cerveza mas, por favor.' This was being said close by, in a soft musical voice not built for the metallic crowspeak of Spanish. It was Mr Muesli. A flush of anger; damn it, it wasn't fair! He was imposing himself on her as imperiously as had those Panamanian louts the night before. Forcing the issue. Two people with nothing to say and a whole language to say it in.

'Hi,' she said jadedly, 'I'm Morgan Moran. I saw you here the other night.'

'Oh, hullo. Yes, I was here with a pupil of mine.' He unnecessarily repushed a small ziggurat of coins across the bar as his foaming beer arrived. Nervous displacement activity. 'I teach at the academy in town. I'm Roger Morrison, how do you do?'

'Hi.' Well, we've explored that one in depth. 'You met Colin. Colin Fox.'

'Yes, impressive man. I was hoping he'd be here actually.' Absurdly he looked around the room.

'He's in Peru.'

'Oh.' There was a moment of stunned confusion in his pale eyes and then a smile, so angelic it lit his face into momentary beauty. 'I don't usually miss by that much.'

She smiled back and suddenly meant it. 'He's due back in a couple of days. They had to leave suddenly. I suppose that's how you didn't know.'

'Oh, it was nothing formal; he mentioned something about a drink one night and this is the first time I could make it since.' A pause. He reached for his beer then took his hand away again. 'I teach from four to ten; English as a foreign language. Right through unless I can get rid of a class.'

'How do you get rid of them?' She had put her elbow on the bar and her hand under her chin, the classic 'tell me about it' stance; from interest or artifice she still wasn't sure.

'Well — may I sit?'

'Sure.' It was the sort of request you expected from an obedient and articulate dog.

He sat, slightly too large to cross his legs. 'You're rude to them, you're late, you turn up drunk . . . It's a long-term operation; you target the smaller classes and try to whittle them down to nothing.' He picked up his beer and sipped. The damp base of the glass dripped beer onto the fly of his light-coloured trousers. He hadn't noticed, and she braced herself for his mortification.

'Your pupil from the other night showed stickability.'

'Yes, he's one of the most profoundly ignorant men I've ever met. He's bilingually uninsultable. He's also my publisher, as it happens. The novel I'm writing has become the class text; I plan to finish it by the end of the teaching year. Well I hope so; I'd hate the rest of the class to leave without knowing how it ended.'

'It's an amazing way to get a book published.'

The angelic smile again; it awed her. 'Yes, it's the only English he knows.' He sipped again, followed the flight of the escaping drips, discovered his damp fly and was mortified.

They talked. He talked, she talked. For hours. She talked with the unbridled, trusting abandon of a verbal one-night stand. She told him things she had told no one but Mary Krueljack. She couldn't help it. It was like face-to-face telephonic adultery. She was captivated, hypnotised, debauched by this large, red, homely man with eyes of faded ceramic and baggy, freckled skin. It was more than simply the soft voice, the deprecating nervousness alternating with startling intimacy; it was . . . that he knew what she meant. The realisation came to her suddenly, and much later. It was like talking to a woman.

Morgan didn't sleep with Mr Muesli Morrison; she didn't sleep with him by the skin of her teeth. She wanted to; not from lust but from generosity; genito-friendship; triple-X platonism. He didn't ask; she knew he wouldn't. He couldn't; he knew his place. And she didn't offer. Because she could see the leering contempt in the eyes of the barman.

'SEÑORITA MORAN?'

The voice caught up with her across the foyer, through the babble of a departing group of Peruvians. She turned. It was the wide-faced, pregnant girl behind the reservations desk. A message? They'd fixed the lines?

'Yes?' She retraced her steps across the foyer, weaving through scattered black suitcases that stood upright like huge dominoes. José Luis was still visible through the steamy window. He had just deposited her at the hotel and was heading back to his van. Like a true macho government official, he was probably going home to unlock the door and let his wife out for a run.

'Is possible that you come to my house this evening?'

It was the most unsemiotic invitation she had ever heard; it was loaded with meaning, none of it evident.

'What for?' It sounded so ungracious. 'I don't quite follow you. For . . . dinner?'

'No. For meeting with my husband.'

'Oh.' Jeezas. Was this an invite into the world of Latin American surrogacy?

'He has something he wishes to show you and cannot come here.'

'Well, is it far?' Still ungracious; we're deep in cross-cultural trouble here.

'Pantasma.' She earnestly studied Morgan's expression, which, from the inside anyway, felt like one of profound incomprehension. 'Is close to Jinotega.' A pause. 'But my house it is in El Nicarao barrio, to east, past barrio Martha Quezada.' Everyone knew barrio Martha Quezada; it had all the markets and restaurants. 'I will write for you the address.'

She did so, and handed Morgan the paper. Large, childishly round letters, like owls on a powerline. 'Show this to the taxi man and he will bring you to us.'

She herself of course would be going home in the bus. Taxis were for los gringos.

'Can you tell me what it's about?'

'No. Is not a converse for here.'

'I see. But he wishes to speak about something he wants to show me in Phantomsville, not far from Jinotega?'

The girl's smooth wide face pleated for one second into a frown of frustration. She glanced desperately round the peopled confines of the desk and said, 'Pantasma. Yes. But not to talk of it here. Is important for you and for he.'

'Okay. Sure. What time?'

'I finish my work at eight, you can come by nine?'

'Yes.'

THERE ARE NO street numbers in central Managua; hell, there are few street names. From what Morgan could gather, you go to the Cine Dorado and work out from there. That's what the driver was doing anyway. He'd glanced at the written directions for no more than three seconds and was now off on a Mister Memory demonstration. Cine Dorado, The Golden Cinema. Flaking honey-coloured walls containing more bloodcurdling threats of death to the FDN in black graffito. 'Al lago' it says on the directions; to the lake. That's how you say north in Managua. They will head al lago of the cine for 'siete cuadras', seven blocks; then 'izquierdo', left, at the 'colmado', superette. They'd rattled through what, from the evidence of occasional majesty, had once been an elegant borough, into the low, dusty and paradoxically well-preserved precincts near the lakeshore. And there it was, the colmado, battered green shutters up, either because they'd run out of food or it was late siesta. Dos cuadras 'arriba', up, which is east. 'La casa con pañuelo blanco.' The house with the white handkerchief. Dangling from the slack metal of a broken filigree fence.

That's how you get round the capital. Because Somoza had refused to fork out for renovations, and the Sandinistas couldn't afford to.

Her mind blipped for an instant into the cockpit of an ageing fighter plane wheeling at dawn above the Camino Real. Down there, in hexagonal splendour, the fatcat Yanquis, eating chicken and pork, drinking imported water, spending the profits of Reaganomic imperialism. The pilot's undernourished little thumbs settle on the little red buttons labeled RELEASE . . .

The House of the White Handkerchief had an entranceway as wide as a cathedral porch, in which was set a great wooden double door with a tiny door in the middle of it. Inside, a wide marble staircase lined with nineteenth-century azulejos — glazed tiles — in lustrous blue. Above them the walls were painted — pinkwashed — in mad pastel. The plaster had fallen off in many places, in tortilla-sized flakes. A recent one lay smashed on a step.

Upstairs, Morgan was led into a wide dark room that looked out onto a complicated raft of rooftops tiled in the serried jumble of 'nuns and priests' — wickedly named, for they lay on top of one another.

She was offered rosquillas, crumbly little biscuits made from — the inevitable. They drank calavera del gato, a special beer, she was told, brewed only in the village of Diriomo. She hoped that Daysi — the pregnant receptionist — had purloined it from work and not spent a year's salary on it.

Nolando, her husband, indistinguishably out of that slight, dark, moustachio'd Nicca mould, was an officer of the Agrarian Reform Ministry. He was based in the village of his birth, Pantasma, not far from Jinotega, and was at home only one week in four. He would continue to commute, however, until the birth of their baby, when Daysi would join him. In the meantime they needed the money.

Nolando hated his job. At first, in 1980 when he had enthusiastically enlisted in the revolutionary cause, all had been positive. He had joined the Sandinista militia and had helped to form a Pantasman branch of the CDS — the Sandinista Defense Committee; a sort of Neighbourhood Watch against Somozan counter-revolutionaries. Since then the triumphs of the Revolution had been steadily desiccating under the arid tenets of Marxism. Young ideologues — 'sin cabello en culo' ('with no hairs upon the arses,' translated Daysi solemnly; evidently it meant they were inexperienced) — had been classifying the locals into 'semi-proletarians' and 'classic peasants' and other obnoxiously puerile categories.

And the farmers of Pantasma suddenly found that they were now to work on state-run collectives under the direction of other juvenile Sandinista administrators. And the unhairy-asses, while glib with Marxist aphorisms, were unschooled in the ways of the land. The state-run farms were failing, and the unhairy-ass answer was to seek blame amongst the new 'classic peasantry'. Suggestions became 'complaints' and were punished by imprisonment, bank loans were to be made only to those who could show party-membership papers, and soon petrol would be issued on the same conditions.

And now, in the acme of lunacy, there was a new scheme, run by new, even more stupid people, which was about to starve the people of Pantasma to death. That, said Nolando, would be the effect of the move they were about to make.

'La gente moririían de hambre. Muerte de hambre, para toda la gente.' Death by hunger, for everyone. He looked at her, somehow pale behind his brownness, gaunt, with slackened skin and leathery eyes. Normal, in other words. The average state of Nicaraguan wellness would require a rest cure in the States.

'Pantasma; presente, presente, presente,' he added gently, then fell glazedly silent. For a second or two Morgan was puzzled, then the terrible significance of something Colin Fox had said, rolled over her: 'When they're referring to someone killed in the Revolution, they say 'present' three times.' Nolando had just declared his village extinct.

Daysi spoke next. Upon acquaintance she had lost that faint air of bovinity Morgan had associated with her wide features and slow movements. 'This reform shall be terrible for Nolando,' she said, reaching across the table to touch his hand, which lay like a land crab beside his bowl, 'because it is he who must force it to the people. They must do what he says or he must put them to prison. This is terrible for him.' Nolando looked up; they were both looking at Morgan now: grim-faced products of every goddam cursed revolution on earth; protagonist and victim at once. 'But it will be terrible also for you.'

'Terrible for me?' Concern for their plight fled before the onslaught of panicky self-interest.

Nolando nodded with a force that caused his jaw to wag. 'Sí.'

Desperately she asked him to explain, and he did; in cracked English, mended in places by his wife's translation.

'The year that comes,' he burbled, 'no Agrisync for we.'

'He say his village will not to grow Agrisync Hybrid the next year.'

'Yes, I understood, but that's madness! You're using every available inch of land now and you're still only just producing enough!'

Daysi was about to answer; Nolando sputtered over the top of her. 'These people say, Pantasma no have Agrisync and I prohibit. I ensure of this. I look over. I see Agrisync, I take; destroy. No Agrisync. In vez de . . .?'

'In place of.'

'In place of Agrisync — Zeacinte.'

'Zea-syn-tay?'

'Sí.'

'What is it?'

'You come. I show.'

'To Pantasma?'

'Yes. You have the need.'

They would go the day after tomorrow. Would Daysi come? She would not; she worked every day at the Camino Real and from two till five each morning on vigilancia revolucionaria.

MORGAN REFRAINED FROM telling José Luis. Caution suggested that if there was indeed more to the Sandinista revolution than met the eye, then his job was to ensure it was never seen by her. From the healthily paranoid point of view, José Luis was a government spy. She must be shrewd. She contacted Roger Morrison from his card: 'The Winston Churchill Academy of Fine English.' Would he like to accompany her on a jaunt into the country tomorrow? The company would be pleasant for her, and the lack of attendance at his classes may be useful to him.

Yes, he would be delighted.

She contacted José Luis and talked to him in large whispers. She was embarking upon an orgiastic tryst with an Englishman tomorrow, she told him. The man was engaged to be married to a noblewoman in London, with well-established Palace connections; no one must know. Thus, from the old principle of 'If you want someone to believe you, convince them you are lying to someone else,' she gained a day's freedom.

The next morning at six thirty she took a taxi to the Cafetín

Mirna four blocks 'up' from the Golden Cinema. There she was met for a 'western breakfast' by Roger Morrison. The food was traditionally Nicaraguan but westernised by the addition of 'tea, like the which makes the mother'.

At seven thirty they were collected by Nolando Benevides in a crepitous World War II jeep and conducted to Pantasma.

MANAGUA TO MATAGALPA in a thrumming of bricks and a blur of off-white churches, circular cockfight arenas and brick walls scrawled with the F words — FSLN and FDN (muerte to, of course); then left and on towards Jinotega.

In all the world there can be few more pleasant journeys than the one from Matagalpa to Jinotega. Fine palms and verdant grasses flourish in the cool and unsullied air; peasant faces are clean, clear and round; limbs glow from colourful costumes. Little roadside stalls sell plantains, carrots, lettuce and flowers, and graceful hills march into an empyrean distance, changing as they go from lush emerald to lustrous purple. Harmony, contentment and tranquillity — the landscapes of the quixotic postcards in the hotel lobby — marred only here and there by burnt-out trucks and tractors, and half-cleared roadblocks.

Roger Morrison made her laugh. He told her about the English language; how you could have a sentence with five thats in a row, or five hads. He also told her about Mr Fonbote's grapple with the fact that you first chop a tree down, then you chop it up.

'My only aim for Mr Fonbote,' he said, 'is to teach him not to pronounce rain as "urine".'

At a signpost saying two miles to Jinotega and eight to Pantasma, they thudded down from the highway onto the gravel Pantasma road, which wound upwards to the right, past serried thickets of bright coffee trees into forests of spruce. It was almost chilly, and Morgan could feel the air hitting the back of her throat as she breathed. Dense tree trunks strobed by; tiny leaves dappled the branches like mildew: the air glowed like a Disney Sherwood Forest. For a time, on their left, the blueness of a lake bloomed through the trees.

In an abrupt clearing they could see blunt hills that rolled to the horizon like a designer salad of manifold greens. 'Honduras,' said Nolando. She stared; somewhere over there Nicaragua became Honduras, the enemy became the goodie, the Yanqui became the Yank, black became white, patriotism became treason, Coke became Pepsi.

They reached the top, still sheathed in trees, and rattled downwards again. She saw a sign: NO CAJAN LOS LOROS — Don't hunt wolves. Wolves! They have wolves here? She asked Roger Morrison, who explained that loro was parrot and wolf was lobo. Oh. Parrot hunters; how despicable and unheroic in comparison.

The trees thinned, then were suddenly lying on the ground as they passed a clear-felling project. A corner on the hillside — a momentary flash of Mount Rose — and beneath them a town, long and thin and made — sensibly enough — of timber, stretching along the valley floor.

They wound down the mountain towards the village, rather as if traversing the canals of an inner ear — they saw the goddam place about five times before they were actually on the straight gravel road heading towards it at its own level.

Pantasma. On the outskirts, the inevitable zoo of disabled EBRO or Pegaso trucks peering out through rusty wire netting.

The town was simply two strips of civilisation along the sides of the road. Halfway through the town Nolando stopped outside — it seemed — no building in particular and said, 'Eat and drink here. I return soon.'

They reluctantly got out, beside a faded red segment of the continuous, dilapidated, single-storey building that ran from one end of the town to the other. Only colour differentiated one edifice from another. This segment was an ex-'Rosticeria', according to faded lettering above the open door. The windows were boarded up; inside, down a deep step, was darkness.

Wrong; it wasn't ex. In fact it was the centre of Pantasman society. Inside, once their eyes became accustomed to the murk, they saw a bar and behind it a hulking man. They stumbled towards him. By now Morgan was seeing quite well. Under the bar was a sign: CUIDADO CON EL PERRO. Beware of the dog. The sign, however, was flush with the boards beside it, and she guessed, rightly, that the sign had simply been recycled into the construction of the bar. They were not alone. Near the door sat a plump young girl in a preposterously tight skirt who crossed and uncrossed her legs for Roger. The banana-coloured flesh above her stockings wobbled. Obviously one of the local ladies of the night — noontime darkness deputising for night on this occasion. Another, with a lion's mane of black hair, was pushing her tongue into the ear of a man in a cowboy hat. There were three other men in cowboy hats around a table. The place smelled of cloacal overflow, cornsack dust and beans. Any gringo, she suspected, who ate in this 'roast meat restaurant' would quickly relinquish rights to their 'I farted in Nicaragua' badge.

Stacked untidily in a glowing freezer — one of the few sources of light — were bottles of Coke and San Miguel beer. On a warm shelf above the freezer were uneven bottles of local popskull, chica wine that would be rancid within two days — and a bottle of Moët! Jeezas! Where in hell had that come from? A leftover from the epicurean days of Somoza? Booty from a raid on the CIA stores in Honduras?

'Well, a brandy for breakfast, why not a beer for lunch?' said Roger. 'Una cerveza por favor. And for you?'

'Moët, thanks,' she replied sweetly.

'Sorry, what was that?'

'Ask him about the bottle of champagne up there.'

'Oh? Good God! Is it real? Compañero, por favor, la champagne; cuánto vale?'

The huge man shrugged; his tiny mouth hung open, pushed inwards by massive cheeks, and his voice came in deep adenoidal snores. 'Qué vale a usted?'

'He wants to haggle,' said Roger.

She shrugged carelessly and looked away. 'Two dollars,' she said with her head towards the cowboys.

'Dos dollares?'

The man shrugged. The deal had been made! A bottle of Moët for two dollars! Praise be to provincial ignorance! She turned back. He was reaching up for the bottle, his tight white shirt riding up his haunches as he did so, revealing a deep, hairy cleavage above his drooping trousers. No 'unhairy-arse', he. He turned to the bar with the bottle, soundlessly pulled out the cork and filled a whiskey glass with warm, flat, piss-toned liquid. He pushed it across the bar. 'Dos dollares,' he grunted.

THEY BOUGHT TORTILLAS from the glassless window of an old woman's house and ate them as they waited for Nolando, who was feasting on beans in the Rosticeria.

Nolando emerged and farted almost immediately. They set off, turned right and bawled on up the road, through farmland that featured cows. Then left, down a trail of mud, to a locked gate. Nolando got out and opened the gate with a key which was separate from the bunch that jangled irritatingly on his belt. He'd obviously gone to his office to get it while they purchased Moët. They drove on, past lush, muddy fields of lime-coloured grass.

Without preamble Nolando began rattling away in his language, not looking at anyone but obviously addressing himself to Roger. After about ten sentences of gurgles and clanks he stopped and Roger turned to her. (They sat three abreast in the front, Morgan in the middle, his arm resting comfortably along the seat.) He was, she calculated, the ugliest man who had touched her without her flesh creeping.

'We are going to the farm of Humberto Tapia,' he said. 'He is a "pigheaded old bastard" who has grown corn all his life on his cuatras palmas de tierra — literally four palms of land, but it just means not very much. Señor Tapia is famous for the bravery of his mulishness; he hated Somoza and wouldn't do a thing he ordered, even on pain of death; so he wouldn't plant Agrisync when told to. He stuck to the old stuff. In the end the Somosistas just left him alone. But he wasn't any more gracious after the Revolution. He hates the Sandinistas as well, and won't do anything they say either . . .'

Nolando cut in here like a machine-gun. She waited. The noise stopped and Roger returned to her. 'Humberto hates the modern ways, and he was proved right. One day a government agent came to demonstrate a fine new plough made of steel. It was the plough of the future, said the agent; far more efficient than any wooden plough could ever be. Donations were to be called from all the local farmers to buy a steel plough for the district. Humberto would have none of it. 'It won't work,' he declared. The plough was hitched to a pair of oxen; it set off, hit a rock and stuck. Every time it hit a rock the new plough buried itself. Humberto was right; the wooden ploughs bounce right over the top of the rocks.'

'Is Humberto growing this zeacinte?'

Burbles. Gurgle, clank.

'Yes. The only crop of it in the whole country; in the whole world, they say. There were many types of old corn once, but now they have all been destroyed. Pulled up to make way for Agrisync, which is much bigger and juicier, and because Somoza ordered it. Here and there, along roadsides or beside stone fences, there is some 'old stuff', but only on Humberto's farm is there zeacinte.'

'What's so special about it?'

Gurgles. Not many.

'You will see.'

Silence. They slowed at one stage to pass a mule without frightening it. On the mule sat a ferocious old man. Ahead of him walked a ferocious old woman bent under a bundle of sticks.

'Señor Tapia?' asked Morgan.

'No,' said Nolando. 'His brother.'

Sloppy fields of lush grass and pinto cows. She suddenly realised the absence of cheese in Nicaragua.

Then, on the other side of a thicket of bamboo that rang with birds, they stopped at a river. 'Rio Pantasma,' muttered Nolando. It was no more than twenty yards wide at this point, and glassily clean. Its pleasantly curved waters bundled themselves by, chuckling glottally over bright white sand and sinuous weeds. Downstream was an island, flecked with tracks — as if a four-legged animal had dragged a sack of sand ashore. 'Tortuga,' said Nolando, following Morgan's gaze. 'Lays here many egg.' Turtles. He crashed the jeep headfirst into the shallow stream and they brayed across, causing minor tsunamis up the grassy banks ahead of them. 'Cocodrillo also lay many egg here.' Inexhaustible font of info was Nolando. The river downstream to the right darkened and disappeared into a murky arbour of hunchbacked alcanfor trees.

Fields between stands of dark trees, several houses of primitive construction. The trees, Morgan suddenly noticed, were straithed with white straps, like the ceremonial banderoles of a company of troops on parade. Rubber trees. Insolent monkeys give them the fingers from high branches. 'Much turkey, tapirs and jaguars,' says the unquenchable Nolando. 'Also yellow-fever mosquito.'

Oh well, a change from your boring old malaria.

And then, almost incidentally, they were there. Out of the window beyond Roger's profile, a tiny valley, and in it, a field of corn. Bonsai corn, almost as tightly knit as the bamboo thicket they had passed, and in dazzlingly regal colours of gold and purple. They stopped, got out and gathered on the passenger side of the steaming jeep.

'Estamos aquí!' declared Roger.

Nolando turned to him from a perusal of the corn, his face long with perplexity. 'Qué? Estamos aquí? Sí. Supongo que sí. Sí. Estamos aquí.'

'What?' said Morgan.

'I think I've been a little overexistential,' murmured Roger. 'I said, "We are here." It obviously doesn't translate too well; he's pondering the cosmic implications.'

The air was cool and still, refulgent with hysterical animal life and, once the last billow of solid diesel had fallen out of the sky, so gleamingly clear that distance came nearer and somehow contorted perspective.

'Well, I agree,' Morgan said. 'We're here.' And she stumped stiffly across the narrow gravel road and onto the damp grass on the other side. Immediately the ground tilted downwards to a ditch, which she easily jumped. And she was 'here'. In the field of zeacinte; Humberto's famous zeacinte. Strangely beautiful. The tassels glowed bright golden like crowns. There was in fact a general spikiness about the crop. What was it? Ah, the husks stood stiffly upright in points, rather than drooping in the traditional beagle ears of Agrisync corn. There seemed to be only one or two ears on each stalk, although it was rather hard to tell, they were pressed so tightly together. She could now see that three or four stalks surfaced from the same root, the outer ones growing laterally a short distance so they could then all grow upwards in parallel. Wiry black tillers grew downwards from the stems, battening the plant to the soil. She walked into the field, pushing through the spikes rather more cautiously than did the men — she was wearing her red peasant dress and if she sank into the mud while straddling plants . . . Penetrated by zeacinte; what a lot of symbolism.

The ground between the dense plants was indeed soggy; it crackled with their movement. Then suddenly the exercise seemed pointless. What was there to gain in walking through this stuff? In fact what was the point in being here at all? Certainly it was beautiful and unusual, and as the newly elected head of a company that made zillions out of corn, she maybe should be more interested than most. But, hell, she'd done it now. It was, as someone once said, like so many famous sights: well worth seeing but not worth going to see. Two minutes after travelling three and a half hours, she'd seen enough.

The nauseatingly sweet, flat taste of lukewarm Moët came back to Morgan in a belch. They'd come halfway across Nicaragua to drink stale champagne and look at spiky corn! And march into a goddam war zone! She looked around; the trees on either side of the valleyette were oppressively dark and suddenly leapt forward into her eyes across the untrammelled air. Ahead of her stretched unprotected forest and hills, to Honduras; to Somosista-land, Pepsiville. That land ahead of her was official war zone; a theatre of war where the Danse Macabre was showing! She tasted fear; it tasted of pewter. A new cycle of reality passed through her, leaving her tingling electrically; the ghost of Che stank of sweat and cordite. Wars killed people! Damn freedom and liberty and defending your country and that crap; wars hurt; made you dead! And this stupid nowhere place she was in right now was traversed by people who had legal and spiritual authorisation to aim a gun at someone else and turn them into meat! Jeesaz! — which translated as: Help! She loved life with a grovelling passion; she wanted to wail, weep and faint; sink to her knees and beg somebody for mercy. 'I want to get out,' she called to Roger across the field. 'Tell him. Tell him we have to go.'

Roger looked back, grave and rather chillingly unsympathetic. He waded through the dense, stunted crop to Nolando, and a conversation ensued in incomprehensible murmurs. Roger called to her.

'The Contras aren't here, in case that's what's bothering you,' he said.

'It could be. How does he know?'

'There was a fight in Jalapa a month ago. They killed ninety Contras. That probably means nine. The Contras are back over the border; the next attack will be on July the nineteenth.' He looked around as if suddenly conscious of being overheard. She looked round wildly as well. 'It's the anniversary of the overthrow of Somoza. Both sides observe it annually in a battle. They're both preparing.'

She glared at him, shaken by a sudden eructation of mean-spiritedness. And what in hell did it have to do with him? What was this New Zealander gaining by charging through a patch of semi-extinct, useless cereal?! Corn meant nothing to him; how dare he! Why couldn't he mind his own goddam business! Her mouth had dried, leaving a desiccated deposit of bad Moët, metal and resentment.

'Also,' he said, 'Battalion 4015 is between us and the border.'

She looked towards the hills. Nothing. Trees, a skyline that suddenly turned inside out and became the jagged edge of a gigantic eggshell of sky with a green nothingness glowing under it. Black and white cows grazed in the field behind the ridiculous corn crop. And there was a goddam army in there somewhere! Calm down; it's ours. Ours? Who the hell was ours? Ours was the government José Luis was spying on her for. Ours was the army lying in wait for an attack sponsored by her government. One tiny flip of the point of view and 'ours' became the enemy!

Spiralling above the cornfield was the scare-crow. She wailed, in the very act of recognising it as a vulture. Holy . . . Who organises these goddam symbols?

There was a movement, achingly high in the sky; either a molecule floating across her retina or more birds. By screwing up one eye and glaring into the blazing sky she could see another vulture, incredibly high. Then another. The leading zipilote landed amongst the cows, converting the first two bounces of its landing into a spiderously ugly hop that made her feel sick. There was a dead cow in the middle of the field; on its side, stiff as a capsized sawhorse. The zipilote was bounding towards it. The others were circling lower.

When she looked down, Nolando was walking towards her with an uprooted plant over his shoulder. Roger was following him, jostling a track through the stalks of zeacinte, which closed seamlessly behind him. She had jumped the ditch and stood once more on the roadside. Nolando joined her there, dumping the plant like a soldier unshouldering arms, and began to yammer.

'It's ready for harvest,' translated Roger, puffing slightly. Sweat had blackened his polyester safari jacket. 'Humberto does not mind if you take one plant — they've been in telepathic communication, it would seem — and here you see the leaves are dry, which shows the plant is fully grown.' Nolando was tugging at the husks as if following Roger's instructions. They were cracklingly dry and bright puce. She could see inside now; the cobs themselves were largely purple, with yellow speckles. The seeds were smaller than standard, and seemed like bright tadpole eggs clinging to a reed.

Then Nolando was holding up the knob of roots. It was massive, far bigger than the roots of any corn she had seen before — and she had seen some as tall as sugarcane. The tillers tangled themselves around a solid, massive, earth-covered knot, which looked like a giant tuber. Nolando was pointing.

'You see,' decoded Roger, 'the roots are like the compact teeth of the garlic. They grow together to make the one great bulb. While at this end —' and Nolando was suddenly pointing to the top of the plant, 'it does not have many ears. Many seeds but few ears — thus zeacinte is a poor producer; there is little to eat, and Nolando thinks Humberto is mad to grow it. It is unproductive because so much energy goes into storage here —' And he is pointing at the root. 'The plant puts energy into storage instead of into seeds, thus only one or two ears on each stalk. Although each root has perhaps three or four stalks, it is still not superior to Agrisync, which is superior to all. I think you're being congratulated.' He had looked up at her with a smile, and then his features suddenly swooped into a frown. 'Are you all right?' she heard him say from somewhere.

She was staring at the fleshy, mud-scarred root. She was in a garden store somewhere, looking down bright rows of gladioli, daffodils and tulip bulbs in black plastic pots on shelves. FOR SALE. And a rushing feeling — an orgasm going the other way — engulfed her as she watched; sickened her. It was horror. For she saw, amidst the rows of plants, this plant also. This zeacinte, thriving on the shelf, with the daffs and tulips, in their little black plastic trays; all of them beneath a sign. And she knew the sign and the knowledge caused her to moan in her head, Oh God. Oh hell. Oh no!

The words resounded in the hollow roar of crashing blood as a nightmare bloomed brightly into the daylight of her awareness. The death of grass; she was looking down at the imminent destruction of her world.

She swallowed horror; pulled her cheeks into a public smile to stop her lips trembling: 'And it dies down for the dry season and comes up again in summer?' she asked ashily, praying for the negative.

It didn't come.

Yes, that was correct. It died down in the dry season and came back in the summer, affirmed Nolando through Roger. Here you may see the thin brittle line just above the root. This breaks and allows the stem to topple down. The stem is soft and spongy and rots most quickly. By summer it has become the soil, and food for the new plant. Miraculous, a complete and never-ending cycle of growth . . .

A never-ending cycle of growth.

Her brain was throbbing: she cursed her inability to be wrong. This thing was eternal, annually feeding on the death of itself; girding its loins to become the death of Agrisync Hybrid Inc. For it was a perennial. Perennial! Immortal, never-ending. It was the ultimate nightmare of monopolism; the bad dream of capitalism; the horror story of supply-side economics — it was a product available to the masses free of charge!

She reached out and touched the thing. As she did so, the last of the Mr Fellucini lookalikes landed in the field of cows and lurched towards the bovine corpse. She touched the zeacinte; the enemy. No, it wasn't clammy, it was not repulsive; it was crisp and wet and warm to the touch. Innocent. She suddenly felt awed. Awed by a plant! — But then how often do you meet a piece of grass worth billions? They could plant this fellow's little zeabrothersandsisters all across Nicaragua — all across the world for that matter, and they'd never have to do so again. It would grow and prosper, thrive and multiply, and take away the need. The need for seeds. The need for capitalism. The need for Agrisync.

She drew herself inward, into the den where survival lived, deep inside her. As proof of her conviction she stretched her hand gently forward to the thing again, reached through the clotted mud, the bed-spring-like black tillers and grasped a tendril of root. It was faintly yielding to the touch, like parsnip. She bent it; bent it until it crisply snapped, revealing bright whiteness. It bled white milk. 'I'm going to kill you,' she said, not as a thought but in the very lowest of whispers. She dropped the bleeding fragment on the sterile roadway and walked away. She was, she acknowledged darkly, the daughter of her mother.

THE LIGHT BLED from the sky in a violent sunset as they curled down from the hills and rattled into sight of the black, perfect silhouette of Momotombo. The low crack of light on the horizon to their left sucked in all remaining light from houses, stalls, the high white walls of the innumerable rooster colosseums and from eyeballs. The last glintings hung in the telephone wires like molten musical bars, then darkness and silence fell, and not another word was said until goodbye.

ROGER WAS DEPOSITED outside his lodging in barrio Maria Quezal, a sadder and no-wiser man. He had set out this morning with bright, perhaps even carnal expectations; by early afternoon he had realised that, somehow, a plant had come between them. He waved, vaguely stirring a hand held up as if wearing a catcher's mitt. His lumpy white face was crumpled into a glowing beacon of rejection. Damn him! Why didn't he learn the manners of deceit?! No one should have to see so clearly how much pain they've caused! She fluttered her hand at him angrily and whisked her sight away. Too bad. Too bad! This was life and death. Out there was a prehistoric, supposedly extinct weed that could bring down a modern, high-tech corporation. Was that fair? Was that what God wanted? No it was not! After all, if Humberto's pernicious zeacinte prevailed and brought down the Agrisync Corporation, what would be the effect? To starve the entire nation of Nicaragua to death! That's what the goddam effect would be! Is that what God wanted? Of course not! She must save the innocent people of Nicaragua. It was her bounden, Christian duty to destroy the zeacinte! And by such rationalisation does panic-stricken self-interest come to peace with itself.

To keep discussion away from zeacinte, Morgan had maintained an imperious silence in the jeep, which shut down all conversation. The journey home had thus taken place in a faintly hostile void. Nolando was outraged at the snub and, now they were alone, he exuded the effete, wrathful body language of the Latin hidalgo. Even unprotected by the presence of Mr Muesli, however, she easily withstood his wordless censure.

'I'm sorry if I seemed rude,' she said, with no concessions to his inadequacies of comprehension, 'but I couldn't afford to allow him to realise there was anything significant about the zeacinte. I don't wish to be taken home yet, I wish to speak to Daysi.'

It is how her mother would have handled the situation; she would have made herself clear by sheer, malevolent force of will.

In powerful silence they bobbled across the patchwork surfaces of Managua's inner-city streets — and with mixed feelings she realised he had understood. They were in El Nicarao, Nolando's barrio.

Daysi was home. She simply placed another ceramic bowl on the rubbed wooden table. The room was misty with the divine smell of gallo pinto — rice and beans. Nolando sulked in the tiny yard amidst the rooftops, where he kept three fighting cocks in bestially tight confinement.

'Daysi,' said Morgan as she sipped black wine, 'what Nolando has shown me is desperately important. I need to call Chicago. I think you have not told me the truth about the telephone at the Camino Real?'

Daysi's easily reddened cheeks darkened almost to purple, but her wide, pretty face did not fold into weakness. 'Perhaps a little true and a little not,' she said, almost smiling. 'In Managua there is only one source international, and that is Telecor; that is true.'

'But I think you could ring Telecor at any time and get an international line, no?'

'Yes. But we are instructed by government when we may do this and when we may not. At this time of year, when it is close to July the nineteenth, the Camino Real is told to keep all lines clear of internationalistas. These lines are not many and are required for the government. Internationalistas, they call very often and for long times.' She almost smiled again. 'And sometimes for things not very important. At these times when we are told to keep closed the lines, it is — how you say — more good for the dignity, to tell the internationalistas that las Contras cut the line than that they talk too much, no?'

Morgan nodded and for the first time in some hours allowed an expression to take its place naturally on her face. It was a smile. 'Yes, we are drawn to the unimportant I'm afraid. But this is very different. I need to get through to Chicago now, and I don't need another two-hour wait in that damn Telecor building.'

'You can call from the colmado. I can arrange this for you.'

'Now?'

'First we must eat.'

'Yes. And I could have a chat to Nolando. If he will?'

'He will speak to you,' replied Daysi firmly, and for a second her face glinted with a blood-curdlingly recognisable resolve.

She retrieved her husband from his brooding place among the fighting cocks. They sat in a tensely polite triangle around the table.

'Nolando, why will they ban my corn in Pantasma?' began Morgan.

Daysi regurgitated the question in Spanish. 'For poison to die,' was the answer, and Morgan shuddered with embarrassment. Her hosts had tactfully dropped their eyes. 'The land must be fallow two years so not to be poisoned by the chemical seeds.'

They all knew! They dutifully planted their shiny new Agrisync seeds every year, knowing they were pumping another twenty-four months' venom into their soil! She felt — decidedly unheroic; Big Business could seem very small at point of contact. Still, she must persist: 'And in two years you'll start growing zeacinte there?'

'Yes.' It was Nolando who answered, then he babbled to Daysi for about a minute without breathing. Daysi put it into sense: 'Not only in Pantasma, but also in many parts of Nicaragua, land is to be kept fallow for two years. After that the zeacinte is planted more and more until all corn in Nicaragua is zeacinte.'

Holy St Hiram T. Cornpone! They meant it! These ingrates were out to shoot Agrisync down forever! She breathed any shakiness out of her voice. 'You won't get anywhere nearly as much corn, you know. The yield will be much lower.'

'Nolando knows this. This is his concern. But these people say that you can cross this corn and it will produce more.'

'Yes, but it may not stay perennial if you do that. It probably won't. You'll lose that quality and end up with low-yield rubbish that won't even grow again.'

'This he knows. Then Pantasma will die. And many other places. This is why he shows you the zeacinte. He can do nothing himself, but you . . . Well, I think now it is in your hands, no?' Daysi answered softly.

In her hands. She would be the saviour of a nation. There would be statues, Morgan Days when flags were flown. Coins would be minted with Tomás Borge on one side, Morgan Moran on the other. Mother of a country. All through the simple act of blitzing a field of scraggy corn.

'I'd like to make that call now,' she said.

THE MUSACEOUS SMELL of plantains, the potatoes of the tropics; and of ham, although ham existed now only as an olfactory ghost of good times past. Bacalau — dried fish you could cut shoe uppers from; lentils, beans, rice; a sack of saffron in the midst of poverty — it sold at about the same price per pound as gold; and it sold. Vegetables — the produce, one week on, that she had seen that morning, gleaming on roadside stands. Tubs of washing powder, laundry starch, soap, glue — oh yes, such things in plenty because they're all made from corn. Also, things as mad as warm Moët in a shanty bar: Rinso — in an off-white packet; Silvo — to keep the ceremonial teaspoons up to par in case the Duchess of Windsor pops in; goldfish bowls in the land of the silverfish.

Daysi is lisping into the phone in the corner, beneath an incongruous thicket of aluminium ladders. An old woman says something to Compañero Rodas the proprietor, that causes him to reach to an overhead rail and take down one of three strangled chickens suspended there. The pale bulb illuminates only shiny things here, and one of these is the head of Compañero Rodas; bald, brown and wrinkled like the surface of a field mushroom as he bends to his work. With a huge pair of scissors bolted to the counter he cuts off the head of the chicken, manicures it in four scrumping clips, then amputates its feet. He puts the feet onto paper alongside the head and adds the shiny silver-blue ball that first appears when you disembowel a chicken, followed by the guts. Then he hangs the rest of the carcass back on the rail, wraps the bits and sells them to the woman as Daysi hails Morgan and holds up the receiver.

She takes the phone. 'Harvey?'

'Hi babe! Hey, how's . . .'

'Shaddup, Harvey. What do you really know about corn?'

'A lot.'

'Yeah?'

'Yeah. Corn brings in two eighty million a year an' tha's a lot.'

Daysi is diplomatically wandering to the entrance of the colmado. 'Yeah, that's a lot, Harvey. And it stays a lot while they have to buy sterile corn from our lines in Peoria. What happens if they replace it with a corn that grows everywhere, like a weed; that seeds itself and comes back up every year without anyone doing anything to it?'

'Hey, man! You're talking pee-rennial here; you's referring

'bout this leg'ndry pee-rennial stuff that don' exist!'

'Don't it? Doesn't it?'

'You tellin' me it does?'

'Yes.'

'Hey now we's gettin' pretty close to a litigatory situation here, Morg! Jeesaz, I'm the recipient o' misleadin' advertising! Your mom tole me they could never make pee-rennial corn; I mean I's been misled, man! I's ventured all my pawnshop capital in a project that could go down the john on accounter some commie peasant joinin' up two bitsa weed . . .'

'Now hang on, Harvey . . .'

'Hang ona what, man? Lucky I's sitting down here, 'cos right now my rectum is in deep need o' hangin' onto! Your mom promised me an ongoin' monopoly situation with Agrisync, Morg, an' now some ex-Aztec is fixin' to bust that monopoly wide open! I might jus' be speakin' to my lawyers on this matter, Morg, in that she has broken a firmly bound non-pee-rennial guarantee!'

'Shut up, Harvey, pull yourself together!'

'Yeah, might as well,' he wailed. 'Your mom obviously figured me for a wanker way back!'

'Is this the famous Harvey the Toot I'm talking to?' she hissed. 'I'm standing in front of three gutless chickens here, Harvey, and every last one of them reminds me of you!'

A pause, in which she exulted at her own oratory.

'Sorry, Ma'am Chairman,' she heard him mumble chastenedly. She was a leader! 'Yeah, I should think so. Now, all we have to do is keep our heads (Stop looking at those chickens!) and calmly go about putting this stuff back into extinction where it belongs.'

'Yeah, yo' right. Yeah, okay; *nil desperandum*, huh, Ma'am Chairman? Hee hee.' And his mood had manically lifted.

'The way I see it,' she went on, suddenly soaring into leadership mode, 'is . . .'

'Wha' we need is the Stealth.'

'The what?' Her leadership was draining.

'Yeah, tha's it! Hey! The big black Stealth! We can fly down at night, no noise, no detection, drop a poison pill on that Black Knight goddam pee-rennial weed an' hightail stealthily outa there without no one can point no fingers! Yeeha! Right on! We's got contacts with Stealth through Cere-star, but we'll need to square this whole thing with Bobby jus' so it don' come leaping onto the

Innernational Issues plate from outa nowhere. So, we gotta get you up to Bobby, Morg; you tell him the story an' say that we'll be back in touch, soonest, with the co-ordinates . . .'

'Now listen to me, Harvey!' The loudness of her resurgent leadership caused Compañero Rodas to turn and Daysi to stare down the aisle of the shop from the dark doorway. 'Have you finished raving?'

'Jeez, Morg, this is an emergency an' . . .'

'Why don't *you* go see Bobby with that preposterous story?'

'I kinda think he'd rather hear it comin' from you . . .'

'Yeah, in G-string and wet T-shirt, asshole!' Compañero Rodas and Daysi show covert interest. She lowered her voice into a vicious aspirate that probably carried just as far. 'Get in touch with my mother, tell her what I've told you. Discuss it with whoever you need, and then get back to me. If you come up with a plan that makes sense, we'll do it, if not, I'll do something at this end. Ring me back in . . . oh God, listen, Harvey; I will ring you in — at exactly this time tomorrow. It's the best I can arrange with the phone system here as it is. Okay? Get it organised! And Harvey, don't make any of your plans dependant on me sleeping with a crazy geriatric! Okay?'

'You mean Bobby?'

'Yeah, I mean Bobby.'

Imbued with leadership, she turned to slam the receiver into its cradle. It was a heavy, old-fashioned Bakelite instrument and took her several clumsy seconds. Harvey's voice continued throughout. 'Jeesaz, Morg, you don't sleep with Bobby! No one sleeps with Bobby, babe. Bobby got drunk one night twenny years ago an' cut his dick off. He jus' likes talking about it! . . .'

NOTHING IS EASY in Nicaragua. Nothing — not time, space nor logic can be relied upon to act with consistency. Nicaragua is a strange and magical place. Consequently, 'exactly the same time tomorrow' was not exactly the same time. It was exactly one hour later!

WHY IT WAS AN HOUR LATER

IN 1609 THERE lived in Leon a priest by the name of Amador who had, miraculously, somehow come into possession of the ability to make miracles. He was a benevolent man and used his powers only for the good of others, causing fish to leap out of the lake (this was when Leon was at its original site by the lakeside, before destruction by the earthquake of 1610) into the cooking pots of needy people, crops to grow prodigiously, hens to yield eggs in astronomical numbers and wicked people to become abruptly good. However, the Bishop of Leon grew increasingly concerned about the state of Amador's humility — especially as Amador's miracle count now equalled Christ's. The Bishop therefore summoned him one day and ordered him, kindly, to desist from further miracles before he outscored the Son of Man.

On his way back to his cell, however, Amador spied a fellow priest topple from a four-storey balcony . . .

'Stop!' he cried to the falling priest, whose ties with gravity were immediately cut and his plunge was halted. 'Wait there,' said Amador, and hurried off to find the Bishop and explain.

An emergency meeting was held by the Bishop and his conclave to discuss the possible effects of a mortal having a miracle count higher than Christ's, and after an hour Amador was told he could perform the last miracle and allow the suspended cleric to float unharmed to earth. Then, so as to cause no status problems with Heaven, the hour in which the miracle had occurred was officially expunged.

Amador was inevitably canonised, and every year, on St Amador's day in Nicaragua, an hour is expunged from chronology. Morgan's call took place on St Amador's Day.

The Perennial Question

'Where have you been, you inconsidering, self-thinking damnable daughter?'

'Look, I'm sorry, Mom, they have this goddam saint's day here that . . .'

'And why are you contacting a loose unit like Harvey?' she snapped. 'If you have problems, you call me!'

'I didn't call Harvey, Mom,' she whinnied in the voice of lost leadership, 'I called the company and he answered.'

'Pah! Well, now you have caused me to come up to this accursed hog-vending town; so this emergency had better be serious!'

The most bloodcurdling quality of her mother's threats was often — as in this case — their violent irrationality; the Company had better be under threat of doom or Acomazuni wanted a refund on her ticket to O'Hare.

'It's real, Mom, believe me.'

'I will believe what I choose to believe. How do you know this plant is a perennial? What do you know of these matters?'

'I've been taking corn lessons from Dr Daniel, Mom. I go down to Peoria now and then. It's a perennial.'

'So what is it like?'

'From what I saw, it's about a quarter as productive as a hybrid. Trouble is, that's not too bad for a wild variety. But they'll never get anywhere near the production we can give them.'

'That is of no consequence to them; they are accustomed to starvation. These people see masochism as patriotism.'

'How much sense was Harvey making about the Stealth bomber?'

'None.'

'I didn't think so. I mean, Jeezas, which planet is that guy on?! Hiring the goddam Stealth, for chrissake!'

'Oh, that is no problem. We help to manufacture it.'

'We what?!'

'We sold to Northrop a protein-based phenolic that is mixed with asbestos for the cutting edge of the wings. It is used also in rocket nose-cones.'

'They make bits of spaceship out of corn?'

'Yes.'

'So why don't we just . . .'

'The plane is under litigation. There is a copyright wrangle. We sold our phenolic to Aerospace Defense Command while PennFuel were selling a coal-based product to Strategic Air Command. And at the same time Four Star sold a petroleum phenolic to Air Force Command, and Floricarb sold a salt-based one to Systems Command. Four phenolics to four departments. All of us have been in court for a year now. When we prove the Stealth belongs to our product, then it will fly. Enough. Tell me about this perennial corn. Who is growing it?'

'Well, the government, of course.'

'Why are you so sure?'

'Well . . . who else?'

'Any capitalist.'

'Mom, this is no time for wild-goose chases! The goddam Sandinista government's growing a plant that could blow us out of the *Fortune 500*! There they were sweet-talking me one night, when all the time they were planning to dump on us!'

'I will call you again tomorrow; now I have a few calls to make.'

'Hang on, Mom! What do you mean . . . You can't just . . .'

'Hold your noise, Morgan. Why do you always persist in being wrong?'

'Mom . . . Look, I'll call you, it's hopeless the other way; make a time and I'll . . .'

'Are you still wandering around with cloth in your ears, child? I said I will call you. Be in your room at ten thirty tomorrow morning!'

'They won't put you through, Mom! . . . Look, what do you mean I'm wrong? . . . Look, Mom, I'll . . .'

'Sometimes I wonder where exactly your father was stickin' that thing, to come up with you!'

Click.

The Night of the Fox

MORGAN THANKED COMPAÑERO Rodas for the use of his telephonic device. 'Ees myee pleesures,' he boomed in a language that was not quite Spanish.

It is nine thirty p.m. On the Night of the Fox. Okay, so she's in the middle of a company crisis, but if there's nothing more you can do about it for the night, forget it. Move on to other things . . .

Nine thirty. One hour before the Aeronica flight gets in from Panama, where Colin Fox will have joined it from Peru. She farewells the mushroom-headed proprietor, shakes his hand and departs with Daysi.

Nolando insists on driving her back to the hotel. It is a gesture; evidently she has been forgiven. They set off.

'You are bruzzers?'

Oh God, he's going to make small talk.

'Yes, I have two brothers. Farrell and Gordon.'

'Ah. I are bruzzers; siete.'

'Seven?'

'Jes. Seben. Maria José, Maria Carmen, José Maria, Roberto, Conchita Maria, Gil González, Pedro.'

'Oh. That's very interesting . . . Um. Donde?' She knew this word; it was an important part of asking for the bathroom.

'Quatro Managua. Dos Jinotega. Uno . . .' He shrugged and glanced at her shiftily. 'Uno Honduras.'

One in Honduras. A defector. Probably a Contra. She was looking at him steadily in the fitful orange glow of the lights of the Northern Highway, and could see him looking back from the corner of his eye.

'You, Honduras? You, Daysi, Honduras one day, maybe?' she said carefully.

He rolled his bottom lip over his top one, wriggled. 'Mabbe,' he said. 'Prehaps.' Then he shrugged. Then they were there. And it could well be he'd just told her he was going to defect to the Contras.

He leaned over the seat she had just vacated, to the door she was about to slam. 'Coshecha,' he said. 'Coshecha zeacinte.' He held up five fingers. 'Coshecha cinquo días. Fife dies. You are only fife dies.' Then he revved the jeep and rattled away through the cactus and palms that protected the hotel from the monotonous parade of military incompletion on the highway.

What the hell was a coshecha? Whatever it was, it was going to happen in five days. And it was going to happen to the zeacinte.

SHE WENT TO her room. She showered. She laved the secret clefts of her body, then swilled them free of soap. She let the deliciously soft water of Nicaragua have its way with her; invited a million little tongues she had never met before to run where they would across her wantonness. By bending or leaning forward she could direct them in hot rivers down courses of her choice. Drying was done briskly to whip every nerve ending to attention and to ensure all-over smoothness. Ah yes; smoothness was the order of the day on the Night of the Fox. Standing contentedly in front of the mirror, she rubbed herself with talcum.

On the bed lay her black camisole; her wide panties of silk. When she stood exactly to attention, she knew, the hem of the bodice — which came down to the bottom of her ribs — stood out four inches from her abdomen. Perhaps four and a quarter inches when her nipples were hard. The panties curved gently from her navel to her groin at the front, and so tightly across the swell of her buttocks that they shone like silver. At the sides they hung loose and open at the hem. She will put them on in ten minutes. The plane will be here in fifteen minutes.

She was walking from the mirror to the bed when she remembered it wouldn't. It would be suspended in the sky, like a dangling priest, for another hour! Because it was St Amador's damn Day! Another hour of waiting! Dammit! Why today? This was Fate's fault! Fate must be taught a lesson. She would tempt Fate. She detoured from the bed and the sumptuous, Miss Driffeld-inspired lingerie, to the wardrobe, and there extracted a wide denim dress and matching halter. She hauled them on. And nothing else.

Quivering with the risk, she walked barefoot into the courtyard. Beneath the circular inspection of Freddy the Friendly Fruit Bat she walked to the pool; looked down at herself in the motionless waters, looked up at herself as she held her hem over the edge. The light faded into darkness about halfway up her thighs. How discreet. Could Freddy see any further up her legs with his little sonar? Vreddy the voyeur; Preddy the pervert.

She shivered with warmth and went into the bar. Clad only in denim. Her riggish bits were so real to her, so powerfully in attendance, it was like entering with a group of friends!

She drank a Nica-libre. She checked the skulking shadows for poor old Roger; this was the very night he'd turn up of course. Mind you, let's be honest here; if Colin Fox were to go down somewhere in the Costa Rican jungle, or if St Amador's Day were extended, she'd be on the phone to the Mr Muesli Relief Services before you could say, 'Get your plumbing snaked!'

She had another Nica-libre.

And . . .

BLAZING LIGHT. BIRTH! Arrrgh! Stipples in the light; sand dunes. No; ceiling. Her eyes are open. Pullulations of irate mosquitoes, caught in the spotlight. Somewhere to her right a voice, urgently childlike. 'Morgan!' She turned her head, closing down nine-tenths of her sight. Colin Fox, grinning like a skull. Beside him, La Swartzkopf, Bianca, somewhere between a smile and a pout;

sucking small lemons. She had the abdomen of a wasp. She had a lot of wasp about her, come to think of it. 'We've just got in.'

'Wozztm?'

'What? Time? Oh, twenty past two. The plane was delayed in Panama. But we're here now.'

Are they? Is he?

'I was asleep.' She was leaning upwards on her elbows. Her voice was absorbed in her throat by a quag of fleshy, foul-tasting phlegm.

'Would you like a drink?' He held out a bottle of Zinfandel as you hold out steak to a guard dog. She took it, swilled the acrid liquid round her mouth. Some of the caked phlegm dissolved in the acid and went down with the wine. Colin Fox was sitting on the bed. He bent down and kissed her temple. His breath reeked. Or was it hers, bouncing off his cheek?

'What does coshecha mean?' she croaked.

'Harvest,' said Bianca.

'Listen, Morgan,' whispered Colin — why was he whispering? — 'Remember the night I went away?'

'You stayed here,' she said. Bianca's eyes narrowed.

'Yes. Well, this is the time we talked about then.'

'You've been to Peru.'

'Yes.'

'Up a mountain.'

'Yes.'

'Did it work?'

He glanced at Bianca then bent down and engulfed her in fumes again. 'Do you want to find out?'

Morgan was staring at Bianca through one eye. Bianca was looking over her head; there must be something interesting on the bedhead. A lizard perhaps. She was trembling slightly, as if jiggling her foot.

'Would you like me to stay?'

'If you want.'

'I do.' A long pause. Their stares formed a triangle: she looked at Bianca, Bianca looked at Colin, and from the corner of her eye Morgan could see Colin staring at her. 'It's my last night.'

'Yes. You can't get out of it.'

'No. I leave at three p.m.'

'My mother's phoning at ten thirty a.m.'

'Oh.' The pause re-formed. The significance of her statement was analysed and found wanting. It was dropped, like a leaf in the coppice. 'Bianca — doesn't want me to go.'

Bianca was looking rather as if she wanted everyone to go.

'You have to. You can't get out of it.'

'What I mean is, Bianca doesn't want to go.' Silence. 'Bianca wants to stay here. With us.'

'Here? In this room?'

'Yes.'

'In this bed?'

'Would you like that?'

'You mean . . . all of us.'

'Have you ever done that?'

'No. Not with a woman. What do you . . .?'

'Do?'

'Yes.'

'Well. I ganch and she gamahuches.'

'Pardon?'

'Well,' and he bent near and whispered, 'why don't we demonstrate?'

In this bed, her bed, Colin Fox will demonstrate the ganch and Bianca the gamahuche. Ganching and gamahuching will ensue. Or vice-versa. Or both at once . . .

Suddenly, like steam through her veins, roared the spirit of the Manitou, the wrath of Ojibwa, the mother in the daughter! She, Morgan Moran, Practising Non-Virgin, was not enough! She was inadequate; alone, she was insufficient to quell the fire in this man's haematose loins, to exhaust the potential of his super-charged intromitter! Is that the case? Is that how the world is seen? Well, then let war be waged upon cobs other than corn!

Her denim halter buttoned at the front. She undid the two stiff brass buttons. Incongruously the thing stayed in place. She shook it down her arms and away. She could feel the pressure of his eyes upon her nipples.

Of her skin she showed him plenty
Turned his thoughts to furside inside
Get the bastard's skinside outside . . .

'Colin,' she said, 'could you go and have a drink? For me? Come back in ten minutes. This is new, I need . . .'

She could see thoughts crossing his eyes, flicking like the letters on those big information boards at airports. Then he glanced at Bianca and back to her. He nodded. He stood, moved behind Bianca, kissed her on the nape and said, 'All right. Ten minutes.' And he pushed Bianca gently forward. He departed; the door clicked.

Morgan held out her hand . . .

From somewhere, in a language last used when she was less than one, she was communicating with the dour, beautiful, dark woman. She was heady with a feeling of peace. And trust; but also of power. She was master here; the relationship was established by the touch of a hand. She was free; there were no games to play! Well, only one . . .

Bianca unsmilingly unbuttoned the black muslin blouse she wore. It opened to the middle, then she hauled it over her head. She had unshaven armpits. Her skin was white, with a smattering of faint freckles between her breasts. Her ribs were prominent and her breasts small. But so astonishingly did she taper from her shoulders to her waist that, had she been six inches taller, she would have come to a point at the navel. And below there, her hips swelled at an angle of consummate generosity. She was a marvel of compact geography, swooping voluptuousness created by a few inches of physical difference. She leaned forward, placing one knee on the side of the bed.

'One moment,' whispered Morgan. She sat up. Suddenly the very faintest of smiles insinuated itself upon her lips and her eyes flicked, for a second, past the glossy black, already-tousled hair of Bianca, past her cheeks and lips, already deep deep red — to the door. Their eyes held again, then Bianca smiled slowly for the first time, stood, walked to the door and locked it.

DRINNNNG! ARGGGH! LIGHT. Birth. Damn. Estuarine smells. A faint, hermaphroditic dissatisfaction. Ten thirty! DRINNNNG!

Morgan grappled for the phone.

'Jeez, Mom, I'll never know how you . . .'

'And I'll never know how you could do that to me.' Colin Fox. Holy Toledo! The spurned man!

Bellicosity. Front it out. 'I guess men will never understand women, that's all.'

'If I completely understand what you just said, I presume it makes absolutely no sense to me at all.' Peevish. And way too clever for her present mental state.

Pathetic collapse. 'I'm sorry, Colin, it was all very sudden.'

'At least Bianca had the good grace to come and apologise.'

'She came to see you?'

'Yes. She apologised for locking the door. Then she locked my door — from the inside.'

Frailty! Good. Frankly the experience had disappointed her. It was like drinking a cup of tea in a moving vehicle. You can never quite come to grips with it; its substance eluded you somehow; at the bottom of the cup you're still thirsty.

'She's just left actually.' A hint of testy pride. 'At least she dignified our farewell with an appearance.'

Oh God! Thirty-five after ten! 'Colin, look, I'm sorry, I need to clear the phone.'

'I see. I know. International call is it? We mere mortals must troop off down to Telecor, but you get your calls in your room, right?' His disbelief had a ring of pessimistic conviction; the sort of perverse conceit of Eeyore.

'Yes,' she said, and braced herself through the sighs and tuts of telephonic melancholy that followed. 'Look, come on over,' she said. At least it would get him off the phone. 'I want you to.'

And she meant it. As she waited for the door and the phone, she realised she really meant it. What you miss, ultimately, with a woman is sacrifice. For true physical release there must be an offering to the pantheon of coitus; a giving of bread and wine at your naughty little Eucharist. There must be a great messy bursting forth of the fruits of your endeavours, then a shrivelling, a sadness, a death. You've killed the bastard yet again.

It's got to be a man; it's built into the family genes, and it's manifest in every culture — get 'em, drain 'em; suck out their essence! Their end is built into their beginning: beast of burden, lamb to the slaughter. You can't do that with a woman; there isn't the tension, the prodigious difference; you're both from the same planet. She looked forward to his arrival.

'I KNOW IT'S not the most loving way,' she'd cooed to him. 'But she's going to call any second now, and anyway, who wants to start with superlatives? You're only halfway through the twenty-four-hour super-cycle, don't forget.'

She had the phone on the floor and reached for it easily when it rang. There was the usual graceless prelude: 'Well, I have done my best to rescue us from the mire in which you dropped us, and I have succeeded. I could not get in touch with Bobby because one is not allowed to ask him about things he officially does not know, and there are many things about Nicaragua he does not officially know. Nor does anyone, it seems.'

And with half a mind Morgan listened to one of the most important phone calls of her life. All anybody seemed to know about Nicaragua, said her mother, was that they had never heard of someone called Ollie North. So many people had not heard of him that she telephoned the Old Executive Office Building and asked for him. He had answered immediately and, after listening to her problem, kindly put her into contact with one Aldolfo Calero, who by fortunate chance was about to mount a jet attack on the road out of San Rafael del Norte. It was to be rendered unusable before the annual Somoza Day battle. It was the deepest raid the Contras had made into Nicaragua for many months and, as it happened, Señor Calero knew exactly where Humberto Tapia's farm was. He had stayed there once. In fact he was a relation. 'He is a very kind man, this Señor Calero,' continued her mother, 'and his fee was very reasonable. He called me one hour ago to say that zeacinte was made extinct last night.'

There were lots of questions Morgan would have asked under other circumstances. She didn't ask any of them.

'You are well?' her mother said finally.

'Yes, sure, I'm fine, Mom. Seems our troubles could be over?'

'Yes. Perhaps I expected you to be a little more — emotional about this matter.'

'Oh, I'm emotional, Mom. I'm emoting here, don't worry about that.'

She had replaced the receiver.

'Thank God,' muttered Colin Fox. 'Now please allow me to get out of this preposterous and humiliating little doggy . . .'

The phone rang. Uncanny. An eruption of calls on a hitherto dormant line. 'Stay there,' she said. She reached down for the phone.

It was Compañero Salas-Ostrada. 'I know it was you,' he hissed. 'It could be nobody but you. And I know why!'

'I'm sorry, Mr Salas . . .'

'No you are not. You made a vicious and unprovoked attack on a farm in Pantasma last night, and . . .'

'Mr Salas, that's ridiculous. How the hell could I . . .'

'For revenge! Because Coca-Cola destroyed Acomazuni Enterprises. You are a pillager of my country!'

'Mr Salas, I don't have to listen to this.'

'Don't you? Do you deny planning the destruction of the only crop of zeacinte in the world?'

'Well of course I do!'

'You were seen there! Two days ago!'

'Your daughter doesn't work in a restaurant there, does she?'

'What? What daughter? What nonsense is this?'

'Never mind. I think I'm entitled to go anywhere I like in this country, Mr Salas, without being accused of treason by a hysterical fizzy-pop maker!'

'You are a pillager of my company!'

'This has got nothing to do with your damn company!'

'You destroy Coca-Cola property and then you . . .'

'Come again? Listen, Mr Salas, I think I'm losing the plot here. Coca-Cola property? What property?'

'Oh, very clever, young lady! Yes, you act the sweet innocent! Well, I didn't come down in the last shower! We would have been completely independent of Agrisync within three years!'

'Who would have?' Wraiths of remembrance, intimations of Nolando's voice. It hadn't been the unhairy-arses, it wasn't the government. It was 'other people' — Compañero Coca-Cola!

'Coca-Cola Nicaragua! With access to our own source of HS 90, we could have put out a Diet Coke at half the price of Pepsi!'

'What the hell has this got to do with me? What the hell are you talking . . .?'

'It's impossible to take HS 90 from Agrisync Hybrid; you know that! We can't get enough and the price is too high. With zeacinte we would have our own national supply of High Syrup 90. Twice as sweet as aspartame, half the sugar content! We would have wiped Pepsi off the map!'

'And Agrisync, incidentally.'

'Not incidentally, no,' he returned nastily.

'Well, I'm sorry you lost your crop, Mr Salas,' she grated, relieved to have a knoll of high moral ground, 'but it seems to me you were going to turn this nation's major food source into a cash crop! You would have starved your country to death!'

'We would have increased the GNP by a billion córdobas; two hundred million US dollars! Is that starving it to death?!'

It was no use arguing; anyway, there were more pressing imperatives. 'How was it done?'

'Jets. Napalm. Total destruction.'

Yeeyha! 'Well, just ask yourself, Mr Salas, where on earth do I lay my hands on jets and napalm?'

'Honduras.'

'Look, use your brain, Mr Salas!' she shouted, disconcerted by his intransigent belief in her guilt. 'You personally know the trouble I've had getting calls into the States, let alone a country I can't speak in!'

'Calero! You used Adolfo Calero.'

'Never heard of him!' She meant it when she said it; remembrance flooded over her a second later, but she said nothing more.

'You've allied with Pepsi to bring down Coke! You're trying to destroy the only Real Thing!'

Before he could go into his mantra of the Pepsi/Coke cosmogony, she hung up. 'Who's Calero?' she said.

'Oh God,' said Colin Fox, 'oh God, oh darling, oh . . .'

'HE'S COMMANDER-IN-CHIEF of the FDN Armed Force in Honduras,' he said later. It was her second time and his third; she didn't count the little doggy.

It was that glorious ending — or interlude — when you lie smiling secretly, the libation to the two-backed gods drying across sheets, thighs — everything!

'Why would the Coca-Cola man hate him?'

'Calero used to be the Coca-Cola man. He ran the company here. He left Coca-Cola for the Contras.'

The first Mr Coke had emigrated to Pepsiland.

She lay in the crook of Colin Fox's slightly musty armpit and closed her eyes. When she opened them again she saw, for one second — herself — with perfect clarity. Unmistakable; smug; in a mirror her mind had conjured on the ceiling. She examined herself in the memory of the mirror. Fronds of light black hair had been whisked from the restraints of her braids by tumult, the peaks of her severe cheeks were red. Her dark eyes were lustreful with triumph over anarchy and her deep-lipped mouth was open as she panted. Her! She closed her eyes. The mirror was now on her lids and there was Mr Salas-Ostrada; behind her; deeper inside her head. And so was Nolando, José Luis, Roger Muesli, Humberto, the jet pilots . . .

By thinking of them, one by one, then quickly opening her eyes she could momentarily see what they saw. What they would see if they were really here. Remarkable! Astonishing! Somehow she had tapped into the male visionbank. She was a rogue female computer nerd who'd hacked into the mainframe of masculinity! In her mind's eye she placed these male orbits over her own, like spectacles, and rose from the bed. .

She wandered, so it seemed, through the corridors of the hotel, through the streets of Managua and of Matagalpa; she mounted the back of an Aeronica quetzal and soared above the bright, jungly gradients, the tightly cropped plains, the nacreous steppes of mangrove and marsh — long fields of dynamic Agrisync, the scar tissue of blasted zeacinte; over silent towns pompeiified by war, violent armies with muddy guns, three-wheeled military vehicles going round and round; plodding oxen, leaving behind them in rocky fields their grooves of boustrophedon infinity. And what did she see as she looked down, naked, through her new eyes? What did she descry across the face of Nicaragua? The answer did not surprise her; it made her laugh. She saw Pepsi at war with Coke.

She left Nicaragua that day with Colin Fox and the desperados.

FIVE MONTHS LATER she learnt that zeacinte was being grown in New Zealand.

BOOK THREE

PART FIVE

Space: The Final . . .

In early '83, Agrisync put a proposal to the National Reconnaisance Office of the Pentagon. The proposition was as follows: to build a fleet of ten spy satellites, each equipped with a VLT (visible light telescope), an IR (infrared) imaging and spectroscopy instrument, and a pointing and telemetry system for transferring information to the ground. The space-age-old problem of keeping the infrared detectors cool enough to ensure they didn't photograph their own heat would be solved by suspending them from the outside of the craft. The spy satellites would travel in convoy in a wide north–south orbit, from longitudes 30 to 185 degrees, monitoring the crops of the USSR, the Middle East, India, China, Indonesia and the Far East, and South and eastern Africa — the agricultural produce of every enemy the Pentagon could possibly conjure.

That was proposal #1, christened Mapping Agriculturally Interesting Zones on Earth — MAIZE (because all such projects must have a clever acronym). #1 MAIZE, especially its budget, did not exactly set Pentagonal enthusiasms afire. After all, satellites retailed at a hefty ninety-three million, and there were covert growls along the lines of 'What's the goddam military application of a field fulla hominy grits?'

Proposal #2, however, immediately rekindled patriotic interest by equating crops with death. From a combination of the MAIZE charts and the Aeroflot domestic timetable, explained Agrisync experts, more destruction could be wrought upon the Evil Empire than would result from a 20 MIRV strike. The method was simple, cheap and undetectable: where the route of an Aeroflot service (the only other airline to issue umbrellas to its passengers) was found to lie over a substantial agrarian zone, a small disseminatory device — made by Agrisync Engineering in Kalamazoo, Michigan — would be attached to the outside of the plane by a secret agent posing as a passenger. When the plane was over the crop, the agent would electronically trigger the release of a cloud of Agrisync chemicals from the device. This pot-pourri of viral diseases would dust the crop and poison it, ensuring regional starvation, famine, plague and the probable collapse of local infrastructure. From two hundred miles above, the KH-11 cameras of the MAIZE craft would monitor the results. Videos would be available for the Pentagon.

Preposterous clap-trap! The beastly little disseminator was a myth, and never built. But the satellites were. Oh yes, the satellites were built, for that was the idea; that Agrisync would obtain a fleet of hi-tech crop monitors in the sky, complete with command and pointing systems and data-crunching HQ in Kalamazoo, all paid for by the National Reconnaisance Office of the Pentagon. Since early '84, Agrisync had commanded the world's only private agricultural space spy system.

ONE OF THESE satellites circled the earth at longitude 175 degrees. It was called Strategic Observation Base #10; SOB 10 for short. SOB 10 was primarily programmed to scrutinise the huge bilberry farms of eastern Siberia, but far to the south, after curving around the South Pole, it came within observational range of the bifurcate islands of New Zealand.

The agriculture of this ungripping nation was of no consequence to Agrisync, but the intense thermal area of the central North Island was a useful calibration point for SOB 10's infrared instruments. And thus a fragment of New Zealand was monitored by default. Every three days the Key Hole (KH) camera of the silver spy would lock on to the abrupt cliffs of Cape Palliser. As if aroused by land, after five thousand miles of ice and sea, the penile lens would protract and aim itself down through the shimmering ozone vacuum above New Zealand. Click, click, click. Photographs, by the thousand, in grids of two acres, click click click, of the oblongs of agriculture — fields lying on the ground like discarded tickets after race day, amidst the black of forests. Then, click click click, at 38°30' the disturbing, female colours of vulcanism; then the chemical green of Waikato grasslands and Coromandel swamps, click click; sea, a final droplet of land — click — Great Barrier Island: then infinite ocean once more. Unclick.

Of all New Zealand — two long islands containing every known form of geography — only this northerly stripe was scrutinised. For once SOB 10's compendium of instruments was calibrated and primed, the tiny silver ball would close down, ignore the verdant jigsaw-puzzle-piece of northern New Zealand and, battening to the nebulous bow-wave of its never-ending fall, sleep across the Pacific until Siberia, where, Kraken-like, it awoke.

The fly-over of New Zealand, from Cape Palliser at 41°35' to Needles Point at the tip of Great Barrier Island at 36°1', took four minutes. Fifty-two seconds into the traverse, SOB 10 passed over Massey University, Palmerston North. The SOB photographs showed an uncluttered, pleasingly vegetated campus. Experimental crops of grain grew on the warm flat fields that extended jaggedly out from the university like a compass rose. Click, click. The fate and progress of these crops was sent to HQ Kalamazoo in the form of a thousand intangible Cubist photographs. There they were translated and perfunctorily monitored: 'Standard cropping patterns: 3,300 acres of barley, 2,300 of wheat, 600 of peas and insignificant but consistent quantities of sunflower and canary grass . . .'

Special, if not overly enthusiastic attention was of course placed on Massey's corn: 'Corn: 600 acres. Sown: 10/20/86. Canopy closure: mid-December.' Canopy closure was the sprouting process; from mid-December the corn was detectable as a bright green mass of young leaves, and the percentage of the company product being grown by New Zealanders could then be gauged.

There was sometimes a minor event of which to take note. For example: 'Massey University has developed corn variety with high alpine tolerance; of some interest to general agriculture. Market intervention suggested if commercial contra-advantage to Agrisync ensues from new variety.'

Then in mid-December 1986, an extra field came into the focus of SOB 10; a three-acre plot of corn, planted, unusually, two miles due east of the major cropping area. It should have been of little significance. It wasn't. It was of stupendous significance. For SOB's read-outs showed that the crop had a unique spectroscopic signature.

Which revealed a unique molecular structure.

MAIZE HQ Kalamazoo assigned full-status analysis to the Massey crop. For weeks before Morgan or Harvey the Toot was aware of the crisis, Agrisync white-coats in Kalamazoo pored over blurry IR photographs and crazed spectroscopic graphs of wavelength and intensity. Until Friday, 2/1/1987 . . .

2 January, 1987

At the beginning of that day Morgan Moran was in a deep meeting with the Board. The subject, coincidentally enough, was Cere-star, which controlled MAIZE, the cereal spy in the sky. Harvey the Toot was speaking.

'That's right, a leveraged buy-out. It's a slider, Ma'am Chairman; we jus' put Cere-star into hock and raise the duckets we need fo' buyin' the whole company off the stockholders without botherin' them with petty details like that we're actually doin' it. Plus we raise a l'il extra bank fo' our individual wherewithall fo' buyin' into the scheme at a rate that will jus' so happen to give us complete ownership when we sell it back to the public. In this way, fellow perps, we don' forward no personal funds into this scheme, but we take personal charge of the divvy, which my people calcolate'll be nett half-billion in three years' time!'

A phone jangled on Morgan's desk. She raised it and swung away from the Board on her high-back swivel chair. Back-on she must have looked like a tawny version of the Slab in *2001*.

'Yes, yes. Fine, anytime,' she murmured absently. A routine request for a meeting from someone in Kalamazoo. She looked idly at the wall in front of her. It contained a framed Mondrian — lots of little squares and straight lines in uncharacteristically dull colours . . . Hell, that's the window! Reality was a little deceptive at forty-five storeys. You were too high to see the ground but not high enough to see the sky, which was somewhere behind that wall of seventy storey blocks out front. So nothing moved out there. No people, no clouds. The window became another painting, and got treated as such.

'Fine; yes. Ten thirty tomorrow, here. Did they say what it was about?' She confined irritation to her face, keeping it from her voice as she acknowledged the reply. No. Top secret. She'd learn tomorrow at ten thirty. The power of the lackey. She swung away from the living still life. 'Some guy from Kalamazoo. Harvey and I will deal with it tomorrow. Okay, where are we?'

Where indeed? In the depths of paranoia, that's where! Since the takeover, every action had had an equal, opposite and sinister reaction. Haunted Board members, still raw from the viciousness, cowardice, fear and deception released by the takeover, hunched across the table once more, poached eyes slithering from one untrusted member to another. There is half a billion dollars in the offing here, and some percentage of it will accrue to each of them. But what percentage? What if their percentage is the smallest?

LBO: Part of the Story

PART-CAUSE OF THE paranoia lay in the web of ownership in which Agrisync was entangled.

Agrisync held a fifty-five percent interest in Ebony Enterprises, which held a fifty-one percent interest in Cere-star, owner of the MAIZE Project.

Cere-star invested in Agrisync, which had large minority interests in MAIZE, as did Ebony Enterprises, which also invested in Agrisync. All of the Board were on some of these companies, some were on all, and several were on one. So who owned exactly what, and how much of it, was a deep conundrum. It would have been of little moment had not Harvey the Toot waved the irresistible carrot of a leveraged buy-out; an idea based, of course, on his pawnshop experience. Ah, the problems of a member of the Board; how to get more money than your friends and colleagues. Tacit little battles of proprietorship were fought desperately, politely and daily in the corridors of ITT&T, where the Board now permanently resided.

Kalamazoo

THE 'GUY' TURNED out to be a woman. Forty-five, untall, badly dressed in a yellow catsuit thing that rustled, thin hair already falling out of the perm she'd doubtless had yesterday to come to Head Office, and stained, bulging eyes — perhaps the wind had changed while she was glaring into her microscope. But she was from Kalamazoo — where they did things. Kalamazoo gave Agrisync a soul; in Kalamazoo they didn't make money, they made things. Well, they had to; Kalamazoo was smack between the broad-shoulder cities of Chicago and Detroit — exactly 148 miles from each. Kalamazoo made real things; things Hank would appreciate — tools, and trailer homes and ventilators, and taxicabs! In Kalamazoo, business was stuff you did in a factory or a yard, not a boardroom; and Agrisync, when it came to town, had been shamed into the same no-nonsense values.

In their mainstreet Kalamazoo Research & Development Section, Agrisync did things. Chemical things. Because Agrisync itself was owned by a chemical company.

In glowing laboratories within the seven-storey building, immense vats of crop pesticides, veterinary medicines, animal-growth regulators and food supplements gurgled and noxiously stewed. And it was on the land outside Kalamazoo, amidst the city's famous pansy fields, that Agrisync boffins had painstakingly tested the combinations of chemicals with which to coat their seeds. Some had been too virulent and killed the soil, some had reacted bizarrely with the seed's own enzymes, creating freaks; some killed the seed. But one — first found, ecstatically, in 1973 — sustained the delicate hybrid seed to perfection whilst gently toxifying the soil in which it grew. An industry was born.

Nowadays on that land dwelt the cattle, hogs and poultry — fattened upon company corn — that unwittingly tested the chemical products of Agrisync House; sometimes to their advantage, sometimes not. Here were created, with steroids, bile acids and hormones, new varieties of beast undreamt of by God; here were devised the prototypes of every American non-vegetarian meal: the nation's dinner never left the precincts of Agrisync Kalamazoo. And if that churns your stomach, Agrisync Kalamazoo has no doubt concocted an organic chemical compound to mend you.

Anyway, a woman called Dr Irma Tetley (the sort who says, 'Call me doctor' — although to be fair, she hadn't), with bloated eyes and sussurating suit, had come from Kalamazoo to talk about SOB 10. Specifically about the SOB 10 photographs being taken daily above New Zealand.

Harvey had heard of New Zealand: 'Noo Zeelan'?' he exclaimed. 'You come all the way over here to talk about Noo Zealan'? — Noo Zealand ain't banana an' it ain't republic, but it's all the res' o' that phrase.'

'Bananas are not our problem right now,' said Irma Tetley in a broadshouldered voice that backed Harvey up, ever so slightly.

'We nearly went to war with that place a couple of years back. Might have to go the whole hog this time.'

'We're in trouble with New Zealand?' said Morgan, respectfully but without great conviction.

'Well, we don't know what their motives are, but if they're doing what we think they're doing . . .'

All this time she had been wrenching open wide, flat leather satchels and extracting plastic-coated sheets of paper.

'Which is?' said Morgan, looking at Irma Tetley rather than the sheets. Let's get some authority imposed here.

'Well, here's your standard corn spectroscope spectrum,' said Irma from Kalamazoo, holding up a smudgy sheet in front of her face and advancing until it took up most of the perceivable universe. If Irma Tetley wanted you to look at a sheet, you looked at a goddam sheet; Round One to Dr Tetley. 'This is the sort of graph you'd expect to get, say, over cornbelt Illinois.' On the sheet held by her square, no-nonsense fingers was a jumble of squiggly lines. A series of figures ran up and down the edges of the page: WAVELENGTH was written across the bottom, INTENSITY up the side.

It was not very interesting. Then Irma Tetley's equally uninteresting face reappeared for a moment, said, 'Whereas here . . .' then vanished once more behind another incomprehensible sheet of craggy scribble. Line drawings done by an artist with compound Parkinson's, St Vitus's dance and the DTs. 'This is what we've been getting on the SOB 10 spectrographic read-outs since December; taken over Massey University, New Zealand.'

There was indeed a quantitive difference in the daubs. The New Zealand one had used up more pencil.

'So what exactly have we just learned?'

The question didn't even rate a pause. The graphs were cast aside and two photos held up; portraits of tiny blocks of colour, some of it spilling out, like those mad, flickering cubes they hide murderers behind on TV news items.

'Hydrolysis shows that the prolamin zein in this new stuff — photo on the left — has got the same DNA fingerprint as the protein in corn, but the molecular structure of something else. You see?'

No, Morgan couldn't see. They were simply spattered cubes in slightly different configurations.

'Nope,' announced Harvey the Toot.

'Thought not,' said Dr Tetley. Harvey flinched. 'You get an idea from this.' She dropped one portrait and pointed to a dense block of colour on the other. Yellows, green, brown, sudden red — like a wound — yellows again, black . . . 'Look at the heat coming off from this thing! Massive, it's radiating over three hundred times the tryptophan and lysine of standard *Zea mays*!'

'So what's our Agrisync corn missin' out on not havin' all this tryp . . . all this Latin stuff you mentioned?' enquired Harvey, commercial greed overcoming his fear of rebuke.

'Swings and roundabouts really,' replied Dr Tetley, surprisingly uncontemptuously. 'This new thing's got incredible protein content but almost no yield. The protein's all down here. Underground.' She pointed an unsharpened finger at what was presumably the ground. Near to it was the red. 'The only sane conclusion you can come to is this new stuff's got a giant root mass . . .'

Understanding dropped, with a clunk Morgan heard in her head, onto the lighted floor of her brain. Massive root mass . . . like a tuber . . . 'Oh God,' murmured Morgan, and a frog flopped from a swimming pool croaking 'Platero and I' to a zinging insect, whilst a whore with an Elvis-cut spewed flat champagne into the ear of a cowboy. 'Mr Muesli,' she breathed, and she was shaking. He'd betrayed her. The aroma of Nicaragua came back to her, refulgent with saffron, mud, cum and the neck of vultures. He'd shoved some seed into his pocket that day. He'd realised the significance. He'd set off back to Managua, arm around her, cobs of perennial corn in one pocket and a raging blue steeler pushing into the other! He'd headed back to Managua with stolen corn and aspirations of sexual congress! She shivered with the coldness of her rage. Well, let this be a warning. Baggy-faced, fubsy, nervously intimate Roger Morrison was an enemy. He had wished her ill. He had taken a move towards her destruction . . .

In the crystal of her watch she suddenly caught sight of her mother's adamantine features. No; hers! It was her.

'You okay, babe?' quacked Harvey the Toot. 'You's gone the colour o' asparagus pee.'

'I'm going to New Zealand,' she whispered. 'Friend of mine down there's got something belonging to me.'

The Day the Earth Spun Out

Once, a long long time ago, even before Lucille Ball, the earth was spinning moltenly along when suddenly a big blob of it flipped off the side and into space, where it kept spinning. Now, spinning things tend to become round, and before long the blob was globular and had turned into the moon. And the big hole it left behind became the Pacific Ocean.

For thirteen hours non-stop, Morgan would be travelling across the void where the moon had been.

Well, that was Harvey the Toot's explanation anyway, which tended to tread somewhat on the corns of the Gondwanaland theory and Wegenerian continental drift. Never mind. You couldn't gainsay the fact that for five miles under her backside right now, there was void. Serious void. It started out, about twelve feet under her seat, as stratosphere, thickening into atmosphere in the next few miles down to sea level. There it became the thickest void of all — ocean. Wet void; stupifyingly large, five miles deep and made up of water, salt, minerals, sharks, rays, plankton, whales, containers (some yachtsmen regarded the latter two as the same species), Japanese golf balls, treasure, kelp, jellyfish, plank-walked pirates, sardines (although she had heard there was no such fish, it was simply a name for any species that fitted in a can), airplane doors, tunny, bottled messages, horseshoe crabs, dolphin (Risso's), failed liferafts, John Dory, eels, dolphin (bottlenose), bathyspheres, toilet flushings, herrings, coral, driftnets, icebergs, desert islands, krill, Very pistols, turtles, oilbergs, squid (standard and giant), John West salmon and nuclear submarines. It would all be going on down there for the next half day of her life as she floated by in the jetstream. Floating in the jetstream. Flotsam and jetsam. Evidently, flotsam was what got washed overboard in storms — like containers; and jetsam was what got deliberately expelled — like the Japanese golfballs, belted over the side from driving ranges on the afts of Nipponese oil tankers. She plugged into her headphones, then into brandy, then into sleep. Her life was solicitously divided, by Air New Zealand, into segments of eating, drinking and sleeping, while behind her — beyond the curtain dividing her from Economy — the aluminium tunnel turned into a housing project.

'ORRR KLAND,' SHE HAD said very slowly and meticulously at LAX. Okay, so it said Auckland NZ on the ticket, but you couldn't be too careful — it was from one of these counters that some biffo, travelling domestic to Oakland, had been sold a ticket to Auckland in the Antipodes.

Now she sat in a blue seat, at the top of five miles of void, following his trail.

'I'll tell you, some of those prices are going to seem chickenfeed in a year or two.' It was a woman with severe purple hair and gigantic teeth, beginning the litany that would drive her as mad in New Zealand as 'compañera' had in Nicaragua. Stock market speak.

The food was good, and worth being woken for every three hours. She liked the fish every time. One hour out, the beef-eaters were apologised to: '. . . who chose beef as your first choice, but we are sure you will enjoy our . . .' Holy cow, they'd run out on the first meal! At standard airline culinary turnover rates there were another half-dozen to go! Dessert was a white compound of sugar crystals held in suspension by cream. And hey, they had kiwifruit down there too. The Sauvignon blanc was like razor-blades; maybe that accounted for the wrinkles round the lips of everyone who said they were from New Zealand.

NEW ZEALAND. SHE had been briefed. It wasn't such a small place. Sure, it was in the South Seas, but its GNP wouldn't halve if you stopped selling local culture at the airport: it wasn't simply one of those ukulele'd 'island paradises' — atolls made entirely of beachfront, with heavy-breasted maidens, weenie roasts of turtle and concrete-block shacks with sand floors and noisy, round, air-conditioning machines set in the non-opening windows, housing Chase Manhattan, Continental Illinois, First National Chicago and every other institutional laundromat. And its people weren't happy-go-lucky either; take your throat out most of them — just like people in any civilised country. No, it was a fair-sized, viable nation, which had split the atom then banned nuclear shipping — and you need a high degree of political sophistication for a volte-face like that.

The briefing had come from Mr Fellucini, of all people. It seemed a consortium of New Zealand businessmen had got in touch with . . . some of his Family, about setting up a casino.

They wanted expertise, they said, and were looking for the best. So they'd contacted Mr Fellucini. A price was set, then several New Zealand consortium members were flown out to Las Vegas and schooled in the arts. And the grafts, of course — black paint soaks into the wood, red sits on the top; the roulette ball skids on the red, so it's going to fall more often into the black. And so on.

Payment was made by the consortium, and the cheque bounced. It was not a great sum — under a million, but principle was involved. A member of Mr Fellucini's Family flew down to New Zealand and, in the way these things are done, got into the consortium's account. There wasn't enough to cover the cheque. He topped up the account until it covered the cheque and withdrew it all. People have to learn.

LBO: The Rest of the Story

Five miles up is a great place from which to get an overview. And one is needed about now, because there is more to the company Morgan is on her way to save than meets the eye.

For a start, as revealed earlier, Agrisync was not the trunk of the family tree. While Agrisync owned Ebony Enterprises, Cerestar and MAIZE, it was itself owned by Mauser Chemicals.

Chemical companies love seed companies, because chemico-seed companies provide a highly profitable catch-22. 'Use my pesticides, herbicides and fertilisers, and your crops will grow. Don't use my chemicals, and you must buy more seed — my seed'. Perfect. The no-win-for-you situation that capitalism is based on. Eagerly, great companies — Bayer, Ciba-Geigy, Monsato, BASF, Dow, Union Carbide, ITT, Du Pont and Sumitomo bought seed houses, planted their hybrid catch-22s and watched them grow.

So the Agrisync family tree is wider than imagined. Is it wider still? So wide that its branches can be seen from here? In the sky? On the way to New Zealand?

Perhaps. For the sap of the family tree is oil . . .

The History of New Zealand: Lesson #1

'There's this old cemetery on Cheltenham Beach,' said the wheezy historian as Morgan retched into an airpocket, 'down the end of North Harbour, across the bridge from Auckland. — No no, use mine, you're welcome. — Anyway, in this cemetery there's this grave of this old chap called Potatau. Well, he was buried on the year that Ernie Leonard's grandmother was born, and she passed away just a year or two back. Well, the point is, you see, that when he was a boy, this old Potatau met James Cook! Potatau died at one hundred and fourteen, and Ernie Leonard's grandmother reached one hundred and eight. Two people cover the whole span of the whiteman's history in New Zealand! Amazing isn't it?'

It certainly was. She'd helplessly wagged her head about seventeen times before he looked away; that's how amazing it was.

'And that's not all!'

She had suspected it wouldn't be.

'There's this parrot they had in Farmers — that's a big shop — anyway, it died a few years back now, but the point is, they say it was born in 1840! One parrot, going back to the year they signed the Treaty of Waitangi! Makes you think, doesn't it?'

It certainly did. She was heading towards a country that measured its history in parrots. She was thinking all right; my God was she thinking!

The History of New Zealand: Lesson #2

'Now you jus' be careful down there, chile. That country was made English in 1769 — an' at that time we wus at war with England! Jus' you keep in mind that they's all traitors down there, an' watch your back.'

The History of New Zealand: Lesson #3

In the early 1840s, the railway mania died down temporarily in England, and there was a short and curious stampede to that far pavilion of speculation: colonisation. Strange new sites were chosen for business — cattle companies in the Falklands, Eugenical Colonies in Chile, magnetic rock mines in Australia — and a 'Steam Navigation and Colonisation Company' was established to trundle capitalists to their loony new destinations.

And a street smart Londoner by the name of Edward Gibbon

Wakefield was cranking up interest in a place called New Zealand.

The Wakefield plan was compelling: you bought your parcel of New Zealand at one pound an acre, which was admittedly fifteen shillings more than an acre of America, but, as EG pointed out, the buyer of America still has to get there. Whereas! — buy New Zealand you get a seventy-five percent rebate off the purchase price for a first-class cabin including table wine!

The rebate worked so well that Australia-bound emigrants bought New Zealand Company, and made for the outback via Wellington! The other feature was, you got town land for the same price as rural land, which made the town property a real snip.

Naturally enough, most of the land was bought up by speculators. These London-based stockmarketeers were called 'colonists' to distinguish them from the poor schmucks, called 'settlers', who were actually going down there, to the dark side of the world.

To get the right sort of buyer, the land orders were called 'shares', and they changed hands in the heady 1840s at about twice the pace of ordinary commercial stock, and at profits of between a thousand to three thousand percent.

And here's why: the lottery. Every greed-frenzied, rotten-boroughed, malmsy-sucking, semi-gentried London-lubbered doddipol with the rack rents of fifty starving peasant farmers in his purse loved a good bet. And Mr Wakefield's colonies were a good bet. For example, a prospective new Wakefield colony — say, Nelson — is designated as a thousand-share region. When the thousand are sold, the book is locked off and your number is put in a little black metal barrel and twirled round. The order in which your number is then extracted is the order in which you could choose your site from the Company survey map. So the last share bought has as great a chance as the first of getting the prime real estate! The New Zealand lottery was the hottest gambling game in town.

(And as the winners celebrate in the Devil and the Cheshire Cheese, the ship that carries EG's brother William — who will actually buy the land — is still far out to sea.)

So, by the time the emigrants get to Nelson, the system is a sellout — but most of the buyers — the 'colonists' — are safely at home. However, Edward Gibbon Wakefield is also at home, so when the settlers find the Company map is wrong and there's actually about a tenth the amount of land they need for colony-building, to whom does Edward give the sites? To the colonists of course, because they're in the same town as he, probably in the same club or theatre. To hell with the settlers, they're twelve thousand miles away and flat broke, and so can't hurt a fly. So EG builds a town with nobody in it, while poor brother William desperately sets out into the backblocks to survey some more land for the extremely grumpy settlers.

That's why, in 1843 he's surveying in Wairau, sixty miles out of Nelson.

And that's when he comes into dispute with the guy who says he's owner: Te Rauparaha, Esquire.

And that's why, after hearing William's side of the story, and being a reasonable man, Te Rauparaha kills him.

So Morgan read, in *The Disreputable Scramble* by Sinclair Keith; background reading.

THE HISTORY OF NEW ZEALAND: LESSON #4

MAY 1980; THE CIA and Gecko Oil used 'their man in Australasia', a mild-mannered little stamp-collecting obsessive-compulsive who looked like Roland Rat, to establish a new banking operation through which they could launder heroin dollars in one of the quieter corners of the world.

This was told to Morgan by her mother. 'This might be useful if you need cash,' said Acomazuni Moran. 'Seeing as how Reagan has put a secret embargo on US venture capital into New Zealand now that they have gone anti-nuke.'

LANDING ON NEW ZEALAND: THE PRESENT

IT IS STUNNING to realise that people can live so far away and yet look so much the same. And look so unconcerned! Don't they realise? Are they not aware of their isolation? Have they never been warned? Maybe everyone coming to warn them has overflown the place and gone home via the Pole? Or do they know, and suppress the knowledge? Or are their fears just numbed by existentialism? 'Hey, you're alone out here! There's nobody else here! — Can you hear me? Are you listening? . . . Is anybody? Is anybody out there listening? Arrrrgh!'

Morgan's plane had landed at the same time as another jumbo, which had hoved into view, out of a mile-high mashed potato of cumulus, an hour or so back, and 'as if it were a Christian soul, they hailed it in God's name'. Paradoxically, having another tube of human beings alongside had exacerbated Morgan's sense of emptiness; coming across other life once was okay, but the odds on doing it yet again were astronomical.

They flew side by side in a little aluminium formation that somehow filled her with pride — until the last few minutes, when it occurred to her that there were another four hundred Customs-clogging baggage carriers aboard that other plane, and this was likely to be a one-jumbo airport. Damn them, damn their eyes; crash! crash! crash!

The enemy landed first. How dare they! Where were they from? Had they travelled five times farther than Columbus? Had they traversed the horizon a thousand times? Dollars to donuts they were from some woofie little nearby suburb like Tahiti or Guam. Equal rights for long-distance travellers! Rush the doors! Remember the Bastille!

'Welcome to Auckland International Airport, ladies and gentlemen. We would like to point out that New Zealand Ministry of Agriculture regulations require . . .' The rest is drowned by hissing. Two overalled men, abreast in each aisle, approach, arms aloft, propelled by steam. Mini heavier-than-air machines? Personalised jet propulsion? No, there seems to be no levitation . . . Fly spray! The waiters are dousing them with Agent Orange! '. . . as a precaution against fruit fly . . .'

'My husband's a chemist,' says the purple-haired woman, *who has a share portfolio of Kupe, Chase, Ariadne and New Zealand Salmon*. 'He says the spray doesn't kill flies at all. Just knocks them out. You'd never know would you? Flies all look the same to us.' Ye gods, the Mortein conspiracy; unscrupulous chemical companies recycling the same flies, causing consumers to expend their product on mistaken identities! She must tell Kalamazoo.

They disembark first! The doors of the enemy jumbo remain closed. Maybe some fruit flies have been discovered over there and are putting up a rearguard resistance.

First class first. Past ranks of hostesses wearing the crazed smiles of synchronised swimmers. 'Goodbye,' they intone gaily, but with funereal sincerity. When Air New Zealand say goodbye, they mean goodbye. Do you tip? The wheezy historian does not. Morgan does not also. When in Parrotsville . . .

Submarine-grey walls and ceiling, blue carpet. Blue carpet! Her dismay circuits are immediately catalysed by the colour, and she is awash in nostalgia, homesickness, fear and despair as she is swept like a neuron down the corridors of bleak memory and of Auckland International Airport, until, almost weeping, she bursts into a metal anteroom as bright as a surgical theatre. Free trolleys! She secures one and waits by the motionless baggage conveyor until a tractor drives in, towing a cage of luggage.

AMNESTY BIN. Subtle. On the Mexican border this bin is labelled CONTRABAND. Into this far friendlier Auckland receptacle you fling your heroin, cocaine, crack, firearms, explosives, Libyan dinars, auto-erotic magazines, snapping turtles, alligators, toucans — and exotic agricultural products. Here, the last stop before Customs, Roger Morrison should have discarded his zeacinte.

He had not done so.

He must be punished.

She has nothing to declare, and says so to officials in white, shortsleeved shirts and blue shorts. Shorts! Knotty, hairy, khaki-coloured legs protrude from children's clothing. It charmingly subverts the leering threat of officialdom; makes for a carefree givingness — she finds herself thinking up something to declare, just to participate. How sweetly unthreatening; how heartening it must be for the nervous drug courier.

She passes through blue screens into daylight, and her journey stops dead. There is no more of it left; she is here. Where?

In a long, narrow, sparrow-spattered airport foyer not far from the South Pole.

'Yes, just buy and hold on . . .'

'. . . going to a thousand, they say.'

Who are these New Zealanders? What do they look like? She observes them for the first time. Thick-waisted! Hooray! In the land of the thick waist the 26-incher is Queen! They dress tightly, emphasising in pastel the bulges above their kidneys and their round Akhenaten bellies. Their biceps are monstrous.

The men are thin; the tall ones stoop.

Natives; huge and square, mocha-coloured, flat-faced, heavy-chinned. They stand, like brown Kelvinators, in smiling groups. Sandals, and red and white sarongs. Activity! They rush towards the disembarkation point like flotsamming containers. Ah, relatives of the other jumbo's contents. Whoops of pleasure, reminiscent of Nicaraguan landing joy.

There are no porters.

Morgan walks to the taxi rank with her luggage and selects a cab. She stares through the gloom of the tinted window; a bushbaby sort of stare is returned through the glass. Impasse, until she faintly makes out the nail of an index finger. Ah. The cab ahead.

No, she discovers; the cab at the front of the line. Always and only, the cab at the front of the line.

'To the South Pacific Hotel, please,' into which she is booked for at least two nights. She sits in the back seat of a cab that has a Greek driver and no bulletproof screen!

'Don't you feel — vulnerable?' she enquires.

No no, she is told. No screens in this country. 'Anyway, with screen, no get stockmarket tips from back seat! Ha, ha!'

Once they are past the airport hangerobilia and the standard necropolis of airport motels, the city widens generously into views. Ahead is a low, curiously prominent hill with what is perhaps a Hiroshima memorial on the top. It's a mushroom cloud on a buckled stalk with a Polaris missile beside it. The nuclear cloud is actually a tree. Complex symbolism.

There is a feeling of almost stultifying harmlessness about the place, manifested by the cautious consideration of the driving. Cars tiptoe past each other like visitors to hospitals, and the signs — CAUTION, SLOW, GIVE WAY — bespeak a land of safety, laws, moderation and order.

She looks about her with wide-eyed wonder and is instantly asleep.

No money! She is awake, with none of the sheikels or pesos or zloties or whatever the hell they spend down here, and this goddam cabbie won't take US dollars! Won't take dollars! How come the Greeks got so dumb when they modernised from Ancient? The hotel will change her money, he tells her. Ah. The hotel does so. The cabbie drives his cab away, bearing rags of local currency. At least the exchange rate is not as baroque as the

Nicaraguan — instead of a dictionary-sized parcel, she receives a healthy Norman Mailer/Edith Wharton-sized wad.

Transactions at the lobby desk take place beneath the gaze of a fish. A swordfish it is called. She has seen them on the label of cans. This one is about as long as a tennis court. It is probably the biggest fish hanging on a lobby wall in the world. In Nome airport, so Hank had told her, is the biggest polar bear ever shot. Shot because it was the biggest polar bear ever shot. Sorry, fish; it's a tiddler's world.

Life's tuner has been turned down a little here; the pace of activity has perceptibly decreased. Noises are softer, people fewer, time moves as if under water. There is a resistance to movement, gravity is stronger, the molecules of the air are more tightly packed so that nothing free-wheels. Cars come to a halt more rapidly, pedestrians lean improbably far forward at WALK signs before toppling into motion again. The conditions impose a curious sense of purpose; you feel compelled to do things, otherwise nothing will happen.

Morgan sits in the house bar, shaken by the discovery that antipodean Black Russians contain no Kahlúa.

'They say the railways and the post office will be on the stockmarket by the end of the year.'

She has made a friend: Alain, of France. Alain has devised a new video method of teaching his language to English speakers, which he is unsuccessfully selling to New Zealand schools. He is slight, young and with an earnest baby face that makes him younger still. And of course a French voice; that most potent male instrument known to woman. In all, his youth and his voice inspire an urge for a night of passionate breast-feeding.

Within two Black Russians she is asleep. She is told this by a manager in yellow waistcoat who informs her, 'We are closing now, madam.' It is one twenty-five a.m. He has left her here all night? Why? Has she been sleepdrinking? Are New Zealand bars a place of rest? Irrationally irritable, she lurches towards an aluminium lift, electrocutes herself into wakefulness and spends the night weeping and alertly dozing in her silent room.

Plans

Breakfast. Coffee and Danish. Danish? No one here has heard of that stalwartly American breakfast. Ah, well . . . The menu. Yes. Hey! No hominy grits. No hominy grits! Now there's civilisation for you; any country that doesn't serve hominy grits just has to be sophisticated. Great! Celebration time. What's this here? 'Porridge'. Yes, she will have porridge, thank you. Anything that isn't hominy grits is just fine with her . . .

It's a long white room with a ceremonial overhead fan slicing the air conditioning; windows overlook a plaza dominated by a ferociously antipodean version of Rodin's Balzac, and on the walls hang portraits of South Pacific Hotels in Melbourne, Sydney, Brisbane, Singapore and Rarotonga. VISIT ANY OF OUR SIX HOTELS. Presumably you gauge your whereabouts from the one whose photo is missing.

'. . . dickheads who sold short thinking the market was about to collapse will have to buy back in now . . .'

The narrow end of the room is wall-to-wall-to-ceiling mirror so you can watch yourself eating: kinky.

You can also watch yourself thinking. She does so. Okay, so what does she know? That the zeacinte is on university land. Can she buy the land? No. Universities tend not to subdivide. Can she buy the crop? They would probably give her some samples, but would they sell her the entire thing? No. Scientists are iffy about entire things; extinction is an entire thing; they'd keep some back.

They would already be intrigued by zeacinte; the odds are very high that they've never seen anything like it before. Did they yet know what it was? From its structure they doubtless had a fair idea, but they'd be waiting for flowering and fruiting before they came to any conclusions. Scientists never come to conclusions, it's a known scientific fact. But they will be intrigued.

What about Roger Morrison? Did he know what it was? No one, as far as she could remember, had actually used the word 'perennial' that day, and he hadn't seemed to have any agrarian understanding. But he hadn't put the goddam stuff in his pocket for nothing, had he? He had somehow known it was important. It must have been her face; her expression. She glanced into the wall of mirror and dispassionately examined her face: stern, high-cheeked, clear-chinned, full-lipped, divine — no, modesty forbids — semi-divine. But with a mind of its own! The damn thing put its own expressions on, not hers. Damn it, whose face was it anyway? Her face was momently wearing an expression of peevish resentment; hers or its? Jeezas, a dualistic duel with her own face! She glared away from the mirror, across the murmurous room, searching for Alain. Gone; peddling his wares. 'Allo? Joo ouant le ouey for learn spik ler bootifool lengarge mine?'

She returns her mind to her mission and awaits her breakfast.

'*. . . so Tip Top sued the strikers and went back up thirty points on the index . . .*'

What was Roger Morrison's aim? To destroy capitalism? Feed the starving masses? Make a fortune? Silly question.

Well, one thing she mustn't do: barge into Palmerston North all guns blazing, and no plan. She'd have to stake it out, appraise the situation. At the moment she had surprise. No one — outside a UFO freak — seriously expects to have their gardening perused from Space. So, they didn't know she knew about them, great; but she didn't know enough about them, or anywhere near it. Information was vital. Her porridge was approaching on a little trolley, beneath a silver serving dish.

'Can you tell me, please, where I might find a good PI? . . .'

The waitress is walking away; Morgan is watching the rise and fall of her broad kidneys beneath the shoulders of her black skirt. Oh dear. The enormity of the task ahead quailed her. She'd painstakingly explained what a PI was, and the waitress had listened with her head cocked to one side. 'Citizens' Advice?' she'd murmured.

Morgan shook her head, slightly humorously, then lifted the lid on her breakfast . . .

DAVID HAY WAS his name; he'd been in the Yellow Pages under Prevention and Detection. He was big, strong, dark, good-looking — despite a mole and a gold-capped incisor — and with that sleazily, innocent, masculine confidence that sees double entendre as a compliment.

He was an ex-cop — a frontline hitman during a series of nationwide football riots they'd had here once — and doubled as a bodyguard when private-eyeing was slow. He'd once dived into the Tasman Sea from a marlin-fishing launch to rescue the gold watch of the Imir of Kuwait. In fact that's how he'd got into the business; he'd been seconded from the force for this Imir-guarding chore, been paid at the rate of five thousand a day, and had immediately resigned from the force to go into private practice.

He specialised in finding disgraced footballers who'd fled public outrage. He then either blackmailed them or sold their whereabouts to the papers.

He was as good as she would get here; a mélange of amoralities carefully copied from pulp fiction. He was hired and despatched to Palmerston North immediately.

TREES; IN STRAIGHT LINES! She'd taken a sightseeing flight while she waited, and they'd winged her down to some volcanoes.

'He's CEO of Forest Products and EMCO, which own Healing, Motor Corp and Group Rentals . . .'

On the way you fly over forests — with trees in straight lines! Unswerving ranks, mile after mile! Is further proof needed of The Great Watchmaker? The Ordered Universe? Trees lined up like they're on parade! Sheesh! God works in immaculate ways down here!

David Hay called from Palmerston North to say he'd need another day.

She went with Alain to Devonport, which is where the Cheltenham cemetery is, that houses the Farmers' parrot that had once asked Captain Cook for a cracker. Or something . . . Anyway, it soon became apparent that Alain had a hidden agenda. He wanted to see the ship that French agents had blown up in Auckland harbour.

It was, he had been informed, on the third quay to the right when you look back towards the city. It wasn't there! Passionate tears. These monsters had sunk the ship his country had blown up. Don't worry, she soothed, they would find it on the way back.

They had lunch in an upstairs restaurant '*. . . one quarter percent per quarter-hour, as long as it's for the stockmarket. Clock loans they're called . . .*' that looked back across the water (and empty quays) to the city. From this vantage there was a skyline; the only one in town. For some quaintly perverse reason, Auckland had turned its back on every method of arriving there — by road, rail, air — except the sea, the way by which nobody arrived. The air was astoundingly — disorientatingly — clear; distant things toppled distinctly over the horizon instead of fading into it; there was no haze, no shimmer, and consequently no perspective. The clean, crystalline little skyscrapers and the standard stone-pilastered, commercial palazzo-banks and municipal buildings lay undiminished by distance like a naïve medieval city portrait.

'. . . *twelve points up on last night's closing price!*'

They found the ship, the *Rainbow Warrior*. It had been moved two quays to the left. It was small, red, low in the water and listing, but it was enough. Alain stood at the bows, hand on heart, tears in eyes. 'We did that,' he whispered.

DAVE THE DICK returned next day.

Grisly! They get 'hacked off'! Morgan had shuddered and discreetly flicked her attention across Dave's clothed frame for evidence of mutilation. What has been hacked off? Hands, fingers, feet — all present. Surely not his . . .

Ah. It's a phrase, an idiomatic phrase. 'Hacked off' meant irritated, and Dave had been irritated to find when he arrived that Buzz Mehrtens was out of town for the day. He'd caught up with him eventually, however, and had 'an evening on the piss'. Buzz Mehrtens was owner of the bar frequented by Roger Morrison, and was an old and talkative friend.

ROGER'S STORY, BY BUZZ

BUZZ MEHRTENS HAD attended university with Roger Morrison. They had flatted together for several years. Then Roger had graduated, left town and disappeared without trace for ten years. Now he had returned some months ago and was living with his sister and her husband, who worked for the Statistics Department. Roger's departure, ten years ago, had been in some haste and had involved disgrace. Well, that was the official view; to many free spirits his departure combined haste and glory. Whichever, the said exit was occasioned by the exposure of an elegant scam he had been operating for some years. Roger was locally famous for his feats of brilliant subversion, but this was his masterpiece. For three years, between 1974 to '76 inclusive, Roger Morrison had been three bursaried students at Massey University, and three bursaried students at Victoria University, Wellington. He had enrolled his airy compatriots in a series of Stage One papers each year, assiduously completing assignments for them, as well as for himself. For safety's sake, his protégés always failed, to be replaced the following year by a new stable of bursary earners. Roger spent the first half of his academic week at Massey, then on Wednesday afternoons trundled down to the capital in his yellow Morris 1000. It was hard work, and none of the six of them ever scored much above C, but overall Roger earned an unofficial government salary of $18,000 a year, at a time when the average wage was seven thousand, five hundred.

He himself graduated from both universities in 1976, and was not exposed until his post-graduate year. Clutching BAs in History and English from both universities, he was sent down by a combination of faculty boards.

He had then decided to travel. He needed funds. He applied to Teacher Training College, received a post-grad studentship bursary and bought a ticket to London with his first six-monthly payment. His guarantor, Mr Morrison Snr, was obliged to pay off the bond, but, as ten years elapsed before he again saw his son, Roger had long been forgiven and the reunion was a fond one.

He had roved the world in those half-score years — Europe, Asia, northern Africa and South America. He had resided in Nicaragua for the last four years, then returned to his home town six months ago, to complete a translating commission for Fonbote SA, Nicaraguan publishers. He was rendering three pornographic novels, *Hot Nurse*, *Going Down at Trentham* and *Cunning Tongues* from English into Spanish (*Enfermera Caliente*, *Bajando En Trentham* y *Lenguas Astutas*). In return, Fonbote SA, had contracted to publish his novel, *The Death of the Inquisition* (*Muerto del Inquisicion*), in Spanish.

He spent his days working at his translatory chores, and his evenings either drinking at the bar of the Idiot & Peer with Buzz and friends, or escorting a Sri Lankan girl called Bindi to restaurants, theatres and cinemas.

'What does she look like? Is she beautiful?' What a ridiculous, irrelevant, unprofessional question!

Dave looked up from his notes and gave his thinking grimace, which consisted mainly of balancing his sliver of golden tooth on top of his bottom incisors. 'Nah, not beautiful. Bit scrawny for that. Though she's got a bit of meat when you think about it. They're funny — they can be thin, but have thick skin at the same time; know what I mean? Thin and soft. Western girls can't do it.

Face is all right; not . . . you know, not knockout stuff, not like someone else not a million miles from here, haw haw, but okay. Yeah, she's all right.'

Pity help the client who had to identify someone from Dave's descriptions. Anyway, it was ridiculously immaterial — and vaguely satisfying.

'She could go to fat, though; her father's got an amazing little pot belly. Holds his sari up with it.'

'What does he do?'

'Lecturer at Massey.'

'What in?' she said sharply.

'Something agricultural. I could find out.' He had failed. His tight bright leer sagged for the first time.

'No. It's okay. I'll find out myself.' It was time to go. 'What's a good time to meet him in this bar? Without the girl?'

'Early weeknights. From about half-four usually. They get a band in later — at eight — he generally goes home about then.'

'Who does he meet?'

'Oh, there's a little group of them; eggheads, all educated beyond their intelligence. Lawyers, journos. You know the type. Drink wine and eat feta cheese. The Lemonade Brigade we generally call pricks like that.'

THERE WERE NO Lemonades on view two days later when Morgan walked into the dimness of the Idiot & Peer. At uncomfortable tables made from barrels, two groups of three sat with copies of the local paper open at page eleven.

'. . . rule of thumb is they should be selling at at least twenty times earning.'

Roger Morrison, with his back to the door, was talking to a Maori man with reddish-black hair battened down with heavy gel. Mr Muesli was unexceptionally dressed in an overtight green sweater and unmatching jeans. The Maori guy was of stooping middle height, in a grey pseudo-Armani suit, white T-shirt and dark glasses.

The gelled Maori looked up at her, across the pellucid light of the empty bar. For several seconds he didn't move and there was near silence.

'. . . when City Realties re-listed . . .'

Then he pushed himself upright into a stealthy stoop.

'Hey, lookit this!' he said. He spoke in a growl, but in that babyish stacatto she gathered to be the native accent. Roger had, of course, turned. She didn't look at him.

She approached the bar. Roger, from the corner of her eye, was running his hand through his hair. She studied him peripherally. The granola colours of his face had turned inside-out — presumably in horror — taking on the piebald hue of a pepperoni.

Mr Gel was holding a cigarette like a pencil in his right hand and dipping up and down from the shoulders somehow, like a great crested grebe in mid-courtship ritual. She walked past the entranced Mr Muesli to the other side of Mr Gel and sat on a stool.

'Is this place fully automated or is there a barman?' she cooed sweetly.

Mr Gel paused, then seemed to come out of hypnotic sleep. Roger, behind him, was obscured. 'Hey! Buzz! You gotta customer out here!' said Mr Gel in Bob Marleyspeak. He turned back to her and began his dipping dance again. Was it for her or because of her? He had fine features, but over the bones of his face lay the drinker's standard lumpy mattress of flesh, bunching into creases around his action lines, as if his skin was slowly freezing.

Buzz arrived, short, sweet and in an apron. He had a face of startled redness, seemingly boiled in good nature. And a scaffolding of bristles on his head, supporting, like the aluminium frames of a greenhouse, a non-existent whole.

'Hi,' he beams. 'Sorry about that, I'm the cook tonight as well. Unless you're not doing anything?' He laughed, not waiting for an answer. 'What can I get you? Have you seen the wine list?'

'No, a Black Russian thanks.' She would not tempt Fate. 'Where I come from that's two of rum and one of Kahlúa.'

'Yep, I've done it that way,' said Buzz. 'You Canadian?'

'From the States. Nevada.'

'Yeah, I thought it wasn't quite Canadian, but we had a couple here from the university who used to have Black Russians this way, and they were Canadian.' He turned to her, suddenly humorlessly solicitous. 'Hope I haven't offended you, have I?'

'No. Not at all. I mean you might be English for all I can tell from accents.'

'Hey, no way!'

All this inconsequential jolliness — the hominoid version of bottom-sniffing — was icily cut through by the bubblegum voice of Mr Gel. 'Hey, do we get an introduction, or what?' He was still bobbing away in front of her, cigarette held in pencil mode.

She smiled forcefully. 'I generally don't converse with people in shades unless they're blind.'

There was a pause in the jigging; she was tensely aware this could be a dangerous moment. Then he amazed her by meekly discarding the shades, which he wrapped and put into his inside pocket, releasing a faintly pleasant smell of warm kapok. His eyes flared in what for him was intense brightness, then he said, 'Hey, Buzz, give us an introduction, man.'

'Oh . . .' Buzz was momentarily overwhelmed by the responsibility. 'Well, I'm Buzz Mehrtens for a start, this is Ted Nea, and that's Roger Morrison.'

'Well, hi everybody, I'm Morgan Moran,' she nodded to Ted and then turned comfortably back to Buzz, obliterating Mr Muesli with inattention, 'visitor to your beautiful little town and loving every moment of it. Tell you what you've got here, a nationwide golf course; the whole thing's so green and well cared for. It's beautiful, and so varied.'

'Yeah, they say it is,' said Buzz, taking the compliment personally. 'That's how a lot of people react to it. You staying long?'

'Oh, a day or two.'

'Great! Good to have you here. Staying locally?'

'In a place just down the road here, it looks like a stockade, the ah . . .'

'The Coachman?'

'That's the one.'

'Hey, come on, that's not how we do it!' Mr Gel — Ted. The feeling of danger returned. He was still standing there as if dangling from an invisible coathanger. The cigarette was now in his mouth and a hair of fine campfire smoke headed upwards into his left eye, which was dripping tears. He blinked only once. It was exquisitely painful to watch.

'Welcome to Aotearoa, girl.'

With excruciating care he put the cigarette in an ashtray, then approached, sexually harrassed her with both hands and jabbed his nose down on hers three times. He smelt of kapok and ash. It was divine! His nose was mouthwateringly soft and burnished smooth — perhaps by forty-odd years of nose-jabbing. It had the velvetness of a puppy's tongue. Her loins, to her horror, gave a little spasm of surprised interest.

'You're the Red Indian, right?' He reached his right hand across himself to retrieve the cigarette; everything he did seemed awkward. 'You're the one Roger was talking about.'

She leaned round Ted and looked at Roger Morrison for the first time. The treacherous Mr Muesli. His fawn skin now glowed palely, his expression was one of intense expressionlessness. 'Oh yes, I'm the one Roger was talking about, all right.' This was the moment.

You're in the spotlight, Mr Muesli, take the microphone.

Buzz has opened a bottle of white wine on a rather violent skewer attached to the bar and is replenishing glasses in readiness for the floorshow. She waits for Mr Muesli's apoplectic explanation.

'It hasn't been easy here, you know,' said Mr Gel. 'No way. You minorities over there think you're the way and the life; you think you carry the can and we all follow. But just think of it from the other way round. Put yourself in our shoes, eh? I wore a patch then — leather jacket. Not this Cardin stuff.' And he held out the lapel of his dark local suit like a menu.

Damn it, the moment was getting lost in social comment!

'Rode with a gang,' continued Mr Gel. 'Solidarity. Against who? Eh? Who'd we have to be staunch against here, eh? You had the KKK, the White Knights, the Bureau of Indian Affairs; you had James Meredith being shat on and shot at; you had riots against the Passamaquoddy and the Wampanoag; you had Wounded Knee and Martin Luther King stirring up white arses everywhere — and the Black Hills of Dakota. You had it made. What did we have? Hell, we had the National Party! We had the Society for the Promotion of Community Standards! Patricia Bartlett! We had *Listener* editorials saying we were scruffy. How the hell're we supposed to start the revolution on that?'

He looked slowly from Morgan to Buzz to Roger. They were nodding. They were glancing at her. Much was going on beneath the surface. At least it was a relief to get out of the glare of the fervent Ted, but hell, she didn't need this right now! The impact of her arrival was being dissipated in sociology.

'I mean it, you know, Rodge, Buzz?' attests Mr Gel. 'It's true. We didn't have a shit show.' Fervent nods. 'You'd cruise town — mean, full of hate — and people would ask you if you were Johnny bloody Devlin! You'd set about fortifying your headquarters with fences and barbed wire, and the damn Rotary Club turns up with a working bee! It was hard, Rodge, Buzz; I mean it, it was hard then, I'll tell you.'

She had by now joined the mass metronome of nods.

'We were ahead of our time, see? This country wasn't ready for us. Conditions were hell for us. I mean, jobs were easy, housing everywhere, no segregation, no racial tension. Shit, if you wanted to go to the pictures, you just went! Anywhere! Downstairs, circle — anywhere! No one tried to stop you. It was hard; you lived life in a void. Ten years we lived like that, that first generation of us; ten years of waiting, wondering if you were doing the right thing — you know, thinking what were gangs for? It was hell, Morgan, I'll tell you.' Her name startled her into attention. Holy Hell's Angels, there may be a test on content afterwards! 'This was the hardest place to be, all right; harder than where you were. While you was getting dumped on, we were just sitting here waiting to become necessary.'

'Sounds hellish,' she murmured, triggering a nodding frenzy.

'We wrote to Stokely Carmichael once,' he said suddenly, directly at her. 'Invited him out here. Know what he said?'

She didn't. She said so simply.

'Twenty-five grand. On top of expenses. And he wanted photos! Photos! Arrgh.' With a grimace of disgust he picked up the lonely cigarette, swilled it and held it in his strangely prissy grip.

'They'd gone loony by then anyway. People like him had all gone Moslem. Malcom X. I mean, what the hell do Moslems have to do with blacks?' His lips pursed in sudden suspicion. 'Indians haven't gone Moslem, have they?'

'No,' she said, 'we're still Christian.'

Buzz laughed. His brows shot upwards, sending a concertina of furrows across his forehead and into the skeleton of hair. He laughed long and hard, and she could see he was trying to clear a break between this conversation and another — any other. She would help. It was time. 'Well, Roger,' she purred, 'so you've been talking about me, have you?'

'I think people will always talk about you, Morgan,' said Mr Muesli in that soft, fine, brownly delicious voice. 'And I would defy them to do it negatively.' His eyes were calm; he had had time, during Ted's lament, to become accustomed to her presence. The faintly mocking humour of his tone smacked of confidence — he had also had time to plan. 'It is wonderful to see you, and I'd love to meet you soon to talk about old times, but I really do have to go. My sister is going out, I'm baby-sitting. I know I leave you in good hands,' he smiled; a wan copy of the sudden angelic radiance of Nicaragua, 'with my old university buddies here; and I just know I leave you with topics of conversation.' He stood up ungracefully, bid his adieus and departed. Oh yes, the wily Roger Morrison, king of the university stuntmen, had had time to devise a plan. The oldest plan of all — run!

In the Breakfast Room

Another breakfast room. She enters warily.

'It crossed the one fifty this morning . . .'

Was everything about New Zealand treacherous? Roger Morrison had betrayed her and her very first breakfast in the land had been a double-cross. Porridge! Porridge was hominy grits! Nothing could be taken on trust; she would rely only on *a posteriori* knowledge. Fortunately the Coachman, a curious mixture of real river stone and kitset fixtures, provided provable breakfasts: buffet. She had seen her fruit and yogurt before ordering, her eyes had rested upon the omelette and bacon that lay waiting in the steam tray. She was onto her third cup of coffee at the conclusion of a satisfyingly authenticated breakfast when Mr Muesli walked in. He was not unexpected.

'Put a coffee on my tab,' she said chillingly.

He did not seem chilled. He nodded and padded off to the bottomless-cup stand. He wore a pigeon-coloured sweatshirt, loose at the bottom, which his light-bulb figure filled out into a pyramid. Beneath, he wore beige slacks. In all, he looked like a small Christmas tree. He returned and sat on the stiff black chair across the table from her. Behind him, tense kitchen attendants refilled stainless-steel containers. Waiters scuttled librarially by. The mood was fitting.

'Look, I wasn't trying to cheat you, you know,' he said with a worried, raw sincerity. He sighed and spread his soft, pink, thick-fingered paws. 'It was mere curiosity. You were upset by what we found; I could see that. I didn't have a clue what it was, and you were absolutely not going to tell me. So I slipped some in my pocket, planning to get it analysed at Massey. I didn't know . . .'

'What? You didn't know what?'

'How on earth did you find it, anyway? It's only been out of the ground a couple of weeks, and you arrive from the other side of the planet. Satellite?' He gave a gag and went instantly white, as if he'd swallowed all colour in his face. 'You're not going to nuke it are you?'

'I wouldn't be allowed,' she said crisply. 'Nuclear war is not yet available to the private sector. I have, however, come here to get it back. All of it.'

His eyes held a disconcerting combination of confidence and concern. 'You can't get it back,' he said softly. 'I'm sorry, but you can't. I mean, it's not yours anyway, is it? It was as much mine as it was yours. You've got no legal right at all. And they want to know all about it now, so they're not going to hand it over just because you say so.'

'Aren't they?'

'No.' Said with a gentle adamance that irked her.

'We'll see about that. I very carefully read the laws of your country on the plane. I was handed a form telling me all the ways I could go to prison in your green, friendly, nuke-free little land — you seem to have as many methods of imprisonment as you have sheep — and bringing in exotic germ plasm is one of them. If I told the appropriate authorities that there was a crop of illegal alien corn growing here, they'd come in and destroy it. It's the law. It said so on the form. The seed police will march in here to destroy it, if I tell them, but from what I know of scientists they'd rather hand that stuff over to me, in the end, than let the rest of the world's zeacinte go up in flames. I'll go to them; explain the situation.'

He nodded. 'Very good,' he said. 'More coffee?'

'No.'

He stood and refilled a cup for himself.

'. . . *If everybody bought in, the whole country would be rich! No poverty, no unemployment! I think shares should be made compulsory.*'

He had probably been creating a dramatic pause, because on

his return he said, 'But among those "appropriate authorities" are the people who are dealing with it now. Massey's what you call a GRC — genetic resource centre. It's getting germ plasm in from all over the world all the time, it's part of a global network.' He sighed, genuinely miserable. 'Please believe me, I know what I'm talking about, because I've just finished learning all this. I'm a hero; I've given them the Mona Lisa of the cereal world — a primitive cultivar. I'll be on a stamp before long.' He leaned forward, his hands unconsciously forming a pudgy cathedral of mercy. 'Will it really mess up your company?'

'Yes.'

'It just never occurred to me. It wasn't until I saw the reaction that stuff caused here that I realised it could have repercussions for you. Look, I am really sorry, but you may as well know that they'll be growing that stuff out and sending it to every GRC in the world.'

'How many's that?' she said quietly.

'Twenty,' he replied. 'At the moment. They're trying to expand.'

There was not a great deal more to say. She went into silent mourning beside the sorrowing figure of her enemy. A waiter sidled over. 'Will the gentleman be ordering a full breakfast?'

'No,' she said, 'the gentleman's coffee will go on the lady's tab. And could a Black Russian be put there too — beside a . . .?'

'Lion Brown,' murmured the gentleman.

'WE CAN GET out of this, you know,' he said later. A further Black Russian later in fact. There had been a moment of vivid *déjà vu* when Mr Muesli had lifted his second Brown Lion from the table and the coaster upon which it had rested rose with it for a second then plunged damply into the lap of his beige trousers. His cry of strangled anguish transported her across oceans and jungles to the Camino Real.

'We? We're a *we* now, are we?'

'Yes.'

'Why?'

'Guilt, I suppose.' A pause. 'I can get us out of this.' A repositioning; his hand goes to his mouth. Standard body language: talking from behind his hand. Here comes his price. 'And if I did, well, who knows, you might feel — grateful.'

'I might,' she breathed. She gently transformed her body into a commodity. 'And in return you might just want . . .?'

His freckles glow in the paleness of his nervous pallor; his eyes flick guiltily across her venerean surfaces.

'About a million dollars,' he murmurs.

Dollars? This asshole is talking money! He has spurned her! Her head reels with outrage, humiliation and hatred of the post-pubescent corn that bloated her waist. She can't even entice Mr Muesli!

'Put it this way,' he continues mildly. 'If we fail, your company loses billions. If we succeed, it simply loses one million: to me.'

She glowers at him, willing a twinkle to interpose between her wrath and her retina: 'Why stop at a million?' she purrs, 'I'll make you a better deal; I'll pay you the market price of that crop at the time of harvest.'

'More than a million?'

'Hell, that's up to you; *you could bid for it yourself!*'

Roger Morrison gnawed his lip in troublement, then shrugged. 'I think it would be churlish of me to refuse,' he said gracefully.

'Then it's a deal. Now, what's your plan?'

Mr Muesli discloses his plan. 'We negotiate from a position of strength.'

'Oh brilliant!' she withered. 'Pure Harvard Business School! And what's our strength, may I ask?'

'Blackmail and corruption.'

'Ah.' She relaxes, rather more impressed by his grasp of the situation. 'The big two. Go on.'

'The land under the university. There just happens to be a deed of sale in a certain office in Wellington . . .'

'Blackmail!' she cried.

'Well, corruption first; then blackmail. The document is a forgery.'

'Jeezas, what the hell are you trying to do to me!' She glared at him in ferocious disappointment, then added, 'A good one?'

'World class.'

She feels a spasm of optimism. 'Tell me about it.'

And while waiters cleared the dining-room of breakfast, with the alacrity of Wombles clearing Wimbledon Common, Morgan Moran and Roger Morrison sprawled in their high-backed chairs, over their Black Russians and Brown Lions, as Roger told his story.

In the Morgue: 1975

THE STORY HAD an improbable beginning. It began on Wednesday, 12 February 1975, when Roger Morrison went on an errand for his mother . . .

His mother's elder sister, Mrs Marjorie Probert (née Nimms), had been captain of the Towngirls' 'A' team at the inaugural Manawatu Netball tournament in 1928. It was, in retrospect, the highlight of her life, and, as an eightieth birthday gift, Roger's mother wished to present her with a memento of the event: a framed copy of the newspaper report, which, she remembered, included a glowing reference to her sister's sporting skills. Roger volunteered to seek out the report, knowing his mother's eyes were 'not the best these days'. He would find the review and photocopy it.

The morgue — as they call it — of the *Manawatu Evening Standard* was a blisteringly cold cellar below the paper's offices in Church Street. It was reached by buying the editor a whisky, receiving a key, then edging down impossibly steep steps and ducking through a Lilliputian doorway. On the low concrete beam above the last resting place of the province's newspapers, a wag had scrawled 'Rip'.

Roger pushed open the grey wooden door and entered at a stoop. Light switch to his left. Yes. Racks of dead news stretched away from him, into the blackness beyond the last photic beams of the single bulb that dangled like a suicide from a ribbed concrete ceiling.

He closed the door behind him and stood beside edition number one. He glanced at it. 29 November 1880: SHOT US PRESIDENT DIES.

He took a step — 28 August 1883: DARKNESS AT NOON AS KRAKATOA EXPLODES. He took another — 26 January 1885: DERVISHES SPEAR GORDON IN KHARTOUM.

He walked on; 1928 was exactly halfway down the aisles of ancient headlines. He stopped at 3 June, King's Birthday.

Kia Roa had beaten White Star 3–0 in the rugby, Thomas Hardy had died in Dorchester; the Turks had changed their alphabet from Arabic to English; and Harold Lloyd's *The Kid Brother* was on at the Regent. And in 'Public Notices' the government announced that it had compulsorily purchased land on the east side of the river for the construction of an agricultural college.

His aunt's story was on page two: CONVENT OLD GIRLS OVER TOWNGIRLS: 14–3. His eyes skimmed down the pallid copy: '. . . was Marjorie Nimms, who many felt would be instrumental in winning the first prize — of a loudspeaker — for her team. Miss Nimms has the reputation of delivering a "bullet pass" which the shooters must be attentively ready to receive . . .'

His mind was wandering. Where to? He followed it. It had returned to 'Public Notices'. The government was still announcing that it had compulsorily purchased land on the east side of the Manawatu River for the construction of an agricultural college. Hmmm. The government, Roger knew, has to publicly announce all such purchases; either in a newspaper or in the official *Gazette*. Here it was, in this single copy of an ancient newspaper. Perhaps they hadn't seen the need to gazette the purchase elsewhere? Such information was of interest to the gimlet mind of Roger Morrison.

He dedicated several days to a search of the *Gazette*. He was correct. The elderly newspaper he had purloined from the Morgue (for its account of his aunt's ante-diluvian athletic feats, of course), was the only record of the acquisition. Roger's heart sang. Much use could be made of this discovery.

— 'You wanted to screw your *alma mater*?' interrupted Morgan, rather crassly, Roger thought.

'Of course not!' he replied heatedly; 'but it's prudent to have the means, isn't it?'

'Yeah, knowing you've got an obliteration card up your sleeve certainly seems to bring peace of mind,' she conceded.

'So I put the information aside for a rainy day.'

'Okay, well here it is; it's Rainy Day day. Including thunder and lightning. And frankly, this story's gonna have to get better to be worth a million dollars.'

'Ah. Then let me introduce you to Ngati Harakeke.'

'Marty who?'

Roger patiently explained.

IN THE MIDDLE of the Manawatu swamplands, many years ago, lived a tribe called Ngati Harakeke. It wasn't their real name, which everyone seemed to have forgotten; it was a derisory sobriquet imposed upon them by the surrounding tribes. It meant 'the flax people'. They were a small tribe with little mana, who were fearfully aware that all around them dwelt much stronger tribes. And even worse, on the coast to the south west was the dreadful Te Rauparaha, a misandrous midget who'd turned genocide into a sort of hobby.

What Ngati Harakeke needed were some of these ferocious new settlers called Pakeha, who had arrived bristling with hi-tech weaponry. Unfortunately, they showed little interest in the lowly lands of Ngati Harakeke.

Then, by sheer chance, a white-faced foreigner walked smack bang into the midst of the tribe! His name was Mr Montefiore, an entrepreneur from Sydney. He had come to New Zealand in search of investment opportunity.

'Aue!' cried Ngati Harakeke, 'have we got just the thing for you!'

After several days of feasting and sightseeing, an agreement was drawn. In return for twenty-five muskets, Mr Montefiore would have tuku whenua — 'the right to use the land' on Ngati Harakeke property. The deal was made, and drafted most carefully to ensure no future title wrangles could ensue. 'It must be placed in written form,' insisted Mr Montefiore, 'for, while you hold your land by communal title under customary law, the whiteman must register his rights under individual Crown title.' Thus James Barrow Montefiore inscribed his claim on vellum, appending it with a neat little map of the land. The tribal members signed it with their thumbs.

Mr Montefiore was to reunite with his Sydney-based vessel at the coast, off Entry Island, in one week's time; that is, 23 December 1830. In Sydney he would put his affairs in order, then return immediately to Manawatu, via Wellington, where he would register the deed with the Land Deeds Department. Then, with his family, business partners and muskets, he would set up a flax and timber business beside the freely navigable Manawatu River. And off he went.

For many months Ngati Harakeke awaited the return of Mr Montefiore. Then the duration of the wait turned into years. Then tens of years. Eventually it turned into history. The tribe lived on, huddled beneath the broodingly contemplative brows of the surrounding tribes.

Then, in 1861, the son of Mr Montefiore arrived waving the vellum agreement over his head and *with twenty-five muskets in tow*! And several bullock-loads of rum. Raucous celebrations ensued; the river was drained of ceremonial eels. Three barrels of rum were broached, and midway through the third, Mr Montefiore Jnr was strategically bedded and quickly wedded to Mereaira, fulsome daughter of Te Motae, the chief.

The highly satisfied Mr Montefiore announced he would send home for several more shiploads of European civilisation. Tino pai! Very good, very good! Off to Wellington they all went, to send messages to Sydney and to visit the LDD, the Land Deeds Department — there to register and ratify, at last, the vellum deed entitling Mr Montefiore Jnr to rights of tuku whenua on his new tribe's land. Tino pai!

Paradoxically, just as Ngati Harakeke obtained the means to resist external threat, the threat itself was nullified. In 1864, a governmental offer was made to the mighty Manawatu tribes for much of the land to the west of the river. The offer was accepted. The power of the anti-Harakeke tribes was sold, their mana gazetted. The town of Palmerston North was built.

Ngati Harakeke would have gladly contributed to the sale but *their* lands, east of the river, were unwanted. Anyway, their estate was now tatty and undrained. The tramlines into their flax forests were uneven and waterlogged; their forests had been mauled into unprofitability by inept axemen. For Mr Montefiore Jnr, alas, had proved a woeful businessman, a lazy worker and drunken husband. An *affectionately* drunken husband it must be added, who spent inordinate amounts of time in bed with his plump and seeping wife, lolling in lubricious interclutchment on his mattress, while outside, the flax that was profitably stuffing the mattresses of the nation went unharvested.

By 1880, Mr Montefiore Jnr's liver had hardened to rock, his wife had gone to seek his fortune in Sydney and the tribe had disintegrated.

He was long dead when, in 1928, by the Public Works Act of 1924, the area east of the river was compulsorily purchased by the Crown for the purposes of the building of an agricultural college (announced in an edition of the *Evening Standard*). But in a dusty pigeonhole in a Wellington office lay a vellum deed.

WITH A SMILE, Morgan acknowledged the refined plausibility of the story. 'Wonderful! Mr Montefiore is a bit like someone out of Nathaniel Hawthorne; is he?'

'Oh no,' frowned Mr Muesli. 'He was extremely unfictitious.'

'There was actually a Mr Montefiore?'

'Absolutely.'

'I see. And what has he got to do with you?'

'Well, he's sort of related to me.' From a pocket, Roger Morrison extracted a square of greasy paper that unfolded into an extremely convincing family tree. 'It begins with James Barrow Montefiore, Hereford, 1807.' The chart octopussed out to include, on the tip of one tentacle, 'Henry Morrison m Annie Jane Stevens 1891'. At about the elbow of the tentacle, Annie's mother had married a William Cabot Stevens. She had been a Montefiore.'

'And Henry Morrison was —?'

'My grandfather.'

'By blood?'

His pale eyes swivelled like eggs in a Teflon pan. 'Well, more by ink, actually.'

'Ah.'

'I have this friend. Extremely good calligrapher.'

'Who also does deeds and thumb prints?'

'Yes.' He leaned back, causing his chair to creak dangerously. At the same time he somehow reached forward for his glass of enamel-coloured beer.

'What about the tribe?'

'Extinct, I'm afraid,' replied Roger Morrison, his pre-startled, Churchillian face slack with sadness. 'Gone. Every last one.'

Morgan was running her finger round the rim of her fourth Black Russian as Roger finished the tale. 'So you are — what do you call it? Heir?'

'Owner,' he rejoined. 'Why fiddle round with namby-pamby words like heir. Owner!'

'And now,' said Morgan admiringly, 'you are ready to announce your ownership? How gallant.'

ROGER AND MORGAN travelled to Wellington in a rental car. They stayed in extremely separate beds at the Plaza International, and next morning hurried to the Land Deeds Department. Was the deed still there?

Yes!

They hugged each other as the document was produced by a stern woman, who then smiled at their joy and asked if they were engaged. There was the ancient vellum title, replete with little map: Mr James Barrow Montefiore Jnr, by right of tuku whenua, landowner; owner of the land beneath Massey University.

They bore three photocopies of this message back to Palmerston North, and drank chablis at the Idiot & Peer. Next day they set to work.

Into an envelope Roger placed a photocopy of the deed and a typewritten account of the history of Ngati Harakeke and the Mr Montefiores.

Then he added three magazines, tightly printed and yellow with age. All three bore the same title in tusk-white letters on a blue background: *NEW ZEALAND GAZETTE*. To the top copy he affixed a note:

'I enclose the *NZ Gazette* for the months May, June and July of 1928. As you will note, the compulsory purchase of blocks Q112, 3, 4, 5 and 6 were not gazetted within the stipulated thirty days. Referral to subsequent volumes — which can be delivered to you on demand — will prove that the purchase was not in fact gazetted at all. This oversight is *ultra vires* the Public Works Act of 1924. The government purchase is therefore null and void and the land returns to the previous owner. The previous owner is the hapu Ngati Harakeke. As no members of the hapu are extant, possession devolves, by right of tuku whenua as registered at the Land Deeds Department, Wellington, 1861 (refer to enclosed deed), to the descendants of Mr James Barrow Montefiore. Please refer to genealogical table attached.'

And a photocopy of the convincing family tree was included.

Roger then signed his name and addressed the parcel to:

THE VICE CHANCELLOR
REGISTRY
MASSEY UNIVERSITY
PALMERSTON NORTH

It was eleven fifteen p.m. Roger Morrison would post the

parcel on his way home to his sister's. Morgan was restlessly excited; she would take a walk before bed.

The Lemonades

MORGAN HEADED ALONG Fitzherbert Avenue in the direction of downtown. Ahead of her was a three-building skyline; a mirror-glass low-rise vicariously illuminating itself in streetlight; opposite it a blocky edifice like a car battery on its side, and between them a clock-tower in the colours of Signal toothpaste. Above it blazed a cross; obviously the clock had been colonised at some stage by the KKK. The city's other bright lights were courtesy of McDonald's.

Across the road, a block or so ahead, K Mart had erected one of its obnoxious barns. With its usual consultant-led/macronomico-profit efficiency/feedback-feedout system, K had built its Mart back-on to the main street. Across its elephantine façade someone had spray-canned the message WHUCK THE TREATY. She suddenly realised she was reading the graffiti with daylight clarity; the façade shone with a brightness mere streetlighting could not achieve. The extra light came from the uncurtained windows of the Idiot & Peer. It was open! A bar was open! Respiration, ingestion, perhaps even conversation were occurring within! She was already disgustedly aware that New Zealand bars closed at ten, but here it was, eleven thirty and the Idiot & Peer still blazed with life. Uninert. Indead. She was intrigued. She entered.

Inside, across the murky air, at the bar where she had met Mr Gel and Roger, the Mad Hatter's Tea Party was in session. The Hatter was a small, nimble, grey-haired man with unmanicured brows and a plangent voice. The Dormouse was asleep with his head on the bar, one large ear sticking upwards like a dorsal fin; and the March Hare was a tall, sinuous, long-nosed man, wearing shortie pyjamas.

The Hatter was telling the Hare that a mistake found recently in the calculation of the Hubble Constant meant that the speed at which the stars are rushing away from each other had been erroneously doubled, and that in fact infinity was only half as far away as had been previously believed . . .

He stopped at the end of this narration — just as Morgan had stopped until it ended, transfixed by a New Zealand story that did not involve the stockmarket. He turned to her with all the care of a Zulu woman turning with a bale on her head. 'Good Lord!' he exclaimed, 'an angel. Are you before or after the pink elephants?'

Buzz emerged with tea towel in hand, and introductions were made. The Mad Hatter was Trevor Johns, editor of the *Manawatu Evening Standard*, the March Hare was Ross Rassmussen, unionist, and the Dormouse was Basil Stolle, journalist, who awoke on cue, shook hands and returned to sleep.

'I thought your bars — pubs? — your pubs closed at ten,' she said. 'I couldn't resist when I saw one still open.'

'Ah!' cried Trevor Johns. 'Aha! Mystery! And what's the opposite of mystery? Solution! Solution — food! Food! You see, the New Zealand male turns into a werewolf if given access to alcohol after ten. It's true. I've seen it with my own two eyes!' Which glimmered like opals beneath the bracken of his brows. 'It used to be worse; in the olden days men turned into werewolves at six. Beer had to be taken away from them at that hour. Our blood's thicker these days. We can last out till ten. But! Food!' he cried and flung those eyebrows — wild as the front of a crayfish — up his head. 'Food is why we're here! Because Buzz serves meals!' He patted the hot glass façade of an incubator in which a congealing pavement of stroganoff and a kelp forest of fettucine fought for life in small drawers of stainless steel. 'Meals are the lifeline of the drinking industry! Food makes us immune from lycanthropy. Food shields us from the creature within! With meals, drinking time is infinite!'

And so she fell in with Trevor Johns and the Lemonades. As she departed that evening she enquired if they always drank here on Thursdays, and was told that yes, indeed they did.

On a whim she returned the next night to find they drank here also on Fridays.

And Mondays through Wednesdays.

Ted Nea — 'Mr Gel' as she'd dubbed the shimmering Maori pre-radical — appeared on only one other occasion. It was late; he stayed an hour or so but, blessedly, spent most of that time closeted with a bleary Roger Morrison. It seems they had been university buddies. There, through a study of geography, educational psychology and political science, Ted had learned enough to become a slaughterman. Slaughterman! Her desperately whispered fears were resolved by Ross Rassmussen.

'Freezing worker,' said Ross Rassmussen, the lids above his long, almond eyes marcescent with rum; 'Like Chicago. He works at Hawera; works with the guts.'

Ross Rassmussen should know. He was a union man; of the Meatworkers Union. His job was to organise strikes when they were needed. The rest of his time was spent in organising the need. He was a strikingly handsome man with golden hair, eyes and beard. And a large nose. Ross Rassmussen was, said Basil Stolle, the probiscal proof that Christ was a Jew.

The early-evening floor, she learned, was often held by Basil Stolle, the Dormouse, with small pink eyes and ears the size of cupped hands. He spoke in a rolling growl, usually about far-off lands. 'If you want to pinpoint tomorrow's trouble spots, look at the soccer teams. Look at Melbourne; scuffles every Saturday between Serbo Athletic and Bosnia. There'll be a race war in the Balkans one day.' He held forth with insight and intelligence until about seven thirty, when he usually fell over. The floor then devolved to Thomas Jeffries, a Welshman who talked in melodies of breathtaking beauty and couldn't sing.

She was accepted as a member of the Lemonades and quickly learned that the term applied only in contemptuous metaphor. Lemonade was not consumed.

SHE FELT LIKE the Connecticut Yankee in Arthur's Court. She brought insights from a technically superior culture. She persuaded Buzz to serve baskets of buffalo wings and squid for sixty cents, as was standard in the US. He exclaimed that the procedure would be disastrously uneconomic. She patiently explained that it would revolutionise the bar industry and hugely increase patronage. Three weeks later, there was a net increase of zero customers. The procedure was ahead of its time. In other words, disastrously uneconomic.

But she was forgiven. She was one of the boys. She still felt the occasional covert eye, however. Imperfectly waisted she may be, but at 36-26-36 she remained a pulsating boy.

People have fights in New Zealand bars. Not in the Idiot & Peer of course, where the clientage was genteel — and unathletic; but news was often exchanged of battles in the Grand or the Dom or the Grenadier. Morgan was puzzled. 'Why don't they sue?' she asked.

This remark, in return caused puzzlement.

'Sue who?' said Buzz.

'You,' she replied. 'The management.'

'Hey? Come again? What are they going to sue me for?'

'For being hit in your bar.'

'Holy suffering cow!' Buzz was negatively impressed. 'Is that the law in the States?'

'Sure is.'

There was silence amongst the Lemonades, broken only by several softly whistled bars of what she believed was the national anthem.

SIX DAYS AFTER the sending of the parcel, Roger Morrison received a telephone call from a woman who said her name was Ruth Kirby from the VC's office. She said she was ringing on behalf of a Dr Duncum and had the following message from Dr Duncum to convey to Mr Roger Morrison.

'Yes?' said Roger.

'The message reads as follows,' said Ruth in a low but rather breathless voice. '"Massey University is responding with marked repugnance to certain overtures made by a disgraced ex-student. A special caucus of the Board meets to discuss the matter on the twenty-fourth of this month, and Mr Roger Morrison will be informed forthwith whether the university intends to instigate legal procedures." That is all,' concluded Ruth.

'My regards to Dr Duncum,' said Roger.

CHARLIE

CHARLIE BENJAMABOPITR, FATHER of Bindi, was not a regular Lemonade but was known and loved by them all. There was a general cry of good cheer as he entered the Idiot & Peer one evening with Thomas Jeffries and waddled beamingly to the bar.

'Oh well! How very beautiful indeed you really are!' Charlie cried as he was introduced. 'I must tell you without embarrassment that Thomas has brought me here expressly to meet you. So how do you do, my lovely young friend? I shall sit beside you, if you do not mind.'

His head wobbled as he spoke, in rhythm with his cadence. Was it because he came from a land of cobras?

He was perhaps five three, in a well-bought blue suit and firm black shoes. He was of a milk-chocolate hue with a slightly square head. Well, let's say his face had slightly square corners. He wore small, John Lennon specs with a wide bridge; too wide in fact, because his eyes had been forced to travel slightly too far away from each other in order to follow the lenses. His black hair shone like Reagan's and was tightly pressed down into a point and two curves — rather like the 'Calling Batman' signal over Gotham City. And on his face at all times was a smile that had drunk the milk of paradise.

'Aha! You see, Morgan, how well I am treated in this establishment! Thank you, my good friend Buzz, thank you prodigiously.'

For Buzz had brought Charlie a big brown cup of Twinings Relaxative Tea.

'. . . Of course getting rich is very good for the economy; it's no wonder they all get knighthoods.'

Charlie told her Sri Lankan stories; of how the monkeys were put into the coconut trees in the morning to spend the day leaping from palm to palm and throwing down the coconuts; of how the elephants turn up out of the jungle at seven thirty each morning for work, and 'knock off' at precisely three.

'Good union they've got, those elephants,' muttered Ross Rassmussen.

'. . . It's going to happen any day now, the billion-dollar day.'

Charlie Benjamabopitr was from Kokuvil, near Jafra, in the north of Sri Lanka. His father was an exporter of goldfish, and had converted two of the village paddy fields into holding pens. 'And you must know what a prodigiously dangerous vocation this is, Morgan my friend; dangerous for business and also unfortunately for the fish, because in the north there are no rivers, you see? None at all; simply a single stream, which is far from our village. So therefore the water for our holding pens must come only from our wells. In my childhood I spent many hours running up and down the tula of the well in order to glean the necessary buckets of water. This was a most tedious occupation but was of great importance. I was the perfect wallah because although of short stature I had feet of great width that gave me excellent purchase on the slippery beam. Many many hours of my youth I spent upon the tula, but did I have discontented thoughts? — oh no! — for my endeavours were of great importance to my family. And I loved the little fish, just as did my father. We were very happy.'

He told her, in gurgle, of the famous cigars of his village, the silver, the beauty of Keerimali Beach and the qualities of the local mangoes — best in the country and therefore best in the world. And of the templefuls of gods: Lord Shiva, Muruga and his brother Ganesh, with the head of an elephant.

There is something deliciously 'other' in speaking to the devotee of a semi-elephant — who, incidently, runs round heaven on the back of a rat! It's that groin-tingling adventure of 'enemy-as-friend'; talking and laughing and hugging a short, wall-eyed, tea-drinking alien whose way of thinking you will never understand.

And why was he here, so far from his goldfish and mangoes?

Charlie was a Tamil. The government was not. In 1960, when seventeen and ready for university, Charlie was told he must 'apply to another university, further afield'. He did so. And was accepted. After the monsoons of that year, Charlie, accompanied by his father, walked from Kokuvil to the border at Vavunia, then travelled by train to Colombo. There his father saw him off on a plane to Massey Agricultural College, Palmerston North, New Zealand.

Charlie had returned to Kokuvil three times since: to be blessed for graduating, to collect a wife, and to show his parents their granddaughter. Since 1965, Charlie had been on the teaching staff of the Animal Psychology Department at Massey.

'You must come to my house tomorrow evening, Morgan, and there you shall dine with my wife and my lovely daughter Bindi, who is an especial friend of Roger. And you of course must come also, Roger my very good friend!' With angelic artlessness Charlie had arranged for his daughter's beau to arrive with another woman.

Then he squeezed Morgan's knee, immoderately high up, and revolutionised her preconceptions.

RUTH FROM THE university had telephoned for a chat. Mr Morrison was to know that the Board had resolved to meet with Mr

Morrison to gain further details before deciding upon its final course of action. Dr Duncum would meet Mr Morrison in the conference hall of the Consumer Studies Department on the third floor of the City Council Chambers at two thirty p.m. on Tuesday, 11 February. Thank you.

A week away.

Dining with Charlie

MORGAN LIKED NEW Zealand homes. She had been in several. She had been to a party in the blank little bungalow of Danny of the racing page, had partaken of 'afternoon tea' and vodka beneath the eaves of Thomas Jeffries' superbly New England farmhouse, had boozed at Ross Rasmussen's little patch — as carefully working class as a rolled-up sleeve, and had taken pizzas and/or chablis to the homes of several of the other Lemonades.

The houses had varied in status, but all evinced an antipodean self-sufficiency. New Zealand houses reminded her of the toolbox of a Lada that Hank had once tested. It was compendious, it was all-encompassing. The Lada toolbox carries the answer to every problem in the universe — presumably because it is going to encounter every problem in the universe. Well, New Zealand houses were much the same. Within them, or in the inevitable sheds and garages that surrounded them, was everything needed to carry out a life. There was no need to ever leave a New Zealand house. In Nicaragua you leave to eat because you have no kitchen; in the Chicago projects you meet in the street because you have no living room. In New Zealand you can independently cover all aspects of living, at home. Consequently there is no real need of restaurants, and there are none. There is no vibrant street life, and they are silent and empty. Everyone is at home.

She was saying this aloud as they journeyed down gracious Fitzherbert Avenue. Above them the arbour of plane trees glowed like sherbert clouds. 'Ah, but here is an element of surpassing strangeness in connection with this very topic,' cried Charlie. 'You see, the very same thing occurs in Nature! You must look at the native birds of this country, and what do you find? That they are private and territorial, much like the people you have described! Whereas the birds of Australia are garrulous and extremely noisy; once more, just like the people! So, you see, we are presented with a conundrum; did the people of these countries get their character from the birds, or did the birds get their character from the people? Will we ever know? Ah, here we are.'

They had arrived at Charlie's house. It was, explained Charlie from the back seat of Roger's Honda, a boarding house. He and his wife had lived here when first they married, and had been charmed by the place and the proprietorship of the Dutch couple who owned it. But the couple were, as Charlie put it, 'in need of emigration to Yogakarta', and were ready to sell. Charlie bought, in order, he said, 'to allow my wife to integrate into her new society'.

Charlie's boarding house, in the light from lamps in the trees around it, was a revelation. To start with, it was pink. Worse, it was a pink mélange of every dreadful feature of the unspeakable Bauhaus frenzy of the fifties. The façade was segmented, like a staircase of about seven steps lying on its side. At the end of the first step — the widest — was a door of dark glass, and above it, a wildly inappropriate rounded corner. The windows came in clumps of three; mean little things, about the size and shape of upright apple boxes. The building seemed at first to be single-storeyed, but extrusions towards the back, which Morgan initially took to be chimneys, then revealed themselves as windowed. The whole mad thing was festooned with the flags of many nations and the letters

E
L
C
O
M
E

spilled downwards from a large W to the right of the door. The house stood at the far end of a square gravel carpark, empty at the moment except for a green Mack truck without its rig.

'Welcome to my home,' beamed Charlie as they pulled up beside the bobcat. 'Please walk this way.' He clambered out and opened the passenger door for Morgan before waddling proudly towards the porch, making that chewing-celery crackle of footsteps on gravel.

Only upon walking past the semi-detached truck did Morgan see the sign propped by the door:

OPEN
MT PIDURUTALAGALA INN. B&B.
CASUAL B'FAST $3:50.
BYO DINNER $6.50

Charlie stopped beside it to explain. Charlie was one of that type — Gerald Ford is another — who cannot do two things at once. Just as the former President couldn't walk and chew gum, so Charlie Benjamabopitr could not walk and talk at the same time.

'Mount Pidurutalagala Inn, you see? A very fine name my wife herself chose personally. You see, we wanted a name that was familiar to the people of this country . . .'

It was their first encounter with Charlie's Jerry Ford-like idiosyncrasy, and with their being unprepared for it, there was a slight pile-up behind him.

'. . . And we felt there would be little use in naming our establishment after, say, our home town, you see, because of course no one in this country would be familiar with such a name. So my wife suggested that we call our boarding establishment in honour of our most high mountain, which of course is Pidurutalagala, as everybody knows. By using this familiar name people will not be alienated by the strangeness of the appellation. Come this way please.' And he ushered them in the only possible direction.

The door was of dark blue glass, with a setting sun sandblasted into it. 'Come in, come in; my wife and daughter will be greatly pleased to see you both.' He held open the door. Above it was a dragon, carved from black wood.

'For good luck,' explained Charlie, following her gaze to the terrible thing. 'It is carved from ebony, which is made in my village by scrubbing teak with Kiwi nugget. You see, we had affinities with New Zealand even in my youth.'

They entered, instinctively ducking beneath the salivating monster of good luck although it was several feet above them. Beside her, Roger Morrison was frowning slightly in preoccupation; perhaps the situation had just occurred to him. She was in form-hugging blue-and-white sailor-striped top and trousers, and was looking good. How was she to be explained to Bindi?

'This way please.' A short passage opened into the dining room, and immediately you were somewhere in Aroostock

County, Maine, in early fall — until you realised it was actually a wall-sized photograph of a golden forest. That was the end of tranquillity; the rest of the room was a riot, based mainly on Dutch kitsch. A dozen stout tables with candles, vases of paper tulips, ashtrays, water jugs, napkins and a few miscellaneous inches left over for dinner plates. To the left of the room, a candelabra'd piano supporting a line-up of puppets and dolls. Above it a cuckoo clock and, dangling beside that, a porcelain clown holding a bunch of bright petunias. Around the walls, another five or six clocks; barometers imbedded in huge wooden spoons or clogs; paintings of dinky houses leaning into narrow streets or of plump-cheeked maidens in black frocks and casual astronautical headgear, standing by dykes; plates with blue windmills; T-shirts enscribed with GREETINGS FROM MT PIDURUTALAGALA INN '82; porcelain cows on the windowsills; a gas heater with a plastic bronze David upon it; and a bar, overrun with presumably drunken pot plants that entwined several of the high, sticky Bolls and Green Fish bottles.

There was a single fellow diner, at the table by the door; presumably the driver of the semi-detached Mack. He looked up to nod worriedly then hunched back over his clear soup. A tonsure of baldness shone from the middle of his head.

Charlie had marched into the middle of the room and was gesturing past the bar. On his right were French windows that led out into another mass of cultural bedlam in a garden setting lit with kerosene torches on bamboo, still bearing price tags ($9.95). Beyond the little bar was an arched doorway, and in it stood a small, seriously sari'd woman and a taller, semi-sari'd girl. Mrs Benjamabopitr and daughter, ready to be greatly pleased to see them.

'This is my wife, and she will serve us presently with a splendid meal, and this is my daughter Bindi, who is a very good girl and who this year has passed all her subjects in business studies at the university.'

Charlie's wife, it seemed, was to remain nameless. She glided forward. 'How do you do?' she gurgled, and her head wobbled slightly, just like Charlie's. She shepherded them to the table beside the piano, under the porcelain clown and in front of the arched kitchen door. 'Please to sit down here. Please to let me take the shoes.' Twenty-odd years of integration into her new society had not ironed out certain Sri Lankan bumps and hollows from her speech.

Bindi had remained in the doorway, and Roger had hurried over to place a peck on her cheek; passively received. She was prettier than Dave the Dick had led her to believe, but he'd got one thing right at least: these people did have the ability to be fat and thin at the same time. Bindi's enkissed cheek was a podgy little thing, and she also had the faint makings of a double chin. Yet her wrists were as fine as plucked sparrows.

She had thick black brows, sienna eyes and full, pale lips. Beneath her eyes, as beneath the eyes of her mother, were aubergine smudges in perfect half-circles. The eyes of both women were fully rimmed in black — in the heavily kohl'd style of the silent-movie heroines — but tacit inspection revealed the rims to be natural. In the meantime, Morgan, Charlie and Roger had taken off their shoes.

'Bindi, you will see to the dining room whilst I prepare,' said Mrs Benjamabopitr, bearing their footwear onto the cluttered porch beyond the French doors. The notes of a radio from a guest room somewhere, seeped in through the aperture: '. . .*Carter Holt 560, Cavalier 602, CDL 228, Ceramco 890, Chase 722* . . .' She re-entered and blessedly closed the door.

'Please, you will sit here, Morgan my young friend,' said Charlie, 'next to me. My wife presently will arrive with some tea for us. Fasting Tea at this time of day. Did you know there are teas for each part of the day, Morgan? Roger knows this thing because I have told him of it before.'

She said she did not. Bindi was returning from the Mack driver's table with his empty bowl. She nodded in a manner that seemed somehow to exclude Roger, then swept on to the kitchen. Roger followed her with his eyes. He was obviously not quite comfortable.

Tea arrived and was accommodated among the bricabrac on the table. Morgan was saved from the hideous faux pas of adding milk to Fasting Tea by its absence. You put lemon in your Fasting Tea. Was sugar permitted? Indeed it was; Charlie had three spoonfuls.

'Nowhere nowadays,' he lamented, 'can you find the sugar lumps. Such a shame, and so many utensils of great beauty have been rendered obsolete. My wife and I have several sublime sugar tongs of sterling silver that now languish in a drawer without use.'

Exquisitely coloured little bowls of dried peas and lentils arrived. They were extremely hot — as in piquant. Poppadoms and hot chutney. Other little bits and pieces. Bindi passed by again with a plate of meatballs and yellow-sauce-covered vegetables for the Mack truck driver.

Rice-filled vine leaves arrived at their table. So did ducks' feet. Bindi went by, carrying a tray of mustard pottles for the transport man.

She returned. And sat on the kitchen floor! Just beyond the doorway. Sat on the floor! Behind her was a refrigerator and a shelf containing a block of wood into which a fan of black-handled knives were stuck like domestic Excaliburs. Her mother placed a plate of noodly things on their crammed table, then returned to sit on the floor as well! Silently, side by side, the two cross-legged women watched them partake of their hors d'oeuvres.

'And what are your impressions of this small country, Morgan?' enquired Charlie. 'Has it enraptured you with its beauty?'

'Oh yes, it certainly has. I suppose there are parts of the States just as beautiful, but they're all so far apart. Here you go through ten different types of scenery in ten miles!'

'And you haven't even been to the South Island yet,' said Roger. 'That's where the real beauty is.' He frowned quickly, in the midst of crunching something that was either a won ton or a calamari or both. 'I must go to a place called Granity some time. Colin Fox mentioned it for some reason. Oh yes, he has an aunt there. We must . . .' He stopped abruptly and glanced at the watchfully impassive Bindi on the kitchen floor. 'You should try to get down that way before you go. Do you ski?'

'Yes, I do. When I can.'

'Here you can,' said Roger.

Bindi's mother had levitated herself without effort and was gliding towards them to replace dishes. The gold sari she wore reached the ground, and there was no evidence of her form of locomotion. She placed down two plates of tiny spring rolls, which surely could only have been made with tweezers, then hovercrafted back to sit with her daughter. They sat at motionless attention. It was eerie; like being stared at by two does at the forest edge.

'And why have you come to this place, Morgan my friend? It is indeed unusual for one to come so far to so — dare I say this without insult to your delightful town, Roger? — so unremarkable a place?'

It was a question that set her squirming. There was much the delightful Charlie must not know, and the necessary evasions seemed somehow grubby. Roger Morrison must have been feeling the same, for he made evasions on behalf of them both.

'Well, you've lived in this unremarkable place long enough, Charlie,' he said. 'There must be some good in it.'

'Oh indeed! Oh gracious I should say so!' And he did say so; Charlie extolled the unremarkable virtues of the town for ten minutes and the situation was saved. For safety's sake Morgan steered the conversation to his work.

Charlie worked with sheep, he told her. He had worked initially with possums but had graduated to sheep.

Charlie was a world expert on sheep, Roger told her, as he had once been a world expert on possums.

Charlie wobbled his dear little head and made modest declaimers while his face shone with delight and fame.

'We have treated the sheep very badly through the years, you know,' he said.

'Yes, I've heard,' she murmured, looking downwards. New Zealanders' relationship with their sheep was internationally notorious.

'Oh no! I do not mean the buggery!' cried Charlie. 'Oh no, not at all. But I must tell you a most amusing story, my dear Morgan; oh how you shall laugh. You see there was a most comical trial here some years ago at which I was called as expert witness. You see a man had been charged with buggery, but in his defence he maintained that his entry had in fact been per vagina. I was called to testify as to the feasibility of the situation, and as it was a two-tooth and not an elderly ewe with which he had been caught *in flagrante delicto*, it was entirely possible he had indeed made entry per vagina; and as common law must always give the bene-fit of the doubt to the accused, and as buggery applies only to anal sex, then the judge had no recourse but to acquit him and he left the court a free man!'

Charlie laughed and laughed, his little face radiant with bonhomie. There was quite a long pause. Bindi passed with a plate of apple strudel and ice cream.

Charlie composed himself and wiped salt from his eyes. 'No no, when I say we have treated the sheep shamefully,' he went on, 'I mean another thing altogether. Tell me, Morgan, what is the food that you dislike with the most intensity?'

'Oh, tapioca.'

'Ah.' A very slight pause. 'I myself am extremely partial to tapioca, but never mind; one man's food is another woman's poison, yes? Ha, ha! Imagine then, a world in which you have been forced to eat tapioca and nothing else, for the entirety of your life! Is that not indeed a nightmarish scenario?'

It was agreed to be a truly nightmarish scenario. Bindi's mother materialised and soundlessly conducted empty plates back to the kitchen.

'And yet that is precisely the life to which we have condemned the poor sheep! Rye-grass is their tapioca. All the fields of this country are of rye-grass; we are the experts of the world in the growing of rye-grass. It is tough and durable and can be trampled upon with equanimity. It is the boon of the lazy farmer. Eighty per cent of our grass is this, and twenty per cent is white clover. Now, we grow the white clover not for the delectation of the sheep, oh no, but for its leguminous properties — for its abilities to nitrogenise the soil. Well, you need to know that sheep hate rye-grass! And white clover also! I know this from my experimentations of some years ago when I wished to wean sheep onto herbs such as coriander that would give their meat a delicious flavour in later life. I found then that sheep will eat almost anything else in preference to rye-grass, and so I began to give them choice. And choose most wisely they did! Oh yes indeed! Those sheep with worms will immediately go to the plantain — for although worms are now becoming resistant to drenches, these worms are quickly murdered by a chemical in plantain. And of the red clovers, I noticed they eat much more of a variety called G27 than of pawera, which is the more common variety. And why? Because, I found, pawera has twice the quantity of estrogen! Pawera was a natural contraceptive, filled with the chemical we put into your Pill, Morgan, and thus those ovine ladies eschewed it most haughtily! Ha, ha! And chicory; this I found to be their favourite food of all.

And of great benefit also, because their desire for this herb is so great that they will eat it right to the ground, and in this way the spores of the insidious facial eczema cannot thrive, as it does in the rye-grass, which they never eat down to ground level. And other such boons come from providing them with food they desire — a sheep that dines on chicory will reach its market weight much quicker than on rye-grass, and will consequently gain the high prices of the early market!'

Bindi's mother had silently glided into the room on the little satin hovercraft of her sari, and had curtsied down to give Morgan her next course. It was a turd on a plate. A white plate, coated in fluffy white rice. And on the rice lay a turd. A stool. A faece. Steaming. Freshly laid. Bindi glided in with a turd for Charlie; her mother returned with a turd for Roger.

Morgan sat at the table beside the piano, in the company of her two dining companions, each with a plated turd in their laps.

'It was from these early experimentations, Morgan, that I developed my great work. You see, I realised the effects of these generations of unpalatable foods on the psyche of the sheep.'

He stiffened the fingers of his right hand and tweaked some rice into a ball, which he dunked into the yielding flank of the turd and popped into his mouth.

'The similarity with corn in South America is quite astonishing. As you will know, corn is not a complete food but has been used as such for many hundreds of years. It is this that accounts for the lethargy and pessimism of these peoples, you see, and their irascibility and torpid susceptibility to dictatorship. Well, are not sheep the same? Indeed! A depressed race. I firmly believe so! You must know, my dear Morgan, that I see it as my mission to save them from the dreary fate we have imposed upon them.'

Roger was also making little sticky balls of rice, dousing them with turd material and cheerfully consuming the mess. From the kitchen floor Bindi was watching Morgan with anxious eyes.

'Tomorrow perhaps you will come to see my groups? You will notice I do not call them flocks. Oh no; my ovine groups. Perhaps you would care to meet my star pupils, Beryl and Murray?'

Charlie was smilingly, chewingly awaiting an answer. His eyes dropped, as did the eyes of so many men, into Morgan's lap. But Charlie had eyes only for the untouched turd upon her plate. She forked her right hand and fashioned a ball of glutinous pellets.

'Consider for one moment, Morgan my delightful friend, the concept of intelligence. Now, although it is insulting to our vanity, I must inform you that intelligence could have come in fish, trilobites, insects or reptiles — there is no neurological reason why not. None at all! Anatomical changes would have been made, and, there you are, Einstein fish! Ha, ha! There was no reason at all why it had to be us. On the other hand, I must tell you that there is no reason why intelligence needed to develop at all. The world would have got along quite nicely without it. Perhaps better! Who knows? Ha, ha! Not even us, and we are the only ones with a mind.'

Morgan had held the wad of rice in her fingers for an unnaturally long time. The next step must now be taken. She pushed it into the creamy brown pulp, arcing her fingers to ensure they were not contaminated.

'Most animals cannot have a mind, you see, because they are completely without cognition; only orang-utans and chimps have this. Not even gorillas! Strange, because they are equally as closely related to us. And here is an amazing thing, Morgan. The inner workings of your very body have also a mind! You see, the immune system in your body must be able to distinguish between self and non-self, or it would not attack flawed cells. So, you see, those little lymphocytes of your immune system must be classified as conscious! Possessed of cognition; minded! Is that not quite amazing?'

It tasted of . . . there was no way of knowing what it tasted of, because she did not have a reference of past experience. She was without cognition. She apologised to those aware little body cells who must next deal with whatever it was she could feel lurching peristaltically down her gullet.

'Now, I must tell you that the effects of our misuse has been catastrophic upon the ovine breed. We have brought this breed to the very abyss edge of extinction with our thoughtlessness! Oh yes we have! You may say, Morgan, "but Charlie, there are many millions of sheep," and I would reply, "Ah, but are there now?" And the answer is, no there are not! You see, so similar have sheep become that they act as clones rather than as individuals. Every day the sheep of the world approach nearer to the state of the anthill rather than the ant. A flock of sheep is no longer a group of separate mammals, Morgan, but a single entity! This is dreadful! Sheep are losing their identity! The terrible dangers of this situation will become clear to you when I tell you that there are not millions of sheep in the world at all; there are perhaps one hundred! Perhaps fewer! You see, that is the number of breeds. And every member of that breed acts in precisely the same manner, so they are in effect the same sheep. And those hundred sheep are all in extreme danger of extinction! You see, even evolution itself is beginning to see the flock as the individual; and once evolution loses interest in you personally, well, you have been consigned to extinction I am afraid!'

The turd was having no adverse reaction upon her stomach. The stomach cells had probably called a mass meeting to cognate on this new material and hadn't yet come to a decision. She had consumed two further mouthfuls in the meantime. The jury was still out.

'Extinction, you know, is an ominous word. Oh indeed it is! So ominous that we cannot bring ourselves to say it, you know. We have turned it into an adjective — we are quite prepared to "die", but we must "go" extinct, you see?'

Death, extinction. Words to conjure as she took her fourth and fifth mouthfuls. The turd, she calculated, contained material for a potential seven mouthfuls.

'It is commonly known by animal behaviourists that domesticating a breed of mammal leads to a reduction in the size of its brain, you know. Oh yes indeed. A most great reduction! Domestic pig brains have shrunk by thirty-three per cent in comparison with wild ones! Cats by twenty-seven per cent and in sheep the brain has reduced by twenty-three point nine per cent! We are able, I am afraid, to speak of "regressive evolution". Evolution that works backwards, and which, alas, was invented by us. We have created, I deeply regret, the domesticated moron.'

One mouthful to go. Her stomach remained quiescent. WHY? Oh God! She was a coprophiliac! She was possessor of a stomachful of all-knowing, excrementivorous, merdivorous cells, partying on a small brown faecal pryamid in her belly!

'My own studies have found that in sheep the olfactory archicortical structures of the brain have reduced by twenty-seven percent. This disastrously reduces their ability to select food. And the hippocampal formation is reduced by forty-one per cent! A figure that almost makes me weep. I think of the fearful reduction in ovine qualities such as aggression, temptation, curiosity and drive, and I cry, "How can we ever repay sheep for the dreadful depredations we have visited upon their species?" It brings me sometimes, Morgan my beautiful friend, to the brink of despair!'

As he said this she was finishing mouthful number seven, and there was a relief in her heart that was easily converted into loving concern for the grieving Charlie. 'Oh you must never despair, Charlie! I'm sure your experiments will be a great success and you'll turn every sheep in the world into an individual!' she exclaimed as if on her fifth Black Russian. Then she rocked forward and, under the inscrutably troubled gaze of Bindi and Mrs Benjamabopitr, kissed the little man on his square, impeccably hairless forehead.

Further courses came and went, none of which evoked *déjà vu*. Morgan departed that evening a living encyclopedia of ovine ways and racked with shame at her treatment of the breed.

A notable evening; one in which she may or may not have consumed a faece. How would you ever know?

Think hard before you answer.

CALLS

THE NEXT DAY Morgan received two phone calls.

'Hi! I just wanted to let you know how neat it was meeting you last night. And your clothes . . .'

'Who is this please?'

'Oh. Bindi. Sorry.' An avalanche of giggles like collapsing blocks. 'Roger's friend. It was great meeting you. You must find us a pretty boring lot, I suppose?'

'No; not at all.' Bindi? The inscrutable, floor-sitting Sri Lankan! Do Tamils say 'Hi'? Maybe Hi is short for Hindu?

'And I just about died when I saw you looking at the panyi dooley last night; I mean fish and rice — fish and rice! You know? I've tried to tell Mum a million times before, but you can't get through to them; it's engrained, you know? I tell her, I say, "Mum, fish is protein and rice is carbohydrate, and you should never put acid with alkaline." But you can't tell them. I'm sorry about that, but they're just locked into the old-fashioned way, you know?'

It was fish! She was saved! The turd was a fish; sulphuric,

sour, saline, corrosive, litmus-enreddening ole acidulous fish! Let's hear it for fish! She was a fishphile; an icthyian; an acidbelly! For all she knew the acid from her fish and the alkaline from her rice were right now combining at molecular level into an alimentary neutron bomb. But who cares? Turd-free!

'Just tell me if I'm being cheeky, but I'd just love to see your wardrobe some time. You must have amazing stuff, you know? Stuff we'll never get here in a million years.'

'Oh, any time. I haven't got much with me at the moment, but anything I've got you're welcome to look at.'

This new, telephonic Bindi was bubbly, giggly, silly, flatly un-Asian in accent — and young. There was already an older-younger sister hierarchy growing around the conversation. It suddenly occurred to her that Bindi wasn't much more than half Mr Muesli's age. Mr Muesli was an older man, a sugar daddy, a dirty old man. And there was no hint of combative protectiveness in the girl's voice; she didn't seem to feel her man was under threat . . . Jeesaz! It hit her like a squall — the girl regarded her as old!

'Well, if you're not doing anything this evening, that would be awesome.'

'Well, I might be busy this evening, but I'm not doing much right now.'

'Really? Right now? Well, I could do that, yeah; we're just down the road. I can come up in about half an hour. How would that be?'

'Fine.'

'Oh great! That'd be fabulous! Wow! Thanks. Oh, and the other thing. I was wondering if you'd like to join our share club? We came into it a bit late, you know? We only started last October so we didn't get any of the rock-bottom deals — in fact a couple of them like New Zealand Salmon and Kupe have gone down a bit. I think we purchased at top dollar, which is absolute stink for your reputation as a broker, you know? I'm sort of the club advisor, you see. Anyway, perhaps we can talk about it when I come over? Roger says you've been in that sort of business in America? I'd love to hear about it, it must be amazing, it's so big!'

It was all a little exhausting; arid little sentences that seemed to curl up at the ends like ticker tape left out in the sun. Morgan replaced the receiver in her room feeling vaguely insulted, vaguely amused and very vaguely jealous.

SHORTLY AFTERWARDS, SHE received another call, this one accompanied by the buzzings, black holes and undersea whinings associated with Nicaraguan telephonics.

This call, however, came from no further away than Hawera, fifty miles away. 'How do you do? This is Ted here, Ted Nea. We've met in the pub a coupla times?'

'Oh yes, of course we have. Hi Ted.'

'Hi. Hullo.' Mr Gel was carefully elocuting his bubblegum words as if speaking to a foreigner. Well, he was, wasn't he? She felt alien in a new way.

'I was wondering if you and Roger would like to come up to Hawera and have a look around the Works? I don't suppose you've ever seen a freezing works?'

No, that was certainly true. She had never walked into an animal Auschwitz, mainly because she had never felt the desire to projectile vomit before fainting.

'Well . . .'

'We've got the biggest pre-breaker in the country; had it in for over a year now.'

'Really?'

'Yeah. I thought tomorrow at about eleven. I've talked to the foreman about it and he said just before lunch would be fine. It's an early day tomorrow, so we can have a couple of beers afterwards.'

'Well . . . I'd have to see Roger about it. I . . .'

'It's okay, I've already spoken to him. He just said to square it with you. So I'll see you at eleven. Better go, the chain's building up again. It'll be great to see you again. Catch you tomorrow.'

THE PRE-BREAKER

PERHAPS IN COMPENSATION for the terrifying outer distances, the inner distances of New Zealand were compressed; squeezed up.

Around her, the geography of a standard prairie state extended to the skyline — but this horizon, you somehow knew, was closer; the distance didn't create that twitch in your vision that happens in Kansas or Arizona as your eyesight goes into fifth gear in order to cross it.

The landscape was trying as hard as it could to become archetypal; flood stopbanks tried to look Pleistocene, irrigation ditches attempted to blend into the geography as streams. But it was unassimilated somehow; new, unworn, not broken-in; crops lay upon the surface like discarded parachutes, and behind her Palmerston North seemed like a blob of flapjack mix that God had dropped onto the plain.

Over to the right, an untidy pile of rock and snow lay heaped on the horizon: Mount Ruapehu, one of the many volcanoes that 'do no longer function' — Charlie's description; as if they'd broken down.

Farms created large, unvarying patterns; every three miles or so they had passed two fields of wheat, one of corn, three of grass (rye-grass of course), three poplar windbreaks, a copse of pine and a white bungalow surrounded by a macrocarpa hedge. Geography as wallpaper. The corn, she noticed with sly pride, was invariably Agrisync Hybrid — identified by little notices on the roadside. Except one. HARDACRE ALPINE, said the little tin sign. It was the only time Roger Morrison glanced at her. He smiled. The bastard had probably been waiting for it.

Towns were Wild Western; long, thin things clamped to the sides of the highway, which became known as Main Street or High Street for the urban duration, and consisting of two-storey shops with a verandah bisecting the storeys. In the dark, plate-glass window of one shop, called AGRICULTURAL IMPLEMENTS, she had seen a wheelbarrow and a pair of rubber boots, and nothing else.

They stopped at a dairy — a store selling milk products and *Playboy* magazines — in one such town. The verandah was oppressively low as they walked towards it; it caused you to stoop. They all did, now she came to think of it. They ate ice creams, of almost orgasmic deliciousness.

On the outskirts of every town, a farm machinery supplier sold the products of Peoria and Kalamazoo. Also on the outskirts of every town, usually on the same post as the Rotary wheel, was a sign saying DUMP. No traveller to New Zealand could ever lose their way to the local garbage tip.

In glowing fields, Caterpillar harvesters rolled hay into great wheels, which John Deere binders then cocooned in black polythene with arachnid delicacy.

They plunged into a valley-like cutting that rose steeply on each side, like the banks of the Panama Canal. The raw soil had been planted with grass to bind it, and for several miles the world was transformed into a weaving, two-tone abstract painting by the flat green of the embankments and the untainted blue of the sky above them.

They burst from the cutting, and symmetry was splintered into amber fields and dark blotches of imported vegetation.

And then a mountain leapt out of the landscape. Its peak was in line with the sun visor. It must have been above them for some time, therefore its advent was startling and somehow offensive. It had not come into her view as a new feature but simply as an object about which she had changed her mind; had seen from another point of view. One moment it was another explosion of cumulus on the horizon ahead — then suddenly it took root. The darkness beneath its white billow was no longer shadow or a storm but the black flanks of a mountain below the snowline. Its sudden presence had shaken her; the fact that she had been unwittingly in its presence for some time filled her with unreasonable resentment. Even when she marvelled at its beauty she never warmed to it; never quite forgave this malignant giant, which Roger said was called Egmont then paused, glanced at her and said, 'No it's not — it's called Mount Taranaki.'

A sign told them they were thirteen kilometres from Hawera. Where the freezing works was. With its almost-new pre-breaker. She had a regurgitation of memory . . .

'I mean, have you ever seen a lion eating a lion? On the TV, I mean. Not the real thing.' It was Bindi.

Morgan had shaken her head and said no. Then the devil had taken her. 'Not unless it's a conspiracy, like getting to the moon.'

'How do you mean?' said Bindi, taking her eye for the first time from her own lankly plump form in the mirror.

'Well, lots of people think they never landed on the moon; that Hollywood just did it in a studio.'

'Really?'

Oh God, she'd just made a convert to the Hollywood moon landing conspiracy theory! 'Well, all I meant was wildlife photographers might be like that; they see dozens of lions eating lions, but they never film them — so they won't spoil the conspiracy.' Why the hell didn't she just shut up? She dutifully allowed herself to be told how very wrong that conception was, and hadn't she noticed on wildlife programmes how lions always unzip the zebra's belly and hoe into its guts first, because that's where all the predigested, high-water-content food is, which you don't get from a diet of lions. Lions, she learned from Bindi, are vegetarian. Having eagerly consumed the sustaining greenery within the zebra's gut, the replete pride then wanders off and leaves the meat to hideous carnal scavengers such as hyenas and vultures.

It was a complex mix of recollections; semi-naked Bindi, of the soft, protruding belly — indented like a very large apricot — trying on Morgan's clothes in front of the wardrobe mirror in room 177 of the Coachman Inn, lecturing on the herbivorous ways of the big-cat family while an avalanche of slimy, knotted, steaming green guts spilled from a bright blue bull hanging by its tendons from a humming metal rail in a slaughterhouse in Hawera beneath the surreal glower of a mountain made of solidified cumulus.

Because the memory came back to her in the skinning room as she stood between Roger and the proprietorial Ted Nea.

Half an hour earlier, just after she had had her first remembrance of Bindi trying on her clothes, they had come upon the town of Hawera, tilted, perhaps one degree, by the beginnings of the long, ashy flank that curved up, with the perfection of an exponential graph, to the cone of Mount Taranaki. Ten minutes later, they were watching black cattle, eyes imbecilic with fear, waiting in profound distress on a shit-darkened ramp to take the place of the leading beast, which was momently being slammed into juddering oblivion by electricity, then flung down a shaft onto a steel table, where its throat was deeply cut, in Muslim halal style. The beast, it seems, then dies facing Mecca.

In the olden days, Ted informed her, before the philanthropists of Saudi Arabia and Iran had insisted on halal, the blood would have hit the roof. Nowadays it was slower — in Texan oil terms, a gurgler rather than a gusher. After fifteen seconds, a sharp knife is pushed along the occipital bone and a tendon is knicked. The head tips back and the neck yawns open in a vast, scarlet laugh.

The weasand — quaint word — is then bound by string to stop the stomachs disgorging shit out the neck, and the floppy beast is hydrauled upwards by the tendons of its knees and propelled through steam, stainless steel and white tiles of oppressive sterility to the skinning room, where the hide is peeled by strong men, to reveal the vulnerable blue nudity beneath.

Fat is startlingly yellow. It is cut away. The blueness soon fades into purple and then into browns.

'That's the electricity in it,' explained Ted as it happened before her eyes. 'Full of electricity right now; that's the meat tenderising.'

She remembered the tenderness of his warm, bronzed nose. And, for a moment that never returned, the electricity.

There were hydraulic machines of many kinds, and switch boxes with buttons; some with standard names: STOP, GO; UP, DOWN. Some not standard: BLOOD.

Artists in white capes and caps painted perfectly straight red lines down the flinching blue bellies with knives, and guts ballooned out. They leapt head-first, these guts — like lemming/jellyfish — into drums, which were then wheeled away. Beneath were the stomachs. 'Rumen, paunch, honeycomb, omasum, abomasum,' intoned Ted as these items were extracted.

Hypnotised by horror, Morgan followed the lurching commuter carcass to its next station, where dark organs were plucked from the glowing coral of the backbone. Kidneys, liver. Real, refrigerator-real kidneys and liver! Impossible! Carbon copies of the kidneys and livers you bought at the meat section of the supermarket! How had a famous source of Vitamin A, D and Cs 1, 2, 3, 5 and 6 got stashed into this messy hole? It took some moments to come to terms with the back-to-frontness of this logic and to realise what was going on. A beast, put together by Nature or God or Allah, was being taken to pieces again by Ted and his mates. This was the archetypal disassembly line.

Ted worked in the tripery, where they tarried a considerable time. 'See, the food is swallowed and comes down into the rumen, then it's tossed backwards and forwards with the honeycomb, and then it's pushed back up to the mouth for some more chewing. That's your cud.'

Every worker, she suddenly noticed, was chewing on gum.

Squirming, green, hundred-pound bags of stomach plopped sporadically down an anus of metal from the skinning floor above, and men cut them open and, with hoses, blasted shit from the egg-carton-like dents inside, called villi. You could see, if you wished, the precise moment at which chewed grass became excrement — alkaline of course; a natural complement of rice.

Prides of lions were led in by Bindi and set down under the steel tables to munch through balls of honeycombed flesh and doughy doodoo to get at their predigested, high-water-content, purely vegan nourishment.

The stainless-steel room was flayed with boiled fog, and everything in it was either red hot or freezing cold, adding to the steam that hissed out of monstrous vats. Astonishingly enough, Morgan had not once felt ill.

She realised this when their group burst out of the innards of the building — so to speak — onto a small iron balcony, perhaps three storeys up, set into its corrugated-iron flanks.

Directly below, grey roofs shielded them from the horrors of biblical massacre — Koran style — and in the pleasant swards around, unwitting cattle grazed, contently plugged into their rye-grass. The midday air was pleasingly tepid and birds sang over the now-distant roar of ventilators, boiling vats, bone saws and the clattering of steel. Beside their feet was a shallow metal tributory in which running blood was bearing scraps of gut, weasand and skin down to a much deeper metal river of junked beast. 'Down there's the pre-breaker,' said Ted, alert with the fear that they were not interested.

They re-entered the building and, after five minutes more of Dante, burst out again into daylight at the foot of a black iron cauldron, perhaps a storey high, into which the river they had looked down upon deposited its detritus. The thing made the grinching growls of a billion stomachs on a Bindi high-water-content diet of onions and prunes.

'Everything that's no good goes in there,' shouted Ted. 'Diseased stuff, bad bones, broken skulls, scraps. Not that there's many scraps, eh? The only thing we can't find a use for is the muscle round a cow's cunt.' He didn't smile. 'I'll show you something that's really beautiful.'

It was in a drum, in the shade of the pre-breaker: a viscous liquid of the clearest, purest, most beautiful emerald green Morgan had ever seen. 'Spleen,' said Ted. 'Squirts out the gall bladder and swills round the gut. Helps digestion.'

The net result of the most heavenly colour on earth was shit. There is much we shouldn't know.

'They reckon a woman got put in here once,' chatted Ted. 'One of them unsolved rape murders. Ended up in here.'

Somehow she'd known he was going to say that. It exposed the sad, banal tautology of so many legends; the Minotaur as urban myth.

He glanced contentedly up at the pre-breaker. 'Do you want to go up and see it working?'

'No,' she said emphatically, but as she spoke she was searching for the brand name. HOGGER & HOGGER LTD, KALAMAZOO, MICHIGAN, USA. A local company! She would certainly tell Mr Fellucini about the machine. The Family could well wish to invest in one.

THEY WERE IN the Railway Hotel. It glowed with the amber of old varnish and the yielding brown of the linoleum that clung cracklingly underfoot and made progress as tedious as traversing a field of sellotape. There were sounds new to Morgan — the clack of pool balls was familiar enough, but sporadic roars from the tables startled her every time. On her way to the LADIES she realised it was a Niagara of balls arriving from the belly of the table for the next game.

A quarter-hour ago they had divested of their white overalls in the bathhouse, and she had been whistled at by politely leering slaughtermen. Not because she revealed anything — she still had her jeans and top on underneath — but presumably because of the act *per se*. Okay — went the theory — so they're overalls, and underneath are jeans. But it could have been knickers, and underneath could have been skin. She felt like whistling back in admiration at the feat of imagination. Anyway, they were now seated at a sticky formica table by a white-painted window near a dartboard.

'. . . *and they're going to have to close on Saturday to give the brokers a chance to catch up* . . .'

She was seated on a high stool, the two men were evidently 'leaning' — the table was called a leaner. Ted had bought two jugs of beer and a Black Russian for her, which came in a pint beer glass. She lifted the iceless brew to her mouth. Her jaws were prised impossibly apart by glass and she gagged. Molten Coca-Cola filtered through the gaps between her top teeth. 'Cheers,' said Ted Nea.

He had lit a cigarette and was holding it in that strange quill-like grip of his. Most of the clientele were Maori, and those who were not seemed ready to evolve. They walked with the same pot-bellied waddle — pot-bellied or not — and spoke with the same infant-like inflection.

The atmosphere was friendly and jolly until strange anthems came across the radio, at which times the patrons stood slowly to attention and their faces immobilised into expressions of nostalgic contemplation. Morgan had seen the same expressions on faces of migrants listening to songs from faraway home. She thought at first it was a succession of patriotic melodies in a South Sea tongue, until the babble translated itself into horse-race commentaries.

Ted and Roger drank two jugs, and then two more. She 'sits on this one, thanks' with her lukewarm Black Russian.

The hub of the bar is an immensely fat Maori in black singlet, grey trousers and white rubber boots, who leans with four compatriots at his table whither he is paid brief obeisance by patrons from all corners of the bar. She is watching now as he pushes off from his table in the middle of the room and goes to a telephone, which he picks up and dials without hesitation. He talks into the receiver while referring to a small tabloid in his hand called *Turf Digest*.

The voice of Ted Nea intervenes. 'Thought I might have a hangi on Saturday,' he is saying to Roger. 'You know, some friends, the whanau. Usual thing; few eels, bit of pork. Wanna come, Rodge?'

His gaze rested on Roger like a finger resting on an eyeball. Roger frowned restlessly. 'I'm not quite into that sort of thing, Ted.'

Ted jiggled stealthily behind his glass. 'Old time's sake, you know? You and me? And I thought Morgan might like to get in a bit of culture; you know, us ethnics all in there together. That sort of thing.'

He had turned to her. The smoke had made unerringly for his eye, which was seeping. 'Me an' Rodge go back a long way, Morgan; we were at Massey together. He had all the brains though, eh? I reckon you should have got one of those degrees for me, Rodge, you got enough for yourself! Hee, hee.'

'Look, we should be getting going, Ted . . .' Roger stopped, mainly because there was nothing more to say; there was absolutely no reason why they 'should be getting going'.

'So you don't reckon a hangi would be on then, Rodge?'

'No. Afraid not, Ted.'

'Not even for Morgan, here?'

'You'll have to ask her, won't you?' His voice had broken out in a cold sweat. Roger was not at home in this bar; she could feel his alienness; two cultures meeting like tectonic plates. 'Never play leapfrog with a unicorn,' she murmured in her head. Old proverb, getting newer every minute.

Ted had never taken his partly disabled gaze from Roger. 'Pity, thought I might have some of the whanau round, you know? Some of the family. The ole Flax Family, eh Rodge? Bit of a reunion for Ngati Harakeke, you reckon?'

She tensed, locked solid by congealed adrenaline.

'What in hell are you getting at, Ted?!' hissed Roger, not impressively. His voice retained its majestic tone, but there was no majesty in it. His outrage was of the hand-wringing not the fist-clenching kind.

'Hey, Rodge, Keep Kool till After Skool, man. Me and Ngati Harakeke go way back.'

'There isn't a Harakeke,' Morgan said.

'That right?' said Ted. His face went down to his beer and his eyes went up. When he looked from one to the other of them his eyes seemed to roll along the rim of the glass. 'Did you know that, then Rodge?'

'They died out,' she said.

'Well, I reckon if you came down to the Polytech grounds Saturday, you might be surprised, eh Rodge?'

'Listen!' she snapped, and Mr Gel gave a start, which he tried to turn into an old neck injury. 'You guys better learn up pronto that I don't stand having grown men playing jerk-games under my nose. If there's something going on here, I want to know what it is!'

'Ah well, Rodge, sounds like you're on, mate. I'll take a slash.' Ted moved slopingly away.

'He's making a pathetic attempt to blackmail me,' said Roger loudly. Ted stopped. 'In fact, under the circumstances, it's blackmail on you as well.'

'Go on,' she said.

'Yeah, go on, Rodge,' said Ted quietly. He hunched the three steps back to the table. 'You go right along explaining.'

Roger wasn't looking at him. 'Ted wishes to make a deal. Perhaps that's why he wanted us to see his damn pre-breaker first, so we'd know he bargained from a position of strength.'

'Hey, that's heavy, Rodge! No need to get nasty, mate!' Ted was offended, not angry.

'There are certain things about Ngati Harakeke I didn't mention . . .'

'Yes, like that they're not extinct at all!' she blazed.

Ted gave a high whinny of giggle.

'No.' Roger Morrison squirted a sigh, looked up and around the dense bar and back at her. 'That they never did exist.'

'You skunk!'

'Roger's very own hapu, eh Rodge? Hee, hee.'

'I invented them. Not Mr Montefiore Snr, he's real of course; in fact I wrote a radio play about him. But his son, and the tribe, I invented them. And now Ted is gently telling me that a tribe that has been invented can easily be reinvented. If we don't cut him in, we'll be face to face with a hapu Harakeke about ten-thousand strong. Is that not so, Ted?'

Ted shrugged with lugubrious modesty.

'You were lying to me all the time!' exclaimed Morgan.

'I don't think that's the point any more. How the hell did you find out?'

He had turned to Ted, who smiled. 'Don't think that's the point either, do you, Rodge?'

THE OFFICIAL STATUS of the hapu Ngati Harakeke had suddenly changed to: 'extinct, minus one'.

NEGOTIATIONS

THE UNIVERSITY RENTED a floor of the City Council Chambers, a preposterous downtown building the shape and size of a New Brutalist aircraft carrier. Here was housed the Consumer Studies Faculty, and here they met, in a lecture hall that had once been the boardroom of the City Council. A table had been set up in one echoing corner of its steppe-like expanse.

Dr Duncum was a short man of nearly sixty with a plum-coloured face and an impressive shock of silvery hair, shaped like the front fender — in an Italian Modernist painting — of a 1920s

Bugatti. His features were extremely regular, but on the tip of his nose a small group of blackheads dwelt, like grains of spilt pepper. Someone had drawn a thin grey line under his nose. Or he had a moustache.

He was quick, intelligent — and trapped. Under kindlier circumstances he could well have been witty. He described himself amorphously as 'Deputy Assistant of Special Assignments to the VC'. He said it quickly and out of the side of his mouth. It was probably an assumed title.

He stood as they entered, but declined to shake Roger's hand. 'I know who you are,' he had said icily. 'I also know what you are. Why are there three of you? This meeting will not convene until I have a satisfactory answer.'

'Events have progressed since our last contact,' ventured Roger smoothly. This, Morgan realised, was his milieu.

'Events in tawdry little episodes like this do not progress, Mr Morrison.'

'To our delight,' gusted Roger, unrebuffed, 'we have discovered a true descendant of Te Motae, chief of Ngati Harakeke.'

Dr Duncum held Ted in a Gorgon-glare. 'I remember you,' he drawled, 'I failed you in Geography I.'

'Well, on that note let us continue introductions,' said Roger. 'As a consequence of meeting Ted, we have set up a company, Te Harakeke Limited. It consists of Ted, myself, and Morgan Moran. Morgan, Dr Duncum.'

'How do you do?' churled the Deputy Assistant of Special Assignments to the VC. At this stage he sat, and they did likewise. The meeting was convened.

'You are aware, are you not,' Dr Duncum said in a carefully incidental tone as he sat down, 'that this whole thing is an outrageous waste of time?'

Roger gazed at him with centred majesty. 'No, I wasn't,' he replied mildly. 'How nice of you to set up this meeting to tell us.'

'The government can simply pass a retrospective Act.'

'Yes. It could. It could do just that thing. And it might.' Roger smiled.

'And we are gathered here today because it might not, eh?' said Ted Nea.

Dr Duncum said nothing in reply; extremely loudly. When he

spoke, it was to change the subject. 'The university will need to know that the claim has been settled in perpetuity. There is a tendancy for land claims to re-emerge . . .' and he glanced at the affably attentive Mr Gel, 'just the other side of the memory span.'

'There's no need to worry on that score,' replied Mr Muesli kindly. 'The company will sign a disclaimer forgoing all rights to the land in question, forever.'

'Let me make it quite clear,' hissed Dr Duncum, 'that the university does not concede that this damned company has any rights to the land in question!'

'Of course.' Roger Morrison smiled. 'Now, shall we continue? This disclaimer will be in effect a complete estoppel against Ngati Harakeke for any future claim . . .'

'In return for what, Mr Morrison? When do we come to the nub? When do we find out what you want in return for your scrofulous little blackmail attempt?'

'Terms will be outlined in due course.'

'You're not going to tell me?'

'Of course. Eventually.'

The subject had been allowed to drop into a sour slough of silence.

'Miss Moran has one percent of the company,' continued Roger briskly. 'She is the only outside shareholder in the company . . .'

'Ah.' And Dr Duncum suddenly swung the neat little prow of his face to aim at her. 'Yes, Miss Moran, how do you fit into the equation?' he said.

Confusion. The situation was changing. They hadn't discussed this; she wasn't ready. His tawny gaze was fixed upon her with the arrogant intimacy of the once handsome. He was waiting for her to speak. Her. To her mortification, her voice began badly. She coughed and started again. 'Oh, nowhere. I'm a friend of Roger's. I'm just visiting. From Chicago.'

'Chicago?' The new master of the occasion swung back to a suddenly disconcerted Roger Morrison. 'Mr Morrison, is there some — what do business politicians call it? — 'hidden agenda' here? Why has someone come from Chicago to take up a one percent share in a company of blackmailers?'

'Well — she's —' He regained a little composure. 'Miss Moran is an American Indian. We thought, as a gesture, hands across the sea, that sort of thing, symbolic, ethnic solidarity — we would invite her to be a member — an honorary member of the hapu.'

'I see,' sneered Dr Duncum. 'An honour it must be indeed to bring one so far.' He swivelled his fine-hewn face back to her, once more the magnificent bully of the lecturn. 'I am mortified to have to say this to a beautiful and presumably intelligent young woman, but anyone who consorts with this man — I can say nothing of Mr Nea, whom I remember only by his absences from my geography tutorials — is inevitably tarred with the same brush. With deepest respect, my dear, I must confess I do not trust you.'

He stood, not a long way up, but firmly. 'Before the university can finalise any deals with this company, we must have triplicate copies of the company registration and complete and definitive credentials of all its shareholders. All of them.' He smiled at her mirthlessly. 'We will have to check you out I'm afraid, Miss Moran.'

And he was gone.

THERE HAD BEEN two subsequent meetings with Dr Duncum.

The first was for the perusal of documents. On the pine-topped trestle table in their meeting corner were four piles. PILE ONE: was formed by the company registration folio. Capital: one hundred $1 shares; ninety-nine shares in the possession, by right of communal title under customary law and individual Crown title, of the descendants of James Barrow Montefiore and the hapu Ngati Harakeke; one share in the possession of Morgan Skei Rastegai'sa Moran.

'I'm Sinagua Indian,' she'd said in reply to Dr Duncum's unspoken question as he looked up from the name.

What was not enunciated on the certificate was the fact that her single share was a B share. It gave her total voting rights in the company. The truth was, the company belonged to her.

'It's got to be part of the deal,' she'd said to Roger Morrison.

'HQ of Te Harakeke Ltd moves to Hauble Ceyapi Towers, Central Avenue, Phoenix, Arizona, USA?'

'Yes.'

PILE TWO: was of originals. The original deed of sale and the original genealogical table that bound Roger to the estate of Mr Montefiore. Two splendid originals by Karl Feodore Sim.

Karl, a friend of Roger, was an enthusiastic and accomplished forger.

'It was a lovely job, and he was very proud of it,' said Roger, of the ancient vellum deed upon which Karl had inscribed the signatures of the Montefiores and the signs of the elders of Ngati Harakeke. 'It took me all my time to stop him signing it. Anyway, then I went down to the Deeds Office in Wellington, asked to search the titles of 1861, and slipped Karl's masterpiece into the dossier.'

'And how did Ted find out about it?' enquired Morgan.

'I don't know,' gritted Roger, 'but I damn well will!'

Roger accosted Ted. 'Who told you about the deed?'

The answer surprised him. 'You did,' replied Ted mildly. 'The day you did it. You came back from Wellington with a 'secret' to celebrate. Then you got pissed to beat the band and told me all about it.'

'Shit. Hang on, that was years ago.'

'Yeah, but you got pissed to beat the band again the other night and told me another secret. I was chuffed, man; I've been waiting years for you to use that thing, so we could be partners.' And he smiled good-naturedly and did a little jig.

PILE THREE: included a stick, intricately carved and luminously polished. Beside it was a sprig of wide flat green leaves, propped up like a praying mantis.

'Your whakapapa, I presume Mr Nea?' sighed Dr Duncum without touching either object.

Ted smiled and nodded.

Dr Duncum's eyes moved on to the fourth pile; the quite hefty pile of Morgan's own documents, sent, on request, by her mother.

PILE FOUR: information on a Sinaguan life, some of it humiliatingly intimate. Baby photos for crissake! The Deputy Assistant of Special Assignments to the VC was awkwardly tweaking through the chronicle with a determined expression of imprurience. He finished and looked up.

'A vivid life,' he said.

'Thank you.' She assumed it was a compliment.

'But who has lived it, I wonder?'

She frowned. He was looking at her steadily. Behind him the cavernous chamber stretched almost into darkness, shrinking them down to the size of Nebuchadnezzar and guests seeing the writing on the wall, by Rembrandt.

'I don't quite follow.'

'Why didn't you provide a birth certificate with all this?'

She shrugged, willing her blood not to rush into her face. Damn her mother — and her mother's meandering loins! 'I assumed one would be sent with the rest of this stuff, but my mother obviously spent so much time gathering my swimming certificates and math grades, she forgot.' They exchanged a rare smile. 'Does it really matter?'

He paused, tutted, pouted thoughtfully, shrugged, then said, 'To be on the safe side, I suppose it does.'

'You think I'm an imposter?'

'An imposter of whom? That's my point, "Miss Moran"; quite frankly you are the — well — the unknown element here. Your part in this scheme, in fact your very presence here . . .'

'But look.' And she tossed a sheaf of photographs: museum pot displays, Washington-with-the-ollas, on-the-trading-floor-with-Johnny, in the jungle with Diana, in the boardroom with Harvey — into the air. 'This is the person I am; this is the life I have led. What more do you need?'

Their present conversation had until now been untinged with dislike. The steel now returned to Dr Duncum's voice as he said, 'It may seem a little pettifogging, Miss Moran, and maybe it is, but I am of the opinion that the official scrutiny of anyone's life begins with the simple and definitive proof that they are who they say they are. Despite the inevitable inconvenience, I must insist on a birth certificate. After all, if the university is to negotiate with a band of desperados who wish to . . .'

And here the conversation yawed off into obsessive speculation. For Dr Duncum had a theory. A theory on what it was that the 'band of desperados' wanted in return for the land beneath the restlessly dreaming spires of Massey University.

'The Cross-Slot drill! Am I correct, Mr Morrison? You are keen to get your squarrose little fingers on the Bioblade?'

How uncanny. Roger Morrison had predicted, days before, that the university would assume it was the Bioblade they wanted. The Bioblade — the Cross-Slot™, a cumbersome clump of wheels, tubes and gears that was poised to revolutionise agriculture and earn billions for its inventor, Massey University. It would introduce the 'no-tillage' system of planting; injecting seed into the soil without collapsing the wormholes, without distressing those little microbes that aerate the earth. In one lurching bound, the Cross-Slot would reduce world erosion by ninety per cent.

Come to think of it, it wasn't so uncanny — the Bioblade was the first thing any sane university would assume you were blackmailing them for.

'And that's what we want them to think,' Mr Muesli had explained to her. 'The longer they don't know what we're really after, the less time they'll have to find out why we want it when they do.'

THE NEXT MEETING, three long weeks later, was called at the insistence of Dr Duncum.

'Miss Moran,' he said, sitting upright in his chair in the echoing cavern, tendentious as Sam Eagle in the Muppet Show; 'this birth certificate issue had — initially, I admit — an element of over-bureaucracy. However, with the ever-increasing length of its non-arrival, it has become an issue in itself . . .'

'I know,' she replied, as evenly as possible. Her blood thudded in small blows through her veins, her mouth tasted as if she had swallowed moth wings. 'For some reason there's been a breakdown in communication with my mother. Is it possible to get one from here?'

'I . . . well, everything's possible; but are you saying your mother is refusing to send you a birth certificate?'

'My mother is a very difficult woman.'

'Could someone else over there get you one? Surely it's just a matter of applying?'

'Yes, I suppose so. I don't know. I'm not there, I haven't got my finger on the pulse. I don't know why this is happening. Look —' she could feel the beseeching whine pervading her voice but could not stem its arrival, 'it's a goddam piece of paper. I am Morgan Moran. Born 1960 in . . . (Jeesaz!) . . . Nev . . . Hotwa Vo? . . . ada. Mother, Mavis . . . Acomazuni . . . Father . . . (she could see the great Magician, he was hitting the eight iron, or was he catching the ball?) . . . Look, why can't I just go to an attorney and swear all this stuff to him?'

When she looked up, even Roger's eyes told her why not.

'MOM, LOOK,' SHE had said three weeks ago, 'they need a birth certificate.' She was shaking; her temple throbbed in her voice.

'What for?'

'I don't know, they just do. It's a hidebound little country.'

'It's more than that, child! We have checked it out; it's as overheated as Chernobyl. You are in the only country that has a stockmarket worth more than its economy!'

'Yeah, I've noticed. Now, Mom . . .'

'Do not ask me to do things that need presidential okays, okay? You have heard about Bobby down there?'

'No.'

'Gone. Got into a power battle with Nancy's astrologer. The astrologer predicted that Ronnie would fire Bobby and — zappo! — Bobby is gone. Policy here has gone haywire; the country is completely rudderless.'

'That's terrible, Mom. But getting back to the point . . .'

'That was the point, child! What is a bigger point than the United States without a firm hand on the tiller of the Ship of State?'

'Mom, if things are bad up there it's best that we don't make them worse down here. The university is getting twitchy about seeing my certificate of birth, and we don't want them any more prickly than they are now. All you have to do, Mom, is . . .

'What has when you were born got to do with getting my corn back?!'

'Not a lot, Mom, but they have their own way of doing things down here; and down here is where the damn zeacinte is!'

'What do they want a certificate for? Do they not believe you have been born? Show them your goddam belly button!'

'Mom, you've got to take it more seriously than that. Everything's going well. The thief and I have got them over a barrel, and I've got the thief over a barrel. All I need now is a few little bits and pieces of documentation and we're home!'

'You had better be! I do not wish to panic you child, but if you do not get that corn back we are ruined.'

'Thanks, Mom, that's just what I needed.'

'You are welcome.'

'But don't you see, Mom, that's why you have to send me a birth certificate!'

But it had not arrived. Three weeks and three phone calls

later and still it had not arrived. She knew why. Oh she knew why . . .

The Corn Mother, child, that is me. I rub my body . . .

And are you my mother as well?

And beneath my hand form beads of flaked skin, flaked skin rubbed into balls. My skin; to plant in the ground . . .

In the story she generally adopts an orphan child . . .

It disgusts them, but without it they die.

May I venture to surmise that in this version you have substituted the orphan for an illegitimate daughter?

They burn me as a witch.

Sired by a man whose tribe . . .

And my body grows.

Is it me?

And they are sustained.

The Sinagua?

She invariably woke with a hangover after this vision; caused not by the vision but by what had caused the vision.

SHE HAD MADE a fourth call ten minutes before joining Dr Duncum and Roger in their empyrean meeting place. 'Mom, about the birth certificate. If there are things on it that embarrass you, it doesn't matter, it's all a hell of a lot bigger than that now . . .'

'Give me time!' her mother had bellowed and hung up.

Morgan had been flustered when she arrived at the echoey meeting. And it showed.

PHONE CALLS

ONE MORNING SHE was blasted out of sleep by the phone at her bedside. It was 10:09 on the radioactive grains of her clock face, and so she feigned lack of sleepiness.

It was Basil Stolle; she could tell from the rolling speech. The distinctive voice was telling her who it was, in tones that revealed its identity anyway. The two sources of information clashed, and cancelled themselves out somehow.

'Who?' she said stupidly.

'Basil. Basil Stolle. I'm ringing you in an official capacity.'

'You arresting me or something Basil?'

'Nope. Interviewing you. Tonight in the pub I'll be a drunk and a womaniser; right now I'm a journalist.'

'Okay, shoot,' she replied; jollity, she hoped, covering her slight wariness.

'You're being very provocative, Morgan,' he rolled.

'I am?' She glanced into the long mirror beside the bed. It was offset slightly so that it could be used for sexual purposes by guests, but only with awkward twisting.

'Yeah, to an old hack journo you are. You've got a great story, Morgan, and you're dangling it in front of my nose.'

'No great story here I'm afraid, Basil. Not from boring little me.' She laughed carefully.

'Come on, Morgan. Why're you here, eh? Visiting your old chum from Nicaragua?'

'Yes, that's right. You know it is.'

'A busy businesswoman spends three weeks in a boondock visiting someone else's boyfriend she met for a few days in the jungle? Come on, Morgan. By the way, I want to be friends after this; this is just work. But you've got to see it from my point of view; my instincts are out.'

'Way out. If you knew how peaceful it is here after Chicago, you'd know why I'm lingering.'

'I see. So you're not going to come peacefully?'

'What do you think this great story might be, Basil?' She is still watching herself in the mirror. She is stroking her hair, lingeringly. Obviously she is trying to put a little sex into her voice: she's worried.

'Okay. Well, you're in the agribusiness, so it's going to have something to do with Massey. Right?'

'Some brilliant intuiting going on here, Basil. Ever thought of applying for the *Washington Post*?'

A booming laugh that wrung itself out into the stringy wails of a dying bagpipe. 'Can't take all the credit I'm afraid, Morgan. Modesty demands I admit I've had help.'

'Help?'

'Yep. Someone's been helping me with my enquiries, as they say.'

She could feel blood draining from her face, and she worked it to ensure it didn't change the timbre of her voice. Damn those loud-mouthed pot-noodle airheads! Which one had blabbed to

Basil? Muesli or Gel? 'That right, Basil?' she purred. 'And who's been doing that?'

'Tommy Timu.'

Who? From the inside she watched her eyes widening. Parts of the ceiling and floor, once obscured by eyelid, now came into view. 'Who?'

'Tommy Timu. Local lad; good rugby player . . .'

'I've never heard of him!'

'No, that's right. Why should you?'

'Because this rugby-playing genius I've never heard of has evidently told you why I'm here!'

'Yes. Well, only indirectly.'

'I'm all ears, Basil.' Oh Lord! She had a momentary vision of Basil's fin-like ears.

'Lucky fluke really. I was doing a feature piece on the tunnels under Massey University yesterday — whole place is riddled with them — and my guide, Tommy, happened to mention that he owned them. "Hullo," thought I, "that's a new angle; the ole Maori land claim has gone subterranean." He said the tunnels went through land that belonged to Ngati Harakeke.'

'I've heard that tribe was extinct,' she said warily.

'Well, Tommy didn't look all that extinct to me. Ha, ha, ha!'

'He's one?'

Yep. I must say he's a tribe I've never heard of. But then it's just a subtribe evidently. And anyway, I'm not really up on these matters.'

'Did he say if there were any other members of his tribe still around?'

'Well, he mentioned Roger Morrison, who evidently married into the tribe a couple of hundred years ago or something.'

'But other members of this tribe? Are there any more?'

'He sure seemed to be talking in the plural — the quite large plural from what I could gather. Mass tunnel ownership. Gives a new dimension to the land march, doesn't it? "Bring your own miner's lantern." Ha, ha, ha!'

So there was a whole tribe of them. This was uncanny; somehow it teetered on the brink of Creation . . .

Basil was talking again, and the timbre of his voice had changed. 'Anyway, getting back to the subject in hand, which happens to be you, my proud young beauty. Agribusiness, Massey and thou. Look, I had a hard night last night; what about a hair-of-the-dog sandwich at the Dumfries? Say at midday?'

'You're not threatening now, are you, Basil?'

'No,' he chortled, 'I'm paying.' But from his tone they both knew she'd said the wrong thing.

THE DUMFRIES BAR, full of two-handed swords and maps of Celtic Britain, was empty as yet, except for Basil and a benighted Japanese tourist, who sat bewilderedly alone, despised and ignored by the denizens he had come across the seas to photograph. Basil sat beside a bottle of Matua chardonnay with one glassful missing. The midday sun heated the plate-glass window. It shone through Basil's wide ears, causing them to glow translucently.

'Well, to balls, I suppose,' he rumblewheezed when Morgan had settled in.

'Yes? And whose in particular, Basil?'

'Massey's. It's a quote from Tommy Timu. You've got Massey by them, from what he says.'

'I have?'

'Well, the way he puts it, he has — his tribe and Roger Morrison. But the way I see it, you're in on it as well.' He held her in a sly gaze but revealed his nervousness by distractedly adding to his glass of wine when it was hardly in need. 'Let's just look at the situation from a newsworthy point of view. Roger Morrison and some local tribe or other are putting the screws on Massey as underground ground owners; you, a big-shot American corporationist, are shacked up in a stagnant little burg called Palmy North. Now, why? Huh? No logical answer. Too much coincidence going on I'm afraid, Morgan. Can't be left alone. Any decent journalist is duty bound to check it out.'

'That right, Basil? That what you think? Well, you chose the wrong turf I'm afraid — to keep to your own analogy.'

She had been, until that moment, quite prepared to keep things elegant, but then Basil swivelled on his barstool and said, 'Now, don't take me for a fool, Morgan!' He wore those grey nylon trousers that old men wear, and that show stains.

Something snapped. Morgan was suddenly drained of all desire to banter. She could feel her face turning into her mother.

'What the hell are you on about, Basil? What are you talking about? Is this national Make Enemies Day or something?'

'No! No, not in the slightest!' Semi-distraught, he put out a shapeless hand to make a comradely gesture on her shoulder, and she shuddered but relented. Anger was not good politics at this time.

'I'm sorry, but it's a story. You, a beautiful young executive of an extremely large American company, come to our little town for undivulged reasons. Hell, Morgan, that's soap-opera stuff! You can't expect me not to be interested. See it from my point of view; I mean, someone who could buy this town with one hand behind her back has got to be more interesting than last night's council meeting or a cat up a tree!'

'So?'

'Massey's got something you want, and Roger Morrison and/or this tribe have got a way of getting it for you. You can't get it without them, and it's no use to them unless you want it. How's that?'

'About where we were on the phone this morning.'

'Right. Well, moving right along. Why would you want Massey by the balls I wonder?' He reached for the bottle and poured another light green glassful. 'Not saying? Well, what about this?' And he put up his hands in standard hold-up fashion. '"Hands up, gringos, and give us zee plans to zee Cross-Slot drill!" How about that, Morgan?' And he sipped from the shimmering glass, then held it up as if appraising her through an aqueous monocle.

She felt irritation, contempt — and elation. Good old Cross-Slot™ to the rescue again! 'Yeah, it's the big one, Basil,' she said with mock heaviness. 'You could knock Irangate off the front page with this one.'

'So, want to tell me more? I'll find out sooner or later.'

She smiled that split-in-the-side-of-the-tomahawk smile inherited from her mother and said with savage sweetness, 'No. Because I don't think you will. I think that's all you know. And if that's all you know, Basil, you'll never know any more.'

'You make it sound very much as if there is more to know, Morgan,' he growled triumphantly. He was smiling at her beadily, then the smile disappeared as if he'd swallowed it. 'All right, I'll be honest with you,' he said, almost hangdog. 'That's all I know.

Tommy clammed up after that.' The smile reinvented itself. 'But let me just take another stab in the dark here. How's this? You've come here to get your hands on the Bioblade. You've heard the Bioblade patent rights are up for grabs — maybe they've already turned your offer down — you're here to get your hands on it by hook or by crook. And the crook is Roger Morrison. Somehow he's set up a land claim. That's what I reckon, Morgan.' He sipped and smacked his lips, either with pleasure at his words or at the acidity of the wine. 'Something like that. There, that's my best shot. How'm I going?' The smile seemed to convert itself into a self-satisfied leer, but that was probably just her point of view.

'You're wrong, Basil,' she gritted through a pearly smile. 'You know how wrong? About a hundred percent. In fact exactly a hundred percent. In fact you're wronger than anyone I've ever known.'

'Am I?'

'Yes!' There was even a sudden modicum of sympathy for him in her feeling. 'It's a pathetic job, isn't it? Journalism? I mean, what is it? It's scavenging, isn't it? It's just goddam scavenging. Look, if you want, I'll give you the scoop of the century. I'll tell you about a guy named Bobby . . .'

She suddenly realised he was angry.

'You want to bet I'm wrong?'

'How do you mean, Basil?'

'Come on, what will you put on it? I'm wrong. Okay? You're just passing through. Okay? You're not here to get your hands on the Cross-Slot? Huh? That's what I am to believe? A journo of thirty years? Well, what are you going to put on it I'm wrong?'

'Come on, Basil, lighten up. You started this and I don't like it. Surely your job doesn't demand you lose friends?'

'Maybe not, but nor does it demand I lose my marbles! Now, you don't have to tell me why you're here, but you can't expect me to fall for bullshit either. What amazes me is how prominent people squeal privacy when it suits them. Well sorry, Morgan, but that's not how the system works; if you put yourself in the public eye, you're public.'

'I'm not public for chrissake!' she cried, amazed. 'There's not a handful of people in the States know who I am! I'm an ordinary, normal . . .'

'Millionaire head of a transnational company who's turned up in a mid-New Zealand railhead! Sorry, Morgan, you may think you're normal, but not here you're not. This country's got ways of making you abnormal!'

She had departed shortly after, bidding sayonara to the Nipponese tourist at the door.

PART SIX

Massey

Massey University was beautiful: open, green, afforested and pastured. A sylvian institute, an academic Garden of Eden, a Kew Gardens with brains. Also a Shangri-la maimed by architecture.

They set out from the Coachman down an avenue of plane trees and petrol stations, with pleasing houses peeping timorously from behind agapanthus and white concrete fences. On the right a sudden open expanse; paddy fields! Elderly white-clad peasants bent to their toils on the flat fertile sward.

'Bowling green,' said Roger Morrison presciently.

They crossed a wide river densely crammed with logs; seventy-five percent water, twenty-five percent timber. Beyond, east of the river, large fields delineated by geysers of poplar; a steep scarp on the left that gave expensive houses a fine view of the approaching erosion. How different it all seemed when not viewed spectroscopically.

MASSEY UNIVERSITY: a strident wooden sign, and beyond it a glowing arbour of lindens that dappled the sunlight into a vast hologram of the freckled paws of Mr Muesli. Banks of riotous flowers and lakes of lawn, puce eucalypts, flowering trees in violent cyclamen or granny-colours of lavender. Buildings with the good sense to hide; and also, alas, those without it. Ranks of 1960s 'new institutional'-style office blocks lay like horizontal Miës van der Rohe skyscrapers.

Holy Abelards! What was that?

'Judder bar,' says Roger Morrison.

'Judder bar? You call speed bumps judder bars?'

That all-male, subversive glance that will always define the vast gulf between sexes is exchanged between Mr Muesli and Charlie Benjamabopitr. She had juddered, oh yes, she could tell from that sly reciprocal delight that she had juddered just fine.

The deep olive leaves of an orchard on the left, several more mammamotive judders, a settlement of yellow pre-fabs; fields, a little hill. Buildings called WOOL, signs leading to the FELINE

NUTRITION SECTION or BOVINE OBEDIENCE. On the right a hayshed in the shadow of a boiler house chimney; some sheep and three skeletal horses, one with its tongue stuck out à la 'Guernica'. SICK HORSE ENCLOSURE, explained a sign.

On the left, the zeacinte.

It was in a cirque, a tiny hanging valley, in a cliff of black soil. Beyond was a field in which grazed pinto cows, and beyond them again, purple hills. Spooky! Where were the zipilotes? Where the dead cow? Where Humberto Tapia? Not far away, surely, because the vista was exactly the same as before! Zeacinte had recreated the scenery of Nicaragua! It had recreated the scene. There sat Roger Morrison, on her right in a vehicle. There, as before, was an arm draped carelessly across the seat behind her — even if this time it was the arm of Charlie. There were differences, but there were uncanny similarities. She waited for the scare-crow.

The zeacinte was lime green, bright with newness, but already half its final height. None of the regal colours, the purples and golds, had yet emerged, but the black flying buttresses of aerial root were there in rudimentary form, battening those engine rooms of tuber to the soil. Zeacinte. Again. It hypnotised her, entranced her with loathing. Its wide tendrils waved in the slight breeze like Sargasso weed.

Far above her in the sky she saw the scare-crow become the first vulture . . . No, this time it was a molecule crossing her retina.

'What it has been necessary for me to do, you see, is to induce a little evolution, Morgan,' Charlie is saying. He is standing beside her, but his back is to the zeacinte and he is pointing into a field across the road. There was a moment of disturbed incomprehension, then the situation gained form. Of course. They are here to meet Charlie's sheep. He has no interest in the zeacinte.

He set off across the road and down a narrow path of dry mud. She followed; so did Roger. They walked away from the zeacinte. To see a sheep.

Charlie stopped halfway down, causing them to concertina and scrabble for balance on the thin, uneven path. 'I must endeavour to create a mutation, you see: point mutation. You must know that these mutations are happening all of the time in Nature, but they are generally eliminated at an extremely early stage by natural selection. If, for example, a mutant gene should slow the speed at which a deer can flee, that gene will be quickly eaten by a tiger. You see? So most of these point mutations are tending to commit suicide by coming into existence, but I continue to hope I can mutate the brain of my sheep. To make it grow, you see. To do this I have subjected my prize specimens to a course of injections of isocortex, a substance found in the mammalian brain. You see the largest volume of isocortex of any mammal is in us, in *Homo sapiens*, therefore it is logical to assume isocortex has much to do with intelligence. I have been subjecting Murray and Beryl, whom now you shall meet, to massive doses of isocortex.'

And, homily delivered, he turned and hurried down the path towards the field of scruffily uneven grass at the bottom. What a ghastly field! Morning-after in the grass factory. It lay about in mismatched hunks, stalks, clumps — a mongrel mixture of shapes, colours, species and stages of generation and decay.

'In this paddock, you see, Morgan, is a great variety of grasses and herbs. Also you will see around the back there, small trees and hedges. My aim is to change the basic behavioural nature of the sheep. My sheep shall evolve from grazers to browsers. In this way they must constantly make choices that will in turn constantly exercise their brains . . .'

A sheep appeared.

'Aha!' squealed Charlie in pleasure, 'here now is Beryl herself!'

Forget the scruffiness of the field — get Beryl! Beryl was appalling! Beryl was a disgrace to the ovine race. She was a disgrace to the female race. Beryl was a mess. Beryl resembled nothing more than a small yak. Her fleece had lost that blooming, cauliflower compactness of well-groomed sheep, and dangled in lank, brown Rasta ringlets. Her tail had not been docked and resembled the infamous 'wiping rope' of Turkish latrines.

She trotted briskly up to Charlie, inspected his hand for gifts and, finding none, bunted it into a patting motion.

'Say hello to Morgan, our visitor from America,' said Charlie.

'Maaa,' said Beryl. Hell! The thing converses!

It — she — scraped out from beneath Charlie's hand and approached Morgan, trailing with her the smell of old Chicago. She reached up her nostrils and it suddenly occurred to Morgan that twenty-seven-year-old human females may smell equally bad to sheep. And it — she — was looking at her. In her tawny eyes with their eerie square pupils swam a . . . cogniscence! Beryl was actually making appraisals!

'The mammalian brain, you must know, Morgan, is a hierarchy of miniature nervous systems. Think of it as a complex computer programme. I must ask if you are familiar with computers?'

'Vaguely, yes.'

'Well, you see, I am not striving to change the BIOS — the basic input/output system — of Beryl's brain, and nor am I striving to alter its command words. Oh no, I am simply striving to modify its top menu and identify the addresses of its various subroutines. You see? By a recombination of the subroutine addresses, the programme of Beryl's brain might be altered substantially and work without crashes.'

Charlie, it occurred to her, probably had more raw material to work on here than poor old Cyrus Rust ever had.

Beryl was shitting in little dry pellets. Perhaps she was clearing the system for a demonstration, because she then trotted determinedly off to the low bushes across the field and nibbled and hauled upon their branches. She moved with authority, with purpose and a vigour that was distinctly un . . . sheeplike.

'She seems much fitter than a sheep somehow,' said Morgan. 'Is that the diet?'

'It is the diet in part, oh yes. You see, the human brain operates exclusively on glucose, so I have introduced glucose into the diet of Murray and Beryl. They eat now a ration of fruit, and also of corn, which they like very much indeed; and in this way I hope to influence their brains in the direction of the hominoid. But also Beryl's condition is the result of hormones I have administered to retard the ageing process. In this way she retains the vigour of the lamb, you see?'

Maaaa!

It was not Beryl answering. It was an immense ram in the hayshed in the next field. He strode into view from the shadows and stood atop the bales, blaring triumph and acsendancy over all beneath him.

'Murray!' cried Charlie. 'How did you get up to there?' He turned to them, not entirely unpleased. 'You see, I have devised an experiment in which he must push a box to a certain spot, at which time a portion of chicory will fall into it. But now his box is at the base of the haystack. He has put it there in order to climb the stack and consume the entire supply of chicory! He has solved a problem of his own accord!'

'He's mutated!' she cried. 'He's cogniscent!'

She wrapped her arms around the triumphant Charlie as he cried, 'He has modified his top menu and identified the addresses of his various subroutines! He has recombined his subroutine addresses to alter the programme of his brain!'

'And it didn't crash!' added Mr Muesli exultantly.

The Treaty

TIME WAS SCUDDING by. The zeacinte was now tassled, and dunked in the breeze in a blaze of regal coloration.

Time was bunching up, like a file of people following Charlie. This thickening of time and her mother's stealthy evasion was sawing at Morgan's equanimity:

'Mom, for God's sake, just get me a damn certificate down here! I don't care who my . . .'

'They tell me this deal of yours is based on a treaty.'

'What? Look, Mom, we can go into that later . . .'

'Well what's the truth? Are you telling me this whole deal is based on a treaty?'

'It's not so much on a treaty, Mom, as because of it.'

'You mean it's not even based on a treaty? Landsakes, child, that is even worse!'

'Listen, I don't want to go into this thing right now, Mom . . .'

'Do you know how many treaties we made with the government up here, child?'

'Look, don't worry, it's different.'

'How different? Let me guess. The locals signed an amalgamation deal with the new honky arrivals a few hundred years ago. Then the deal turns out to be a hostile takeover in disguise and the locals squeal. Correct?'

'Guess so, yes.'

'And then the locals find there are not too many White Knights around for defence against the buy-up and asset-stripping. Right? Like when the Boomers turn up in Oklahoma and promise they are just passing through? What they must do is . . .'

'That's not quite the way . . .'

'No? So you are calling your mother a liar?'

'Of course not!' Then courage flashed into her heart, riding on the blood-red roan of anger. 'Not about that anyway, Mom. Who's my father?'

'Jimmy Carter! Never forget that, child! Without the ethnic guilt invented by that good man, we would be nowhere!'

At which stage, inevitably, her mother had a pressing need to hang up and do something else . . .

CUZZIES

A FRIDAY EVENING. Morgan and Roger are in Room 117 of the Coachman Inn. Morgan lies on the bed. Roger sits in the purple plush armchair by the window. Outside, in the hotel gardens, the sun sets on a plaster Pompeii.

'It has to be Ted.'

'Nope.'

'Was it you?'

'Nope.'

'Well, it wasn't me, so why are you so goddam adamant it wasn't Ted who told this Tommy guy?'

'Because the Maori people are possessed of a rather noble concept of communality, a sort of pre-democracy: a beautiful, uncynical generosity that Western civilisation has long since forgotten. If one of them is in luck, they want to share it.'

'Well, there you are!'

'No. Because Ted's the only Maori I know who's totally devoid of it.'

'I've got more faith in human nature,' growled Morgan. 'It was him. Call him.'

The truth lay about midway between their opinions. Ted had indeed shared the secret, but with extreme reluctance and without beauty or generosity. The knowledge had been extracted from him under duress, by Bunny Todd, to whom Ted owed $300. Bunny had accepted a quarter share of a million dollars in lieu.

'Well, how many other people has he told?' howled Roger through the New Age reverberations on the line.

'I don't know!' wailed the voice of Ted.

'Find out!'

The news when it came — an hour later, by phone from the Railway Hotel, Hawera — was shattering. Morgan's faith in human nature was resoundingly affirmed: Bunny was bounteously possessed of that noble concept of communality described by Roger Morrison.

He put down the phone, limp with horror. 'There're millions of them,' he croaked. 'How can they do this to me? It's my tribe; I invented it!'

'Have they got no sense?' she snapped, offended at the lack of commercial logic. 'Don't they realise the more they bring on board, the less of the divvy they get?'

'They're from a pre-capitalistic background,' murmured Roger, staring blankly into the mirror on the wardrobe. 'He says thirty-three and rising.'

'Okay, enough! Let's get some Tough going here. Get hold of Ted again. Threaten him. Tell him, any more numbers and we confess. We tell the university it's all hogwash. Then no one gets anything.'

'The trouble with Ted is he's not stupid. There's too much money in it. He won't believe we'd do it; he's a student of human nature.'

She angrily rattled the ice in her depleted Black Russian. 'He'd better believe it; you'd better make him believe it, because otherwise you are one of the people who ends up with nothing!'

He was not as cowed as he should have been; in fact her words seemed to snap him out of his semi-coma of remorse. 'It's no use you getting on your high horse, it's going to backfire on you as well.'

The hideous injustice of the remark caused tears to splash across her eyes. 'What! You keep me out of this! How? I don't care how many ways you have to split the money; how can it affect me, dammit?'

'It's going to scare the university off. How can we sanely expect them to believe the claim is all tied up when there's more Harakekes climbing out of the woodwork every day?'

From that calm nub, that eye-of-the-storm in her brain, Morgan awaited the answer. It came. 'We'll make the deal immediately.'

'How?! The university won't make the deal till you produce a damn birth certificate!' He had suddenly found some high ground to clamber onto. His voice firmed. 'It's not me undermining this deal, you know. It's you! Why in hell are you dragging the chain on this certificate thing anyway?'

'That's just become irrelevant. Get back to Ted. Tell him to organise a grouping. Every single last member of this fantasy tribe.'

'Then what?'

'Then we have a signing; get them all together, both sides; we sign a treaty of estoppel.'

'That doesn't solve the problem. They won't deal with us until you . . .'

'Then we sell them the company! My credentials become irrelevant then!'

Great Day for a Hangi: Sunday, 21 February

THE WIND, OF which Palmerston North seemed to be made, was tangled in the high wall of macrocarpa behind her, susurrating in the thickets like a million little librarians demanding silence. To Morgan's left, a honeycomb of nets and netting on a tennis court, and beside it a stand of bone-white eucalypts. Between the trees lay great strips of fallen bark, like exploded retreads on a motorway.

Across the park two male sprinters strode with supercilious elegance around a four-hundred-metre track, arms held up to their chests in tyrannosaurus pose. They pounded to the line and their form disintegrated into a flurry of limbs, then they looked down in unison at the watches on their wrists. Behind them a blotch of sunset, elegant houses, a lake peopled by ducks.

A voice beside her, crackling with age. 'I told you to go real slow!' It was an old woman she now knew as Hannah. 'We put you in at the same time, as a privilege, and you have abused that privilege!' Morgan assumed she was referring to the sprinters. She wasn't; she was talking in singsong to a chickenwire basket of tubers called kumara.

Another old woman, called Betty, leaned over the basket beside Hannah and prodded at the steaming tubers with her finger. 'They're okay. Not to worry, Hannah, they're fine.'

'I told them. I said, "Don't cook too fast." I took them on trust!'

'They're fine! Don't be picky!' Betty waddled to the side of the pit to unwrap cheesecloth from another excavated basket.

'Do you talk to all the vegetables?' enquired Morgan lightly.

'Oh no,' replied Hannah, distractedly unloading the basket's contents onto a plate. 'None of the others understand, only kumara. They come from heaven. Not that that makes them always listen!' she added severely, glaring down at the plate of rebellious vegetables.

Morgan was at a hangi. At hangis you bury food then dig it up and eat it. The trick is that you put heated stones in the bottom of the pit. Not just ordinary stones either — river stones, for example, are not very good because they often split with the heat and blow up the food. The best stones are volcanic, and Waka Harris had brought some down from Auckland in his truck yesterday.

'You get the best-sized ones in Remuera,' he explained. 'That's where the walls are.'

Waka was now shovelling soil from the last corner of the cooking pit. Hemi, Pete, Pete, Terry and Diesel were hauling steaming sacks from the hole, revealing bright green vegetation beneath. The process was disturbingly reminiscent of the activities of the skinning room.

Around and about, in the rosette light of evening, were the cuzzies. Dozens of cuzzies, bright as Smarties in their contrasting football jerseys; dozens and dozens of cuzzies, and all of them members of the hapu Ngati Harakeke. The cuzzies came in three age categories. The old: picturesquely wrinkled and with the quiet hepness of the near-dead; time had eroded anger from their faces — honky was merely a rude stranger who had burst in one day without wiping his feet. The middle-aged: the generation of the damned, wrought with the cattarrhs and dementias of paleface drugs, unversed in their own language, fearful of the anger of their children and the anger it will provoke in return. And the young: cursing Whitey in Polytech-perfect Maori.

In fact the hangi was taking place in the Polytech grounds. The buildings loomed to their left; Pentonville-chic, windows like Darth Vader's eyeslits; 'Have a nice day' in reinforced concrete.

The layers of sacks and flax and leaves had been cleared, the meat had been inspected by experts and declared done — an announcement greeted with relieved cheers.

'An underdone hangi is a deep disgrace,' explained Roger, who had come to stand beside her. 'It portends great disaster.' She caught his eye and he nodded. 'Yes, and we got exactly that.' He wandered off into the mêlée of sudden hapu members, with whom he must divide the profits of his company. She'd counted forty-four new company shareholders so far, and, with the comings and goings in the distant carpark, the numbers were not yet complete. She laughed; what gall! What aplomb these people had!

Cloth-covered baskets of food were extracted from the pit with the reverence of treasures from Tutankhamen's tomb. Beneath the baskets the volcanic stones were translucently white with heat.

'I hate to say this,' she whispered to Bruce, the giant bookie from the Railway Hotel and now her best friend, 'but it's much like a wide grave.'

Bruce smiled. He had four teeth — two up, two down — and probably the same number of balls. His voice was a thrilling bass rumble. 'In the olden days,' he rolled, 'they used the same system for curing wounds. Medicinal hangi. Special secret wood, layers and layers of special secret leaves. Lots of flax mats, then the patient was put in and covered with more mats. The steam and the prayers cured the wounds.'

'What if the steam . . .?'

He shrugged. 'Well, we were cannibals in those days.' He looked quickly away, presumably to hide a four-toothed smile.

During the evening Ngati Harakeke members approached her, alone or in little groups. The approach was formal, often with a little jiggle of the back foot on the way, and upon arrival there was often a disconcerting silence as they studied her. Despite initial daunting appearances, she realised the greetings were warmly genuine, and in most instances she was sympathetically adjudged a near-miss. Hannah summed it up. 'There is us and there is Pakeha. Before they came we didn't have a name for us — didn't need one. Well, they came and we gave them a name. And what are we going to call you? Nothing! You don't need a name.'

From this Morgan assumed she was not a Pakeha. What she was, conveniently, did not need to be defined.

It was universally agreed that she 'looked like Hinerangi'. Hinerangi was evidently a local beauty who had 'gone up north' (sometimes she'd 'shot through') some years before to seek her fortune in Auckland. Morgan had braced herself for the bit about how she now worked in a south-side cathouse, then was told she was a principal dancer with the New Zealand Ballet.

They evinced a flabbergasting uninterest in her roots. Well, it had been flabbergasting initially; later she realised that as she wasn't Pakeha, she was more or less one of them, and they knew all about themselves. But they loved tales of Indian one-upmanship. She easily found herself in Uncle Remus mode, retelling the history of the US with the natives of America as Brer Rabbit: the stories of Deganawidah and Hiawatha, Tammany, Tecumseh that she'd learnt at school — plus the blood-and-guts stuff of course — culminating in Sitting Bull's big win over Custer.

A BLACK HOLDEN Executive VP had cruised into the carpark and was now surrounded by a knot of half a dozen or so Ngati Harakeke. From behind the knot emerged Ted Nea, pushing a wheelbarrow. It had been washed smooth and was lined with sacks.

Two figures emerged from the tinted interior of the Holden. From the driver's side Dr Duncum, and from the passenger side a slim figure in a gracious charcoal suit, the best, by far, Morgan had seen since her arrival.

Roger was still standing beside her and she could somehow feel tension humming from him like electricity. 'Oh no,' he was muttering. 'For God's sake, no!'

The hapu members had gathered unthreateningly around the newcomers, nodding, trudging up and down on the spot, wringing their hands behind their backs. The impression, even from this distance, was of an awedly nervous football scrimmage. The elegantly clad gentleman was standing silent, surrounded by a nimbus of saintly dignity into which no tribal member dared to step. They gathered beyond it, staring in. Ted, who had parked his barrow, and two other clansmen were now in energetic discourse with grey-suited Dr Duncum, who was making the staccato movements of an angry man. His wrath was not reciprocated — the mood of the tribe, as manifested by wide-spread palms and shoulder pats, was of conciliation. Then Dr Duncum strode the three paces to the dark-suited man and spoke to him. The man listened, white-crowned head held high, a point of serenity in the midst of bustle.

From there on in it became even more preposterously biblical: the dark-suited man stepped into the wheelbarrow, supported by Ted and another. Immense Bruce the Bookie picked up the handles. The convoy headed across the carpark towards them. Christ was on his way into Jerusalem.

Oh no! There were spilt leaves of flax on the ground!

Roger was moaning quietly and repetitively. 'I said the Governor-General! I said "Governor-General"!'

Morgan was gaunt with helpless mystification. 'What's going on? Is this some sort of traditional ceremony?'

'One day, in the Camino Real, Managua,' mumbled Roger, not taking his eyes from the outlandish scene, 'Colin Fox told me that when the Governor-General visits Massey, he is traditionally carried to the meeting place. I told this to Ted one night; somehow he's turned it into this.'

'Who's that in the wheelbarrow?'

'The Vice-Chancellor.'

THE VISIT OF the Vice-Chancellor lasted for no more than fifteen minutes. He carried out his duties with unsmiling poise, then, graciously declining to partake of hospitality, he departed. He was escorted back to his vehicle by Dr Duncum and a formation of respectful hapu members. He went on his way without ostensible signs of rancour or outrage.

But it was a quarter-hour of nightmarish unreality; one of those segments of time when the mind, having said, 'this can't be happening,' is so convinced by its own opinion that it numbs out all but about a tenth of its awareness.

At the beginning of that quarter-hour the Vice-Chancellor had been borne, delphicly upright in his wheelbarrow, to a trestle table, unadorned with food, where he was offered a chair. On the table were several sheets of dense paper, replete with heavily Gothicised headings and large round seals. The title page bore five paragraphs in exquisite print, below which the Vice-Chancellor affixed his signature and the date, and Dr Duncum did likewise. Then the Vice-Chancellor turned the document around and, one by one, the members of the hapu Ngati Harakeke stepped forward and signed it, filling the next three heavy pages in the process. Thirty-four males, twenty-one females — the imprimatur of every twig of the Harakeke family tree, there on the document of disclaimer. Solemnly and bindingly, the Harakeke signed away its rights to the land beneath Massey University.

At the conclusion of the signing ceremony the document was rolled, fixed with royal-blue tape and handed to Dr Duncum. He bowed from the neck and, after showing it to an impassive Vice-Chancellor, thrust it into a leather hold-all from which he then produced a BNZ chequebook and wrote a cheque for $100. This he presented to Roger, who passed it to Morgan, who put it into her black kid-leather handbag from which she then extracted the registration documents for Te Harakeke Ltd. She handed them to Roger, who handed them to Dr Duncum, who showed them to an impassive Vice-Chancellor and then put them in the hold-all.

From the hold-all Dr Duncum then produced a document that he handed to the Vice-Chancellor, who ceremoniously read it to himself, knowing full well its content, and signed it. Dr Duncum did likewise, then handed the form to Roger, returning a duplicate to the hold-all. Roger handed the document to Morgan.

And so she came into possession of the zeacinte.

THE TERMS OF disposal were brisk and thorough. Under Morgan's supervision the crop was to be dug up and placed in metal containers, doused in petrol and burnt. The containers were then to be dumped at sea. The land that had supported the crop was to be soaked with Agribiocide, a product of Agrisync, Kalamazoo, available under licence and known (by her) to be two and a half times more toxic than Agent Orange. A tarmac carpark was to be built on the land within a week of the removal of the crop, and she was to be given open rights to have the university searched for stored zeacinte. If the crop ever emerged, the disclaimer on the land was invalidated.

These were the terms within the last document signed by the VC and Dr Duncum, both of whom then rose and departed.

('Do you wheel them back as well?' Ted had whispered. 'I don't know!' Roger had hissed in reply. 'Colin Fox didn't say.')

Across the invisible pathways of incomplete tradition the return was made on foot.

After the tension and unreality of that quarter-hour, Morgan assumed she would desire as little food from the hangi as had the Vice-Chancellor, but she was wrong. She tried some pork, and it fell down the sides of her tongue like the saliva of lust.

She ate deeply and drank bad, sweet white wine. It was wonderful. She talked deeply too: with Diesel, Pete and Pete she discussed which US cars had the most 'grunt'; with Hannah she discussed the best burial place for detached braids; with Bruce and his brother Garth, who was studying to be a lawyer, she discussed the story that American Indians discovered Europe while Columbus was on the high seas.

They performed a war dance for her. 'Car mar tay, car mar tay,' they chanted. 'Cow hearer, cow hearer.' It was ferocious but curiously melodic. She realised it was in waltz tempo. She sang 'We Are the World' for them in return, so successfully that all joined in for at least ten minutes. Diesel, a thin, twitchily rhythmic type, knew F, G, C and A minor on the guitar. They sang rowdy ballads; she with the wide-mouthed gusto of Dolly Parton, they with the dangerous cleverness of the barbershop.

'Sooner or later of course,' she shouted to Roger Morrison, her throat throbbing from the thick, dreadful notes of 'Cheryl Moana Marie', 'you have to tell this lot about the change of plan.'

'That was a lot of ceremony we went through, eh Rodge?' It was Pete who spoke, his chin shiny with pork fat. It was after midnight, and the trestles sagged with a supper of cold collation under the lights of the tennis court.

'Sure was, Pete,' replied Roger.

'I reckon we must be filthy rich now, eh?'

His face had the square, feral cast of a Bolivian peasant. So did that of his friend Pete, who now joined them. In fact, to Morgan's slight perturbation, the Petes called each other 'bro' rather than cuz.

'How much do you reckon we're worth now, Rodge?'

'In round figures, like,' added Pete.

'It's a bit hard to say offhand,' said Roger shiftily. 'It'll take a few days to find out.'

Others had joined them. There was a subtle change of atmosphere. Ted was a short distance away, standing side on, as blackbirds do.

'I reckon we should put Bruce in charge of the accounts,' said Pete. 'He's the boy with the head for figures.'

'Yeah?' jeered Pete. 'Since when's he had to count up to a million to give you your winnings, eh? Hee hee.'

'A million?' cried someone. 'They reckon that drill's worth a billion!'

Roger sighed and scuffed at the dampening ground with his toe. He looked up and glanced angrily across the darkness, first at Morgan and then at the hovering Ted. 'Of course, no one actually said it was the Cross-Slot, did they?'

Silence. Morgan noticed she was holding her breath.

Ted had peeled off from the conversation he had been having with Waka, the collector of Remuera walls. He strolled over to the periphery with a dangerously careful swagger he'd probably learnt from *West Side Story*.

'How do you mean then, Rodge?' he said quietly. His voice carried from one end of the occasion to the other. He stood at the edge of the light-silhouetted group, rather like Judas at the Big Supper. Oh no, biblical imagery again!

'It was a common assumption that it was the drill, and a logical one. But it's wrong — there's something else.'

'You saying we've been cheated out of our heritage again, Rodge?' Ted, gelled red hair gleaming in the high light, was doing his curious little jig again.

'No, Ted, I'm not. Just that there were certain things we couldn't tell you because we didn't want it to get out to the university. Well, we drew up a contract, which the university agreed to tonight. It was one of the papers they signed. We take possession tomorrow.'

'Of what, Rodge?' Ted with the same ominous serenity.

'Morgan will explain,' said Roger. 'It was her company until tonight.' And he turned smilingly to her; a mask of cherubic assassination.

Asshole! Traitor!

'You sold our company? To them university types?' It was Waka, outraged; as was she, for a different reason.

'Yep,' said Roger vigorously. 'A hundred one-dollar shares; we owe you all about forty-five cents so far.' He flashed a lonely smile.

Ted had cleared a little wold in the crowd with his jigging. 'So

— uh — if we're not getting this drill as compo for our tribal land, what are we getting then, Rodge?'

'You're getting the market value of a rare and important type of corn, found nowhere else in the world,' said Morgan. She waited for a response, suddenly finding herself on the balls of her toes; poised, she realised, in flight mode.

'Corn, eh? They do corn chips?' asked Diesel.

'Cornflakes, eh? Hee, hee.' She wasn't sure who had said it, it could have been any of them. The astonishing thing was there was absolutely no recrimination. Their expectations had migrated from a machine to a plant in less than a nanosecond.

There was a strange, potlatch sort of carelessness about material possessions here; a charming uninterest in the particulars of their fortune. Just as innocently beautiful was their unshakeable faith in the fact they did have a fortune. They had instantly become a proud bevy of middle-class stockholders; owners of . . . something.

'What's it worth, Miss Moran, our corn, like?' asked Terry, one of the most villainous human beings she had ever laid eyes on, with the disposition of a lamb.

'Market value depends on the market,' she replied promptly.

Roger Morrison gave a jolt, as if her reply had been electrified. He was gawping at her now, and even in the mothy light she could see he had paled. Poor Mr Muesli. She smiled into his horror; watched the moonrise of realisation as he walked for the first time into the cold brutal light of Big Business. He would accost her at the first private opportunity, she knew. And he did . . .

THE TRESTLES WERE being dismantled, sacks, wire baskets and other cooking utensils were being shaken clean, dogs were being shooed away from buckets of surplus food. Diesel was singing Billy Joel from the top of the remaining woodpile.

'I've just realised something!' gritted Roger Morrison, glowing livid in the now-misty light.

'Really?'

Just beyond the light, the macrocarpa hedge reared like a black tsunami.

'Market value depends on the market. I've just realised the market value of zeacinte!'

'Really?'

'Yes. Nothing! Totally nothing!'

'Well, well,' replied the daughter of her mother.

MAIL: MONDAY, 23 FEBRUARY

MORGAN WOKE, NEXT morning, in need of Berocca, and had some sent to her room. She later asked for orange and coffee. She read a newspaper called the *Dominion*. The attitudes and philosophies of everyone within, except the Phantom, were profoundly alien to her. At nine o'clock the desk called ('rang' as they said here) to say a gentleman was asking for her, should he be sent up to her room?

No, she would come down. It would be a university official, come to conduct her to the overseeing of the zeacinte blitz. Put him at a table with coffee and she would be down in fifteen minutes. And she would have a light omelette at that time, thank you. Destruction Day should not be embarked upon on an empty stomach.

She 'rang' Harvey the Toot. 'The world's last zeacinte gets put to sleep this morning,' she cooed.

'What morning's this?' croaked Harvey. 'We ain't havin' a morning. We ain't even havin' the same day as you.'

'Shut up, Harvey,' she smiled. 'Tell Mom, tell everybody; it's all over.'

'Good girl, Morg, I will. Afternoon to you.'

She ran the shower and thrummed through her wardrobe for something tight. 'I'll tell you what, Miss Moran,' Terry had said last night, 'you're a well-mangoed woman all right.' She owed it to her audience.

When she descended, she was informed by an assistant manager — the third since she'd been here — that the gentleman had not waited but had left a letter. Odd. Who was the gentleman? Was it one who had been here with her before? Yes, it was the gentleman she had been with in the bar several times.

Roger Morrison. Yet the letter was on university stationery. She took it to her breakfast table. After reading it, she returned to her room, her fast unbroken.

In the envelope there was a birth certificate and a short note from Dr Duncum.

Dear Miss Moran,
Our curiosity was aroused by your reluctance to produce a birth certificate. Consequently, we commissioned a search of your public credentials from the genealogical library of the Church of the Latter Day Saints. Coincidentally, the results were awaiting me on my arrival at the university this morning. I enclose a photofiche copy of your birth certificate. When you have read it, please contact me immediately at 354 4331.
Yours faithfully
William Duncum.

She turned to the copy of the document.

CERTIFIED COPY
BIRTH REGISTERED IN NEW YORK, USA
After declaration duly made according to law.

SURNAME: Mordkjosbotnan (Moran)
OTHER NAMES: Morgan Skei Rastegai'sa
SEX: Female
DATE OF BIRTH: 13 March 1960
PLACE OF BIRTH: St Carmel Hospital, Brooklyn, New York

PARENTS OF CHILD
FATHER — SURNAME: Mordkjosbotnan (Moran)
OTHER NAMES: Marritte Isachsdr Lemmbutte
AGE: 43
OCCUPATION: Entertainer
PLACE OF BIRTH: Bensonhurst, Brooklyn, New York

MOTHER — SURNAME: Ynzynstenzy
OTHER NAMES: Mavis Thora Mocba
PLACE OF BIRTH: Unionville, Monroe County, Indiana

DATE OF MARRIAGE: 1957
PLACE OF MARRIAGE: Sts Volodymyr and Olha Orthodox Church, Kings, Brooklyn, New York
PREVIOUS CHILDREN OF MARRIAGE: Two males living
INFORMANT: M.I.L. Mordkjosbotnan (Moran) Father, Brooklyn, New York

PARTICULARS OF REGISTRATION: Ervin A. McKenna,

District Registrar, Brooklyn, 4 June 1960
Number 72133/2200

Mordkjosbotnan? Ynzynstenzy? Names she couldn't even pronounce! Her names! And where was the Sinagua blood? The nearest her heritage came to Indian was Indiana!

She'd secretly come to accept Hoppy Sideways as her father. And with him had come acceptance of her Sinaguan heritage. Now, suddenly, brutally, Hoppy had packed his tepee and left her; had strode off forever into the fasts of the Sonoran Desert and Hotwa Vo, where she could never follow him.

She was buffeted by a wave of strangeness; she sat, a stranger to herself, in a strange country, fighting for a company that sold a crop that had just become profoundly alien to her . . .

Even the short walk from the dining room was difficult; she handled her body with the fumbling diffidence of a beginner driver. In her room, in front of her mirror, when she asked the inevitable 'Who am I?' question, a mental voice enquired coldly, 'Who wants to know?' Holy St Genes! How much further down the schizo/dualistic road can you go than that?

Yet strangely, paradoxically, it was towards her mother that she leaned for identity. But then was that so surprising? Okay, so this was all the old shrew's fault, but what were the options? Who was her father after all? What did she know about him? Who was he, this Marritte Isachsdr Lemmbutte Mordkjosbotnan? What was his history?

SHE DIDN'T CONTACT Dr Duncum 'immediately'. Why the hell should she? She knew where events were heading: she was shafted. 'The contract as it pertains to you, Miss Moran, is invalid. Your persona does not, unfortunately, correspond with reality.' Something like that.

Did this invalidate the entire contract? If it did, Mr Muesli's bogus tribe were out as well. And if it didn't . . . hey, then they'd legally signed their rights away! Either way, they were screwed down too! In the disastrous day's only moment of exultation she telephoned Roger Morrison.

'GOOD GRIEF!' HIS lovely voice had said when they met, 'what have you done with your hair?'

He stared at the empty space where once her braids had been.

'It was you who got my birth certificate, wasn't it?'

His mouth hung open as it awaited operating instructions from the LIE/ TRUTH centre of the brain.

'Yes.' TRUTH. 'When it became obvious that your mother was not going to front up with the certificate, I thought that if I could get hold of it from the Mormon family-tree department, I could pass it across and get the show on the road. Do you a favour. Then, to my horror, I saw what it said, and kept it out of sight — for your own good. In the meantime I hoped something else would turn up. I hope you realise that what I did was . . .' TRUTH was about to disintegrate into earnest supplication.

'And then you passed it over to the university.'

'Well . . .' The soft dappled paws were spread beseechingly. 'Look, I didn't do this to hurt you, Morgan, and it's no real threat to Agrisync. It's just that — well, let's face it, you did me like a dinner, didn't you? "Market value" — what an idiot I was! I mean, what's the market value of a crop that's about to be obliterated? Okay, I showed my financial naïvity, but that left me with a hideous problem: how do you tell a fictitious tribe of cut-throats that there's nothing in it for them? Do you think they'd let me get away with that? It was self-protection!'

The same earnest, somehow intimate sincerity; the same vulnerable honesty . . . Jeesaz! This was exactly what he'd said last time! This asshole kept stealing her corn from her in exactly the same way!

'All I wanted to do was — well — put a bit of pressure on you. Look, all you have to do is front up with a bit of cash that I can spread out among the —'

'Cuzzies?'

'Yes. And all will be well. We'll destroy the stuff as planned and everything is sweet.'

She stared at him, almost marvelling at his gall.

'Twenty times earnings? That went out the window months ago, thirty times at least!'

Then she hissed quietly to him, 'Roger darling, do not try and pull your pathetic little pranks on me. You are out; you have nothing. You have crashed out as cataclysmically as I have. We organised a little ceremony, you and I — remember? — by which we unitedly signed away our prospects.' And she blew him a little kiss, which he fielded with the centred fondness he'd hitherto reserved for Dr Duncum.

'I don't want to embarrass you, Morgan,' he replied, 'but your — may I say venomous? — triumph is a little misplaced. In the light of proceedings, the company lawyers met with the university's lawyers this morning and concluded that what had been invalidated by . . . events was the signing away of our rights to the land. So the rights 'devolved' as we say in law-speak. Te Harakeke Limited owns the rights again. The only difference I'm afraid is that you're not part of it all. Darling.'

She could feel her lip curling. It was a common activity but had never occurred to her before. She had often wondered what caused it. Now she knew: a desire to bite. 'Listen, you scumball, what if I go to the university and tell them there's no such tribe as the Harakeke?'

He sighed. Deeply and with great sincerity. 'I think Dr Duncum would take you to the Race Relations Tribunal,' he said mournfully.

THE STOCKHOLDERS: 23 FEBRUARY; 2.30 P.M.

MORGAN CALLED A cab. 'To the university,' she said. 'Go in the back way, left off the main road to Shannon; top of the hill.'

THEY WERE HARD at work. Ngati Harakeke were fortifying their company assets as if Te Rauparaha were coming. Or E.G. Wakefield's settlers. Or Attilla the Hun.

Or her.

Yes, that was it; her. They were barricading the zeacinte against her.

Terry was there, and Waka. Bruce, Pete, Pete, Diesel — several women. Some of them were inexpertly rolling barbed wire around the crop, others were erecting tents behind the dishevelled pines on the plateau above the tiny zeacinte-glowing valley. She watched for an hour.

The cabbie stirred worriedly. 'You got the money to pay for this, lady?'

She watched the attempt to ruin Agrisync. 'Dunno,' she murmured.

It was not a thing of beauty. It had none of the formidable

'barrierness' of a classic fence. It looked rather more as if the crop had been untidily gift-wrapped.

Morgan shivered. Her body temperature had actually been lowered by her wrath. There really is a state of cold fury.

'On TV,' she murmured, 'several times I've seen this primaeval wlat striding across fields with a telephone pole on his shoulder . . .'

'No, not Watt,' explained the driver. 'That's Colin Meads. Pinetree.'

'Really? I thought it might be hardwood.'

'Come again?'

'Where do I get those posts?'

'Oh, Mitre 10.'

'I'd like to go there.'

A group of men in bad suits walked up the road from behind the first line of low-slung, Prairie House-like agricultural buildings. With them was Roger Morrison, paleface leader of the famous Ngati Harakeke. Chief Hominy Grit; walking with the studied inexorability of the overweight.

'Drive down the hill,' she said, 'into that group of men. Not necessarily gently. Pick up the tubby guy with the freckles.'

From the cut of their suits and the wear on the seams she gathered that they were middle-salaried officials, probably agricultural technicians. She didn't recognise any of them as they glared angrily into the cab.

'Get in,' she said to Mr Muesli. 'Take us to town, driver.'

'I've got a car out here,' he said as he levered into the back seat with her.

'He can bring you back. Now we can talk. Presumably you want to talk?'

'Yes.'

They set off past the little valley and its bulwarked crop. The stockholders worked on, protecting their stock with a will, every worker a Ngati Harakeke hapu member with a heritage stretching back to the day in 1975 that their tribe had been forged into creation.

The crop blazed with rainbow fecundity. It had seeded, and the field swayed like molten lava. Soon the company shareholders would harvest their zeacinte.

'Well,' he said, with cautious vigour, 'what do you think?'

'Pathetic.'

'Look, I know . . .'

'I could build a better fence than that myself. In fact I'm going to. Driver, will these Mitre 10 people know where I can find some decent fence-builders?'

'I reckon.'

'Good.' She turned back into Mr Muesli's frown. 'If you want to keep me out, then by God you'll do it properly. That thing is an insult to my skills of breaking and entering.'

'Look, it's more . . . symbolic really. I didn't really think you'd . . .'

'Yes you did. And if you didn't, you're mad. I will build you an entirely unenterable fence, and I'll leave provision in the budget for you to buy as many locks as you like. Now, you said you wanted to talk?'

'Yes I do, but why do you want . . .?

'Talk!'

'Yes. Right. Well. Let's . . . I'll bring you up to date with the situation.' The earnestly presented palms. 'The situation with the university is that we harvest this crop, return the ground to its original state, and then officially renounce our land claim again. The situation with the company is that it sells the crop to you.'

'You're going to sell me my own crop?'

'We've been through all that, Morgan. I am going to sell you this crop; not your crop, this crop. Okay? The whole thing — lock, stock and barrel. No other negotiations will be entered into unless you decline to buy or forfeit your rights to. Upon sale — and transfer of funds — my fellow company shareholders will immediately begin the total destruction of the crop, if that is still what you wish.'

'You know it is.'

'Then it will be done.' There was a pause; she allowed it to hang in the air untouched. At last he summoned the courage to break it. 'Well really, that just leaves the matter of — the price, doesn't it?'

'Yes. You start.'

'Well — how will I put this without crassness creeping in? Let's say we had come to an arrangement and had signed on it, and I was looking at the contract right now and it said, "We the undersigned undertake to completely destroy the zeacinte in return for compensation to the sum of . . ." What do you think that figure might be?' And there was that flash of angelic radiance.

'Oh, it could well have been a billion,' she replied airily. She looked away with glowering mini-triumph. Beside her she heard the click of the condoyles in their glenoid fossae as Mr Muesli's temporalis muscles slackened and his jaw fell open. She looked back. 'But it isn't; it can't be; because of your nuclear policy. Ronald Reagan's ban on the dollar has put such pressure on the laundromat system into New Zealand that the whole thing's clogged. I couldn't get a billion in here right now for love nor money; I'd be ten miles down the queue behind your business leaders.'

'Right, right. So, what do you . . .?'

'How about ten million? Much more manageable; I can get it flown over.'

The same click. A pause. 'Fine.' The voice came as a squeak, which overcorrected itself into basso-profundo. 'Fine. They'll be happy with that, I'm sure. I'll tell them.'

'Yes, you do that.'

'I will. US dollars?'

'Is there any other?'

'Of course not — ha, ha. Look, Morgan, I hope . . . I'd like you to leave here thinking . . . well, look, it would be nice if you felt that everything I did was necessary — that it was what you would have done in the same circumstances . . .'

'Roger, don't get craven. Big business is about bigness. Okay?'

'It's just that . . .'

'Don't, Roger. They don't provide barf bags in these cabs.'

'I'm sorry. I'm really, really . . .' Sentimental tears of pacified greed bulged in his eyes.

'We'll sign tomorrow, okay?'

He nodded, unable to speak, his face a mottled caricature of Stan Laurel's. They continued in silence down the heavily verandahed main streets of Palmerston North, through a series of maddeningly hectoring traffic lights, and stopped outside a purple barn set in an acre of concrete.

'Mitre 10,' said the driver.

She disembarked and smoothed down her skirt. 'The gentleman wants to return to Massey; how much is the fare so far?'

'No! No, I'll get it,' cries Roger, still overcome by the emotionalism of ten million dollars. 'Don't worry about it. Last one out pays; local custom.'

'Well,' she emotes. 'That's gallant. It seems a little unfair, seeing I was giving you a lift, but if you insist; thank you.' She flares a four-megaton smile then turns to the passively bemused driver. 'Just by the by, what is the fare so far?'

'Seventy-three dollars eighty cents,' he murmurs.

She smiles into the psychic chaos going on in the back seat. 'Is that okay, Roger? You wouldn't prefer . . .?'

'No, no,' moans the Ten-Million-Dollar Man. 'I'll pay.'

'Well, thank you very much. See you soon. See you, driver.' She leans away from the use-buffeted, pea-green Holden, then, seemingly as an afterthought, leans back and hands the driver five cherry-red $100 notes. 'And there's a little something from me, driver, to go on top of the fare.' She turns to look towards the palely glowing visage of Mr Muesli in the back seat. 'In my business, Roger darling,' she breathes, 'even parables are made of money.'

The Central Figure

Morgan is in luck. The manager knows the foreman of the gang who recently fenced Linton Prison. The structure will be completed by 'two weeks Frydee'. She extracts her chequebook and writes a sum that ensures the structure will be completed by 'Frydee.' Money talks, even in funny accents.

She walks to the public library. There she makes for the reference section. She takes down the *Congressional Encyclopaedia of America*. Between 'Ymir' and 'Yob', is an account of a Gregor Alexi Ynzynstenzy who had been living in the middle house of the middle street of Unionville, Monroe County, Indiana, when, on 30 July 1890, the town was proved by Census to be the population centre of the USA. G. A. Ynzynstenzy was thus declared the nation's Central Figure and for several months knew feverish celebrity: 'Meet Mr Middleman!'

He did nothing else of note. He'd evidently migrated from Voronesh in southern Russia when the Czar made his famous 'watz my lips' pronouncement, promising there would be no tax increases for the rich. G. A. Ynzynstenzy fled Russia because, he said, he wanted to escape capitalism. His favourite phrase was 'Bog vysok, tsar dalyok' — God's in his heaven; the tsar's far away.

Unionville; birthplace of her mother. Mr Middleman was, perhaps, her great-grandfather. Her Central Figure.

Mordkjosbotnan. Norwegian. He'd gutted his name, taken nine letters out of the middle to Americanise it. Moran.

The blood of Norway and Russia pounded at her temples; she had a vision and wept; Hauble Ceyapi — crying for a vision.

AT FOUR THIRTY P.M. she called Harvey at eleven thirty p.m. yesterday and made a requisition order.

'Jeez, Morg, I dunno we can do that.'

'It's flying, isn't it? Mom said we won the case. She said they went with all four phenols.'

'Yeah, sure, that's right. But without Bobby we hain't got access to decisions like that. There's only one guy who could help out at notice this short, an' that's . . .'

She stared into the mouthpiece as if examining the sincerity of the face at the other end. 'Hank?'

'Yep.'

'What the hell's Hank got to do with it?'

'He invented it.'

'Hank?'

'Yep.'

'You're telling me Hank made that thing?'

'That's right, girl. They work out of Tona Park out back of his place. Hey, you must have been there when he was fiddling round tryin' to work out how radar energy gets reflected off things, Morg? Been onto it since the '60s. Started the scheme up in '62. That's when your father . . .'

'What?'

'Nothin'. Jus' what I heard from your mom, girl. Your father worked for Hank for a while.'

'My father built the Stealth bomber?!'

'No. Seems he was more on the entertainment side. Anyway, tha's all I know, an' my advice to you if you wanna fast track this thing is get onto Hank.'

The Stealth. Hank invented the Stealth!

My God, the scare-crow. The radar box beside the ranch house porch!

SHE TELEPHONED HANK, mainly to make arrangements — (for above all she was a businesswoman) — but also to talk. They talked emotionally. Hank told her of her father. This is what he said:

In early 1963 he had heard that 'Mago Moran', the famous golfer, was touring the Western Mountain Region with his wife and young family and his assistant Hoppy Sideways. Hank contracted 'Mago' to perform for his workers on the recently completed Break-a-Heart golf course, designed by Sam Snead. The team would stay a week and play local dignitaries between performances. They would be paid handsomely and accommodated at the Carson City Saloon and Restaurant, where the late Marilyn Monroe had stayed while making the *Misfits*.

They arrived: 23 February, Hank thought it was; a Saturday.

Mago's skills astounded the locals, and yet, strangely, it was Hoppy who invariably won their actual matches.

On the day they were playing a foursome with the mayor of Carson City and his deputy, a violent electrical storm engulfed them; (with Hoppy and the deputy two up). A bolt of lightning hit the mayor's four iron while he was playing his second to the green and the mayor exploded. Much of the detritus hit Mago.

Mago had been screaming at the time and some of the body jelly flew into his mouth. He spat it out but portions, he knew, had gone down his throat.

'Your father never recovered,' sighed Hank, 'from the knowledge of his cannibalism.'

Two days later her father disappeared, and no trace of him had ever been found. Hank had accommodated the widow and her family — and the now unemployed Hoppy Sideways — in cottages on his ranch. He had also, Morgan discovered, supplied them with a small pension.

Morgan had wept briefly into the telephone then sniffed her grief back into herself. 'Thank you, Hank,' she whispered, then her voice strengthened: 'Now — that was then, and this is now. I must ask you an immense favour.'

And the arrangements were made.

SHE CONTACTED HARVEY with the news.

'They'll send a fighter, not a bomber; it's logistically easier and it's still got the necessary payload.'

'Great. Soon? In time?'

'Yes.'

'Great. Hey, how's it gonna get down there, girl? I's heard those things need three computers to hold 'em up and they still fly like a brick.'

My God. A jagged flash of memory; the scare-crow; a succession of changing scare-crows. Then kites. All of which crashed.

'They're going to load one on a Hercules and haul it down to the Deep Freeze base in a place called Christchurch. It'll operate out of there.'

'Hot diggerty dog; so we's back on track, huh? My corn, your corn an' both our asses has been saved. You'd better consider givin' yourself some promotion, girl!'

'I will. Oh, and Harvey. One last thing; tell my mother to cut her hair.'

'Heey! You want that I tell your mom to cut her plaits off? I know what my life's worth, girl, an' that's zilch!'

'Tell her it was me who told her to.'

'Jeez, Morg, hirin' planes that don' officially exist yet is one thing; telling yo' mother to . . .'

'Mention Unionville; she'll understand.'

She hung up.

WITH BREATH-TAKING clarity she was curling down to the sky, beside her mother, brothers and Hank in his big brown Waggoneer. A body lay unrotting at the bottom of a lake. She would play craps and Hank would talk to his national radar enthusiasts.

She gave a gag of dismay at the elusiveness of reality: on the day Hank was lecturing at Lake Tahoe on how to make the Stealth, her mother was planning to turn her into a Sinagua Indian.

THE BARBECUE: 25 FEBRUARY; 5.30 P.M.

WITH NORSE CLARITY of mind Morgan Mordkjosbotnan laid her final plans.

'Yes, a barbecue, Roger. I want to have one. Next Saturday. I'll be leaving not long after that.'

She implanted a wicked pause and listened to the solar flares of distension and contraction in his pupils. Then she added: 'But don't worry; nothing will be left undone. Financial provision will be made. That very night in fact. I don't walk out on deals.'

There was much breathy business on the other end of the phone: 'Of course you don't. Well, a barbecue would be wonderful. And we'll keep our side of the bargain, I promise.'

'I don't do promises, Roger, I do deals.'

'Of course you do. I really wish . . .'

'Listen!' She said it only to accommodate the hiss she felt building behind her teeth. 'There is one more thing. It's probably what you'd call a quick glimpse of the sensitive face of Big Business. The thing is, I want you all to come. It's my farewell party. Now, you will immediately think I want the place left unguarded so I can get at it . . .'

'No no, of course we don't think . . .'

'Don't insult me, Roger! At least have the decency to respect my unscrupulousness. I built a fence that keeps me out of the zeacinte, okay? So, seeing I'm kept out, there's no reason why you can't all come to my party. And, to overcome your last strands of suspicious paranoia, I've done something else to ease your mind. I want you to come out to where I am now to see what I mean.'

'Look, Morgan! We certainly . . .' Not even Mr Muesli was brazen enough to finish the apoplectic disclaimer. 'Sure, I'll come out. Where are you?'

'Dunno. To find me, go down to the zeacinte field and look north. You'll see a marquee up on the hill. It's for the barbecue. That'll be me in the red slacks and black B.U.M. sweatshirt, waving. You get to it off the little road to the left just after the crossroads heading to Aokautere. That's where I am. Come on up.'

'That's . . .'

'Yeah. That's remarkable. And listen, arrange for someone to stay down at the field; tell them, when I wave again, to walk around the perimeter. Okay?'

'Okay,' he replied, restraining his puzzled question in order to annoy her.

He arrived twenty minutes later. She had watched from the vantage of her hilltop as his ordinary little Honda Civic nosed down the Massey roadway, bucking over its many 'judder bars' to the bright cornfield. From there he had waved and she had dutifully waved back. Someone got out and stood self-consciously beside the field. It looked like Diesel, thin, sinuously stooped in black clothing. Then the little red car beetled towards her as if she were winding it in, disappearing behind bits of geography from time to time until it was nosing up the rough gravel road to where she stood. By now, after all this looking down upon its progress, she was feeling positively celestial.

She ushered Roger into the already-musty marquee and showed him a monitor upon which glowed blobs of Cubo-Impressionistic colour.

'Meet SOB 10,' she said. 'He's locked into geo-sync a few hundred miles above us. He's aiming down at the zeacinte — that's it on the screen. He'll be locked in for the next half-hour; keeping himself there with little squirts of retro, at a price of ten grand a pop. On the night of the barbecue he'll be locked in there for as long as the party lasts. Watch this.'

She went outside and waved to Diesel, who set off at a heavy-ankled gait around the verge of the Dachau-like fence she had provided for them. She went back to the monitor. A radioactive dot of crimson was jerking across the screen, like a dinoflagellate under a microscope.

'Hot-blooded boy,' she said. 'That's Diesel.'

'Amazing.'

'Thank you.'

'And amazingly elaborate.'

'And amazingly expensive.'

'All so we can all come to the party?'

'Yes. No expense spared. A "no hard feelings" sort of thing. Not to you; to them. I want to show my respect. They're good. They're the best. They shafted me completely.'

'That's not how they'd . . .'

'They also shafted you. Ngati Harakeke, every last one of them, and there's nothing you can do! Ha! They're the best I've seen. I don't know whether they could sell the Brooklyn Bridge to some of the street-wise Harvey the Toot types in New York, but I reckon they could damnwell hire it to a few! One day I'm going to organise a seminar on modern business methods and get them over to Harvard. They'll be a wow!

FRIDAY, 27 FEBRUARY; 7.30 P.M.

THE VIEW WAS beautiful from the little hilltop. It was an interestingly complicated array of river flats whose bright planes acted like semaphore mirrors, flashing the light of the descending sun into gullies and ravines at improbable angles, emblazoning the entire vista in anarchic technicolour. To the left, a choker of bead-like mountains ran to the west and disappeared into burn-out as it reached the sun. Close by, in the fields just over the roadway and down to her right, the colours were darker and less violent. Hey! she realised, old Rembrandt was right! Colour does start out dark and get lighter with distance! Over there too, a pretty little two-storey cottage, roofed in red slate, clad in brick with dinkily latticed little windows — idyllic. You could sit in your back parlour and look out west across untrammelled Nature, or head to the sofa in the front room facing east and watch the traffic going by on the highway.

Beyond the house, down a pleasingly sweeping hill of rye-grass and disaffected sheep, was a sliver of bright water, a reservoir into which cattle gazed like dim-witted Adonises. A mile or so to the right, a convoy of pines, behind which the chimney of the university boilerhouse stuck crudely into the sunset. And between the boiler and the pines was the zeacinte. A Persian carpet of royal reds and golds, hemmed with steel netting, barbed wire and tanalised posts.

What a pleasant evening. A warm breeze blew and cicadas sizzled in the nearby trees in time with the laden hotplates of the barbecues. They ate massive grey sausages which burst at the ends and ejaculated pink flesh that you doused in crimson 'tomato sauce' and consumed in white bread and yellow butter. The evening dimmed into night, which then released light of its own; a full moon so bright you couldn't look at it, speckles of pale stars in strange configurations, the glare of the city and the shimmering blush of smaller towns across the plain. And a cone of glowing ivory on the horizon: Mount Taranaki. Just as it had once transformed itself from cloud, it grew now from moonlight.

The air was striped with smells: pollen, herbs, manure, silage, hay, smoke, sausage fat, the sweat of cooks, the musty heat of the marquee.

They were all here. They had to be: safety reasons. But not just

Ngati Harakeke; the Lemonades too. All of Morgan's friends were here: her farewell party. She walked amidst them, proprietorial, proud. They were here simply because of her; she was their only bond.

'Statistically speaking,' Trevor Johns was rasping, 'there has to be a loophole in Death somewhere. Nothing is perfect; nothing — not Nature, not physics, not chemistry — there's always a cock-up somewhere. Why not in Death? Death can't be a hundred percent perfect; there must be imperfections — immortal people . . .'

Charlie was here. 'The right-hand side of our brain, you know, does not have the capacity of speech; not at all! And do you know, it has the IQ of a subidiot! If the right hemisphere and the left hemisphere were to meet in the street, they would not realise they were of the same species!'

'Is that a fact?' replied a voice that put Paul Robeson into soprano class. 'Is that the physical basis of dualism?' Dear old Bruce the Bookie.

Mrs Benjamabopitr had not shown, but Bindi had. She was wearing black jeans with the white cotton top Morgan had given her.

'Roger was saying you couldn't get the billion dollars?'

'No. It was a bit tricky to get through Customs.'

'That's a pity. A billion dollars would have been really neat.'

'Yes, I'm sure.' They were talking the GNP of this nation here, but they could just as easily have been talking wardrobe. Morgan strongly suspected that Bindi's brain was the source of the isocortex her father was pumping into Murray and Beryl.

And Basil Stolle was here too. 'I want you at my party,' she'd said. It had surprised him; they rarely spoke these days, joining each other's conversations only at group level, falling silent when they were alone at the bar. 'Yeah, okay, I'll be there,' he'd replied, carefully disguising his troubled pleasure. 'Good,' she'd said. 'Bring a pencil.'

'Great party, Morgan,' he said to her now; nearly midnight. He was bluff, but ready at a second's notice to circle the wagons. 'Pity I don't do society columns.'

'Nor do I, Basil. I just thought you might like that interview that was so important to you once. If you'd been allowed.'

She smiled the smile of a collector pinning a moth to a board.

Basil glared back at her in an unpleasant goggle of truculence and craven distaste.

'Now, now, Basil,' she said, 'the pen is always mightier than the word.' She smiled some more. 'Isn't it?'

Basil Stolle curled his lip; it was perhaps the most actively athletic thing he had done for some years. It was a painful and angry acknowledgement of the fact he had never been allowed to publish a single word about her.

'It's all right,' she cooed. 'It's a special night. I've given Trevor permission to give you permission. Come on.'

Behind his wide ears were the stars and the cape of the night. He looked — although it was probably just association — like Freddy the Fruit Bat. Without moving his lips, he said, 'You are a ball-breaking bitch.' Moving his lips, he said, 'I'll get you another wine and we'll take a walk.'

'Why, what a gentleman you are,' she replied, just this side of a parody of Scarlett.

He headed off.

'Nah, course the margin-buyers aren't deserting! They're coming in more strong!'

Morgan had sung a verse and a wildly out-of-tune chorus of 'Saving All My Love for You' before Basil returned with two paper cups of sudsy white wine.

'Well, let's go,' he growled, still holding both cups.

They set off, leaning into the field of rasping docks and semi-trod thistles. On the way up the hill they effected an on-hoof wine exchange as delicate as a mid-stratospheric refuelling.

They reached the top and leaned against a wire fence that squealed in greeting. They stood, regaining breath, in the deep black bars of shadow from the spinney of pines behind them. Only these dilapidated trees stood between them and Alpha Centauri. Below them, in the moonburnt field, a chiaoscuro carnival.

The monitor converted the marquee into a devilishly glowing Halloween pumpkin. Its infernal effects spread; people who passed were freakishly X-rayed on one side, plunged into darkness on the other, reducing them to voodoo skeletons. The music continued. Its chug-chug beat seemed either to join with the flicker of the stars, or create it. It's official, folks; the stars twinkle to the beat of Bob Marley!

Basil Stolle leaned sourly on the fence, holding his cup like a TV reporter doing a 'piece to camera'.

'So, how long since your last confession, my child?'

'Still want that bet on being wrong, Basil?'

'Okay, so you didn't come for the drill. But you don't own it either; I've checked.'

'Keep checking. Anyway, no. That's what I came for, that stuff over there.' She pointed. Despite the blinding moonshine there was still a perverse thread of sunset on the western sky, and beneath it the ghosts of royal colour seemed to hover over the cropfield. 'It's so hot you can still see it gleaming in the moonlight.'

'Yeah, I heard; perennial corn. Next commonsense question. Why destroy it? Why not use it yourself?'

'Bad capitalistics. Why sell something once when you can sell it every year?'

'Not being a bit paranoid about this stuff, are you, Morgan? You're going to pay this lot a fortune for one little paddockful of scrubby corn?'

'I can't afford not to, Basil. That stuff won't put capitalism out of business tomorrow, but it will one day. That's my little gesture to civilisation — preserving monopolistic control for posterity.'

'You want to pass sado-monetarism on to your kids, huh?'

He spoke with his usual wise-guy wheeziness, but the ugliness of the phrase took her aback for a moment. It had a viciousness beyond the perimeters she usually operated within.

'Yes,' she replied sweetly. The phrase was also, after all, rather sexy.

'It'll make a good story,' he said with nasty jocularity.

She smiled. 'When Uncle Trevor says you're allowed to print it.'

'What's to stop me going to another paper? The Sundays?'

'For what, Basil? Five hundred dollars? Two thousand? That worth your job? Sorry, Basil, but you live in a peanut paradise. You have to wait till something happens that interests the rest of the world.'

Someone was pursuing them up the hill, crabbing sideways to follow the sheep tracks. Foreshortening made it impossible to distinguish features, but it was a woman, in a lank dark dress and light cardigan, with a dotted scarf on her head. Hannah had been wearing a similar one.

It was Hannah. Even before they saw her face she was identifiable by those imperceptible fingerprints of mannerism. She reached their feet and flopped down on the silver grass. 'By cripes,' she gasped, 'that hill's steeper'n a cow's face.'

She sat up, propped by her arms with her back to them and facing down the hill. The legs that stuck out from the hem of her sprawled blue dress were amazingly thin, no thicker than some of the bunches in her gnarled old stockings. 'Hey!' she cried suddenly. 'Well, I never saw that before.' She pointed; her arm made a shadow.

Bouncing across the vespertine brightness was a bumblebee, pouncing on clover flowers and riding their pendulous swaying like a rodeo rider. The light and the warmth must have befuddled the circuitry of its little brain, and it had come out to play. Morgan suddenly realised the cicadas still thrumbed on as well.

'Well, that's the most unusual thing I've seen for ages,' said Hannah. She stood up, perversely at the moment Basil had taken several steps downwards to help her to her feet. She chimped to the brow of the hill and stood upright. 'You came in a car, eh?' she said to Morgan.

'A taxi, yes. It's waiting for me.'

'Yeah? A taxi, waiting?'

'He knows I pay well. Why?'

'Me and Diesel forgot to shut the gate. It was our job. We forgot. I thought you might run me back.'

'Which gate is this?'

'Back at the corn. They'll damn well murder me if the possums get in.'

'Possums? You're worried about possums down there? Ha, ha!' Basil performed one of those hearty cowboy, knee-slapping, attention-seeking displays of pointed laughter that say (pathetically), 'Ask me what I'm laughing about.' He finished. To silence. 'That block would be the most possum-free area in the country!' he hollered, desperately maintaining his own momentum. 'There aren't any possums down there!'

At last he got reaction. 'Bloody better be!' snapped Hannah, glaring downhill at him. We've got a coupla thousand dollars' worth of fencing down there to keep 'em out!'

'Sorry, love, but facts are facts,' shrugged Basil. 'They say possums are dumb, right? Well get this; that area down there —

Sick Horse Enclosure, the little valley the corn's in, the pine trees, round there — it used to be the Massey anti-possum-testing strip. Well, there hasn't been a possum near it for five years! They have to buy possums in!'

'Hannah,' said Morgan slowly, 'who said the fence was built to keep out possums?'

'Roger.'

Holy Judas, could that man betray! He hadn't told them she was off the team. With the warmth of positive conviction she realised he was going to say she'd skipped town without paying.

'How do you know there's no possums? There's possums everywhere! Possums is like weeds with fur!' Hannah's tone was an oxymoron — both ferocious and plaintive at once.

'Yeah, except down there,' said Basil, scowling triumphantly up at her. 'I told you; there hasn't been a possum there since they laid neuroheptaiodothryonine carrots, five years ago. The experts reckon possums don't talk — well, they passed the word somehow; won't go near the place.'

'Listen,' demanded Hannah in an old voice, steely as her mother's. 'You tell me what the hell's going on here! If there's no pests, what the hell did we build that fence for?'

'You'll have to ask Roger Morrison,' said Morgan. 'About quite a lot of things I imagine.'

They had been face-carvers, these people, in earlier times. Hannah's fine, firm old face was now tattooed by wrinkles into a mask of war. 'Roger, he's all right,' she snapped. 'He's ours.'

'Yours?'

'By marriage. One of ours married one of his.'

Morgan reeled, overwhelmed by the power of artifice over reality. A fictitious Pakeha, bonded by marriage to a phony tribe! 'Are you sure, Hannah?'

'Yep. That a problem?'

'No, not at all.'

'He didn't know there was no possums. He was doing it for you. Keeping them from the crop for you.'

'How thoughtful,' murmured Basil Stolle. 'He wanted the corn to be in pristine condition on the day it was destroyed.'

'He's a good boy,' said the old woman. By standing very still with her head raised, she somehow, motionlessly, created that curious, challenging jig.

'Is he?' said Morgan gently.

'Yep.'

'Hannah, he's not being very honest. With anyone. Including you.'

'Ko te koura kei te upoko te tutae.'

Morgan glanced down at Basil, who shrugged. 'I'm sorry, Hannah, I don't . . . You'll have to translate.'

This seemed to surprise the old woman. 'The crayfish has shit in its head,' she said peevishly.

'Oh . . .'

'Course we all know he's a crook; that's why we joined him,' snapped Hannah.

'I think you'll have to translate some more,' said Morgan carefully.

'Quite simple,' said Basil Stolle. 'They're crooks too.'

'Nope,' said Hannah, with crisp unoffence. 'We're family. We have joined him to absorb his crime, reduce it, weaken it with our strength and our numbers. Aue!'

'And incidently gain a fortune,' muttered Basil Stolle, not daring to look up from his already-leaking cup.

'We don't want the money,' said the old woman quietly. 'Just want our mana.'

Basil Stolle's eyes were buoyed upwards into hers by cynical amusement. 'Is that so? All mana, no money?'

'Yep,' she said, ending on the plosive so heavily she cut it in half. 'Might even send the money back.'

He was looking up, she was looking down. A monumental and unusual eyeballing ensued. Hannah had actually dropped her eyes, but as she was on the hill at least a body-length above Basil, her gaze fell on to his. They glared; passing a plasmatic beam of — whatever eyesight is made of — between them; creating a sort of rod of vision. Yes; the rod was now visible. Morgan could see it, glowing very faintly in the sky between them, the most minor of lasers, upon which their eyeballs were leaning. It was about twelve feet long — for that was the distance between them — and extremely straight, because light of course does not bend. She could clearly see Basil at his end, Hannah at hers, of the twelve-foot rod.

And where was she, Morgan? Well, she was somewhere between them. Basil was on the side of the hill below her; Hannah slightly above her on a little knoll. In fact, she seemed to be exactly halfway between them — she could measure the ratio on the eyesight rod, which, she now noticed, was marked in segments. Yes, six feet from Hannah, six feet from Basil.

Cicadas rattled like maracas.

'And where,' said a voice, 'do you want to stand?'

The question surprised her, but without awareness of motion she found, when she measured herself again on the eyesight rod, she was six foot one from Basil, five eleven from Hannah.

Hannah then threw her a line made of . . . good God, braid! — fortunately free of burial mud — and hauled her upwards with one hand while continuing to balance her end of the rod on her eyeballs. Progress upwards was easy.

'I'm making this up,' thought Morgan, 'you have to watch out for this artifice, it can be fantastically real.' And suddenly she heard herself say aloud, 'I'm sorry, Hannah, but you'll have to give me a name. I'm not Sinagua.'

Hannah turned her head. The rod fell, and Morgan would have fallen after it had not the bumblebee, at that very moment, flashed down the empty twelve-foot space. She saw it, a momentary black streak against the lozenge of glowing light called Mount Taranaki. Then it was gone, the bumblebee/rod; heading south. A geyser of flame shot upwards from the earth behind it and engulfed the white mountain, singed the sky into purple, darkened the moon and scorched the faces of all three of them uncomfortably red. There was an inverse tempest — air was sucked out of them, the shabby pines behind leaned creakingly down towards the holocaust as if in obesiance, and the marquee imploded and collapsed. Beneath the canvas folds the monitor blazed like lava.

The cicadas stopped. So did the world.

The flame acted in the nature of a splash. Great spicules of fire reared into the sky, found no grip there and fell back. The pine trees, down by the boilerhouse, detonated into a fireball. They blazed in formless violence, then burnt on as a Calvary of Ku Klux Klan crosses.

The inferno subsided into a blinding line below the much lesser line of the horizon; a subterranean sunset. Sundown over Hell.

Only when air returned — scalded air, rushing katabatically

up the hill — did Morgan realise there had been none to breathe. The trees behind them lurched upwards again with the noise of mad snakes.

And indelibly reburnt into the flesh of her brain was the vision of the scare-crow above a field of shattered corn. The impact of the image was so scaldingly new that it still glowed hotly when she blinked, yet it lay there also with the comfort of a memory. Either she had known about this moment nineteen years ago, or her mind had just duplicated a once-in-a-lifetime impression, nineteen years later.

A chant began below them, throbbing and wailing.

'What are they saying?' said Basil quietly, ever the reporter.

'Praying for rain,' said Hannah. 'This has happened before. Maui tricked fire from Mahuika. She was angered by the trick and set fire to the land.'

There was a thud from somewhere that slightly shook the ground. Morgan knew what it was.

'Hannah,' she said, shakily taking the few steps to Hannah's knoll, 'I think you've just been paid. You'll find it in one of the fields to the south of the cornfield.'

'What cornfield?' replied Hannah, not turning. The conflagration shimmered on her eyeballs. 'The one under the fire?'

Morgan squeezed the old woman's shoulder then continued to the path that led, like a little gravel glacier, down to the main road, where her taxi waited. Basil was watching her. The vision was bizarre, he was simply a head thrusting above the rough herbage at the pathside, like one of those erumpent semi-buried statues on Easter Island.

'There's your international story, Basil,' she said.

'Thanks,' he said emptily. 'Where are you going?'

'Home,' she said. She set off, then stopped. 'Basil, could you give Roger a message for me? It's quite a good quote; you can use it if you like.'

'Sure,' he said. He was more interested in the fact he still had wine in his paper cup.

'Just tell him — it's an old proverb — "Never play leapfrog with unicorns."'

Then she set off down the path to America.

BOOK FOUR

PART SEVEN

CHICAGO; APRIL

IT WASN'T AN international story. At least Basil never turned it into one, and nobody else bothered. A Stealth FII7 fighter napalmed a friendly nation then went home, without evoking comment.

Journalistic stealth.

Enquiries over the next weeks revealed that:

— the Ngati Harakeke had discovered the $US10 million bale of wampum next morning, and were well pleased;

— the napalm strike had been a direct hit, and obliteration of the crop was total;

— Roger was engaged to Bindi, and Charlie was delighted. Evidently it assuaged his grief at the loss of Murray and Beryl . . . Oh God, why this quid pro quo of Fate? Poor Murray, poor Beryl. Had their seared flesh smelt fulsomely of marjoram, rosemary and other wayside herbs? She decided to believe so.

NEW YORK; OCTOBER

COCKROACHES. HOW ON earth do they get up here? Walk? Ride the Otis? Did they come up with the bricks when the place was being built? (Come to think of it, what's a fifty-five-storey building doing being made of bricks?) 'Cockroaches you know,' Charlie had said, 'are the world's most living fossil, along with the shark, the horseshoe crab, the coelacanth and the horsetail.' The apartment was a suburb of roach-houses. The cleaning woman took them away each morning and replaced them with pre-occupied ones.

Morgan had been in New York for two days; her first trip. From her little balcony (which you could jump off if you wished — there was only a waist-high railing to stop you), she looked east, across flat, tarred roofs, through a thicket of stultifyingly efficient people-boxes — the Robert Taylor projects of the upper working class — to the East River and the industrial fleshpots of

Roosevelt Island. Queens, beyond it, seemed to be a flat place, made of smog. The smog came from the four chimneys of what was either a power station or the Queen Mary, whichever was the greater. She tried hard to see further south, down towards Brooklyn, but the view turned into bricks.

She had seen the Brooklyn Bridge; in fact she had set off to walk across it, to her roots. The October wind, blowing from the cemeteries of Brooklyn, held all the warmth of a corpse and brought tears to her eyes. The bridge was endless and soon became a procession of mini-Arcs de Triomphe latticed with gigantic spiderweb. The view ahead of her was . . . footpath, the slight bow in the bridge making a horizon that Brooklyn was below. She turned her head away from the approaching wind; behind her the silver sun glinted from a quarter of the 43,000 windows of the Trade Centre. Another fifty exuberant skytowers, some daffily crowned in Gothic scrollwork cried, 'Come back! What the hell's over there? Ten thousand files of row houses and an ex-amusement park. Come back; the only decent thing over there's the view of us!'

She turned around and walked back.

No, she walked away.

SHE WALKED AWAY again the next day when she visited the Museum of Modern Art. It could simply have been a shortish walk from her apartment, down Eighty-sixth and Fifth, but she had begun the day with a subway journey to The Cloisters. Mr Fellucini had made two cultural suggestions — that she visit the Erotics Gallery in SoHo and The Cloisters in northernmost Manhattan. 'Go see The Cloisters,' he'd said, 'pure Sicily brought home by Rockefeller. That's my roots, Morgan; go there for me.'

It had all been simple enough: the IND Eighth Avenue A train from the station a hundred yards from her apartment, up to One Hundred and Ninetieth Street, then a number four bus to the door. It was beautiful; atmospheric, sublime, Middle Aged. And French. The bits of cloister and chapel, stained glass and relics that hadn't been crated out of France, came from Spain. Not a single stone from Italy, let alone Sicily. It would be her secret.

Over-confidence was her downfall on the return journey. She

crisply disembarked at Eighty-sixth to find herself in profoundly alien territory. From a confident and amused traveller amidst gentle byways, she was reduced to a snivelling foreigner in a hostile wilderness. She appealed to a policeman. Ah. She was at Eighty-sixth West. Her people dwelt to the east, beyond the Park, towards the rising sun. If she would simply return to the subway . . . And Hell will freeze over! She marched across the leafless veldt of Central Park, pushing a bow wave of cutpurses, flashers, muggers, serial killers and multiple rapists from her path, and found herself at MOMA on the other side.

After the silence of the Park, coming back to the streets was like part two of the Mad Horn and Siren Symphony in H minor. She was hot. Harvey had presented her, as she left for O'Hare Airport, with a grubby, green, rubber/plastic raincoat. 'Wear it at all times when you're in the streets,' he'd warned. 'It's an antidote to your figure.' Beneath it now, after her march across the Park, she was steaming. A square-faced man in a black beret was selling papaya juice in little blue cups outside the entrance. She bought one, drank it and was surprised to learn she had just cured herself of cancer.

She had come to see Kandinsky and Edvard Munch; Russian, Norwegian. She wanted to know to which she would most freely respond; it could give her a fix on the direction of her identity. But as she took the elevator to the second floor, the image of Picasso's 'She Goat' and of Rodin's 'Balzac' had so soured her mind against either parent that she marched in a blinkered spiral past nine-tenths of the exhibition and stood in front of 'Starry Night'.

She gazed into the mad whorls, jagged edges and electric colours of Vincent's looniest vision and felt, for the first time in New York, a sense of tranquillity and sanity.

EVENING. MORGAN HAD been napping. The telephone blared; an internal siren. Her car was waiting, she was told. She bid farewell to her new neighbours in the roach-houses and set off for the elevator. Party time.

It was the sixtieth birthday party of Colonel Cotton Irvine of Montgomery-Manville. He'd been born in October, Black Thursday month, two years before the Crash of '29. So the party was to have a twenties theme, with a slight stockmarket emphasis.

Montgomery-Manville had bought into Mauser Chemicals six

months ago (in fact while she'd been offshore in New Zealand), and an invitation had arrived at the boardroom in the IT&T. Mauser Chemicals, of course, owned Agrisync.

The invitation hadn't been specifically for her, but in strong ballpoint at the bottom had been added the words 'Come swing, down at old Man-a-hatta', which was Algonquin for Heavenly Land. So someone had wanted an Indian who swung. There was only one. Well, of course there weren't any, but she hadn't yet found the opportunity to say so. Nor had her mother. Her mother had resigned from all business the day after Morgan arrived back in Chicago. For unspecified reasons.

The party was in a hotel suite — that's how you partied in the twenties — in West Forty-second Street. Seediville. This was partly because the colonel had been born in these parts, but also because it catered to that modern delight in 'living the difference'. In California you got the feeling by hiring a jumbo and throwing a champagne party in Haiti.

In fact, advertently or not, the party fused the values of the twenties and the eighties. The Terrible Twenties; the Execrable Eighties. Clara Bow got drunk at both parties and threw bread around the table; a Lindberg lost his shining manners and tripped up waiters; a Ziegfeld folly gave Fatty Arbuckle a blow job in the Mens. In the twenties young women smoked with bold uneasiness; in the eighties they snorted in the same way.

There were a dozen hanged bankers present, which was evidently one more than the real thing on Wall Street '29.

Seven or eight Rudolf Valentinos of course, one of whom told Morgan, much later, that his real name was Rudolf Alfonzo Raffaele Pierre Filibert Guglielmi di Valentina d'Antonguolla, which was tattooed on his dick and, with a little assistance from her, would be real easy to read. While he was doing his laughing knee-slap she stood up to shimmy with the monkey from the Monkey Trial.

She had gone as a flapper. What else? The trouble was she flapped. Unrestrained or battened, her chest could not be rendered down to the tube-like boyishness of the day, and within her straight, long-waisted, blue silk skirt, her hips resolutely refused to go away. The fact just had to be faced, she was not unripe. But at least, in these post-braided days she could shingle her hair. And she had rouged her cheeks, charcoaled her eyes and converted her mouth into a vermillion wound.

Fifty women dressed *à la mode*. A general minimum of female clothing proved, both negatively and positively, that less is more. Calves swelled below knee-high stockings; plunging décolletage freed dense shoulders and underarms that sagged like turkey wattles. Mind you, strength was a requisite — pound for pound, the well-jewelled flapper in gold-filigree butterfly necklace, chains of golfball-sized amber beads, lapis lazuli bracelets and ruby earrings and rings weighed in at about the same as the average front-line knight. Less weightily there were indulgent maximums of cosmetics, fans and feathers. And it wasn't all nightmare; there were women, usually more plainly dressed in plaids or French circular, who glowed with a willowy obstreperous beauty not seen since that indulgent age.

Oxford bags proliferated amongst the men; unimaginative smoking jackets, blazers and 'Homer 60' hats. The greatest variety was among the shape of the black bow ties.

There were some nice touches, however, amidst the standard Lindbergs, Al Jolsons, Mae Wests and Gretas Garbo. Mickey Mouse was there, for example; and Trotsky (who still lacked charisma) and Laurel and Hardy from a husband-and-wife team who had little choice. Greatest by far was a Mona Lisa with a moustache. Brilliant.

The ballpoint additions to the invitation had been made by Douglas Fairbanks; Snr. Two Douglas Fairbanks Snrs in fact.

Morgan had still been dancing with the monkey when voices behind her chorused, 'Glad you could make it, Minnehaha.' She turned the monkey to peer over his shoulder — and thereby came face to faces with her past. Behind the monkey, smilingly stepping forth from the gossamer-clad confines of teenage memory, was her duet of lovers from NAU.

Time had been good to them — no, had absentmindedly passed them by — both were an upright five feet eleven inches, both a riot of teeth and bland good-nature, both ten unexceptional years on from the polite queue of Checkmate holders in the sickbay of the Northern Arizona University. Holy Andrew Jackson! Holy smallpox-infested blanket! It was them; her first lover in triplicate! . . . duplicate! She jettisoned the monkey.

They suited their costumes well. Unfortunately, both were Fairbanks doing *The Thief of Baghdad* and it was difficult to gauge the firmness of their bodies because they were unavailable for the tactile dances — their curled shoes collapsed hazardously during tangos and waltzes. They merely charlestoned, perfectly still, criss-crossing their hands across their knees while she syncopatedly fluttered in front of them, reeling with *déjà vu*.

They exchanged histories. To her horror, Morgan found that she had forgotten not only their names, but also their identities. How dreadful! How immoral somehow, for the agents of her defloration to linger in her recollection with the unmemorable interchangeability of Rosencrantz and Guildenstern.

'And where do you fit into the philanthropic warp and weft of commerce?' she shouted to them over *Rhapsody in Blue*.

'Oh, I'm way above it all!' one replied.

'Oh?'

'Pilot. I flew Calvin Tunney the oilman in from Dallas.'

'I'm the flight attendant,' said the other. In a light voice. (Ah, she sighed, a faller from the wayside of heterosexuality, I fear. Was it her fault? Horrors!) She shimmied on, feeling the thickness of her sixteen-year-old waist.

'How do you find New York?' continued the flight attendant.

'Well, I'm not quite sure that I have. You're either looking down on it from a great height or you're so embroiled within the ten feet around you there's no time to look further. I think to get used to it you have to be a schizophrenic insect with hundred-way vision.'

'Cheer up, it gets worse. How's the apartment on Eighty-sixth?'

'How do you know I'm on Eighty-sixth?'

They laughed. 'You're learning,' said the pilot. 'That was a pure New York response.'

'The Colonel owns it,' explained the flight attendant. 'It's part of his social hierarchy. If he owns your company, you stay on Eighty-sixth; if you own his company, he puts you in a suite at the Vista International.'

'You've come a long way since . . . that night,' said the pilot.

'Richest wagon-burner in the west, I hear?' said the flight attendant.

Sudden resolution overpowered her; she would practise her

revelation on this insubstantial pair. 'I'm not a wagon-burner,' she said.

'No, I'm sorry. It was only a joke but it was out of line.'

The Fairbanks Snrs became a squirming tandem of discomfort; she'd quite forgotten which of them had caused it.

'No, you've misunderstood,' she bellowed above the music. 'What I meant was I'm not American Indian.' There, it was out. The first public announcement. It seemed to be a show-stopper. It certainly stopped the music: the dance was over.

'Hey? You sure were an Indian when we . . . that night.'

'You're an Indian success story! You mother was in *Time* magazine!'

'My mother is a fraud and a pathological liar. She's been using the system for years.' They had made their way to a couch and sat, Morgan in the middle.

'Well, what are you?' enquired the pilot.

'Norwegian or Russian — pre-Communist of course. Which would you rather be?'

'Norway's beautiful,' replied the pilot, 'but the tax is hell. But then Russia — sheesh!'

'You've been to both?'

'Yep. Well, I've been to Norway — Nato.'

'I've heard about the Russian toilets,' said the flight attendant in his light voice.

In trio, they drank highballs or champagne — whichever tray arrived first. They ate crayfish and radicchio salad.

The Colonel departed at midnight, declaring it was the best sixty years he'd ever had. 'I wish I could stay up with you youngsters till the papers come out, but those days are over for me. Not for you; stay on.'

Most did. The thicket of dancers only began to sparsen at about one a.m. Those who stayed, sat on sofas, talked in brays and dropped ash on the beige carpet — like in the olden days. The band departed at one fifteen. A flapper was found asleep in a cubicle at one thirty-five. This was as it should be; at least one high-born young lady spoke into the Great Telephone at every twenties party.

At two a.m. there is a sudden surge for the elevators; someone knows 'an amazing new coffee house' in Seventh Avenue South. Emotional contagion spreads through the increasing gap in common sense. After all, there is excellent coffee right here, and there're a million 'new coffee houses' down there. Why are we leaving? Who cares! Critical faculties have curled up in their cerebrums and gone to sleep. An odyssey in taxis.

The new coffee bar is closed. Old coffee bars on each side are open. Communication breaks down, the convoy disperses like an armada in a storm. Within Morgan's crowded wide-body Checker Marathon taxi discourse continues intensely past the frenzied gyoza shops, noodleries, shrimp bars, quesadillarias, currydoms, lescos kolbasz outlets, pig knuckleries, coconut-soup stands and mussel kitchens of Greenwich Village, SoHo, Chinatown and Little Italy — and out the other side into the foodless gulches of the financial district. Cameraderie crumbles at this point.

'Let's walk,' Morgan murmured to the Douglas Fairbanks Snrs. They dismounted and strolled Fulton Street: they spied a newsstand. Twenties parties couldn't end until the papers came out. Well, the papers were out. She plucked one from the stand, and instinctively turned to the business section. 'US AGRIBUSINESS IMPERILLED,' it said.

They walked down Nassau, the Douglas Fairbanks Snrs each with an arm around her, mainly to keep her warm, and guide her as she read the story.

A plant had been found (the story told her) that could endanger several large US agricultural consortiums. It was flourishing on the plains of Manawatu, near Palmerston North in lower northside New Zealand. How the plant — called zeacinte — had come to be there was a mystery, local sources said, because a campaign to exterminate it some months ago was thought to have been entirely successful. However, the zeacinte — a perennial cousin to corn — was now so widespread as to be probably beyond eradication. Perennial corn, (said the story), if allowed to gain access to the agricultural market could . . .

Rainbow mirrors of dizziness glimmered at the corners of her mind, and triffid-like tentacles of the hideous plant reared out from the page towards her throat. It was back, and she knew — deeply and positively — that it would never go away again. Zeacinte was immortal. Zeacinte was the Corn Mother. She, Morgan Moran, had killed the Corn Mother, but not before the old woman had rubbed her body, and left instructions for the burial of the beads of flaked skin. Morgan had napalmed her, burnt her as a witch . . . but not before the Corn Mother had adopted her. 'It isn't Ceres on the Corn Exchange,' mumbled Morgan, deep in shock, 'it's Zeacinte.'

The black, gargoylean bulk of George Washington hove into her view and behind it, across the street, the façade of the NYSE.

She was very, very cold; she was reeling . . .

PERHAPS HER IDENTITY had frozen, leaving only the motor neurons of her mind still working. Or perhaps the return of zeacinte had shocked her into a waking dream. The fact was, next to her were two Douglas Fairbanks Snrs, and the people around them were dressed as the first Fairbanks cinema audiences must have been. She herself was a flapper, and the women around her were either flappers or the types who first disapproved of them. She was on Wall Street with a brace of Fairbanks, and it was '29. Or was it '87? She didn't know. It didn't matter: the result was going to be the same.

As she reached the statue she realised there was a crowd, thousands strong, stretching from its plinth to the entrance of the Stock Exchange. The brassy midmorning sun was funnelled by masonry into a spotlight, paling the grey-clad throng, which, she now noticed, stood motionless and silent. Almost as still was the Stars and Stripes above them, and the black flag of the NYSE. The flags hung lankly, like equine heads in the Sick Horse Enclosure.

'One minute to ten,' whispered a Douglas Fairbanks.

A great gong sounded and the crowd gushed forward through the doors that had opened in the darkness behind the columns. Movement somehow transformed them into a mob. They wailed like Islamic fundamentalists as they surged, and, as they disappeared within, baying reinforcements rushed down from Broad Street and Nassau to maintain the crush outside. It seemed to her the population of New York, perhaps of the world, was being sucked into the throat of the NYSE. Inside, the babble congealed into a mad psalm of pain and fear, and outside, the six great columns of the building seemed to tremble like the strings of a granite harp.

Suddenly, impossibly, surreally, the stock board was on the façade of the building, dangling from the flags. Frantic assistants slapped cards onto the LOW and LAST columns, then almost immediately ripped them away to replace them. Stretching like a banner across the narrow street was a celestially glowing screen, through which figures galloped like steeds, gathering speed as they progressed and smashing into the metal frame on the left; constant, innumerable numbers, flinging themselves into oblivion beyond the margin. Hundreds of them a minute.

Upwards from beneath the feet of the assembly the spent tape of the frantic stock tickers reared like growing clouds of fettucini — or zeacinte — entwining the mourners, binding them together.

Clerks on clogged telephones exclaimed and shouted until reduced to answering hysterical calls with nods and shrugs. Men in grey suits and hats were lurching at brokers, hauling them close, shaking them, screaming, weeping, begging, laughing with insanity.

One of the ticker machines, she noticed, was balanced on the back of a crouching hunchback.

Now and then a voice emerged from the crazed gibberish with sense intact: 'Chicago's been closed!' 'It's collapsed in Buffalo!' 'The troops are guarding the NYSE against the mob!' She looked around to search for troopers and found walls. She was inside. Tendrils were coarsely brushing her naked arms; she had been cut by an edge, across the hand. Tape or zeacinte was climbing towards her throat.

'The production and distribution of commodities is on a sound and prosperous basis!' she heard a voice boom, and recognised it as President Hoover's.

'We've got to get away from here!' said another voice nearby. 'The whole thing's going to crash and it will be dangerous.'

'No, the President's right,' she answered urgently. 'The bottom's the time to buy!'

'It will never reach the bottom!' hissed an identical voice. 'Not till Steinbeck's written *The Grapes of Wrath*!' The voice turned into the physical experience of having her arm pulled. She turned. It was a pair of Thieves of Baghdad; a set of Fairbanks. One of them covered her bare shoulders with his brown cape and hurried her down thin streets; the other then spread his magic carpet and flew her away . . .

Of course he didn't! Morgan had awoken from a reverie into reality. She was on a jetty, looking down into the ploughed brown waters of the East River; bankers floated by. The Douglas

Fairbanks Snrs were standing on the Staten Island ferry shouting, 'Hurry, Clara! The revival is a rumour!'

Of course they weren't! This is '87! They were standing on a wide stone jetty on the East River. Over there was Brooklyn, down there the Staten Island ferry. They are at the Downtown Heliport, and the yoke of lovers from her high-school days, dressed as Douglas Fairbanks Seniors, had simply brought her here to show her their machine. She'd been hallucinating.

'Jeez Morgan, you lost it,' one was saying.

'It's the cold. You wanted to pour mulligatawny soup into your ear,' said the other.

She was wearing a wide brown cape, but was shivering. The flight attendant was holding her newspaper. 'I'd like to go,' she said quietly, taking the paper.

'Yes. We've got to get you home. Walking was dumb.' They took her hands — theirs felt like blast furnaces — and hauled her towards the South Street Highway and the white buildings that reared like the cliffs of Dover above it.

She watched giddily as the flight attendant enticed a taxi from the thin stream of three a.m. traffic, waving it in like those men with ping-pong bats do at airports. She got in. 'I meant to your place,' she said to them. 'Take me to your place — places — at the Vista International.'

THERE WAS NO patient, goose-bumped-Adam-naked queue this time. Oh no, indeed! The three of them lay abed together — and how profoundly wrong she had been about the flight attendant!

In the morning, Doomsday would begin, and perhaps its imminence impelled that instinctive 'save the male' campaign that women go on after wars, for Morgan could feel a new pulpousness around her delta, as if the very bones had yielded slightly — dislocated like a python's jaw — to allow entry within herself, to unprecedented distances.

Her worshippers fell upon her, whelming her with their tetrorchid devotions, astounding her with their imaginative venery, amazing her with their troglodytic endurance, gladdening her with their suspirant swyvings, gamahucheing her with their zeal-sodden tongues, ganching her with their identically immense, ripe cobs . . .

No, it was not corn that entered her — not the sterile cores of hybrid corn. It was the insinuant tentacles of zeacinte that came within. Time and again she was transfixed upon those tumid stems that burst forth, died down, then grew again. Tomorrow, hybrid corn would die, she knew; but that was tomorrow, and tonight she writhed with joyous unconcern upon the spouting, respouting, fertile ends of perennialism.

Then they slept. Then she heard, 'Jeesaz! We've got to make tracks. We head Mr Tunney towards Dallas at nine.'

'You fly him to Texas in a helicopter?' she murmured.

'We fly him over to Linden Municipal. We've got a Lear waiting there.'

The phone rang. She knew what it was. Everything came back. She picked it up, then deliberately dropped it into the midst of its own jangling. Silence.

'Hey! That could have been important!' cried one.

'It was,' she sighed. 'It was probably your Mr Tunney saying the sky's falling on his head and he wants to hurry.'

'Well, hell . . .!' cried the other.

'Are you putting your work before me?' she demanded.

'Would you want a man who lies around in bed all day?' chorused her lovers.

She pushed back the covers and sat up in a naked lotus. 'Listen. Both of you. The world has changed. Is going to change. Profoundly. Today. Out there; when the NYSE opens. Can I tell you a story?' They were restless. 'It's a sort of de-Creation myth. You need to hear it.'

'Okay.' As peripherally as possible they were trying to spy the time on the bedside analogue.

'An old Maori woman left a gate open. Two sheep got in to a field. Their names were Beryl and Murray.' She had their attention. They were staring at her, searching for physical signs of insanity to match the verbal ones. 'When Charlie said they'd disappeared I thought he meant they'd been obliterated by the napalm. They hadn't; they'd migrated. But first they got into the field. They ate seeds. Zeacinte. Then they escaped. Before the Stealth arrived. They escaped their pasture and they escaped their past. They had become individuals.' (Four identically troubled eyes stared at her.) 'Together they set off to forage, to mate and to raise lambs. It was an idea they had; an intention! Amazing; a reaction lingers, doesn't just dissolve into reflex action, it becomes abstract, outside itself. "We can gain self-determination! We can make things happen, control our destiny — if we are free." So off they set, Beryl and Murray; the ovine nuclear family, created by Charlie Frankenstein. And as they went, they shat. Little zeacinte-balls; prolific droppings encased in their own fertiliser. The seeds sprouted, grew tubers and waited underground for warmer weather. Then they grew. All over — everywhere Murray and Beryl had wandered till the last seeds had passed through their systems. And in spring the seeds germinated.'

'Are you okay, Morgan?' murmured one of them. They were concerned; for themselves of course. Trapped in a hotel room with a young Ancient Mariner.

'Curiously, yes. Listen,' — she was astonishingly calm — 'this is important, don't interrupt. As we came through Tribeca in the cab last night, there was a spraycan mural on a wall, a very good one. Remember? "I AM THE BEST ARTIST", it said. One of you mentioned it, or somebody did. Well, the words "best artist" were joined up, and the bottom of the B had been smudged. I first read it as: "I AM THE RESTARTIST". Well, for better or worse, I am. The Re-startist. Of the world.'

They had knelt at the side of the bed, facing her in a sort of cunnilingual prayer. They were in range of about ten thousand olfacts — or whatever you measure smell in — of their own seed.

'It would be nice if you told us,' the pilot said quietly, 'what the fuck you're talking about.'

'Okay. Today there will be a hysterical run on agribusiness shares. Word has got out that this zeacinte found in New Zealand is going to devastate the industry. Then the market will realise that if the agribusiness falls, the chemical companies will go too.' She paused; they were sickly white. 'And who owns the chemical companies?' she said.

'Oh Jesus,' her lovers moaned in tandem.

She nodded. 'Yes, my darlings. I think your oilman is more likely to want you to sell his plane than fly it.'

'How rough do you think it's gonna get?' whispered the flight attendant.

'I don't know.' She smiled, swung away from them, leapt from the bed and walked to the window.

'And you're saying that a couple of sheep . . .'

'You hush your mouth!' she said without turning. 'They were very intelligent sheep.' She crossed her arms and looked out across the battleship-coloured morning. Through it flowed the untroubled Hudson; and beyond, New Jersey, about to become Manhattan's prosperous younger brother.

Behind her, to the east, a wan-faced crowd gathers beneath the statue of George Washington, silently watching the flags climb to half mast outside the NYSE. 'Oh well, every cloud, I suppose,' she said, turning brightly. 'It certainly helps you make a choice. I've decided to be Russian, in case Individual Capitalism is on its way out the window with the bankers.'

'I don't think it's the time for jokes.'

'No,' she said. 'It's time for action.' She strode, naked and efficient, to her briefcase on the plastic teak desk. 'We're going for a little ride,' she went on. 'To Granity. You'd better get dressed.'

'A ride?' said one.

'Granity?' said the other.

'Yes; on a little island I know of, on the other side of the universe. We're going to see the aunt of Colin Fox.' She was bent over her cheque book. 'It will be quieter there. She will bake us scones.'

'What're you doing, Morg?'

They had spoken — tremulously — together. (As, increasingly, they did.) She turned to them, fondly, and was suddenly back in Charlie's improbable dining-room in Palmerston North. From the floor, four eyes — two interchangeable sets of lefts and rights — gazed up like those of anxious does at forest's edge.

She smiled down at her brace of paramours; her symbols of fertility; her future. 'I'm buying Mr Tunney's plane before the bank opens,' she replied.

GRANITY; 19 OCTOBER 1987 . . .

'Holy fucking . . .